THE HUNTER

"A suspenseful, gutsy saga which adds fresh variations to the cops-and-robbers theme. Interwoven with . . . Thorson's international exploits . . . swirling personal interest."

—*Publishers Weekly*

"A machismo story about a capable and virile legend in his own time."

—*Chattanooga Times*

"There is an excellent chance that Thorson will not live to see his grandchildren. Read it now and you can tell yours, 'I read about him when he was alive.' "

—*The Cleveland Press*

Steve McQueen

THE HUNTER

A Rastar/ Mort Engelberg Production

Music by
Michel Legrand

Produced by
Mort Engelberg

Screenplay by
Ted Leighton
and
Peter Hyams

Directed by
Buzz Kulik

The Hunter

Christopher Keane

BANTAM BOOKS
TORONTO • NEW YORK • LONDON

*This low-priced Bantam Book
has been completely reset in a type face
designed for easy reading, and was printed
from new plates. It contains the complete
text of the original hard-cover edition.*
NOT ONE WORD HAS BEEN OMITTED.

THE HUNTER:
TALES OF A DIFFERENT PAPA

*A Bantam Book / published by arrangement with
Arbor House Publishing Company, Inc.*

PRINTING HISTORY

*Arbor House edition published August 1976
2nd edition . . . September 1976
A selection of The Playboy Book Club
Bantam edition / August 1980*

*Bantam Books are published by Bantam Books, Inc. Its trade-
mark, consisting of the words "Bantam Books" and the por-
trayal of a bantam, is Registered in U.S. Patent and Trademark
Office and in other countries. Marca Registrada. Bantam
Books, Inc., 666 Fifth Avenue, New York, New York 10103.*

PRINTED IN THE UNITED STATES OF AMERICA

0 9 8 7 6 5 4 3 2 1

For Lori Sacks

Few can attain this man's knowledge,
and few practice his virtues;
but all may suffer his calamity.

—RASSELAS

Contents

PART IV

Foreword

Ralph "Papa" Thorson is a shy man who surrounds himself with people. He shies away from the press because of the nature of his business. He tries to keep a low profile, at which he has been unsuccessful. The West Coast criminal class knows him; the police have teamed with him on pickups; judges, bank presidents, ex-cons, hookers, insurance salesmen and movie stars parade through his home.

The Los Angeles *Times* featured Papa as "today's bounty hunter—and he is known by that name—who still brings in violent types. He ranges throughout the United States, into Canada, and down into the Caribbean and Mexico with more freedom and effectiveness than the police in some ways."

True magazine characterized him as a "big, full-bearded bruiser. Thorson can send his 310 pound, six-foot-two frame charging when he has to."

In the press he is defined by his occupation; and, for the violent and hazardous situations he encounters, rightly so.

There is a different Papa, however: a church bishop; Master bridge champion; renowned astrologer; criminology alumnus of the University of California at Berkeley; child nutritionist, aficionado of classical music.

I have heard a number of people call Papa the most intelligent person they know, and the most charming and perceptive. Others idolize him, and for many he has become a legend.

He has the stuff from which legends are made: growing up in the wild west mining town of Anaconda, Montana, where a man's code is his integrity, is all; choosing an occupation that no other man in the nation holds, an occupation that is picaresque by design and perilous by nature, and to which Papa has devoted almost thirty years of his life.

He is by vocation a bounty hunter. He hunts down fugitives, and sometimes people get killed in the process. His financial security depends upon how energetic he feels. Insurance companies refuse to insure his life. He will receive no social security benefits. He must depend upon tight-fisted bailbondsmen for his livelihood.

So be it. He has made the choice.

Papa has 5,000 case files in his cabinet. We have chosen ten of them on which to concentrate, in addition to another thirty-three to modify the initial ones. Papa considered these particular cases as representative of the types of situations he has found himself in. Some names and locations have been changed in order to eliminate the possibility of lawsuits. Cases are still pending in some instances.

Here then is the story of a man who in many ways has been born into an age where he does not belong, who counterpoints a violent disposition with an artistic one, and who adheres unequivocally to a code he learned as a child that has been reordained throughout his later years.

Papa Thorson is the last of the bounty hunters, a tradition's denouement. The end of a type. And as such—the notion is correct—he has become legend. The stories herein are all true; they reflect the man who lived them.

C.K.

Los Angeles
March 1976

PART I

The Law

TAYLOR VS. TAINTOR, 16 Wall 366 (21 Law Ed. 287). In this case the SUPREME COURT OF THE UNITED STATES said:

"When bail is given, the principal is regarded as delivered to the custody of his sureties. Their dominion is a continuance of the original imprisonment. Whenever they choose to do so, they may seize and deliver up in their discharge, and if that cannot be done at once they may imprison him until it can be done. They may exercise their rights in person or by agent (such as a private detective). They may pursue him into another state; may arrest him on the Sabbath; and, if necessary, may break and enter his house for that purpose. The seizure is not made by virtue of new process. None is needed." (It should also be noted that this rule is not limited to cases of felony, but is applied to every case where a person is released from legal custody upon the giving of a bail bond or recognizance and includes all cases of misdemeanor and even cases of civil arrest out of a civil action.)

An Opinion

"Out of state bailbondsmen apparently have greater rights with respect to obtaining custody of a fugitive from justice than does a peace officer from another state.

"Although peace officers must go through the courts by way of extradition proceedings to obtain custody of a suspected law violator, under existing law a bailbondsman can gain custody of a fugitive without the necessity of resorting to state court procedures."

HON. MARK BRANDLER
JUDGE, SUPERIOR COURT
COUNTY OF LOS ANGELES
STATE OF CALIFORNIA

1

Papa

Spring, 1975

The bright yellow Plymouth raced along the desert highway on a bed of shimmering heat. Sand kicked off the rear
wheels and sent two towering wakes arching high into the
dead, juiceless air. The Plymouth slowed to fifty, to
twenty-five, and came to a stop. The door swung open and
out struggled an immense, bearded man with his shirt
open down the front and barely visible knife scars on his
chest. He stretched his bull-like body and felt the constrict-
ed muscles pull away from one another. Perspiration
beaded on his forehead and streaked down his face into
the thick salt and pepper beard pasted like a sweaty mat
against his skin. He looked with disgust at the car whose
air conditioner shorted out when he crossed the California
border into Arizona. He told the mechanic who wanted
$200 to fix it to take a flying leap. At that price he could
afford to sweat.

Papa reached into the back seat and from the ice chest
pulled out a beer which he drained. He hurled the empty

can at a cactus bush. This was no place for a forty-nine-year-old man with high blood pressure.

"God*damn* air conditioner," Papa grunted, pulling a soaking wet handkerchief from his back pocket. He wiped his brow and his arms and attached the handkerchief to the aerial to dry. From inside the car he heard the police band radio squawking information between a dispatcher and her squad cars. The portable eight-track stereo on the front seat soared with an aria from Puccini's *La Boheme*.

Before climbing back in the car he took a final look down the highway where for the last hundred miles he'd passed nothing but the flat, boring, sweltering desert. Up ahead lay more of the same.

He eased his massive body behind the wheel and stared out through the windshield to the road where a cluster of tumbleweed balls bounced by. His parched lips hung open. He was hot, he ached, his eyelids were half closed and he still had two hundred miles before reaching Ruby.

At five that afternoon he pulled into Ruby, one of a string of small Arizona towns on the Mexican border. Ruby had fought desperately the emergence of the modern age and for the most part won the battle. Hitching posts stood next to parking meters. The bars had names like the Silver Slipper and Fanny's Place. The men wore chaps and checkered shirts and ten gallon hats and walked bowlegged down wooden sidewalks. Mexicans and Mexican-Americans took their siestas on chairs tilted against restored wooden buildings.

Ruby had its neon signs advertising All-State Insurance and a Great Western Motel and the Caterpillar tractor outlet. Leather and Indian goods shops were interspersed here and there; a tobacco store; two banks, members of F.D.I.C.; a McDonald's and a Burger King—all stood on Ruby's main drag.

Papa drove the Plymouth slowly down Main Street. In the trunk: two riot guns, a .45, a .38-caliber Police Special, mace canisters, a Prowler Fouler stun gun, a long black cylinder that shot beanbags filled with buckshot, and an "emergency kit"—plastic bottles filled with Scotch, rum and vodka.

Papa scanned both sides of the street looking for the Golden Horseshoe Cafe where, according to the information he carried, he would find Tommy Price.

He located the Golden Horseshoe at the end of the block, flanked on one side by a graveyard and the other by a funeral home. Papa climbed out and headed up the front steps.

He pushed open the double doors and stood in the entranceway. The Golden Horseshoe was an old-time wild-west saloon. Above the bar on the second floor a veranda ran the length of one wall. A wooden railing guarded the veranda which led to a circular staircase. A television set sat on a platform over one end of the bar. Pabst and Budweiser beer signs hung from the ceiling by thin wires. A half dozen tables and chairs occupied the main floor, along with a pool table and three pinball machines with out-of-order signs Scotch-taped to the glass.

Papa's appearance caused a chain reaction in the saloon where a half dozen cowboys leaned against a brass-railed bar. Heads turned. The place became deadly silent except for the hillbilly waltz blaring from the jukebox. The two scruffy old cowpunchers playing pool rested against their cue sticks and peered at the huge figure looming in the doorway.

What they saw was a six-two, 310-pound giant dressed in a silk Hawaiian shirt, gray military issue trousers with a stripe running down the side and scruffy white bucks that hadn't seen a polish in months. Papa nodded and grinned and walked casually across the floor to a table where he selected a chair with its back to the wall. The dozen or so patrons, the bartender and the fat florid waitress at the silverware tray all trained their eyes on him.

Papa settled in, placing his cigarettes and lighter on the table, and motioned to the waitress who in nervous confusion remained where she was.

"Ma'am!" Papa shouted above the music. "Take my order?"

The waitress looked at the bartender, who nodded his approval, and she waddled towards the table. Her approach terminated five feet from Papa, and as some people tend to do in the presence of evil she ran one hand through her hair, which had thinned out from changing the color too often.

"Steak, medium rare, and a bottle of Burgundy," Papa told her and she made her way back to the kitchen.

Papa then called to the bartender, "Can you turn that down a little?"

"The boys like their waltzes loud," he replied, which drew a laugh from the customers.

Papa shrugged and inserted a cigarette into his Aqua-filter, lit up, and waited for his food. It seemed to the cowboys that the danger had passed so they turned back to their drinks. The pool players lined up shots. The waitress emerged from the kitchen with a bottle of wine which she handed to the bartender who uncorked it.

The waitress carried over the wine and food, served it up and went back to her silverware tray. Papa chewed on a piece of steak and sipped the wine and then he pushed himself from the table and walked out of the Golden Horseshoe.

Out in the street he opened the car door and removed the portable eight-track stereo and a pair of wire cutters.

He marched back inside and crossed the room to the jukebox. He reached behind the machine and yanked the plug from its socket, killing the hillbilly waltz. He caught movement at the bar and turned around to see two cowboys starting toward him. When they saw him turn they reared up and returned to their stations. Papa went back to work on the jukebox. He used the wire cutters to snip the plug and placed it on top of the juke. He carried the eight-track back to his table where he inserted Strauss' *Rosenkavalier* into the chamber, turning the volume to high.

He speared another piece of steak and washed it down with more wine. He raised his eyes towards the bar and smiled.

"That loud enough for the boys?" he called out.

The same two cowboys at the end of the bar had seen enough. They hitched up their pants and began moving in Papa's direction.

He watched their approach and waited until they were just a few feet away when he placed one hand over the .45 in his belt.

The cowboys stopped and turned to one another. Their decision was made quickly; they attacked. The distance between them was short. The big man came in from the right. Papa kicked the chair next to him and it flew into the big man's knees, tumbling him to the floor. The smaller man came from the left, arms flailing. One of them caught Papa on the shoulder, pushing him off balance. With one swift gesture Papa snatched the .45 with his right hand and drove it into the man's thigh. The man yelped, doubled over and sank to the floor.

Der Rosenkavalier crescendoed through the Golden Horseshoe Cafe.

Papa waved the .45 at the two fallen men who rose to their feet and crept back to their positions at the bar.

Papa replaced the weapon and called the waitress over.

"Can you warm this up, sweetheart?" he asked her, handing her the platter.

The backroom door flew open and into the bar marched a stocky, sandy-haired man in his late twenties. He wore a faded Levi outfit, a red bandana around his neck and ornate, pointed boots. He moved his head back and forth and the patch of freckles across the bridge of his nose scrunched up and his wideset eyes scowled under the bushy red brows.

"What the *hell's* goin' on!" he growled.

The bartender nodded to his left and the man spotted Papa, who held the steak knife up and waved Tommy Price over. Tommy hesitated, calculating his next move. The two men stared at each other for what seemed a long time. But for Tommy the answer was clear. The message came from Papa's eyes. They told Tommy not to run away, not to get a gun or start a fight, just to come over and sit down where everything would be worked out. Deep gray and set way back into their caverns, the eyes wore an aura of intelligence so intensified they made no entreaties, but demands. Tommy Price sighed deeply and shook his head in resignation. He walked to the chair. Papa lowered the music.

The waitress returned with the steak and Papa continued eating in silence, occasionally glancing up at Tommy and smiling.

"Nice place you got here," Papa said.

Tommy Price grunted.

"Fine wine," Papa grinned. "Good food."

Tommy grunted once again.

"*Excellent* music."

Tommy leaned forward, placing both elbows on the table.

"You sumbitch, how the *hell* did you find me?"

"Looks like you found me, Tommy," Papa said, offering him the bottle. "Nothing like beautiful music to bring a man out in the open."

Tommy took the bottle and gulped down the wine.

"You packin'?" Papa asked him.

Tommy stood and rotated his body for Papa to check for a weapon. He was clean. Papa motioned for him to sit back down.

"Now will you tell me?" Tommy asked.

Papa pulled out his certified copy of the bailbond on Tommy Price and showed it to him.

"The woman who put up your bail," he said, pointing to the bond application. "Sally Charmody."

"Yeah, that's my girl friend."

"She owns this place, right?"

"She does."

"When you didn't show up for your trial she got worried. Sally put up the Golden Horseshoe here for collateral."

"You mean that bitch turned me in! That goddamn . . ."

Tommy started out of the chair. Papa wrapped one hand around his wrist and pulled him back.

"Tommy," Papa said quietly, "wouldn't you have done the same? She put everything she had up for you."

"I know, but turning in your old man is something else again, Papa."

"Tommy, this is the—what?—third time I've picked you up . . ."

"Fourth."

Papa thought for a second.

"Let's see"—Tommy counted on his fingers—"there was the time in Carson City, and then . . ."

"Let's talk about it on the way. You ready?"

"Do I got any choice?"

Papa nodded. "If you've got three thousand dollars on you?"

"You know I could have my friends here make things rough for you," Tommy pointed out.

"They already tried."

Tommy shrugged. "All right, let's go." At the door he turned back to the bartender. "Take care of my things," he said. "I'll be gone a while."

Outside on the porch Tommy halted abruptly, turned, and cupping both hands over his mouth shouted back into the bar, "And you can tell Sally Charmody to go fuck herself."

Papa held the car door open for Tommy, then went around to the driver's seat. He placed the wire cutters and eight-track in the back seat and drove out of Ruby, Arizona.

They'd gone just a few hundred yards when Tommy, dripping with sweat, asked Papa to turn on the air conditioner.

"Wish I could," Papa told him. "It broke."

"You're shittin' me. All the way back to Los Angeles in this heat?"

"We're not going to Los Angeles just yet."

"We're not?" Tommy said uneasily.

"Nope. Got a little business to take care of in Houston."

Tommy jerked his body higher on the seat and stiffened up.

"Houston!"

"Would you rather spend the weekend in jail?"

"No. Uh uh."

"Besides," Papa said, "I could use a little help. So be a good boy. We've got a long ride in front of us."

2

Richie Blumenthal

It was early evening when Richie Blumenthal rushed from the Los Angeles City Jail with a sheaf of papers under one arm. He adjusted the boutonniere in the lapel of his three hundred dollar suit and scurried off down the street towards his office on Bailbond Row. With short, rapid-fire strides his spindly legs carried him past the construction site and boxlike buildings of the County Courthouse and onto the neon-lit street where his office—Equity Bailbonds, Inc.—was housed.

Equity Bailbonds was almost as old as Richie himself. He started the firm fifty years ago and wheeled it into the second largest in Los Angeles. Richie kept what he made and invested it in a chain of massage parlors and race-horses, two restaurants, run by relatives, and a half dozen hockshops along Santa Monica Boulevard. Richie owned two Bentleys, a Rolls, a Maserati he gave to his son and a half million dollar shack in Beverly Hills. He was still only the sixth weathiest bondsman on The Row.

Richie did however have the distinction of being the smallest. But the way he figured, anybody standing five-four and weighing 132 pounds, the only way to go was up. He was in excellent shape for a man seventy-five years old and could eat and eat without gaining an ounce. "So, I'm short," he once said to his even shorter wife. "That's short in size but not mentality, not in *success*, Harriet. In success, I am a very tall man." He had a huge beak of a nose, two oversized front teeth that formed a perpetual smile on his lips, and no eyebrows. Twenty years ago the eyebrows, along with the mane of thin hair, had turned snow white. The brows disappeared; the hair remained and now swooped back from a severe widow's peak. The skin on his face and hands was like thick, deeply lined parchment, and his eyes were pale green, so light in hue they seemed almost the color of his hair. They were eyes that enchanted. Richie used them to good advantage and attributed a great deal of his success to the power they held over his clients.

Richie stopped by Herb's Deli for cigars and the Racing Form.

"Got a hot one at Santa Anita," Herb told him.

"So?" Richie said, scanning the first race.

"Perry's Girl, in the third. It's a lock."

Richie looked up from the Form at the tall, rail-thin deli owner. "Herbie, how many times I gotta tell you? I place bets on my own nags, nobody else's. C'mon, gimme the change."

Richie pocketed the money and walked back into the street. The Row looked like Vegas at night: a rainbow of flashing signs advertised the bonding companies; throngs of hustlers, pimps, hookers, lawyers, cops and middle-aged couples paraded in and out of the offices.

Richie walked through the door to the glass-enclosed outer office. One of the assistants, Andy Troot, a short, stocky Malaysian with a fat face, met him at the door to the inner office.

"The Bernardos are here," Andy informed him.

"This oughta be good," Richie said, turning the knob and entering.

"Hello." Richie smiled. "Mr. Bernardo. Don't get up. Mrs. Bernardo, how are you?"

"We would have come last night," Mr. Bernardo apologized, "but . . ."

Richie raised his hand. "Hey, anytime. We're open

twenty-four hours in this business. Glad you could make it. Lemme put these things away."

Richie placed the sheaf of papers on his desk, with the Racing Form on top. He removed his suit jacket and hung it on the hat rack against the wall.

The Bernardos sat in chairs facing Richie's oak desk that took up half the small room. This was the office where Richie originally began. He felt secure here, as if making a change might reverse his success.

"Now," Richie said, standing behind the desk, "let's see what we got . . ."

He peered down at the Bernardos, Tony and Sylvia, both in their early sixties and demure to the point of embarrassment.

"Your son, Anthony, Mr. Bernardo," Richie continued, "how reliable is he?"

Mr. Bernardo shrugged. His eyes swept the floor. His gray rumpled suit was much too large and the soft felt hat in his lap was on the verge of slipping off his knees.

"This is the first time . . ." he started to say.

"Mr. Bernardo," Richie interrupted. "There's a first time for everything. It was the first time young Anthony robbed a liquor store. It was the first time he jumped bail. What next? Understand, sir, that you are in as much trouble as your son. The bail was twenty-five thousand. If Anthony doesn't show up in a hundred and eighty days you forfeit your business."

Mr. Bernardo had put up his hardware store as collateral against Anthony showing up for his trial. The kid didn't show and was now loose somewhere, leaving his family to hold the bag. Richie hoped Anthony appeared. He did not want another hardware store added to his collection. He already owned a hardware store—from another forfeiture—in San Fernando Valley, which was losing money. Richie also wanted the kid back because in a moment of grand benevolence Richie took the 10 percent retainer fee on credit. The Bernardos didn't have the cash and Richie felt sorry for them. Feeling sorry for clients was the best way to go broke. Richie played humanitarian no more than once every thousand cases.

"And me, Mr. Bernardo," Richie was saying, "I took your ten percent on credit. Twenty-five hundred's a lot of money."

"And we appreciate it, Mr. Bramenthal," Mrs. Bernardo said.

"*Blu*menthal."

"We *do* appreciate it," Mr. Bernardo added with a smile.

The phone rang. Richie picked it up. "What? Yeah, put her on." It was his wife Harriet, who as usual had nothing to say but she loved to talk, about anything. Richie loved his wife, everything but her mouth. He loved her enough to sign over the house, the boats and the bonding business to his mother-in-law, who owned everything, which made Richie bulletproof against anyone slapping a lawsuit on him. Richie owned nothing, not even the hundreds of items he kept in the warehouse near Griffith Park. He acquired the items from clients who had forfeited their collateral. He owned a twelve-foot-high pipe organ, a totally chromed Harley-Davidson motorcycle, hundreds of radios, televisions and stereos. There was a beehive, very large and, according to the previous owner, the best in Southern California. Who knew? Richie threw it in with the rest. Other bondsmen on The Row got airplanes and tanks, and sometimes children were offered as collateral, and refused—as far as Richie knew. This business attracted strange people.

"Harriet," Richie finally said, "I'm with clients now. Goodbye."

Mrs. Bernardo nudged her husband.

"Ask him," she insisted.

"Mr. Blumenthal," Mr. Bernardo asked. "I took inventory on my business yesterday and"—he looked away as if already knowing the answer—"it seems my hardware store is worth close to fifty thousand dollars, much more than the twenty-five thousand for my son's bail."

"I understand," Richie explained. "It's a rule of thumb in my business to try to get collateral worth about twice as much as the amount on the bond. The reason for this, I can tell you from experience, is after the lawyers and the foreclosure fees I'm just barely able to cover my expenses."

"Foreclosure?" The word stung Mr. Bernardo and brought tears to his old puffy eyes. "Thirty years," he mumbled, head down. "Thirty years I worked my business. *Forty* years I've worked, Mr. Blumenthal. I can't lose it all now. I can't start over. I'm too old. I . . ." Mr. Bernardo snapped his mouth shut and pressed his lips tightly together.

Richie sympathized with the man. It was the reason he agreed to post bail for their rotten son. If he'd been smart he would have persuaded the Bernardos to leave the kid in jail.

Richie paused, twisting the pale jade ring around his pinky finger.

"Let me lay it out for you," he said, standing and walking around the desk. "First of all, chances are your son won't turn himself in, right? He's either too scared or too"—Richie was going to say stupid but changed his mind—"uninformed. He doesn't know any better. I think there's only one way to go."

The Bernardos lifted their heads towards the bondsman. Hope?

"We're gonna have to get somebody to find him," Richie said.

"A private investigator?" Mr. Bernardo asked, wondering how much *that* was going to cost him.

"A bounty hunter."

The second Richie said it he regretted the words. The Bernardos were stunned. Bounty hunter? A killer who brings them back dead or alive? That kind of bounty hunter?

"Don't worry," Richie assured them. "The man I have in mind is very gentle. Hardly ever carries a weapon. He'll bring back your son without a scratch, believe me. He's worked for me fifteen years. Very reliable."

Mrs. Bernardo shook her head. "I don't think so, Mr. Blumenthal. I don't think that's the best way."

"Put it this way," Richie replied. "It's that or you lose the hardware store."

It was Mr. Bernardo's turn. "This bounty hunter. You're sure he'll go easy with Anthony. He is a good boy. I know that."

"In that case you have nothing to worry about," said Richie, wondering how gentle their punk kid would be with Papa Thorson.

3

The Billy Joe Face Case

Papa hauled Tommy Price to Houston to have company on the long stretch across Texas.

"Just who is it you're goin' after, Papa?" Tommy asked.

"Guy named Billy Joe Face. Jumped bail for bad checks."

"Billy Joe Face!" Tommy had to laugh. "For real, that's his name?"

"That's what it says."

It seemed to Papa that half the bailjumpers he went after, especially in the Southwest, were named Billy Joe. According to Richie Blumenthal's file, Billy Joe had "hung paper" in Los Angeles for over $6,000 and got caught by trying to pass one at the May Company department store where, just a week before, he had bounced one for $800. Which showed that Billy Joe Face was either stupid or had an extremely bad memory. He was nabbed at the store and taken downtown to be arraigned. The judge set his bail at $2,100, which Billy Joe's cousin Jimmy guaranteed. A week later Billy Joe left for Texas. When cousin Jimmy found out that Billy Joe had taken off, Jimmy called the bondsman, Richie Blumenthal, who in turn sent Papa to bring Billy Joe back to Los Angeles.

They crossed the border into New Mexico and drove most of the night through the cool, moonlit desert. Tommy slept a good part of the way and woke when the sun appeared over the Texas prairie. They passed through El Paso, San Angelo, and took the expressway around Austin.

During the drive they got to know each other better. They answered each other's questions, argued, had a few laughs. Papa found Tommy Price easy to listen to, his smooth, fluid manner of speaking, one word overlapping the other, and the off-handed humor.

Tommy had spent a total of three years in prison for small-time dope dealing and grand theft auto. Tommy Price was, in street jargon, a scuffler, a lower-case crook who lived by his wits. In between jail terms he dealt blackjack at The Sands in Vegas, tended bar, and lived off women who eventually found out what a liability he was and kicked him out. Papa knew hundreds of guys much like him.

They stopped for lunch in a small roadhouse on the out-skirts of Houston. Tommy had been bugging Papa to show him how the Prowler Fouler worked so after lunch Papa pulled off the road into a cluster of trees. Papa found a two-by-four which he set up on a tree stump and marched back twenty paces. He inserted a nitrogen cylinder into the chamber and stuffed the beanbag down the muzzle. The Prowler Fouler looked like a thick billy club as Papa held it in front of him. He cocked the bolt-action spring, aimed the Fouler at the two-by-four and squeezed the trigger. The beanbag exploded from the muzzle and slammed into the piece of wood at eighty miles per hour, knocking it fifty yards in the distance. Tommy's jaw dropped and a low whistle escaped from between his teeth.

"And that thing can't kill somebody?" he said quietly.

"Not unless you stick it in his mouth," Papa smiled. "No reason to kill a man when you can knock him out."

"Mind if I try it?"

"No. Go ahead."

Papa set up the two-by-four, reloaded and handed the weapon to him. Tommy missed by ten yards the first time; the second go-round he connected. A split second after the explosion crackled through the air the board left the stump and landed almost exactly where Papa had sent it. Tommy handed the Fouler to Papa and walked back towards the car with a big grin on his face.

Back on the road Tommy turned to Papa and asked, "This bounty hunting you do, what's the pay?"

"About enough to live on," Papa said.

"Fifteen, twenty thousand a year?"

"About that," he said vaguely.

"And you been doin' it—what—twenty years or so?"

Papa tallied up the years and said, "Twenty-eight."

Tommy readjusted his body, drawing one leg up on the seat. "Twenty-eight years and that's all you make? Hell, you coulda got an office job and been making twice that."

"Yes," Papa agreed, "and gone crazy in the meantime. I have an aversion to office work, always have. Nine to five and some morning getting canned because the boss had a brawl with his old lady. No thanks."

"S'pose a guy like me, bein' what I am and what I done, maybe wanted to sorta get into the bounty hunting business. S'posin' I'd like somethin' like that . . ."

"How would you do it?" Papa finished up for him.

"Yeah, how would I?"

"First of all you have to be fairly insane."

"Which I am, all the shit I done," Tommy insisted.

"And big enough to take care of yourself in a fight."

Tommy outstretched both arms and flexed his chest muscles. "Say no more."

"Have a steady job because there's not much money in the beginning."

Tommy let that float by with an "uh huh."

"And . . . be a borderline hood with a lot of street savvy. That's probably the *important* thing. You take a priest straight out of the seminary and put him in Watts, the best thing that could happen to him would be to get killed. To make any kind of money in this job you've got to know the criminal, how he thinks, how he acts. Give you an example.

"In L.A. I drive down Hollywood Boulevard, right? Everybody else driving down Hollywood Boulevard looks at people walking on the sidewalk and what do they see? They see people walking on the sidewalk. I see hustlers and scufflers and hookers and pimps and a guy I once picked up for robbery who is staring into a jewelry store window. I'm looking at them through an overlay from twenty-eight years doing this. Cops do it, criminals do it. All of us, we all think the same way. We're all hooked into each other's frequency."

Papa paused to light a cigarette.

"*You've* got that, Tommy," he said. "Pretty much. I can also see some *morality* in you. Not much, but enough so I can trust you. A professional crook has none. First thing you know he's making a deal with the guy I just snatched. If the guy offers him more dough than he's getting from me—whack—he cuts him loose."

"I wouldn't do nothin' like that."

"I believe you wouldn't."

"Jest outa curiosity, what kinda bounty hunter'd you think I'd make?" Tommy lifted his head and his eyes widened on Papa.

"Half the people who've worked with me have been just like you, guys I've picked up," Papa told him.

"So you had this conversation before?" Tommy said, not feeling so special anymore.

Papa shook his head. "All different."

"Uh huh. Different good or different bad?"

"What?"

"Me."

"Different good."

Tommy leaned back in the seat and cocked his head towards Papa. "I knew it," he beamed. "Tell me somethin'," he said after a moment. "What about you? Twenty-eight years ago. Was it so different then?"

JUNE, 1948. Northern California. Thousands of summer vacationers swarmed through the Lake County resort area; weekenders from San Francisco, Idaho and Nevada. Papa spent his summer vacations bartending at Hoberg's Resort Hotel where he mixed highballs for thirty dollars a week. He became friendly with most of the guests, one of whom was a man named Boyd Puchinelli who every summer spent ten days at Lake County resorts. "Pooch" was a big spender from San Francisco who handed out substantial tips and threw one big bash on the last day of his vacation, inviting all of Lake County to participate.

"Pooch drank Campari cocktails," Papa remembers, "which taste like a combination of kerosene and iodine. Every night he'd sit at my bar and order one before dinner. It was the only booze he drank.

"Pooch and I got to be good friends during the ten days. He asked me about myself, where I went to school, how old I was, did I mind getting into fights, was I interested in making a few extra bucks. Doing what, I asked him. He said he was a San Francisco bondsman and he needed a few lunatics to pick up bailjumpers and haul them to jail. I said sure, few extra bucks, I could use it. He told me to contact him after the summer, he'd put me to work.

"I finished with Lake County in early September, drove back to San Francisco and looked him up. He handed me a piece of paper with a name and address on it and pointed me in the direction. When I got there the guy I was after was sleeping. I pulled him out of bed and had him downtown in less than fifteen minutes. Pooch gave me fifteen dollars and said this might be the start of something big. The way I figured it, fifteen bucks for fifteen minutes put me in high-income territory.

"Little by little, one guy a week, then two, three, however many Pooch wanted me to snatch. Sometimes he gave me handcuffs, sometimes a .38 Special, which I fired at a gallery down the street. Then I started expanding; out of town trips, then out of state, then, finally, I went international. Canada, to get a grizzly old fuck who was arrested for shoplifting women's underwear. I found him in Vancouver, in a dress, which I had to haul the old fag back in, all the way to San Francisco.

"Blacks and whites, Chicanos, Chinese, pimps and hookers, junkies, you name it. It was an education.

"My education on the other end, at the University of California, Berkeley, was not doing so well. I wanted to be a doctor ever since I was a kid so I was in pre-med. It eventually dawned on me that I could never afford to go to medical school, no matter how many guys I picked up for Pooch. I transferred to criminology. I was meeting a lot of criminals and they were fascinating. Their brand of morality was ridiculous. I couldn't believe the absolute, total, horrible rip-offs so-called friends pulled on one another.

"Another reason for changing was the part-time job I had in Contra Costa and Alameda Juvenile Halls. Thirty hours a week I worked there, honestly trying to rehabilitate those kids. Then I started to realize that everything I did to help them was fucked up by the judges, the court system, my bosses, everybody. Instead of hassling with the kids they were shipped off to the California Youth Authority or a mental institution. They were *expedited*, a popular word around Juvenile Hall.

"There I was, couldn't afford to help people medically, not able to help them psychologically, and eventually picked up a lot of those kids I once tried to straighten out.

"I have regrets. I would rather have been a doctor, and I would have been a good one. Instead, as millionaires with fifth-grade educations like to say, I got a Ph.D. in life.

"So for ten years I hung around San Francisco. I got my degree, I learned how to scuba dive, I became a bridge fanatic, and I went after guys for Pooch.

"A lot of times he sent me to L.A. on pickups, and I could see right away that the bailbond business was in great shape down there. I was like any young businessman looking to expand his boundaries, and his bank account. I made the move in 1958, been there ever since."

With Houston less than an hour away Tommy Price began pushing hard for Papa to try him out as an assistant.

"From all I know, Papa," Tommy said, "going over state lines to bring somebody back is kidnapping, ain't it?"

Papa nodded his agreement. "For everybody but me."

"How's that?"

"Goes back to an 1872 Supreme Court decision. Bounty hunters can legally do it. Cops can't. FBI can't. They have to go through formal extradition procedures."

"Pretty slick," Tommy smiled. "How many guys like you operating like this?"

"Full-time?"

"Yeah."

"One."

Tommy paused. "One what?"

"One full-time bounty hunter. Myself, me. Everybody else part-times it, slipping in and out."

They remained silent for a time, staring through the car windows at fields of tall prairie grass bending with the wind. Weatherbeaten shacks dotted the countryside, their chipped tar roofs and television antennas visible above the tall reeds.

They crossed over the Brazos River that eventually fed into the Gulf of Mexico. Houston was on Galveston Bay, just north of the Brazos.

Houston sat in a basin, scooped out of the earth like a huge saucer. Overhead Papa watched black rain clouds float in from the east, casting shadows on the fleet of oil tankers anchored in the bay. The men who owned the tankers had offices in the Gulf and Humble Buildings rising above the rest of downtown Houston.

As they drew nearer the Sheriff's Department they passed streets with the names of Texas heroes—Crockett, Lamar, Sam Houston. They watched extraordinarily beautiful girls marching in and out of Battlesteins, Neiman-Marcus and Sakowitz department stores.

By the time Papa reached the Harris County Sheriff's Department the downpour had begun.

The Sheriff's Department, in the heart of downtown on San Jacinto, was an eight-story building with a penthouse and a basement. The Fugitive Division was on the third floor.

Papa and Tommy, soaking wet from the short scramble through the rain, walked down the long hallway and turned left into the T-shaped office. In 1974, according to a sign above the captain's desk, "These Walls Came Tumbling Down." The walls had been torn away, transforming the office from a ten-foot square box with six people huddled inside to a big, brighter office with a six-foot window overlooking the street. Housed with the Fugitive Division were Criminal Warrants and Bailbonds. A bank of fifteen file cabinets lay flush against the bulkhead, holding 50,000 cards among its metal containers. Adjacent to the cabinets sat a half dozen pieces of computer equipment.

Papa approached the watch commander, a fat, jolly man with oversized ears sticking straight out from his head, and explained to him who he was and why he was there.

"Billy Joe Face?" the watch commander said suspiciously.

"The same," Papa said.

"You got papers?"

"I do," Papa answered, producing the certified copy of the bailbond, the power of attorney from the bonding company authorizing the Sheriff's Department to surrender Billy Joe to him. Also in the envelope were mug shots of the fugitive.

The officer looked over the material. His expression was no longer a friendly one.

"Mr. Thorson," he said haltingly. "I don't rightly know what to do with this."

"Just give me one of your men for an hour and I'll go pick up Billy Joe."

" 'Fraid I can't do that."

"What do you mean?"

The watch commander fumbled through the papers and looked everywhere but at Papa. Wrinkles grew on his wide forehead. Tommy played eye ball with a woman officer across the room.

Papa waited long enough and said, "I came all the way from Los Angeles for this man, Sergeant. I want him." His insistence jolted the watch commander who picked up the phone and dialed a number. No answer.

"Mr. Thorson," he said, "would you have a seat? I think you better talk to Sheriff Strong on this."

Papa knew about Sheriff John Strong who during his tenure had become one of those larger than life characters; legendary. His control over Houston in particular and Texas in general was absolute. He instituted the "Strong Hold," which meant all Strong had to do when he wanted a man for questioning was to call up any police department in the state and tell them to pick the guy up and hold him till he got there. Within minutes every available cop was sent looking for the suspect who often spent weeks in jail waiting for Strong to show up.

"Mr. Thorson," the watch commander said when he returned, "this way please."

Papa and Tommy followed the officer down the hall and into Sheriff Strong's office. The room was huge. A picture window looked out over the Houston cityscape. Photos of Strong shaking hands with celebrities lined the walls. Momentoes from the old Texas Ranger days stood on bookshelves and teakwood cabinets. A paperweight of a silver horse rearing sat on the massive desk. Behind the desk, with his back to Papa, was Strong himself.

The watch commander left Papa and Tommy in the center of the room. The sheriff made no move to get up. He remained in his chair gazing out through the window. Papa cleared his throat.

"I know you're there, Mr. Thorson," Strong said in his gruff Texas drawl. "Be with you." Strong's head dropped back and he stood.

Papa was not at all prepared for the size of the man.

Strong stood over six-five. Long white curly hair fell over his ears and an equally white handlebar moustache, waxed at the tips, covered his upper lip. Strong looked as if he'd spent a lot of time at the gym; he was lean and evil-looking and to Papa's mind would have made a terrific heavy in a B movie.

Papa reached over and shook the man's hand.

"Heard a lot about you, Sheriff," he said with admiration.

"Heard about you too, Mr. Thorson. All bad." Strong reared back and let out a belly laugh that must have carried all the way down the hall.

"I hope so," Papa smiled back. "Wouldn't want my reputation ruined."

Strong lifted his head and glanced around the room.

"First time yuh seen my office here, eh?"

Papa nodded.

"They blew it. Moved in all this *modern* furniture, made all these *modern* changes, and tried to make an old-time cowboy like myself into a *modern* man. Course that'd never happen but"—Strong chewed on his bottom lip and scratched his neck—"they sure made it rough for a sixty-five-year-old horsetrader like myself to keep his wits about him."

Strong kept his head tilted back when he spoke, and Papa found himself rising up on his toes to look the man in the eye.

"Now what can I do for yuh, Mr. Thorson?"

Papa handed the envelope to him. "I'm here to take Billy Joe Face back to Los Angeles."

"So I hear." Strong opened the envelope, sifted through the papers, replaced them and handed the envelope back to Papa. "My recommendation to you, Mr. Thorson," said Strong with an easy smile, "is git outa town."

That's when Papa saw the glass eye, the left one, floating in its socket. When Strong moved his head the eye went along with it. Papa had trouble *not* looking at it because it never seemed to be looking back. The eye sort of hung there, half asleep, half dead. It was disconcerting as hell. So was Strong's response.

"Soon as I get Billy Joe, Sheriff," said Papa. "I'll be out of the state by morning."

"I don't think you quite understand me, Mr. Thorson. I want you out now."

"Now?"

Strong nodded. The eye again. "Without this Billy Joe."

"I can't do that, Sheriff. You've seen the papers. I've come a long way."

"And I appreciate it."

Papa wondered what the hell was going on. Strong was congenial enough but something was bothering him. Some punk kid who had written bad checks didn't seem important enough for the sheriff to get riled over.

"Can you tell me this, Sheriff Strong," Papa said with some caution. "Why is it you won't help me get this man, and why don't you want *me* to get him?"

Strong turned halfway around and stared out the window.

"I really don't have to answer any of your questions."

"Well," Papa shrugged, "I'm going after him whether you help me or not."

"Oh no you ain't."

"Oh yes I am."

Strong turned back to Papa and peered down at him. "Don't argue with me, Mr. Thorson."

"Listen," Papa said, half confused, half irritated. "I drove fifteen hundred miles for the bastard. I'm not going back without him."

Strong leaned forward with both hands resting on the desk. With his right hand he reached into a desk drawer and pulled out an old Colt .45 hogleg with the big barrel. He lay the weapon on the desk, cocked it and aimed it directly at Papa's groin.

"Goodbye, Mr. Thorson," he said.

Papa looked at Strong then down at the Colt .45 and back to Strong. He took a deep breath and said, "Goodbye, Sheriff."

Papa turned and left the room. Tommy followed closely behind. They moved back down the corridor to the elevator and rode it to the ground floor. The rain didn't bother Papa as he strode from the building to the car. He climbed in the front seat, slamming the door behind him, and sat fuming.

"What kind of shit . . ." He gripped the steering wheel tightly. "I've *never* run into this kind of crap before."

"What're you gonna do?" Tommy asked, excitement in his voice.

Papa glanced at the third-floor windows and figured that

Strong was looking back. "I don't know. Can't stay here, that's for sure."

Papa drove out of Houston but the further he went the madder he got, until they reached the Brazos River where he pulled into a roadside rest area and turned off the ignition.

"There's something funny going on." He ran both hands through his pockets. "Got a dime?"

Tommy found one and handed it over. Papa climbed from the car and walked to a phone booth standing near the picnic tables. He dialed information and got the Houston number of Bennie Fogel. Fogel was a member of the Houston low-life. He ran booze, dope and broads across the Mexican border for a living and had been one of Papa's informants since the late fifties. Papa had met Fogel through another informant, Jack Ruby, the same Jack Ruby who later shot Lee Harvey Oswald. When Ruby was sent to jail Papa began using Fogel as his main source of information.

"Bennie," Papa said into the receiver. "Ralph Thorson."

"Papa, Papa, how the hell are you! *Where* are you?"

"Outside Houston."

"Jesus Christ. Get your ass over here. Have I got some women you'd like. Three Mexican virgins."

"Every time the moon comes up. Listen, Bennie, I got a problem you might be able to figure out."

"Shoot."

"I just got kicked out of Houston by Sheriff John Strong."

"That ain't no problem. Just go."

"I went into his office, said I was here looking for this guy and, goddammit, Strong gets all bent outa shape and aims a Colt .45 at my balls."

"Sounds just like the bastard. What'd you do to him?"

"Not a damn thing. All I wanted was to pick up this guy."

"Uh huh. What's the guy's name?"

"Billy Joe Face."

There was a pause at the other end, then Bennie started to chuckle.

"Billy Joe Face!" Bennie exclaimed. "For crissake, no wonder he gave you the boot. You know who Billy Joe Face is?"

"Tell me."

"His nephew. Billy Joe Face is Strong's nephew."

"Oh, Jesus."

Papa thanked Bennie Fogel for the information and returned to the car.

"Well," he said to Tommy, "looks like we're going to have to snatch Billy Joe all by ourselves."

Papa wheeled the car around and headed back for Houston. Billy Joe's cousin Jimmy had provided Richie Blumenthal with Face's address: Billy Joe and his wife were staying at his brother-in-law's home in the exclusive River Oaks section of Houston.

It was after midnight when they coasted down the tree-lined street. The homes were in the $100,000-plus bracket, which to Papa said that Billy Joe's writing bad checks meant he was living way beyond his means, probably trying to keep up with his brother-in-law.

Papa turned on the car's overhead light and glanced at the mug shots. Billy Joe was thin and bony, with light hair sweeping over his forehead. A mole appeared at the right corner of his mouth. Papa replaced the mug shots and continued down the street.

"What're we lookin' for?" Tommy asked, trying to catch a number.

"Seventeen-oh-five."

Tommy squinted his eyes, keyed in on a sidewalk mailbox and said, "Seventeen-oh-one."

Papa edged slowly forward and stopped beside a bush guarding the circular driveway to the house. An old green Cadillac sat in the drive. A Black Sambo knocker peered at them from the center of the front lawn. Papa pulled the .45 from its holster, checked the ammo and returned it.

"I hope Billy Joe goes to bed early," he said, stroking his beard.

The house was lit on both floors and the faint musical strains of a country-western station filtered out from the interior.

"You ain't goin' in, pick him up?" Tommy wanted to know.

"Would you?"

"Hell, I'd just bust in, ram that old pistol into his eye and drag him out."

Papa unstrapped the holster and handed it to Tommy. "Go ahead," he said.

Tommy hesitated. He looked from Papa to the house and back again. "You comin' with me?"

"Nope."

"Not even to help me out?"

"Uh uh."

Tommy took another pause. "How come?"

"For one thing I don't know who's in there or what kind of weapons they've got. For another thing, I don't want any shooting. That's the easiest damn way I know of getting killed."

Papa surveyed the house to see if any upstairs lights had been extinguished. None had, so he leaned back in the seat and turned towards Tommy.

"Well," he said, "you going in?"

"Not just yet," Tommy replied, handing the .45 to Papa.

And they waited. And waited. At 1:10 an upstairs light went out.

"Probably the brother-in-law," Papa said, "unless Billy Joe had a fight with his wife."

At 1:55 the final upstairs light clicked off. By 2:00 Papa was ready to move.

"Bedrooms are dark," he mumbled to himself, checking off the details. "Two men, two women. Downstairs light's on." He turned to Tommy. "Whaddya think the situation is in there?"

Tommy thought for a moment.

"Well, at least two people went to bed, maybe the wives. Which means the men are still in the livin' room. Or, if a couple hit the sack, and one other person, there's only one left downstairs. Which I would think is the case."

"Yes," Papa told him. "Except for one thing. *Always* expect more than you see. Far as I'm concerned, there's two people down there. I'll be looking for two."

Papa opened his door and got out. He reached into the back seat and pulled out the Prowler Fouler. "Tommy," he said, "you help me out here and I'll let you turn yourself in back in L.A. That way you'll avoid a lot of court hassles, and you might save my ass in the meantime."

"Okay, Papa."

Papa checked the gas gauge. "Slide on over here. Keep the engine running. And if you see anybody hot on my tail blast him with this thing. Got it?"

"Got it."

Tommy moved behind the wheel and cradled the Prowler Fouler in his lap.

"If I'm not back in fifteen minutes," Papa said, "wait."

With that he crossed the sidewalk and angled towards the house, keeping to the treeline on the edge of the property. He reached the front porch and tiptoed towards the door. He took a thick piece of plastic from his pocket and slipped it under the latch. Just as the door unlocked a second light flashed in the living room. Papa recoiled, pasted his back against the building. He waited, listened, placed his right hand over the .45. Then he eased closer to the door and looked through the parted lace curtains. He saw the back of a man's head but couldn't tell whether it belonged to Billy Joe. Billy Joe's mug shots came into focus and Papa, for the first time, wondered why only a front and side view appeared in mug shots. Here he was looking at the back of the head.

Papa continued along the porch, checking at each window, until at the end of the porch he saw what he wanted. It was Billy Joe, in a bathrobe, with his feet propped up on the coffee table, watching a movie on television.

Papa retraced his steps back to the door, opened it softly and stepped into the anteroom. He pulled the .45 from the holster and crept up behind Billy Joe. He was now just a few feet behind the man. He shot a glance up the staircase. Clear.

Papa's left arm curled around Billy Joe's neck, yanking his body half out of the chair. The .45 was aimed behind his ear.

"Billy Joe," Papa whispered. "One sound and your brains will be on television."

Billy Joe tried to free himself. Papa tightened his neck grip. "Dammit, be a good boy and you won't get hurt."

Papa lifted him completely out of the chair and carried him from the room.

Billy Joe shook violently in his robe and asked in a quivering voice, "What's happening?"

"Nothing."

"I ca-unt go out like this."

"Yes, you can."

Papa took him through the anteroom and out to the porch. Halfway down the sidewalk Billy Joe jammed his elbow into Papa's gut. Papa jammed his gun into Billy Joe's back. "You hard of hearing, Billy Joe? Goddammit!"

At the car Papa handcuffed him and threw him in the back seat. The weapons and mace were transferred to the front floorboard and Tommy got in beside Billy Joe.

Papa had driven just a few hundred yards when he heard loud sobs coming from the rear.

"Why yuh doin' this to me? I ain't done nothing wrong," Billy Joe moaned.

Papa turned his head slightly and said, "You've done a lot wrong. You wrote bad checks and you jumped bail."

"Just a few thousand dollars," Billy Joe whined.

"And look at all those people you stuck," Papa added.

"Stores and banks. That happens every day. I wanna go home."

"How 'bout your cousin Jimmy? He put up his money for your bail. What about him?"

"Oh, that's Jimmy."

"That's right."

Papa drove all night; northwest along the Colorado River, back through Austin, San Angelo and Big Spring. At seven-thirty the next morning he crossed the Texas border into Hobbs, New Mexico.

He pulled up to the first phone booth he found, dragged Billy Joe Face from the back seat and placed a long distance call to the Houston Sheriff's Office.

"This is Ralph Thorson," he told the desk sergeant. "I want to talk to Sheriff Strong."

"The sheriff ain't in, Mr. Thorson, but if you'll leave a number I'll have him return the call."

"I haven't got time for that, Sergeant, so why don't you patch me in to wherever the sheriff is. Tell him it's mighty important."

Papa knew that Strong spent most of his time in a mobile unit where he ate and screwed and slept while he traveled around the state. Strong sounded as if he'd just climbed out of bed when he came on the line.

"Sheriff Strong, this is Ralph Thorson, remember me?"

"Mr. Thorson, I surely do. How you doin'?"

"Oh, I'm just fine. Just called to tell you, Sheriff, I took your advice and got outa town."

"Well, good for you, Mr. Thorson. I kinda figured you would."

"There's just one thing. I took your fucking nephew

with me. Say hello, Billy Joe!" Papa shoved the receiver into Billy Joe's mouth.

"Uncle John?" Billy Joe quivered.

"Nephew, seems like you're in a little hot water."

"Yes, sir, I am."

"Well, don't you worry none. You'll be back home in no time a'tall."

Papa took the receiver back.

"Just thought I'd let you know what the situation was, Sheriff."

"You done pretty damn good, Mr. Thorson. You were doin' your duty. I was protectin' my kin. Yessir, you done real good. Next time you're down Houston way, stop in say hello, why doncha?"

"You bet, Sheriff. Bye."

Papa hung up and sauntered back to the car with a satisfied smile on his face. He shoved Billy Joe in the back and climbed in.

"What'd Strong have to say?" Tommy asked.

"Congratulated me on doing a fine job."

"No shit? He said that?"

"Twice," he grinned.

Papa started the engine and headed west towards California.

In 1886 Great Grandfather Thorson, a staunch Norwegian Lutheran, made his living as a wheat rancher one hundred miles southwest of Oslo. His son, T.B., had the Viking in him and migrated over the North Atlantic to Anaconda, Montana, where he too became a rancher. T.B. possessed a more commercial sense than his father and opened a grocery store, Thorson's, which grew into Anaconda's largest independent. T.B.'s son, Ralph Edgar, Sr., Papa's father, was a rugged, handsome man who became a prominent social and political figure. The Thorson influence, and the Thorson land holdings, expanded until the family exerted substantial power over much of western Montana.

In the year 1635 the Hereford family arrived on the ship *Planter* from England, in Braintree, Massachusetts, and during the next two hundred years established themselves as landed gentry and high government officials. James A. Hayford (Hereford), in 1868, moved to

Laramie, Wyoming, and seventeen years later was appointed judge of the Second Judicial District.

The judge's son, A. C. Hayford, was a railroad man who, like his father, had the nomad in him. A.C. finally settled his family, and his position with the Butte, Anaconda and Pacific Railroad, in Anaconda itself. It was there that A. C. Hayford's daughter Margaret met Ralph Edgar Thorson. They fell in love, and were married in 1923.

Three years later, on July 11, 1926, Papa was born, a Cancer, of dual imagination and sensibilities, a man of divided emotions, a division which would partition the rest of his life into what he wanted to become and what he would be.

Papa has traveled seemingly incompatible routes but has arrived at a fruition, an essence that, understanding his journey, was inevitable.

4

The Eighth House Is Death

Papa dropped Billy Joe at the Los Angeles City Jail and left Tommy Price outside to turn himself in. They had been on the road for thirty-five hours since leaving Houston and Papa was dead tired.

The Ventura Freeway leading from the jail to Papa's North Hollywood home was free of traffic on this bright early afternoon. He left the freeway near Universal City and took Lankershim north towards Magnolia.

When he turned the corner onto Magnolia he passed Bob Hope's massive twenty-three-acre estate with the private nine-hole golf course in the back yard. The incongruity for Papa was that the estate, built twenty years ago when this section of North Hollywood was a huge open field, should now be surrounded on all sides by homes on quarter-acre lots. Bob Hope never figured the middle class would bulldoze its way across North Hollywood; nobody figured it. But they did. Papa always got a kick out of it when he heard someone say, "Oh, *my* neighbor is Bob Hope!"

Papa was less than five minutes from home when a call came over the radio. It was Richie Blumenthal.

"Papa," Richie said in his gruff Brooklynese accent, "how are you?"

"Tired," Papa replied.

"How'd you do?"

"Billy Joe Face is in the can. I let Tommy Price turn himself in; he helped me out."

"Got another case for you," Richie said. "Twenty-five grand."

"Shoot."

"Tony Bernardo. Armed robbery. First offense. Jumped bail the other day on a no-show. His parents were here and very nervous, Papa. They hocked everything . . ."

Papa cut him off. "Shitcan the sob story," he said, not willing to listen to another of Richie's long sad renditions.

"There's more. I'm in for the two and a half G's."

"Richie, Richie, when are you going to learn. Keep the heart out of the pocketbook."

"Lectures I don't need."

"Lectures you do need," Papa said half-heartedly. With all the money Richie had stashed away he could have bailed out Los Angeles.

"Papa . . ."

"All right. All right, I'll take it. I don't know why."

"For me," Richie insisted.

"Why else? I'll be in tomorrow for the file."

"Don't bother. It's in the mail."

"You're a sweetheart."

Papa rang off and quickly calculated what picking up Tony Bernardo would mean to him financially. Normally, he would collect his standard 20 percent of the bail—in this case $5,000. But since he was on a weekly retainer to Richie the fee would drop to 10 percent—$1,250—which he *might* get if Richie happened to be in a good mood the day he brought Tony Bernardo in. Papa could rely on Richie for the weekly check but when it came to collecting fees it was like bucking Ma Bell for a rebate.

During their fifteen years together Papa and Richie have had only one major split, which lasted three years. The split had been coming for some time when one day in June, 1969, Papa paid a visit to the bondsman's office.

"Any two people working together for that long have their arguments," Papa says. "With him it's a perpetual bitch, one bitch after the other. It's all part of the racket. A bondsman and his bounty hunter fit the classic mode, like the landlord and the tenant. Richie's the consummate barracuda when it comes to paying off. I expect it. He expects me to argue back.

"That day I went down to his office we argued for hours. We were getting nowhere fast until I whipped out a seven-point plan which stated explicitly how much I should get for each case. I said, 'Sign it!' and shoved it in his face. He signed and gave it back.

"Six months later we were at it again, same argument—money—and I pulled out the seven points. 'You signed this, Richie—the whole thing is outlined.' I shoved it at him. He shook his head and said, 'I didn't sign it. That's not my signature.' 'Hell if it isn't,' I told him. 'No, that's not my signature.' I took a look at it and, sure enough, the scribbling at the bottom wasn't his name. It was signed 'fuck you!' I walked out and didn't see him for three years.

"We'd talk on the phone every once in a while though and he would always tell me what hotshot bounty hunters he had working for him, and how he didn't miss me. One of these hotshots—who I nicknamed Depitty Dawg—was an ex-cop from Arkansas who was kicked off the force there. The first case he was on Richie sent him to Texas to pick up a dope dealer. Depitty Dawg gets down there, flashes his gun and the badge he kept from the Arkansas cops and—bang—the bailjumper handcuffs Depitty Dawg to a tree with his own handcuffs, takes his car and his wallet, and before leaving smashes him in the mouth with his own gun, knocking out his front teeth. Depitty Dawg had to call Richie collect to send him money to get home.

"Next case out Depitty Dawg went after a hooker who skipped and also went to Texas. Depitty Dawg wasn't real swift to begin with and actually drove all the way down there on a $300 bond. He snatched the hooker and handcuffed her to the dashboard of his car. On the way back they stopped at a café for lunch. He uncuffed her and they walked into the place. As soon as they entered the hooker screams rape. The local cops rush in, cut her loose and bust Depitty Dawg.

"The third and last case had Depitty Dawg driving all the way to Kentucky to grab some sniveling John Smith. He found the guy, slapped cuffs and leg irons on him and

hauled him kicking and screaming all the way back to
L.A. He took the guy down to the Dicks Bureau and told
them he had their man. No you don't, they said, we already picked him up. Then who's this? Depitty Dawg
wanted to know. We don't know, said the cops.

"It turned out that he picked up the wrong guy. The
state of Kentucky brought Depitty Dawg back and put
him in the state pen for two years for kidnapping, false imprisonment and all sorts of felonies.

"He finally got out and went back to L.A. But Depitty
Dawg was a marked man because the second he walked
into the house his old lady picked up a twelve-gauge shotgun and blew him back out the door. So every time Richie
gives me some trouble I tell him to go get himself a Depitty Dawg to handle his cases."

Papa's house sits on a street lined with homes and
apartment buildings whose only conformity lies in the fact
that there isn't any. If Studs Terkel had come to this
neighborhood to find a cross section of the American
middle class he would have gone away babbling to himself. Across the street from Papa's multi-leveled, small-
roomed crackerbox of a house lives Jimmy Doohan, the
pixie-faced Scotty of *Star Trek*. Next door is an old-time
Cosa Nostra figure who has long since retired.

The street has its hopped up Harley-Davidson choppers
leaning on their kickstands; candy apple-lacquered Chev-
rolets snuggled against the sidewalks, their owners spit
shining the polish; dozens of kids dashing in and out of
buildings and racing across the street. Three doors away is
the Mad Dog Coll's mad son, Mad Dog Donovan, who recently won a huge settlement from an insurance company.
Mad Dog, Jr., celebrated the haul by marching down Bailbond Row, stoned out of his mind, with two Colt .45's on
his hip and $40,000 stuffed into his rear pocket, challeng-
ing everybody he met to take the cash away from him.

Despite the odd assortment of characters, Papa's block
is not unlike other North Hollywood neighborhoods. The
homes range in price from thirty-five to seventy-five thousand. Rust-colored pyramids, the result of wayward sprin-
kler systems, climb the sides of houses. Juniper trees guard
some entances; hedges protect others. Two blocks to the
east, lining both sides of Lankershim, are small stores interspersed among the shopping centers. The Xerox-copy

place where Papa duplicates file material and news-clippings of interest is on Lankershim, along with his favorite liquor store and pharmacy. He shops for food at Ralph's, the chain market down the street from the health food store where he bi-monthly loads up on vitamins and natural foods. Also close by are numerous variety stores stocked with everything from antiques to marked-down fashions. Papa is a voracious bargain hunter and will drive fifty miles to a garage sale to spend hours pouring over items for which he has no need, except to bargain.

The house sits on a garden plateau corner lot, a pale yellow adobe-type structure with a garage out back and, on the north side facing the street, a wood fence-enclosed patio with a fish pond in the center. An old, unused, stand-up hibachi takes up one corner of the patio where Papa has frequently picnicked in the eight years he has owned the house. In the back yard is a doghouse inhabited by a pure white, one-year-old wolf. The animal is protected by its father, a dog named Fang, who on Papa's command will attack a man.

Inside the house awaiting his return was Dotty, his girl friend of ten years who has that thin, country-western, close-to-the-bone look and short red hair that sunlight filters through. It was Kenny, Dotty's thirteen-year-old son by a former marriage, who gave Papa his name. When Dotty moved in with Papa in 1965 Kenny never called him by name. At the time Papa was known only as Ralph. That wouldn't do for the three-year-old Kenny; neither would Mr. Thorson. He began calling him Papa. The name stuck.

Also in the house was the stocky, dark-complected Myron Fish who sat in the middle of the living room frantically trying to reassemble the television set whose components were spread all over the carpet. Myron was one of the hangers-on who regularly visited the house. Before Papa had left for Texas, Dotty compiled a list of people who had actually lived in the house over the last seven years. The figure came to one hundred and seven. They consisted mostly of men Papa had picked up and sent to jail. After their release they returned for Papa's special brand of rehabilitation. Not only did he house them and find them jobs where he could, he counseled them, loaned them money, sometimes bailed them out, and only rarely kicked them out when they took extreme advantage. They always returned. The house had become a haven for them, a meeting place where they could rehash old crimes and capers.

Myron Fish was not like the others. Myron bolstered his income by stealing electronic equipment from the places he worked. Twice he was caught and twice sent to jail. The second time, in March, 1973, he failed to show up on the court date and thus became a forfeiture whom Papa was sent to retrieve. Papa had him back in the can within two days and Myron spent a year at Folsom prison. The day he was released he showed up at the house.

Myron was an anomaly. As a thief he was a miserable failure. As an electronics expert he was a genius. He could fix anything—televisions, stereo equipment, radios, all appliances—in record time. He taught computer programming at local schools, including Santa Monica College, and was considered by the schools' administrations as a top-flight instructor. On numerous occasions Papa had witnessed his mechanical prowess—at other people's homes, never his own. Whenever Myron tried fixing something in Papa's house he mysteriously ended up destroying it beyond repair. His failure had to do with Papa himself, an admixture of fear and adulation Myron felt towards him. Myron's genius disappeared in Papa's presence.

Papa learned that Myron's home life was disastrous, classically so, with a dominant mother and an effete, browbeaten father whose chief asset, it seemed, was taking orders from his wife. All his life, Myron wanted a strong father, and admitted as much. He chose Papa.

To please him, Myron tried repairing things that didn't need repairing, for the sake of making them perfect. He destroyed toasters, the refrigerator, the deep freeze, a Mix Master in which Papa blended drinks, the stereo and the television that now lay in a shambles at his feet.

Myron's great ambition was to become a bounty hunter. He asked Papa endless questions about the business and pleaded with him to take him along on cases. Which Papa did, to his everlasting agony. In his desire to please, Myron also botched up the cases. Papa ended up spending more time getting Myron out of trouble than he did coralling bailjumpers into jail. On three occasions Myron discharged his weapon just when Papa was about to grab fugitives, allowing them to escape. Once he ran Papa's car into a light pole. When no one was in the house Myron answered phone calls and took down information that later proved to be so confused that Papa spent hours unscrambling it. Neither Dotty nor any of Papa's friends could figure out why Myron was allowed to hang around. He was a total liability. When the question was put to Papa, he replied that Myron, underneath it all, was basically a good kid. Papa further admitted that he liked the idea of Myron treating him as a father figure and also that rehabilitating the kid had become one of life's supreme challenges.

Unfortunately, the challenge was looking more hopeless every day. Myron knew when Papa got home and saw what he had done to the television all hell would break loose. That's why every few minutes he looked up at Dotty and said with mournful eyes, "How long before he gets back, d'ya know?"

"Soon," she said. "I'd leave if I were you."

"Okay. I'll have it back together in a second."

Papa had phoned Dotty from San Diego, saying he'd be in around three. It was already after the hour.

Since the call Dotty had been moving about the house with a duster in one hand and a cleaning rag in the other, stepping carefully through Myron's mess as she moved.

For Dotty, who did all the cleaning, the house was a testament to Papa's refusal to throw anything away. The rooms were not cluttered but overstocked.

Against one living room wall is a massive stereo setup flanked by 500 albums and tapes, almost exclusively classical, alphabetically arranged. If it's Giuseppe Verdi Papa wants to hear he will immediately pluck it from the stacks. Or Dvořák which sits next to Bob Dylan, which is beside Georges Enesco, next to Manuel de Falla. Above the stereo is the Thorson coat of arms, and beside that a skull with a candlestick jutting from the top.

Tucked into one corner of the room is a circular, padded bar with high-backed leather stools and an ice machine. A specially made chair sits behind the bar from which Papa directs all traffic and conversation, and once there, seldom moves for hours, all the time asking whomever is in the room—usually Dotty—to retrieve cigarettes, mixers, and papers from the massive file cabinets in his office. From his chair he operates like a circus ringmaster, and is given the deference that position holds.

An open bar divides the living room from the kitchen

where a deep freeze takes up one entire wall. The deep freeze is stocked with two hundred pounds of steaks and chops and chicken. The kitchen door has on its lower panel a rubber flap which allows Fang to pass to and from the back yard.

The rear of the house is occupied by two bedrooms, separated by a bathroom into which someday Papa wants to install a Roman tub and Jacuzzi.

Guarding the entrance to the oddest room in the house—Papa's office—is a sturdy sofa worn from the imprint of thousands of asses. Opposite the sofa are three gun racks with 12-gauge shotguns, two 30-06 Woodmasters, two 30-30 saddle carbines, a half dozen bolt-action rifles, an arsenal of handguns, including a .45 caliber nickle-plated one with hand-carved silver grips. The .45, according to Guadalajara, Mexico, officials who have placed a price on Papa's head, will be his ransom if they ever pick him up. In the event that happens, Dotty has instructions to bring the revolver to a prearranged rendezvous spot on the Mexican border near San Luis where she will exchange it for Papa. As much as those Mexicans hate Papa they love the .45 more.

Between the gun racks and the sofa, elevated two steps above ground level, is Papa's office. No one but Dotty is allowed into this inner sanctum of a room with its black leather and steel desk set. The walls are painted silver gray, giving off an eerie illuminated glow. The room has an ashen quality, removed from the rest of the house by a dark Spanish archway. Here Papa keeps files on former and current case portfolios, short stories he has written, a haphazard collection of memoirs, his special library of law books and journals, famous and bizarre cases from history, an extensive collection of books on astrology and the occult. Hanging above the cabinets is a plaque that reads: "Yea, though I walk through the valley of the shadow of death, I will fear no evil . . . because I'm the meanest sonofabitch in the Valley." Stacks of unopened and unanswered letters lay scattered on the desk and overhead shelves.

The room's single window looks out on the street, giving Papa a panoramic scan of the neighborhood. A black velvet curtain is drawn across the window when Papa is on the road. When he's behind the desk settled into the swivel chair he has access to three telephones from which he makes early morning calls to the East Coast with its three-hour time difference. Beside the phones, on the gray tinted desktop, are two tape recorders. A telephone pickup is attached to each receiver and plugged into the recorders. Papa tapes almost every phone conversation, and instead of writing letters he tapes his voice and mails off the cassettes.

On the shelves beside the desk are mugshots of various bailjumpers still at large. Big cases. Hundred-thousand-dollar jobs. Child molesters, murderers, grand larcenists, mostly men, some women.

On the opposite wall hangs a glossy eight-by-ten photo of actress Sue Lyon who inscribed over her name: "I couldn't help loving you." Papa once saved her $25,000 by hunting down and capturing a boyfriend who skipped bail after she laid out the cash. She once remarked to a *True* magazine reporter doing a story on Papa: "He's the only man I know who can do a bastard's job with taste and come off looking like a nice guy."

The office is Papa's cul-de-sac; he's become part of the room. He gives the room an energy when he sits in the chair, calculating, charting a course through the maze of papers and machines surrounding him. Of all the places Papa has ever been, it is here that he feels the most alive.

Dotty glanced out the window and spotted Papa's car crawling down the street. Myron sensed something and raised his eyes to her. Nothing was said. The message was clear when she gently nodded her head.

Papa decided against hauling the guns into the house just yet. He squeezed out of the front seat and stretched. Dotty waved to him from the window near the bar. He smiled and waved back. Fang barked his welcome from the fenced-in back yard.

Dotty came out the front door and met him halfway down the walk. They kissed and she wrapped one of his arms around her shoulders.

"You look bushed," she said. "I have a steak in the oven. And Myron has the TV all over the living room floor," she added almost inaudibly.

Papa halted.

"Which means I might have to kill Myron, and you for letting him do it."

"I was gone all day," she protested. "He had it spread out by the time I got back. I didn't know he had a key."

"Neither did I."

Myron wasn't in the room when Papa entered. The television set was in a single pile in the middle of the floor.

"What was wrong with the set?"

"Nothing."

"MYRON!" Papa shouted.

Myron appeared at the kitchen door with a dumb, terrified expression. "Hi, Papa."

"Myron," Papa said quietly, "how am I going to watch television tonight?"

"I'll get you another one," Myron said, his head wagging.

"I want this one."

Myron's eyes swept the floor. He pinched his fingers together. His body teetered from one side to the other. For a thirty-two-year-old he was a mess.

"Go home," Papa told him in the same even voice.

It was the only thing Myron couldn't bear to hear. He wanted to explain but there was no way he could do it. Papa had commanded him to leave and he had to obey. He dropped his head, turned and skulked into the back yard.

After Myron had gone Dotty turned to Papa and said, "You shouldn't be so rough on him."

Her comment surprised him. "That was *rough?*"

"All he wants is to please you. You're a father to him."

"I know. *His* father wouldn't make a good mother."

Papa turned and made his way back to the circular bar where he poured a drink.

"Speaking of fathers," Papa said, "how's our friend there?"

Papa was gone only a few days but even in that short a time he noticed, especially on a woman as thin as Dotty, the expanded waistline.

She was three months pregnant.

MARCH 15. When Papa woke that morning three months previously he should have known by the cold, smog-infested air outside that the rest of the day was going to be miserable. In other households when a man discovers he's going to be a father there is cause for celebration. In other households, not in this one.

"When I found out Dotty was pregnant, it was one of the great mind-blowers of all time. She didn't have to tell me; I *knew*, an intuition. I asked her point-blank, and she

denied it, at first. By the time I finished the interrogation
she would have admitted to anything. Still, she had the
nerve to tell me she didn't get pregnant on purpose. She
stopped taking birth control pills. If that's not on purpose
I don't know what the hell is. She said since she was ready
to have a hysterectomy she simply forgot to take the pill
for a few days.

"A kid was the last thing I wanted. Here I was, almost
fifty years old, drinking at least a bottle of booze a day,
along with the serious drinking at night, smoking five
packs of cigarettes a day. I couldn't get insurance because
of the work I do. Doctors told me I should have been
dead thirty years ago with all the crap I put into my body.
I didn't want a kid. I couldn't afford one.

"I haven't got many years to live. That's a fact. I
wanted to know who the hell she thought she was having a
kid. How were she and the kid going to live after I kicked
off? Never occurred to her. Women are so fucking stupid.

"I told her to get an abortion. She said, fine, she would.
Her gynecologist, Dr. Furey, wouldn't perform one because the fetus was over six weeks old, which to Dr. Furey
meant the kid was already alive. How 'bout a clinic, I said
to her. The state of California will perform abortions up
to five months.

"I told her straight away that if she didn't have the
abortion I wasn't going to have anything to do with the
kid. The baby wasn't mine. Sure, I got her pregnant but I
didn't have any decision in having the baby. She never
consulted me, she never discussed, never asked. The baby
was hers. If she tried taking me to court for child support
I told her I'd get five other guys to testify they slept with
her.

"Of all the things I fear, utter helplessness is the worst.
That's what I felt that day—utterly helpless. How the hell
did she expect me to support another body when I was
having a tough enough time as it was. I'm getting old. I
can't bash down doors and chase assholes the way I used
to. When I was younger I could pick up five, six people a
day, no sweat. I was faster then, in much better shape.
Now? Forget it. I'll go out on the road every once in a
while but, hell, I spend months at a time right here at
home. As you get older your perimeters start closing up.

"Why did I go all the way to Texas for Billy Joe Face?
Why would I take jobs I wouldn't normally think twice

about? I had to. She wasn't going to have any abortion. Why did I start cutting down on the booze? Why did I start taking loads of vitamins? Somebody had to take the responsibility. Dotty would have the baby; that was her responsibility. Mine was supporting it. Right from the beginning she kept saying the baby was going to be special, going to be a special person. Big fucking deal. I've never *known* a broad who didn't feel that way. She had no right to pull me into a situation like that."

Papa screamed and ranted and raved at her. The baby had to go. Dotty promised to make an appointment tomorrow.

"I've heard that so many times . . ."

The argument was interrupted by a knock on the door.

"Get that, will you?" Papa said.

Dotty remained in her seat, immobilized, on the verge of tears. She rose but instead of heading for the door she turned and walked off towards the bedroom.

The knock came again and Papa slid from the chair, walked across the living room and opened the door.

"Thorson, you're under arrest," the man said.

"Jack, how are you. C'mon in." Papa left the door open and returned to the bar. Jack closed the door behind him and followed Papa in, remaining in the center of the room.

"You look like hell. Should I come back?" Jack said.

"I just got off the road," Papa mumbled, climbing on the bar chair and regarding LAPD Detective Jack Finnegan. "Sit down," he said. "I'm fine."

Finnegan was a dream cop. He was tall and blond and all-American, a fair-haired Errol Flynn. He won more commendations than anyone his age—30—in the history of the LAPD. He had white, even teeth and a ready smile that enchanted juries. Juries believed everything Jack Finnegan said, he said it so well and with such forthrightness and boyish candor. He was so good that prosecuting attorneys never coached him. He was also a crack police officer. His list of informants was as good as anyone's, most of whom he met through Papa. He traded information with a substantial portion of Papa's network of snitches and informants. Finnegan was proud of the fact that he never once worried about meeting arrest quotas. For these reasons, and because he was known to possess impeccable integrity, he rose quickly through the ranks.

Papa had known Finnegan for ten years, having met him on a pickup. Finnegan drove a squad car then and when he came to Papa's assistance they began talking. Papa was impressed by the young man's intelligence, and his wit. He told jokes with a lot of sagacity.

He was currently huddling with Danny Krebs, a cat burglar, and Billy Burnham, an ex-border patrol cop on the Mexican line. With their help Finnegan was tracing heroin and amphetamine distributors in the Los Angeles area.

Before Finnegan reached the bar Papa had the bourbon uncorked and ready to pour.

"A double," Finnegan said.

"A double it is. Why aren't you working?"

He grabbed the lapels of his three-piece worsted and fanned them out. "I am," he said. The .38 was tucked under his armpit. "I'm supposed to meet Danny Krebs at four."

"What's the deal with you two?" Papa wanted to know. "He gives you names and you let him knock off an apartment a week?"

"Something like that," Finnegan grinned.

Finnegan reached inside his coat pocket and pulled out a sheet of notebook paper. "Will you do me a favor?"

Papa compressed his face and squinted at him. "Depends."

Finnegan handed over the paper. "Check this out."

Papa looked it over. "Yours?"

"I figured it's about time."

"That calls for a drink, or two or three."

The paper read: "April 8, 1943. 6:45 p.m. Lansing, Michigan." The data Papa needed to calculate Jack Finnegan's astrological chart.

"Why all of a sudden do you want me to do it?" Papa asked him. "I've been bugging you for years."

"That's the reason."

They left astrology for a time and went on to other topics. Papa told Finnegan about picking up Billy Joe Face, after which the detective reeled off details of a current investigation he was handling, a ring of auto thieves who were operating in Los Angeles. The ring stole cars from the street, drove them to a warehouse where they were repainted and had the serial numbers and tags changed, and sold them out of state.

"The only real lead we have," Finnegan explained, "are two guys who call themselves Mutt and Jeff. Two of the stolen cars were located in Seattle, picked up by the police there. The owners described Mutt and Jeff as the ones who sold them the cars. Know anything about them, ever heard of them?"

"No."

From that, Papa and Finnegan got on the subject of names and nicknames.

"Finding two guys named Mutt and Jeff should be easy," Papa told him.

Normally, it would be, Finnegan agreed. Normally. Nicknames also worked the other way. Both men had often gone after fugitives, having only their legal names. When they approached people who might have known the fugitives and asked for them by their legal names the people either didn't know them by that name—a Manuel might for years have been known only as Chico—or wouldn't say they knew them, even if they did. It was a system by which to filter out cops and enemies.

California is strongly influenced by Mexican culture, in which nicknames are the rule rather than the exception. The Mexican culture, in turn, has been influenced by the Indians, all of whom had nicknames, which they earned. Old Crow's son was always Old Crow's son until one day he caught a running horse. And so on.

Papa likened the Indians to athletes who must also earn their nicknames—Mean Joe Green, Crazy Legs Hirsch, Scooter Rizzuto, Champagne Tony Lema.

Finnegan listened but kept looking at his watch. Finally he got off the stool and started for the door. Turning back, he said, "Don't forget the chart."

"I'll have it for you this afternoon," Papa told him. "Want to wait?"

"Can't. I have to see Danny Krebs. Tomorrow." With that he flashed his winning smile and vanished.

Two of Papa's telephones were hooked up to an answering service; the third was private so that no one at the answering service could listen in. He drained the remainder of his drink and called the service, instructing the woman to take all calls.

Dotty was still in the bedroom where Papa hoped she

was by now asleep. He did not want to pick up where their argument had left off.

As he started towards the bedroom the private phone rang. He picked it up.

"Papa?" the high-pitched voice asked.

"It depends."

"Papa, this is Winston. How, uh, uh, are you doin'?"

It was Winston Blue, a tall black man with a gold tooth in his mouth, whom Papa had picked up a half dozen times. Papa easily recognized Winston because of the stutter. Winston only stuttered over the phone, however, never face to face. No one knew why. Winston said it must have come from a bad telephone experience during his childhood.

"What can I do for you, Winston?" Papa asked.

"It's this way, Papa, uh, uh, I been picked up for posession, you know, and uh, uh, I can't find nobody to go my bail, so, uh, you know, can you do it?"

"How much?"

"Twen-fi hundre."

"Twenty-five hundred! You're kidding."

"Oh, no, Papa. That's for real. Uh, uh, I'm stuck. I promise to show up, be in court, jus' a few days, you know? Please, Papa. Got nobody close no more. You're the only one."

"Hock your tooth, why don't you? Or how about your clothes?" Winston had a wardrobe Liberace would have been proud of. Winston had already hocked one tooth with a small, inlaid diamond in it. That had been three years ago and Winston had moaned about the loss ever since.

"My clothes? How could you s'gest the thing?"

"Sorry, Winston, I must be overtired." Papa took a deep breath and continued. "Okay, but you've got to promise me. I'll give you one month at the outside. Otherwise, I'll come looking for you."

"Oh, Papa, *believe* me, I'm good for it. I'll be there."

"Something tells me . . ." Papa paused. Winston was so damned unreliable, and such a liar, but in the past he had steered Papa to bailjumpers. "All right, Winston, but remember . . ."

"Uh, uh, I got a mem'ry like an el-phant. You know that."

"No, Winston, more like a sieve. Who's the bondsman?"

"Dell Hoey."

"I'll call him right now. See you in a month, hopefully less, right?"

"Right, Papa. Thanks, man. Thank you."

Papa rang off and called Dell Hoey with the information. Hoey thought Papa was crazy to go Winston's bail but it was his money. Papa was glad it wasn't Richie Blumenthal he was calling, not after having chided Richie for putting up his own money on the Tony Bernardo case.

Dotty looked as if she were sleeping when Papa entered the bedroom. He quietly removed his clothes and slipped into the shower. A half hour later, nestled beside her on the king-sized bed, he was fast asleep.

Papa slept for eighteen hours and woke late the next morning with a splitting headache. He climbed out of bed and padded into the bathroom where he spent the next few minutes wiping the cobwebs from his brain.

When he entered the living room and found Dotty in the kitchen cooking he nodded to her, knowing she would not bring up their argument of yesterday. She smiled and handed him a list of calls he'd gotten.

"Jack Finnegan was here," she told him. "His astrology . . ."

"Oh, Christ, I'd better do his chart."

Papa took the steak and potatoes into his office where he pulled out his *Ephemeris,* the book which charts the daily planetary configurations for the last fifty years. He first calculated Finnegan's Rising Sign, from which he'd be able to figure out the rest of the planets and houses. As he found each he entered it in its designated position on the natal chart. He worked quickly but carefully, having done this thousands of times before.

He had drawn back the velvet curtain, allowing the sun to stream through the window. At one point he asked Dotty to have the answering service hold all calls and to take the receiver off the private line. He wanted no disturbance as he did the chart, especially this chart, which unfolded in startling consequence. Papa was so stunned by what he saw that he checked and rechecked his computations. He couldn't believe that a chart like this could belong to a man like Jack Finnegan.

NOVEMBER, 1939. Anaconda, Montana.

The day was bright and the temperature below zero outside the small schoolhouse. Inside the single-room class with the pot-bellied stove providing the heat, Ralph Thorson sat calculating during his algebra lesson. His teacher, a thin, nervous woman in her forties, happened to pass his desk and asked what he was doing. He told her astrology and showed her the chart he had half completed. The woman remarked that astrology was too inexact and too frivolous. Science, not fantasy, determined the nature of man, she said. The young man did not argue with his teacher. Instead he asked if she would be interested in having her own astrological chart done, just for fun. She agreed and gave Ralph statistics on the date, place and time of her birth. He went home that night and did the chart, only to discover that the data indicated his teacher would meet with a violent death in a very short period of time. He returned to school the following day, fearing to give her the information. When she pressed him for it he told her. The teacher was mildly shocked by what he said, then told him that algebra was what he should be spending his time on.

Two weeks later, with the snow piled high against the road banks, the teacher had just left Sunday Mass and was driving home. When she crossed over the railroad tracks her car stalled momentarily. As she tried putting it back into gear a train roared in from the east and collided with the car, dragging the pieces one hundred yards before coming to a stop. The teacher's body was discovered in the wreckage and Ralph Thorson became a believer.

"I studied astrology through high school and college," Papa remembers, "doing charts for my friends. The more charts I did the more I started realizing the unique correlation between the planetary configurations and how our personalities operate. I wasn't some prophet of good fortune or doom, or a fatalist, which most people think astrologers are. I was simply looking at a person's raw materials. I was gathering data, just as any scientist or shrink would—a composition of character. What astrology really does is discover what we are and not how we'd like to see ourselves.

"Astrology's made an interesting evolution over the centuries. Up till the eighteenth century it was considered a science. Kings had court astrologers. Isaac Newton studied it. The list is endless. Anyway, when the 'scientific community' emerged astrology became a pastime, a kind of fad. Only until lately has it taken an upswing.

"What irritates the hell out of me are those one hundred and eighty-six scientists who recently attacked astrology, called it dangerous. And what did these hotshots base their argument on? Blurbs in the daily newspapers. These are scientists? Newspaper horoscopes are as dangerous as breaking open a fortune cookie and finding out you're going to be rich next week. I should think those learned men would spend their time and the taxpayers' money on something a little more constructive. They had no statistics, no data, to back them up. They're guilty of exactly what they accused astrologers of doing—talking off the tops of their heads.

"On the other hand, I personally know psychiatrists who use astrology in treating their patients. In fact, some of them refuse to treat some people because they're not compatible with them. I think that's a damn good idea. Why buck heads when you don't have to? Why not use astrology, along with Jungian, Freudian or Adlerian analysis, as an aid? A prime example is Dr. David Goodman, a New York clinical psychiatrist, who called astrology 'a good diagnostic adjunct' in treating his patients.

"A similar thing happens in my own business. I use astrology a helluva lot. Example: I look at the fugitive's birthday. Two weeks before and two weeks after his birthday is a bad time for him, a bad time for anyone. The sun has returned to its natal position, which usually indicates trouble with the law, with any authorities. The guy is vulnerable, a perfect time to pick him up. I'll sometimes wait months for his birthday to come up before going after him.

"Tony Bernardo, for instance. I put Richie Blumenthal off by saying I was after the kid. I was really waiting for his birthday. First of all, picking up a fugitive is an energetic situation. Why chase after a guy when his energy is high? Where guns are concerned I want the situation as *un*energetic as possible, if I can help it. I don't always have that option. Let's face it, after chasing as many guys as I have over the years, and coming away with only a few scars, I feel lucky. I place a lot of that good fortune on picking the right astrological moment to hunt the man down."

When Papa finally completed Jack Finnegan's chart, he placed it on the table and stared out the window where dusk had settled over the neighborhood. He called for Dotty who shortly appeared under the Spanish archway.

"Would you buzz Jack Finnegan and ask him to come over?" he said quietly.

She saw the despair on his face and asked, "What's the matter? You look . . ."

"His chart."

"What's the problem with it?"

"I don't believe it, that's what."

"Why not?"

"He's loaded in the eighth house," Papa muttered. "The eighth house is death."

5

Boom Boom Jaworski

Jack Finnegan said he would not be able to get away until the next afternoon. Papa was relieved. He could put off the bad news till then. He picked up the list of phone messages and began at the top.

One caller had a Browning automatic he thought Papa might want to buy, another told him to read an article in the morning paper about a mutual friend who had been found dead in his garage.

"He was found hanging from a beam," the friend said. "Three slugs were in his back, the car engine was going, there were stab wounds around the abdomen. And the cause of death . . ."

"What?"

"Suicide."

Papa had known the dead man well and, knowing the caliber of enemies he had, wondered why he hadn't been eliminated a lot sooner. The cops, themselves probably after him, had most likely called it suicide as a way of saying thanks to whomever did the job.

The remainder of the calls were from friends saying

hello and trying to lure Papa out of the house for the evening, to which he answered: "I just got back. Why don't you come over here?" They knew arguing with him would be futile and agreed to drop over later on.

Finally it was Richie Blumenthal's turn.

No "How are you?" or the dirt of the day; Richie began right off with: "What about Tony Bernardo? Got him yet?"

"Richie, for crissake, I've been back less than two days."

"Made any calls, huh? The mail came, right? You got the information?"

"I got it."

"Whaddya think?" Richie said with growing anticipation in his voice.

"Haven't opened it yet."

"Go ahead. I'll hang on."

Papa whispered into the receiver, "Richie, I just got up. Whaddya do when *you* first get up?"

"What do I do?" A long pause followed. "I take a pill."

Papa's voice perked up. "You do? I didn't know that. What kind?"

Another pause. "Mood elevator."

"Speed? You take speed every morning?"

"I have a prescription," Richie snapped.

"From which croaker? I might know him."

"The Bernardo case," Richie reminded Papa.

"I'm on it day and night. I've got informants out all over the place. Should have him in no time."

"Talk to his parents. They know their kid's friends."

Calling the parents was automatic for Papa. Richie didn't care; as the bondsman he wanted to play part-time detective on every case.

"I got another one for you," Richie added, with what Papa thought was excessive enthusiasm. "Boom Boom Jaworski."

"Forget it," Papa said.

"No, no. He's calmed down. Boom Boom's all right now."

"Boom Boom was never all right and never will be. Give it to somebody else."

"You handle all my cases, Papa. Besides . . ."

". . . nobody else wants it."

"I know you just got back from that miserable Texas,

and going after Boom Boom is rough, but . . . like you said, nobody else wants him."

"I can understand their hesitation."

"Papa, listen, he *has* calmed down. Found out where he lives. You can pick him up. No sweat. How 'bout it? I'll throw in an extra five hundred. Bail's at twenty-five hundred."

Anytime Richie Blumenthal threw in an extra anything it meant problems.

"Calmed down?" Papa said. "What's he packing now— five machine guns instead of ten?"

"No, you don't understand. He's tired of running."

"Who are you shitting?"

"A thousand. I'll throw in an extra thousand."

Big problems!

Papa ignored the offer. "Tell me this," he said, "why do you keep bailing him out?" Papa could understand Richie bailing out motorcycle gang members—bikers—who were not as insane as Boom Boom. A biker—and Boom Boom was the El Marino chapter president of the Hell's Angels—is one of the best bail risks. He'll seldom fail to show up for court. If he doesn't show it means his biker club, who always put up a member's bail, will hunt him down. Forty Hell's Angels converging on one guy is instant death. The Angels commit not murder but atrocity as their modus operandi. Slow death, painfully. It's a strong incentive for showing up for trial.

"The insurance company wants him picked up. It's outa my hands," Richie was saying. "One of their investigators infiltrated the Angels and found out that Boom Boom doesn't want to go to jail—or court—anymore. Of course, that was after the investigator was discovered and got the hell beat out of him. I tried to explain to them that Boom Boom was good for showing up. They don't agree."

"That guy has given you nothing but trouble, Richie."

"Have you ever heard my philosophy?" Richie had a way of bulldozing through a discussion as if it were his own personal monologue. "My philosophy," he went on, "is to post bail for anybody whose name I don't see on the dirty board."

Richie's dirty board hung on the wall opposite his desk. It held the names of the dirty sonofabitches who had ripped Richie off over the years.

"I'm talking individually now," Richie continued.

"Group-wise, I will never—*never!*—ever touch cops or lawyers. You know why that is?"

"Yes."

"Because they'll hit the bricks so fast you'll never see them again. A cop not only goes to civil court, he also gets a departmental trial with a good shot at losing his job. A lawyer has to face disbarment. Talk about risk. I wouldn't touch 'em with a ten foot pole." The following pause was so dramatic that Papa considered applauding.

"Now . . . Boom Boom Jaworski."

"Tell you what, Richie," Papa said, "I'll go after him if you come with me."

The silence told Papa that Richie wasn't laughing. "You're the only one who can handle it, Papa. I'm asking you."

"No way am I going to his place. If you can arrange to get him somewhere else, somewhere out in the open, I'll think about it."

"For five hundred," Richie stated.

"What happened to the thousand?"

"The thousand is for his place, five hundred for somewhere else."

Papa decided to take the case for two reasons: to keep his mind off Jack Finnegan; and, of course, the money.

"What's the address?"

Richie read it off.

"I gotta be crazy to go after that maniac for a thousand bucks," Papa said.

"Bull," Richie said. "For a hundred you'd go after God."

"For God, but for Boom Boom?"

Papa rang off and glanced up at Dotty who was standing beside the gun racks. She wore an anxious expression. She knew, everybody knew, about Boom Boom Jaworski. He was not the most overly dangerous biker in the area but the most unpredictably dangerous, which to Papa's mind *was* the most dangerous. Biker gangs worked on impulse. If they saw somebody looking at them, even with casual interest, they would suddenly attack. A gang member might be bored riding around; he might have had a brawl with his old lady; a headache would do it.

Papa attributes the gang mentality to a childhood phenomenon where most children attach themselves to their peers for both security and out of the fear of isolation. Bike gangs have retained that attitude and refused to outgrow it. They commit outrageous acts which they feel will be excused, or for which they will only be summarily punished.

"Children have their own rites of admission, less sophisticated and bizarre than adults," says Papa. "With a strong group orientation during childhood a guy will join a fraternity, a civic group, a coven or a gang. While a children's gang will accept a new member solely on whether they like him or not, the biker gangs will make him prove himself. A standard initiation requires a new member to eat out a girl's vagina while she's having her period. The event takes place on a motorcycle seat in front of the rest of the gang. If the guy succeeds he gets to fly her Tampax from his handlebars. Another one, and this usually happens right away, is for the initiate to drape a pair of jeans on the ground for the rest of the gang to piss all over. The new member must then wear the jeans and not remove them until they get so ragged they fall off his body. That may seem grotesque—hell, it's *sick!*—but that's mild compared to some of the horror shows put on by fraternities and witch groups I've come across.

"Boom Boom Jaworski was a special case. Before going after him I took a look at Richie's files. Boom Boom had been picked up dozens of times on everything from attempted murder to shoplifting. He spent eight of his twenty-seven years in juvenile halls and state pens. A psychiatrist's report said he was a paranoid schizophrenic; his entire personality had lost touch with his environment and disintegrated into a totally different character. In other words, he freaked out and thought the whole world was against him.

"I was pretty shaky about going after that lunatic. I relied on—it's hard to describe—a *condition* I guess you'd call it, which happens when I confront a situation I'm not exactly sure of, a dream-like state where everything moves in slow motion. Fear is not permitted because the territory around me is my own. I control it. I *expect* to succeed. I'm sure of it. Not cocky, but convinced. It's almost as if some secret force jacks up my perceptions. I know exactly what to do and how to handle the situation. A friend of mine once suggested that by having motion slowed down I was able to predict more accurately the adversary's next move, or at least narrow it down in a hurry. It's a twilight zone. I enter it just moments before the confrontation. It might be the reason I'm still alive."

Papa checked the files on Boom Boom; they were extensive. Los Angeles *Times* and *Herald-Examiner* newsclips dating back eight years mostly concerned the Hell's Angels, occasionally mentioning Boom Boom as the El Marino gang leader. An event not appearing in the news but which Papa learned about from a member of the El Marino force was indicative of how truly bizarre Boom Boom Jaworski really was.

In March, 1973, Boom Boom arrived at the El Marino precinct station after learning of a warrant out for his arrest. According to the source Boom Boom arrived at the precinct, barreled past the watch commander and headed straight for the captain's office. Boom Boom loved to kick down doors but not on the knob side where the door would swing open. He smashed them at the hinges so that the door would fall flat. The captain's door slapped the floor and Boom Boom blew in. The captain almost had a heart attack. He started for his gun but changed his mind when he noted Boom Boom's .45.

"I hear you got a fucking warrant on me, Captain. Why?"

The captain fumbled and stuttered around for a moment. He leafed through papers which he knew didn't contain Boom Boom's RAP sheet, then called the desk for somebody to bring it in. The captain wasn't very happy when he saw one unarmed cop bring the sheet into the office, but he understood why none of his men was interested in confronting the madman.

After reading the sheet the captain said, "Armed robbery on La Mesa and Civic Boulevard. Last night about eleven. There's a witness."

"Shit, I wasn't even awake last night at eleven. I been set-up, Captain. What're you gonna do about it?"

"Uh, arrest you, Boom Boom, what else *can* I do?"

"Good question."

"Well . . ." the captain murmured.

"Well?"

The captain took a deep breath and motioned towards the door where three cops aimed shotguns at Boom Boom.

"So that's the way it is, huh?"

The captain shrugged.

"Okay," said Boom Boom with a calmness that worried them all. "I'm gonna show you what I think of your police department, what I think of the warrant, and what I think of you." Boom Boom dropped his pants and urinated all over the captain's desk.

He was arrested, and out on bail the next day.

Papa knew before he did anything he would have to get help on this one.

Boom Boom Jaworski slept with his eyes open on the army cot in the middle of a barren room, all six-two, 285 pounds of him. Beside him on the cot were two cocked and loaded shotguns. Beneath the cot were four grenades, and under the rock-hard pillow was a heavy .45, also cocked. The foot of the bed pointed towards the room's only door, secured by a police lock and four burglar-proof bolt jams. Anyone wanting to get in either knocked twice and called softly or bashed the door down. In the latter case all Boom Boom had to do was wake up and squeeze the shotgun triggers. That had happened once to a guy who should have known better. Boom Boom attended his funeral. Once a friend—a friend in the figurative sense; Boom Boom had no friends—knocked on the door and had the good sense to stand to one side. When the knock came Boom Boom was having a nightmare and woke up shooting. The impact blasted the door against the wall across the hallway. Which annoyed him because at the time he didn't have enough cash to install another door. He had to rob a grocery store to pay for one. He was apprehended and had to spend eight months in the can. In his own twisted mentality Boom Boom blamed the guy who had knocked and punished him by slicing off the fingers of his right hand. Coincidentally, the guy was a jazz pianist.

It was now early afternoon, about one, when Boom Boom heard a knock. He closed his eyes to wake up, opened them and placed both index fingers on the triggers.

"Who's there?" he said in his high-pitched voice.

"Moose," came the answer, meekly.

Still half asleep, Boom Boom mumbled, "Moose what?"

"It's me, Boom Boom, me, Moose."

A pause. Then: "Just a minute."

Boom Boom crawled out of bed and lumbered over to

the door. It took him a full minute to unlatch the safety catches. He carefully opened the door and in walked Moose who averted his eyes because Boom Boom was naked. For the size of his hands Boom Boom had the smallest cock Moose had ever seen. It looked like a pimple resting there in the bush between his legs. The women Boom Boom fucked—and that's what he did; fucked them; for making any kind of sensitive love was beyond his realm—the women were pleasantly surprised. When that pimple got hard it was said to grow fairly big, about six and a half inches. One of the women nicknamed it the accordion, which pleased Boom Boom. It was the reason he could walk around naked. But Moose didn't know what the women knew and spent the entire conversation looking in an opposite direction.

Always the proper host, Boom Boom asked him if he wanted something to drink. Moose said yes and Boom Boom brought out a four-day-old bottle of Ripple wine, which made Moose sick to his stomach, especially when he had to drink the stuff. If he refused, Boom Boom would have been displeased.

"What's on your mind?" Boom Boom asked, sitting on the cot. Since there was no other furniture in the room Moose had to stand. Moose was a slightly smaller version of Boom Boom and was the number-three man in the motorcycle gang.

"Thought I'd tell you," he said with some caution. "They're lookin' for yuh."

"Who's they?"

"The *in*surance company that put up your bail. They're lookin' for yuh." Moose ended each sentence with a short "ha." They're looking for yuh, *ha*.

Boom Boom exploded. He jumped up from the cot, lifting one shotgun with him, and crossed over to the window which looked out on the Santa Monica Freeway. He raised the shotgun and fired one blast. The pellets meshed with the heavy smog.

"For what, Moose?"

"For what?"

"What's the goddamn insurance company looking for me for? I'm on bail. I ain't committed no crime. They can't pull my bail. I ain't done *nothin'!*"

"Right, Boom Boom. That's all I know. Thought you'd like to know."

"I do! I'm gonna bust some balls down at that El Marino police station, goddammit! You hear me?"

Moose nodded and backstepped towards the door. He'd seen Boom Boom like this before and knew what he could do. Mostly he remembered the time when a rival gang scratched up Boom Boom's bike and how he lobbed a grenade into their headquarters and how they all cleared out fast.

"Some heads is gonna *fall!*" Boom Boom screamed, grabbing his jeans and the leather vest he wore with no shirt. Boom Boom stormed around the room, his hard, mammoth gut ballooning out of him and his short massive arms hanging ape-like just below the belt.

He dressed quickly and ran a comb through his long, stringy black hair. "Let's go," he said and marched past Moose to the hall.

Outside he rammed the shotgun into a leather holster on the bike. He climbed on the big Harley chopper and told Moose, "I'll do this alone. If I ain't back in two hours blow up the po-lice station, yuh hear me?"

"Right, Boom Boom."

Boom Boom started up the chopper and roared off down the street. Big as the bike was, under his frame it looked like a kiddie car.

Twenty minutes later Boom Boom pulled in front of the El Marino station and backed his chopper into the restricted zone. He locked the bike and plugged in the alarm system which would sound off if anybody so much as breathed on it.

The second he hit the front door there was movement. The five cops who were lounging in front of the desk hustled around back and stood behind the watch commander. They all knew Boom Boom and didn't want to mess with him.

"Hello, sumbitches," he said, "how are you?"

Papa Thorson picked up Doc Elliot on the way to the El Marino precinct house. Doc was a biker from a rival gang, Satan's Slaves, who pulled in occasional spending money by helping Papa on pickups. The "Doc" had come from his interest in medicine. Doc was the Satan's Slaves resident physician and dentist when nobody had enough money to spend on the real thing. He patched gun wounds, pulled out raw teeth and knew mumbo-jumbo cures he had read in the book collection his mother had bequeathed to him upon her death.

Doc had the average biker's IQ, which on a good day hovered around sixty, and was consequently thrilled about going after Boom Boom for the points it would make with his own gang, not considering what would happen to him once Boom Boom got out of jail. Papa didn't mention it to him on the ride down to headquarters.

In stature Doc was the antithesis of the mean biker. He stood only five-five and weighed 134 pounds. His clothes were cleaned and pressed and sometimes they even matched. He spoke softly and tried hard not to use double negatives. What made him a threat was the German luger he carried in his shoulder holster.

"So what's the deal with Boom Boom?" Doc asked when he got into Papa's car.

Papa explained about the insurance company's nervousness and the undercover agent who had his head caved in. Papa told him, furthermore, that Boom Boom had committed no additional crime but that any insurance company had the right to call in a bond whenever it wished. Boom Boom was considered high-risk material.

"Uh huh," Doc agreed. "Where is he?"

"All I have is an address on Berkshire in El Marino, but I think we'd better stop by the precinct to see if we can get some backup."

"You think the cops'll come with us? Forget it. They want nothin' to do with that freak. The only way to take him is by surprise, then blow his face off. That dude's got no morality, no respect for law 'n' order. Nothin'. He just as soon blast you as talk to you."

Papa turned off Merrimac and headed down Preston towards the station. He glanced over at Doc who was nervously tearing at his fingernails.

Papa had to pump him up. "Really bad guys like Boom Boom are few and far between, right?"

Doc grunted. "Like the buffalo, man. They almost don't exist anymore."

"It takes a sick combination of insanity and meanness to make somebody like that, right?"

Another grunt. "That man's so sick and insane—I mean they could throw him in the rubber room and he'd be rejected. He's nuts. People like him shouldn't walk the street.

I'm doin' somethin' for society, Papa, picking this asshole up."

"Yup, the guy is lame. In this business," Papa said, "you really get the cream of the crap."

"Don't you know it."

They pulled in front of the station and got out. Papa noticed Doc eying a big blue chopper over in the Red Zone.

"Whaddya know," said Doc. "That bike there . . ."

"What about it?"

"It's Boom Boom's."

"I don't know if this makes it easier or tougher."

"Tougher. That's the way I like it."

"Doc," Papa said to him.

"Yeah?"

"Think easier, okay?"

From the sidewalk they could hear Boom Boom ranting and raving. They climbed the steps and entered the building. There, leaning over the desk towards the six petrified El Marino cops, was Boom Boom. He was banging his fist on the counter top. "First of all, I done nothing! You agree with that?"

The cops nodded.

"Second, I ain't gonna stand for the in-justice. Right?"

More nods.

"Third, when the sonofabitch who's after me finds me I'm gonna waste him. Got that?"

"I got it," said Papa.

Boom Boom wheeled around and stared at them. "I'm that sonofabitch," said Papa.

That took a few seconds to register, and while he was contemplating what Papa said Boom Boom buried his hands in his pockets. Why was anybody's guess. Maybe he couldn't think and aim at the same time. Knowing Boom Boom's mentality, Papa gave that reason a lot of credence.

Boom Boom broke out of his funk and said, "Well, that's interestin'. Lemme tell you: you and your punk friend and all the cops in the worlt ain't gonna take me, no way."

"Yeah, we are," said Papa, with forced nonchalance.

Doc said under his breath, "Let's take him. He's almost in jail as it is."

"He's nowhere near jail," Papa said from the side of his mouth. "The cells are way in the back."

"Hey! Whaddya talkin' about?" Boom Boom roared.

Papa ambled towards him. talking along the way. "Oh, just what a good idea it'd be to put your hands out."

"Put my hands out! You crazy!" Boom Boom cocked his fist at Papa.

Papa halted about two feet away and said in a low, casual voice: "Let me put it this way. There's no percentage in you fighting me. You haven't done anything. Your bail's been yanked, that's all." Papa scratched the top of his head and continued. "The truth is you're gonna have to take a little rest. The question is do you want it to be temporary or permanent?"

Back went the hands into Boom Boom's pockets. Papa figured he would take about three minutes to wade through the question. He gently took Boom Boom's arms and handed them to Doc. Papa took the handcuffs out and placed them on Boom Boom's wrists, snapped the cuffs shut and stepped back.

"Your time's up," Papa said. "Temporary or permanent?"

Boom Boom contorted his face a couple of times as if he had a choice, and said with the only smile he'd given that day, "Hell, I need a rest anyway. I got a lot of pressure. I ain't slept well."

"You'll be back on the street in no time," Papa said with a wink.

Picking up Boom Boom was no sweat until the El Marino cops said they couldn't hold him; the order to apprehend him had originated from the County Sheriff's office twenty-five miles away.

After depositing Boom Boom at the Sheriff's Department and Doc Elliot at his apartment, Papa drove home, arriving just after five.

Jack Finnegan was at the bar with a drink in his hand when Papa walked through the door. Dotty came from the kitchen to greet him.

Papa carried the Prowler Fouler into his office where he lay it on the desk, unstrapped the .45 and checked the phone messages.

For the next ten minutes Papa roamed from room to room hoping something might happen—a phone call, an urgent errand—to postpone the news he had for his friend.

Dotty followed him into the bedroom.

"Are you looking for something? Can I help?" she asked.

"You know damn well what I'm doing," he said.

"Want me to tell him?"

"No," Papa said, shaking his head. "But would you sit close by in case I sound too harsh, and soften it up?"

She nodded with a smile and followed him into the living room.

Papa tried erasing the gloom from his face as he slipped behind the bar and poured himself a drink.

"Boom Boom Jaworski," Papa said. "Know the name?"

Finnegan shook his head.

"Hell's Angel. Ugly bastard."

"That's where you've been?" Finnegan asked. "Did you get a chance to do my chart?"

"Your chart."

"Right. Did you do it?"

Papa looked at Dotty. "Jack's chart. Do you know what I did with it?"

"Right there at your knees."

Papa dropped his eyes and saw the heavy bond paper with the configurations written in all the wrong places. Christ, it was a terrible chart. He picked it up and lay it on the bar between them.

Finnegan glanced down at it and back into Papa's face.

"What's it say?" he asked, with the same childlike quality that wooed juries.

"A lot. So much that it's almost impossible to go into at one sitting. Dotty knows that, don't you?"

"It could take weeks," she said without looking at him.

"Just a short rundown," Finnegan said. "That's all I want. You can fill in the details later."

Whenever Papa didn't want to do something he worked like the artist who fills his canvas by painting around the central object until there's no place else to go. Finnegan seemed to sense it and asked Papa what the delay was all about.

"No delay," Papa assured him. "I'm tuning up. You know. A little pre-game show. All of us fortune-tellers do it." He said "fortune-tellers" with a wink and a smile that quickly vanished when he saw that Finnegan wasn't buying it.

"First I want to ask you a couple questions," Papa began. "How have you been feeling lately?"

Dotty turned around and held one hand over her mouth.

They both looked at her.

"Don't mind me," she said. "Something struck me." She waved them away.

"I been feeling all right. In fact, pretty damn good," Finnegan replied.

"No problems?" Papa said.

"Like what, for instance?"

"Oh, I don't know, a case you're working on. Something in the department."

"Papa, stop bullshitting around and tell me what it says."

Fuck it, Papa said to himself. Might as well get it over with. He picked up the chart and began in rapid cadence: "You've got the Sun conjunct Uranus in the eighth house, square the conjunction of Jupiter and Neptune in the eleventh, which is in opposition to Venus." Papa had studied the chart so long he could have delivered it by memory.

"The progressed Mars is also conjunct the conjunction of the natal Uranus and the Sun, with a lunation on the exact degree that day." Finished, he looked up for Finnegan's reaction.

"Now can you give me the dummy's version?" he said.

"Okay. But first I have to tell you that I've never read a chart like this before. What I mean is, you're nothing like the chart. It's incredible. The complete opposite. Either you got your data wrong or there's a creature living in you I've never met, and, to tell you the truth, don't really want to."

"Neither one."

"Then tell me what," Papa demanded.

"*I* don't know." Finnegan was getting impatient. "C'mon, will you?"

"Yes." Papa drew on his cigarette. "For the rest of the year at least—that's what? six months—your life will be like a tinderbox. With all your planets squared and opposed and with all the conjunctions you had better take it very carefully. *Very* carefully. The lunation I mentioned; that's the catalyst, the spark, the . . . the fire that ignites the situation."

"What situation?"

Papa looked over to Dotty for help. She wasn't giving any.

"It indicates . . ." A long pause followed. "Death. It indicates death. Jack, for crissakes this could be all wrong. It's been wrong before. I might have miscalculated."

Sweatbeads appeared on Papa's brow. He dried them away with the palm of his hand.

"Go on," Finnegan said as if he were interrogating a suspect. Here was the cold determination Papa knew Finnegan possessed.

"The conjunct of Jupiter and Neptune in the eleventh house means that your hopes and wishes will go down the drain. It says you will also be deceived . . . by friends or people close to you, people you trust. This is a ridiculous suggestion but the chart indicates you should stay away from all guns and knives and wars . . . anything to do with weapons. Mars' position in the chart shows the deceit coming from someone official, a law officer, maybe, which might lead to . . . " Papa shrugged.

"My death."

"Possibility. Listen, Jack, you also have to understand that all this is merely indicative; there are no absolutes."

"Until they happen."

"Jack, I . . ." Papa suddenly felt tired. He wanted to escape to the bedroom and go to sleep. He felt as if he had betrayed his friend. Telling someone he has a good chance of dying pretty soon was for Papa a sacrilege.

The laughter began slowly, from far back in Finnegan's throat. Soon it blurted from his mouth like a high-pitched machine gun.

"Finally," the detective announced after a moment, "after all these years of listening to your astro rap, I believe you."

Papa was confused. He looked from Finnegan to Dotty and back again. "What does that mean?"

"The information I gave you; the date of birth, time, etcetera . . . they belong to a guy I found three days ago in Westwood. Ted Moran. It was in the papers. He had four slugs in his body. Very dead."

Papa looked at Dotty and closed his eyes. "Jack," he said quietly, "do me a favor. Next time—and there'd better not be a next time—don't put me through this. Please?"

When Papa opened his eyes and looked at Finnegan he saw guilt on the officer's face.

"I promise," Finnegan said, apologetically. "But now

that I know you're for real, that it's not all bullshit, I'll get my own stats for you. Hey, look, I *am* sorry. You've been bugging me to do it for so long I thought I'd test it out. It's the way I operate, friends or no, you know that, Papa."

"Why didn't you use somebody else's birthday? Like George Washington?"

"I looked at Moran's date of birth," Finnegan confessed. "It was the same as mine and I got the idea."

Papa raised his glass.

"Here's to the nervous breakdown you almost gave me," he said.

6

Watts

On July 10, a Saturday morning, Dotty walked down the steps to the mailbox. She sifted through the letters and one of them caught her attention. The envelope was black with Papa's name scrawled in white. Dotty glanced down the street to see if Papa was on his way back from downtown. His car wasn't in sight so she walked quickly inside and opened the letter.

It read: YOUR TIME IS SHORT. MINE IS OVER. LOOK FOR MY BULLET, PAPA. It was signed: MASON.

Dotty resealed it with glue and replaced it on the pile. Five minutes later she pulled the letter out again and carried it to the bedroom where she hid it in the top drawer of her dresser.

She returned to the living room where she sat and finished her coffee.

A few minutes later Papa came through the door with a sheaf of papers under his arm. He crossed the living room to his office where he filed the papers and lumbered into the kitchen for a glass of orange juice. He drank the juice quickly, paying no attention to the taste, and left the kitchen for the living room where he turned on the radio, paying no attention to the innocuous "supermarket" Muzak. He then took his seat behind the bar and reread the Los Angeles *Times*. He accomplished these maneuvers with habitual determination, interested in them all but with automatic languor. A dreaminess.

Papa says he feels no great yearning, as he did when he was younger, to get back on the road. The road carries problems—fatigue, the absence of excitement it once had, driving with his back lodged in one spot for hours at a time.

"The road is hell," he says. "I get up some mornings not knowing where the hell I am. Every Holiday Inn looks the same, the plastic food tastes the same. It's *Death of a Salesman* all over again. Willie Loman, I can empathize with that poor bastard.

"Staying home is a pleasure. I lounge around, tinker with the trailer out back, read. I read a lot, a lot of newspapers, about five a day. Books, I read sections of. Friends bring books over and mention this section or that. I read them and usually leave the rest alone. I read for information. I watch television for entertainment, what entertainment there is.

"I like *Police Story* for the authenticity that shows up every once in a while. *Barney Miller* is funny as hell. I love science fiction, which you can link up to the astrological stuff if you want to. *Star Trek, Outer Limits, Twilight Zone.* Well made, tight, good drama.

"People ask me how I like cop and private-eye shows. I don't. The kind of authenticity I find in *Police Story* isn't there. I can understand why the networks feel they have to make their characters bigger than life and have them doing incredible things but when it's obvious that whoever wrote or directed the shows were ignorant of certain things—and never bothered to check the facts—I get irritated.

"The movie *Shane*, for instance. Twenty-something years ago Jack Palance sent a .45 slug into Elisha Cook, Jr., who went flying into a puddle of water. That's what a .45 really does. On the TV shows the guys go 'Ouch!' and stumble to the ground. It's a helluva lot more dramatic the way it really happens. That's one example. Another is guys getting hit in the head with a gun and getting up a minute later. All the private eyes do it and most of the crooks. When you hit a guy in the head there's a fifty percent chance you'll kill him; otherwise you'll give him brain damage. A real cop hits him in the arms, in the legs, in the balls. It hurts like hell and the guy is disabled.

"There's one private-eye series starring a big man like me that does it all the time and also happens to have had shows that were direct steals from my own case files, even down to the dialogue. People traipse through the house all the time, some of them writers and producers. They hear a story and the next thing I know it's on TV. It's happened dozens of times.

"When I'm not watching TV—even when I am—people traipse in and out all the time. Aside from the steady clientele I get an army of snitches and informants who have literally turned the house into an information trading center. More information is passed back and forth across my bar, in one hour, than it would take cops a week to get through interrogation. That's one reason so many cops drop by. And everybody talks about his specialty. Dealers talk dope. Thieves talk about heists and fences. Con men talk about capers. Mainly because it's all they know about. The word for it is 'jawjacking.' Back and forth everybody waiting for the chance to break it with his own story. The cops hang around and hear all this but they never ask snitches any questions directly. They'd clam up like mad. So they ask them about everything else but, and the snitches eventually get around to telling everything they know. That's really my network of informants; they come to me.

"I suppose I need people around me. I was such a god-damn vagabond when I was younger that I had no time to make good friends. Now I do.

"Eat and sleep and get drunk and talk and argue with Richie Blumenthal and fight with Dotty and bullshit with everybody else, I sometimes wonder where all the relaxation comes in."

The phone rang. Dotty rose from the sofa and answered it.

"It's Winston Blue," she said, holding the receiver for Papa.

"Winston," he said, "your month's gone by."

"Yeah, Papa, just, uh, uh, understand, I'm callin' to tell you I'm still alive and ready to turn myself in."

"When?"

"Hey, uh, I'm ready any time now. You can trust Winston."

"Where are you?" Papa asked.

"Where am I?"

"Yeah, where are you?"

"Ohhh, out in the Valley somewhere."

"Where out in the Valley?"

"Mmm, uh, uh, I can't tell you that jes yet."

"Why not?"

Click. Winston had hung up. Papa stood by the bar with the receiver held away from his ear.

"Something tells me I'm going to get royally screwed by Winston Blue," he told Dotty. "I should *never* have bailed that sonofabitch out."

Dotty gave him a look that said: You've done it a hundred times already, and complained a hundred times, and you'll do it a hundred more. Papa had to agree; he was a sucker for a sob story and always would be.

Papa had just finished skimming the sports section when Ramsey Trask came through the front door, followed by Myron Fish.

"Look who I found cowering on the sidewalk," Ramsey smiled, allowing Myron to pass him and walk cautiously to the armchair, where he sat. Myron had been over twice since the broken television incident and still suffered from the experience.

Ramsey marched to the bar and sat on a stool facing Papa.

"How are you?" he said to Papa, then turned to Dotty. "And how are you, beautiful?" he said with a wink.

A shy grin appeared on her face and one hand automatically moved to pat her hair.

Ramsey was a good-looking guy. His full head of sandy brown hair and deeply tanned face gave him the appearance of a sportsman just back from bush country. He was a half dozen years younger than Papa, though from a distance looked in his early thirties. Up close one noticed strong facial lines running down both sides of his nose; his pale blue eyes seemed almost white against the tan; and the Howdy Doody grin he wore on his thin, tight lips gave him the look of a prankster. At five-ten he stood four inches shorter than Papa but seemed as tall with his lean, muscular body. Ramsey had a chameleon-like face that by turns was ruggedly handsome and, without sufficient sleep or sun, puffy and pale. Guessing his occupation he might have been a model, a rodeo rider or movie stunt man, a cowboy or a con man. He wore a faded denim shirt and jeans tucked at the waist by a thick brown leather belt fastened in front by a buckle of interlocking bull rings. The shirt was opened down the front, exposing a rug of thick salt and pepper hair.

For Papa, Ramsey was a man who defied categorization. He professed to be a flaming liberal but contradicted that term so often that Papa finally came to understand what Ramsey really was—a liberal thinker. A liberal talker. Disagreement was a tenet upon which their relationship was based. Part of Ramsey belonged to an old hippie who mouthed political slogans that had gone out with the sixties. He was a crusader to whom the sixties' Revolution had come five years too late. He was one of those to whom Nixonitis gave inspiration rather than resignation.

They had met six months after Papa had first run into Jack Finnegan, who introduced them. At the time Ramsey was on the Oakland, California, police force, from which he later resigned after being asked to by the chief. Ramsey had become over-zealous one night and blasted two henchmen belonging to a restaurant owner. It was no exaggeration that he resigned for reasons of health. He later joined the San Bernardino, California, force only to discover that red tape and bureaucracy kept him in court most of his duty hours. He became fed up and quit.

Since that time—summer 1969—he divided his time among writing tracts for political journals, traveling about the country in pursuit of radical causes and part-time bounty hunting.

Of the countless partners Papa worked with over the years, Ramsey was the best. He had the criteria: he was intelligent, he wasn't afraid, he followed instructions, he backed up Papa—and vice versa—at the right times, he was flexible enough to look at situations from many angles. They thought alike about most things. They disagreed politically, the least important element when it came to retrieving fugitives. Bounty hunting comprised only a part of their partnership; they worked together primarily as investigators, for insurance companies and attorneys and private individuals. A Ramsey came along once in a lifetime and Papa knew he was more than fortunate to have him as a partner and a friend.

"Interested in collaring two pimps in Watts tonight? They killed a guy yesterday and the bondsman wants them back real fast," Ramsey said, leaning over the bar.

"Coupla niggers, huh?" Papa said.

"Coupla *blacks*," Ramsey corrected.

"Whatever you want to call them. In Watts, at four in the morning, they're all niggers. Ask them."

Papa loved to bait Ramsey but at the same time he never had any qualms about calling blacks niggers. He called them "nigger" to their face. They also called him "nigger." As one heroin-dealing woman once told him: "You're the only white nigger I ever known, Papa, you're a *real* nigger." She meant it with affection. Papa took it that way.

"Ramsey, I'm not prejudiced," Papa told him. "You oughta know that by now. Just because I use 'nigger.' 'Nigger' has a lot of connotations. I picked up a guy in east Texas one time. The sheriff down there called blacks niggers. Blacks called themselves niggers. It was a word they used for two hundred years and weren't about to change it."

Ramsey sat higher in the seat.

"Well, goddamnit, they oughta start," he said.

"You go down and tell them that. They'll laugh in your face and call *you* nigger. Now, I'm not about to roam through Watts calling everybody nigger. I'd get my ass shot off."

"That's right, you would," Ramsey agreed.

"But the way I see it, there are bad niggers just as there are kikes and dagos and spics and micks and any other damn term that means the scum of the earth. Every ethnic group has its garden-variety asshole who'll rip off his own mother if he has to. *That's* who I'm prejudiced against."

Ramsey admitted he understood what Papa was talking about but still couldn't buy calling a man a nigger.

Papa respected Ramsey's attitudes, at least his right to hold them, if not the attitudes themselves. Papa raised one arm and pointed to the chart hanging in his office. He made the chart in 1970 to celebrate the essential differences between him and Ramsey.

RAMSEY	PAPA
Liberal	Conservative
Revolutionary	Reactionary
Civil Rights	Law and Order
Drugs	Booze
Daniel Ellsberg	J. Edgar Hoover
Rhetoric	.45 automatic
Humanist	Chauvinist

While Ramsey and Papa bantered back and forth Dotty went to the kitchen and returned with two cups of coffee. She placed them on the bar and took the chair beside Ramsey. She waited for a pause in the conversation and said, "Who's Mason?"

"Mason?" Papa asked.

"Someone you might have picked up?"

Papa looked from one to the other and shrugged. "Got any details?" he said.

"Oh, wait a minute," Dotty said, sliding off the stool. She went into the bedroom and returned with the letter she found in the morning mail.

Papa read it aloud. "Your time is short. Mine is over. Look for my bullet, Papa. Mason." He paused for a moment, then shook his head.

"Check under M," he said to Dotty.

Dotty went to the cabinet and filtered through the files. She called out the information.

"Karen Mason. Nineteen-seventy. Hooker. Dr. William Mason . . ."

"Oh, yeah," Papa said, turning to Ramsey. "Nice guy, except that he bilked old ladies out of their life savings. For collateral he tried to stick Richie Blumenthal with a house he owned in Malibu. Only problem was a storm knocked the foundation from under it, made it worthless."

"And Rocco Mason," Dotty called.

"Rocco Mason," Papa repeated. "He'd do something like this. Complete lunatic. Manhattan Beach. About six years ago."

Papa thought for a moment, juggling the sequence of events.

"I think I told you about him, Ramsey. He was a kid, twenty-two, twenty-three. His old man turned him in. The kid was on speed and he was running his father's bar business. Chasing customers away. Jimmy Fox and I went down to pick him up. Walked into the joint, stationed ourselves at opposite ends of the bar. The bondsman went with us.

"As soon as the bondsman walked in Mason freaked. He jumped over the bar, picked up a knife and screamed, 'I'll kill myself before you take me in.' He jammed the knife into his belt buckle and the blade broke in half.

"So we grab him, cuff him and start out. That's when the police arrive. This big fat sergeant leads them in and says he knows about Mason; that he'll go to jail forever. That's when Mason really freaked. He screams at the top of his lungs. He's frothing at the mouth. I mean literally frothing. Spittle and juice down his chin. Then he jumps straight up in the air and kicks the sergeant in the mouth, knocked his front teeth out. The only good thing that came out of it was when Mason came down he landed on his head.

"So we load him in the car and take off. Two minutes later Mason comes to. We've got three guys holding him in the back seat, two in the front. Two squad cars in front, one in back. Mason goes berserk. He's pounding his skull against the roof. The handcuffs are tearing the skin off his wrists. He's screaming bloody murder. He's bitten all of us at least twice.

"The substation wouldn't take him. He was too wild, too fucked up. So off we go to the county jail. They don't want him either. And we've still got this four-car parade taking in one guy. Mason's only five-nine, hundred and thirty pounds, right? At County we take the cuffs off and put him in sheepskin and leather restraints because he's bleeding all over the place.

"We finally get him to the county hospital. By this time he's stark raving mad. The doctor pumps enough thorazine into him to knock out an elephant, and Mason calms down.

" 'All right,' says the doctor, 'you can take the restraints off him.'

" 'Not me,' I tell him.

" 'I'm in charge here,' says the doctor.

" 'Then you take them off.'

"Two seconds later Mason snaps out of his funk. He kicks the doctor in the balls and bites a chunk out of his neck."

"At the same time?" Ramsey asked.

"At the same time."

Dotty clasped her hands and leaned forward. "Where is Mason now?"

"They threw him in a padded cell, shot him up with more thorazine and the last I heard he was in San Quentin."

"I'll bet he hates you a lot for dragging him in," Dotty said.

"I'd say."

"Do you think he meant it, the note? Think he'll try?"

Papa shrugged. "Maybe. He was a crazy bastard."

"Just be careful," Dotty said quietly, and walked into the kitchen.

Papa picked up his wooden backscratcher and scraped it along the lower part of his spine. "If he wants me," he called after her, "he knows where to find me."

At one the next morning Papa and Ramsey headed for Watts. Watts of the riots of 1965. Watts of the five families living in one-room ghetto projects. Watts of the Jewish shop owners chasing down blacks the minute their welfare checks come in.

Watts proper is a small section in South Central Los Angeles where the tiny patches of lawn are watered by urinating children and mowed by stolen cars zipping over them. Dusty brown buildings line the streets. Broken store windows serve as reminders of the hot and heavy summer battles. Watts, like the rest of South Central L.A., is a matriarchal hell. The women make most of the money from welfare and cleaning jobs. The men take their wives' cash, leaving less than enough to feed the kids, and gamble or shoot up the rest away in a few hours. Children don't know who their parents are.

The welfare system is the essential means of support in South Central L.A. When the case workers arrive to check family figures they find women with six children, the maximum number the state will subsidize. Out of that ruling grew the seventh baby death, which means that after having six children women will abort the seventh baby, leave it on someone's doorstep or give it to a family with fewer than six. Before the case worker shows up, children are loaned out from one family to the other so that every family receives maximum benefits. It's been estimated that a child, after being passed from one household to the other, may actually be registered on welfare roles as many as twenty-five times. Watts is a black kibbutz.

Pimps and hustlers roam the streets, predators who stalk one another. For the last twenty years the wealthier families moved out of South Central L.A. to Baldwin Hills, to homes worth $90,000. Baldwin Hills is now known as the Jungle, another testimony to modern-times progress.

Papa tries to avoid Watts. Nobody in his right mind will go down there unless he has to. The cops won't even go. A badge is a moving target down there. Ever since the riots in 1965 cops have been marked men.

"Before the riots, when everything was more peaceful, cops used to walk beats in Watts. The so-called elite squads used to sneak or storm in and blast the more dangerous felons. The Four Hats, for instance, the predecessor to S.W.A.T. teams, made busts in the area. The Hats was a group of detectives working robbery. Big, mean, tough, intelligent—they all wore hats, thus the name—other departments have assassination squads. Whenever there was a big robbery or a kidnapping they put the Hats on it. One of their goals was to take no prisoners. The Hats have all since retired.

"Some squads' tactics were illegal in the strictest sense of the word—but who was going to bust them? They'd break into an apartment and start shooting: bang, bang, halt, bang, bang, bang, you're under arrest, bang, bang, we're the police, bang, bang. They left bodies all over hell.

"They also used 'throw downs,' unregistered guns they'd place in a guy's hands after they killed him—to make it look like self-defense. One time, in the late fifties in Watts, a cop blasted a guy after he was on his stomach in a pool of blood. Squad cars pulled up, other cops arrived. Nobody knew what the others were doing so when the honchos got there to investigate they turned over the guy's body and found four guns and three knives.

"Then there's a section of the LAPD called the C.C.S., which the public knows little about. Criminal Conspiracy Squad, which says exactly what they're into. If two jerks get together and plan something it's a conspiracy, and out comes the C.C.S., the elite of the elite. All these outfits get away with murder. Dead men tell no lies, no truths, no nothing.

"One reason behind S.W.A.T. and C.C.S. being set up was the Miranda Decision, protecting the citizen's civil rights but not allowing a cop to bust into his place without a warrant or some damn good provocation. These outfits also allow the cops to play undercover games without having to publicly answer for their actions. They're the modern day's answer to the old times when a gun did a man's talking.

"But even with all their tough-guy tactics the C.C.S. and S.W.A.T. teams will not easily go to Watts. I suppose Watts or any big-city ghetto is America's last frontier, lawless, self-supporting, self-destructive. The only reason I went after the pimps was because Ramsey asked me to. I wouldn't have let him go down there all by himself."

Papa and Ramsey drove through Baldwin Hills on their way to Watts. Ramsey poured shots of bourbon into a Styrofoam cup and handed it across the front seat. In the trunk was Papa's arsenal. The back seat held the Prowler Fouler, some mace and a long black police "Kel" flashlight that doubled as a billy club.

All the way down Ramsey fidgeted, scratched his neck, squirmed in his seat. It was making Papa nervous. When they reached the end of 3rd Street Papa turned to Ramsey.

"What the hell's the matter with you?" he said.

"What's the matter with me?"

"You got ants in your pants."

Ramsey didn't answer. He looked out his window, then back at Papa. "Something's bugging me. I can't put my finger on it."

"Well, hurry up and figure it out because now you've got me going."

A few blocks later Ramsey jerked his head up. "You hear that?"

"Hear what?"

"That noise."

"Ramsey, for crissakes, take it easy. We'll both be nervous wrecks by the time we get there."

It happened so fast Papa didn't even see it coming. Ramsey whipped out his .45 and threw his body over the seat. The move shocked hell out of Papa who wheeled the car towards the sidewalk and jammed one foot on the brake. The car came to a screeching halt, missing a light pole by inches. Ramsey's gun was pointed into the darkness behind the seat.

"Oh, my God!" he said and broke into uproarious laughter.

"What! *What!*" Papa insisted.

"Take a look," Ramsey said between breaths.

Papa looked over the seat. There was Myron, hunched down on the floorboard, smiling up.

"Hi, Papa," he said.

"Hello, Myron. What are you doing here?"

In his squeaky voice, he said, "You know, I ruined your television and I felt real bad about it, so I thought I could help out on this snatch." The way Myron said *snatch*, something was missing.

"Jesus, you're dangerous," Papa said wearily.

Ramsey was having a heart attack he was laughing so hard. His body trembled against the passenger door. A few blacks ambled over to the car, peered in and kept moving.

Papa ran one hand through his beard and took a long slug of bourbon from the cup. He now had a perfect excuse to turn around and forget about Watts.

"Ramsey, when you're done . . ."

Ramsey was gradually calming down. Tears rolled down his cheeks and his nose ran. He refused to look at Myron. After a half dozen deep breaths he was able to talk. "This is our big chance, Papa."

"Big chance? For what?"

"Getting rid of Myron. Let's leave him here."

"Wait a minute," Myron said. "You can't do that. Not here. Not in Watts. You know what would happen to me?"

Papa didn't say a word. He just turned his head and looked Myron straight in the eye. A grin was upon his lips.

"No, you . . . you wouldn't . . ." Myron stammered.

"I'd love to."

"But you wouldn't . . . would you?"

"No, this place has enough problems."

Myron gave off one of his flat laughs. "Boy, you had me going there."

Papa backed into the street, jammed the gears and the car lurched forward. The pickup was a quarter mile away, in the Bleeker Hotel, on Ramparts Street. Officially, this was Ramsey's case. For practical reasons it belonged to them both. They would split the commission, take the same chances and have to spend at least two boring hours at the jailhouse waiting for the pimps to be booked. That is, if the pimps didn't give them trouble. Papa remembered Ramsey saying that the pimps had killed someone.

The targets Papa and Ramsey sought were the two pimps, Silver and Gold, who the previous afternoon had killed a black male in a Watts bar and took off in their twin Continentals. They had jumped bail a month ago for another offense, Ramsey informed Papa, and Ramsey had gotten a lead on the pimps' location from one of his informants.

The Bleeker Hotel stood in the middle of the block, flanked by appliance and jewelry shops. Across the street was a vacant field with old tires and a makeshift basketball court. In the moonlight the broken chain hanging from its hoop reminded Papa of a Dali painting. Stark, surrealistic, petrified and cold.

He parked the Plymouth, turned off the ignition and settled down for the wait.

"You hungry?" Papa asked Ramsey.

"Yeah. Myron, run out and get us a couple of sandwiches, will you?"

"Sandwiches? Really?"

"Whaddya want, Papa, ham on rye?" Ramsey asked.

"Ham on rye. Good. Toasted rye. Hold the mayo. And a pickle, Myron. Got that?"

"Pickle."

After a minute, during which they could almost hear Myron trembling, Papa leaned back. "What're you waiting for?"

"Mustard? You want a little mustard?"

Papa laughed and thought maybe the wait wouldn't be so boring after all.

They didn't have long to wait.

Turning the corner onto Rampart, one after the other, came the twin Continentals. They looked to Papa like two big white stallions as they cruised in.

"Sometimes I think I should've been a pimp. Look at those machines," said Ramsey.

"You ain't seen nothin' yet."

The Continentals pulled in front of the hotel and out

climbed Gold and Silver. They lived up to their names.
They were dressed in their colors, hats to boots. They
emerged at the same time, in the same way—gliding and
sweeping—and from the passenger doors came their
women, tall, leggy chicks in gold and silver hotpants to
match their men. Every move was choreographed; the way
the women pranced around the cars; the way they lifted
their left arms and placed them lightly on the pimps'
shoulders, the way they sauntered into the hotel. It was the
Pimp & Hooker Review. In Watts. At three o'clock in the
morning.

"Welcome to the late show," Papa said. He glanced at
his watch and then up and down the street searching for a
phone booth. Ramsey had called the cops before they left.
As usual, they were nowhere in sight.

"What room are they in?" Papa asked Ramsey.

"Sixth floor. Oh-two and oh-four. Back side."

"Whaddya think?"

Ramsey scratched his curly brown head and counted six
floors up the building. "We could hang around for the
cops, which might mean till Wednesday. Or wait till our
friends up there go to sleep."

"Which might take just as long. They've gotta be coked
out of their minds."

Ramsey paused, thinking.

"This is your baby," Papa said. "Call the shot."

"Let's hang on for a while. Let 'em settle in."

Ramsey slid further into the seat and lay his head
against the back. "Those hookers looked pretty damn
fine."

"Fine for what?"

Ramsey looked over at Papa and said, "Oh, excuse me,
Your Holiness, I forgot you don't approve of that kind of
thing."

"The only thing I don't like about hookers is they're so
fucking stupid. The massage-parlor broads, unbelievable.
Vice cop comes in, she says, 'You a cop?' Cop says no,
she gives him a blow job and he takes her downtown."

"What about the fifty-thou-a-year call girls. If that's stupidity, count me in."

Papa sat straighter in his seat. "Take it another step.
The million-dollar-a-year actresses and entertainers. An
actress will act in a film; she'll get naked in front of the
leading man, the crew, the director, everybody, climb in

bed with the leading man and *pretend* to make love to him—you think hookers don't pretend to make love?—get paid and turn it over to their old man, who also happens to be their business manager. What about *those* hookers?"

"Hookers, bullshit!" Now Ramsey was up in the seat.

"And the business managers are the pimps, just like our gold-dust twins over there."

Ramsey grunted and slid back down.

"I can't talk to you," he said.

Papa reached into his belt holster and checked the .45.

"Myron," Papa said, "hand me the flashlight."

A moment passed, then: "Myron, did you hear me—the flashlight."

Ramsey whipped around. "Myron, goddammit!" Ramsey looked over the seat and saw the bad news. Myron had done it again.

"Papa," Ramsey said softly. "I hate to tell you this."

Myron's pleading eyes looked up. "Ramsey, no," he cried. "No."

"What now?" Papa asked.

"The flashlight," Ramsey said.

"Yeah?" Papa closed his eyes.

"You don't want to hear it."

"He ate it?"

"He broke it."

Myron started talking fast. "Well, you see, Papa, I brought my own flashlight, you know, and, uh, the bulbs, well, you see, they don't fit. Nope. That's what happened. They don't fit."

"Gimme that goddamn flashlight!" Papa rammed one arm behind the seat and came out with the police light which Myron had disassembled. Myron had tried stuffing the big bulb in Papa's "Kel" into his small one. He had also broken the glass.

Papa ground his teeth. His jowls popped in and out. "Tell me something, Myron, you working for those pimps?"

"Working for the pimps, ha ha. That's funny, Papa. Working for the pimps. Yeah, that's . . ." He didn't get a chance to finish because Papa stuck his massive face over the seat. Their noses almost touched. Papa contorted his eyes and mouth. He became a demon in the darkness. Myron's face compressed. He slid further into the space between the seats. He could hardly breathe. He cried inside.

"I'm gonna punish you, Myron," Papa seethed. "The worse way I know. I'm gonna let you live." He watched the terror set in, then heaved his body back to the front.

A moment later Myron's voice whispered from the back.

"Am I going in with you, Papa?" he asked.

"Going in?"

"To get the pimps. Am I going in with you?"

"Only if I wanted to blow the thing, which I don't."

Papa draped one arm over the seat and looked into Myron's face. "And I don't want you to leave the car. I want you to squeeze down between the seats and stay there until we get back. Understand?"

Silence.

"Understand!"

"I thought I could go with you," Myron pleaded.

Papa glanced over at Ramsey; they were both thinking the same thing. If Myron had the gall to hide out in the back seat he might also have the gall to follow them into the Bleeker Hotel. In fact, with Myron's penchant for screwing things up, they might even have a riot on their hands.

"Myron," Papa said, his voice tight. "If you leave the car I'll kill you."

"Yessir," Myron whispered.

"Good boy."

Papa looked out through the windshield at the hotel and then at Ramsey. " 'Bout ready?"

"Let's go."

They got out of the car, Papa making sure to take the keys with him. They locked the doors behind them, moved across the street towards the Continentals and climbed up the steps into the lobby.

Inside they crossed the lobby's threadbare rug, passing old-fashioned chairs and sofas, and started for the elevator. The desk clerk called after them.

"Who you lookin' for?" he asked.

"Couple old friends," Ramsey told him. "Want to surprise them."

"I'm sorry. I can't let you do that."

Papa pressed the elevator button and the doors opened.

The clerk was on his way around the desk and headed towards them.

"You can't do that," he insisted. "I'll call the police."

"Oh Gawd, don't do *that!*" Papa said as the doors closed.

They took the elevator to the eighth floor in case the desk clerk decided to follow them and walked down two flights to the sixth.

They quickly located rooms 602 and 604. No doubt Gold and Silver owned weapons but, as Papa figured, they wouldn't be cleaning them just now. He hoped they were wiped out on drugs and in bed with their girls. The single problem they immediately had to face was where the pimps and hookers were; in one room, or had they separated and gone to individual ones? Ramsey would have to go through one door; Papa the other.

Papa motioned for Ramsey to follow him back down the hallway where they huddled by the maid's closet.

"This calls for something different, Ramsey," Papa whispered.

"Like what?"

"How 'bout starting a fire?" Papa suggested.

"A fire? As in smoke them out?" Ramsey did not sound wild about the idea.

"Better than us bombing through the door, no?"

Ramsey nodded in agreement. "What've you got in mind?"

Papa opened the maid's closet, from which he took a pail, some old rags and newspaper pages he found piled in the corner. With Ramsey close behind he carried the equipment back down the hallway and set the pail a few feet from the pimps' doors. The newspaper went first into the pail, the rags were placed over them, and Papa struck a match which he dropped on the bundle. The fire started slowly, smoldering at the bottom and sending smoke billowing into the air. Ramsey pulled off his jacket and fanned the flames. Smoke filled their end of the hallway and began drifting down the corridor.

"We better get going before we're asphyxiated," Papa said, placing one hand over his nose and mouth. "Ready?"

"Ready."

They shouted simultaneously.

"Fire! Fire!"

Papa took one side of the hallway and Ramsey the

other as they rushed down each wall shouting through the doors.

"Fire!"

They turned at the end of the hallway and headed back, halting outside the pimps' rooms. Papa saw an old couple peek around their doorway, and waved them back inside. A moment later it looked as if all the rooms had been occupied. A crowd gathered in the corridor screaming bloody murder. Some rushed back to the rooms to call the fire department. Others made a dash for the elevator and waited for it to arrive. Pandemonium. The shouting grew louder. The hallway filled with the smoke. Children coughed. Where were the pimps? Papa wondered if they were too stoned to come outside. With all the commotion something had to happen fast.

Which it did. One door opened and out stumbled Gold, still in his pants, coughing and sputtering, wiping the smoke from his eyes. Behind him was his hooker, naked and hacking away. Papa took a step towards them and with a solid right to the clavicle decked the pimp. Papa grabbed the hooker and shoved her back into the room, closing the door behind her.

Ramsey waited by the other door.

"C'mon! C'mon!" he called inside.

Nothing.

Through the smoke Papa was able to make out the vague formation of people who had still not gotten off the floor.

"Go get 'em," he ordered.

Ramsey raised one leg and sent it against the door. The frame broke at the hinges and fell forward. Ramsey stormed in. Papa followed him in.

Silver and his girl were struggling to get off the bed. She reached for clothing; he was tangled in the sheets.

Silver raised his head and spotted two men coming at him. He made a move for the .38 on the bedstand but all it got him was Ramsey's weapon against the side of his head.

They told the hooker to shut up and dragged Silver from the bed out into the hallway where Gold was still slumped on the floor.

The elevator doors were closing when Papa reached the hallway. They would have to carry the pimps down six flights of stairs.

Papa hefted Gold over his shoulder and started out. Ramsey dragged Silver along the floor. They moved slowly, cautiously, down the stairwell, passing residents coming up while others passed them going down. They received no more than a cursory glance from any of them.

They carried Gold and Silver down the stairs and out to the street where they draped them, one atop the other, in the Plymouth's back seat.

True to his word, the desk clerk had called the police who drove up just as Papa was about to take off. Ramsey explained the situation to them, showing them the papers he had on the pimps and telling the cops where they could find the hookers, if they wanted them.

"Pimps give you any trouble?" Myron asked on the way to the city jail.

"Trouble!" Ramsey said. "We had a war in there, Myron."

"Yeah? They're not drugged out? I don't see any marks on them," Myron said skeptically.

"You ever have miracle chicken, Myron, you know, when they de-bone it without touching the outside skin?"

"No."

"Well, all their pain's on the inside."

Confusion crossed Myron's face. "Hey," he said, "I'd like to see how you do that sometime."

"Whaddya think, Papa?" Ramsey said across the seat.

"I'll show you when we get home."

"Yeah?" Myron said with a smile.

"You can be the chicken."

The smile faded and Myron turned to the front, watching Papa from the corner of his eye.

On the way home Papa stopped off at Richie Blumenthal's. Richie was with a client when he entered the office so he sat on the bench outside his door. Also with a client was Millie Terrazza, one of Richie's five assistants. Millie had been with Equity for twenty-five years, and looked it. She was short and fat and pale; her face fell naturally into a scowl; the huge gray pouches under her eyes were gross, as if they'd been shot with silicone. The only part of Millie that moved was her mouth. She spit forth sentences like a drill sergeant, all of them grammatically correct and to the point.

Across the desk from Millie was a young man in jeans trying to make bail for his girlfriend.

Papa had heard their conversation a thousand times before.

MILLIE: What's the beef?

GUY: Beef?

MILLIE: What's she in for? Why'd they pick her up?

GUY: Well, uh, she, uh . . .

MILLIE: Junk? She's a junkie?

GUY: Junkie. Yes, that's right.

MILLIE: The bail is what?

GUY: Twenty-five hundred.

MILLIE: Collateral?

GUY: I have a car, a year-old worth about thirty-five hundred.

MILLIE: Fine. Give me that, I'll lock it up till the girl shows in court.

GUY: Lock it up? I need the car. You can have the pink slip on it.

MILLIE: Great! And if she skips out? Can I drive the pink slip around town? Lock it or forget it.

GUY (thinking): I have rings.

MILLIE: How nice.

GUY: No, they're worth close to five thousand dollars. Had them appraised.

MILLIE: Five thousand. Appraised? Give 'em here. I'll show them to somebody who can verify. (PHONE RINGS) Hold on. Hello? Yeah, I hear you. Forget it. You burned us once, pal, call the competition. *(hangs up)*

GUY: The rings are home.

MILLIE: Not here?

GUY: No. At home. I'll have to get them.

MILLIE: Uh huh. (PHONE RINGS) Hello? Yes, how are you? (*cups hand over mouthpiece, says to young guy*) Go home, get the rings, bring them back today. Who knows, tomorrow they might be worthless.

Papa watched the young man depart and half-listened to Millie's phone conversation. He was pleased to see, a few minutes later, Richie's client walking from the office. The bondsman waved Papa in.

For the first half hour he was given a lecture on what financially bad shape Richie was in, and how the situation reflected the economy in general. Papa had to listen because he knew Richie wouldn't hand over the weekly check until he finished.

When Richie finally sat down he reached into a desk drawer and pulled out a portfolio on one Paco Carrera who had skipped bail and was now in Mexico.

"I don't want to go to Mexico," Papa told him.

"You have to go," Richie insisted.

"Why? You aren't my mother."

"What about the bail?"

"Which is?"

"Exactly one hundred thousand dollars." Richie drew out the words.

"I'll be ready in an hour."

"By the way," Richie added, "there's no danger."

"His bond is a hundred grand and there's no danger? Richie, you're not being logical. You send me down there optimistic. Okay, I breeze in. The guy *is* dangerous and he blasts me. You don't get him back, I get shot up. All bad news. Why are you so fucking cheap? I'm in the life and death situation, you're home free. I want fifty percent of this Paco Carrera—fifty thousand dollars—because he *is* dangerous, I know it, he *has* to be. Fifty, that's it."

"You got it."

Papa rose from the chair and headed towards the door. He turned and faced the bondsman.

"I hate going to Mexico knowing you lied to me," Papa said, a frown on his face. "Not only are you a thief, Richie, you can't even tell the truth."

Before Papa turned and left the room he saw the pain in Richie's face. There was no real pain. Richie was an excellent mime.

Papa left the office at two-thirty, picked up a bottle of Jack Daniels on the way, and now sat in the living room drinking it.

Dotty complained of labor pains. Papa said it was all the crap she was eating.

"I know labor pains when I feel them," she said sarcastically. "I've had them before, remember?"

"How do I know? I didn't give birth to Kenny."

Kenny, Dotty's son by a former marriage and whom Papa had more or less adopted, had already been taught

to play bridge and gin. He'd met Papa's odd assortment of
cops and robbers and killers and priests and boozers and
junkies and actors and bank presidents. Kenny had also
come to know Papa as a man whose idea of being a father
was sometimes tough to take. Kenny was under the
wing—under the command—of a staunch disciplinarian
who put him on restriction when he broke a rule, who
used him as a go-for whenever Papa wanted something he
was too lazy or occupied to get himself: cigarettes, liquor,
papers, weapons, coffee; anything not within reach. It took
Kenny a long time to understand why Papa had not married his mother; it had something to do with Papa's independence, and his line of work, and a whole lot of other
things Kenny didn't understand. Like his mother still
maintaining her own separate apartment down the street.
He wondered, too, why his mother put up with Papa's
bullheadedness, the way he ordered her around and the
way she obeyed. And there were the times, back in the
apartment, when he watched his mother cry and when he
heard her say how much she wanted Papa, how much she
loved him and how their relationship was like skating on
thin ice. And how having his baby might keep them
together.

"Look," Papa was saying to Dotty, "I have to go to
Mexico tomorrow. I don't want your pains on my mind."

"Then don't," she said and walked out of the room.

"Why?" Papa said aloud after she'd gone.

"Why what?" came the answer. Papa looked up and
saw the beaming face of Tommy Price.

"Tommy!" Papa was glad to see him. "What's going
on?"

"They dropped the charges."

Papa came out from around the bar. "Sit down.
What're you drinking?"

"Isn't it a little early?" Tommy said, climbing on a
stool.

"Four in the afternoon? Do you schedule your drinking?" Papa wagged a finger at him. "First comes the
booze, then the sex, then you buy a gravestone and then
goodbye. What're you drinking?"

"Scotch, little water."

"Attaboy."

One thing Papa never used Kenny for was mixing
drinks. He learned that lesson one night when Kenny al-

most killed off a half dozen of his friends. It wasn't that
the drinks were too weak or strong. They were horrible.
Scotch and ginger ale made for bad company.

Papa fetched Tommy's drink and placed it on the
leather counter.

"Came over to see yuh for nother reason, Papa,"
Tommy said in his effortless Arizona drawl. "I'm lookin'
for a job. My old lady down in Ruby—we ain't speakin'
jest now."

"How come?"

"Says she's tired of hangin' with a criminal. She wants
to move up. I cain't blame her. I ain't never gonna have
garden parties, that kinda shit. Hell, I never even been to
a garden party."

"They're boring."

"I guess but anyway. A job." Tommy's tight-fitting jeans
and checkered shirt showed off the good shape he was in.
"I'd like a job with you. We done all right in Texas,
right?"

"That we did."

"So if you need some kinda partner or somethin' I
could handle it."

"Yeah." Papa studied Tommy closely and tried to visu-
alize how he'd look in a suit and tie and chauffeur's cap.
The Mexican case was on his mind. He knew it could be a
dangerous one. Bringing a Mexican national out of Mexico was equivalent to kidnapping. Papa wasn't too worried
about going down himself, or with Ramsey (as he had
planned), but taking an amateur like Tommy seemed
shaky to him. Still, for what he had in mind, the kid might
be a real asset.

"You're familiar with Mexico, hmm?" Papa asked him.

"Like a jackrabbit knows its hole."

"That good?"

"That *damn* good," Tommy stated with supreme
confidence.

"We leave tomorrow. My friend Ramsey will be with
us."

"I'm already packed."

Later on, while Tommy was out buying toilet articles,
Papa called Ramsey, who sounded high on something.

"Can you talk?" Papa asked him.

"Mmmm, can I talk! Talk your fucking ear off, or your ass, whichever's receiving right now."

"Ramsey, you're weird."

"If I wasn't weird you wouldn't like me."

"Who says I do anyway?"

"This act will never play in Vegas. Whaddya want?"

"I'm bringing along a third on our Mexican jaunt."

"Hold *it!*" Ramsey said. "If that third is Myron Fish, look for another second. Count me—one, two, three—out. Fini. Adios. Goodbye."

"My dear Ramsey, Myron would get us killed."

"Oh, would he get us killed! Before we got to the border, going in."

"Tommy Price," Papa said.

"Yeah? Tommy Price? He did that Texas snatch, right? By the way, what ever happened to Billy Joe Face?"

"What we expected. He paid off a judge and a couple other honest men and the case was dropped. He's back with Uncle John."

"Is that all?" Ramsey said.

"Is that all what?"

"Is that all you wanted to talk about. The phone is really bumming me out."

"Goodbye, Ramsey."

Papa hung up and went into the bedroom for a nap. The thought of going down to Mexico for what could be a week made him suddenly tired. The last time down there he brought back Montezuma's Revenge and enough headaches to last him a year. He didn't like Mexico because it was hot and dusty and barren; it was lawless; and the food gave him the runs.

Then he thought of the $100,000, of which he'd net a hefty share. In that way picking up Paco Carrera was special; he'd seldom gone after a man with that big a price on his head.

PART II

7

The Mission Impossible Snatch

For Papa, San Diego was no great shakes. It was a city that couldn't make up its mind. It wanted to be modern and progressive but how could it be when it was so close to the Mexican border? Its claims to fame: a freeway that every comedian in the world had a line about and sports teams that lived in the cellar.

It was a Monday, just after six in the evening, and outside the TraveLodge motel room kids were splashing in the pool. In the room Papa, Ramsey and Tommy Price watched television.

"Instead of watching the idiot tube," Ramsey complained, "we should be *planning*. How 'bout it?"

Papa didn't hear him; he was involved in one of the few TV shows he enjoyed: *Mission: Impossible*. Papa had looked at the *TV Guide* that morning and noticed a *Mission: Impossible* caper that was similar to Papa's own circumstances with Paco Carrera. He had purposely stopped in San Diego rather than heading into Mexico where television was back in the dark ages.

Tommy sat on the bed weaving a long braid from two

95

pieces of rawhide. Every so often he'd look up and announce: "I've seen this twice."

"Then will you tell Papa what happens so we can get out of this joint?" Ramsey said.

They were already getting on each other's nerves.

"Papa, dammit," Ramsey pleaded. "We need a plan!"

"It's coming."

"What's coming?"

"The plan. Have you been watching this show?"

"No."

"Watch it."

Peter Graves, Greg Morris, Peter Lupas, Barbara Bain and Martin Landau were in Sangrania, or wherever the hell it was. Their mission: to smuggle a big dope dealer out of the country. The MI Force masqueraded as foreign businessmen.

"That's why it's called Mission Impossible," Ramsey said. "There's no way it could happen, *except* on TV."

"Variations on a theme, Ramsey," Papa replied.

The show was ending. Peter Graves and Greg Morris walked out of a lab, with the scientist, and they all piled into a limousine. Papa turned the set off and looked up at Ramsey with a satisfied smile on his face.

"Well?" he said.

"Terrific. All we have to do is build a new Kremlin, get the Secretary to disavow all our actions, find a couple of smart broads who can seduce the Mexican government, and we're in."

"I've got it," Papa said, not listening.

"Got what? I hate to keep asking that question."

"The plot, dummy." Papa stood and moved to the window where he parted the curtains and looked out over the pool. "Paco Carrera is a land speculator, right?"

"Yes."

"My original idea was to have Tommy as our chauffeur. That stays the same. You and I, Ramsey, are rich businessmen interested in leasing Mexican land. A *lot* of Mexican land."

"Rich businessmen in what?" Ramsey wanted to know.

"We'll think of something."

"Yeah?"

"And at the right moment we bang Paco over the head and whip across the border."

"That's a plot?"

"So far."

"For a disaster movie."

Papa tapped one index finger against his temple. "The details I'll tell you on the way down."

They pulled out of San Diego the next morning. Tommy drove the rented black Cadillac limousine south towards the border. In the back seat wearing new $300 suits were Papa and Ramsey. They had already spent close to $1,500 on clothes and shoes and suitcases, the car, Tommy's powder-blue chauffeur's outfit, gold lighters, tie clips and cuff links, all of which they would charge to Richie Blumenthal as expenses.

The six-lane throughway took them into Tijuana, through the newly renovated border crossing and around the city. They continued south. Their destination: Rosarita Beach on the Baja peninsula.

Paco Carrera, according to Richie Blumenthal's file, was a premier drug smuggler and wholesaler. Before getting nabbed in Los Angeles and jumping bail, Paco had done very well. Few men handled both ends of the dope business; few could handle it. Almost without exception the business was divided between the smugglers who got the narcotics out of Mexico and the wholesalers who shipped it throughout the States. Paco was obviously a crafty guy, and Papa knew he would have to be on his guard with the Mexican.

"Without the dope business," Papa says, "Mexico would go broke and have a major revolution on its hands. Dope is the country's biggest industry.

"And like a good neighbor the United States started Mexico on its road to success. During World War II there was a shortage of morphine in this country, so the government scouted Mexico, where the weather and rainfall are perfect for growing opium poppies, and backed the first operation. What the U.S. government didn't figure was how smart the Mexicans were. After the morphine shortage was taken care of, the Mexicans, who knew a good thing when they saw it, kept right on processing the opium and ended up as our biggest heroin supplier, which it is today.

"The opium poppies are grown all over. When the leaves fall off the pod it's harvest time. Field workers take their little Exacto knives with their short blades and cut into the poppies. The raw opium seeps out of the pods. The workers gather the opium gum—or *goma*—on palates and place it in plastic bags. They get one kilogram of pure opium per acre.

"The opium is transferred to small portable labs behind farmhouses where grandmothers, armed with menus, boil the *goma* for hours at exactly two hundred thirty-eight degrees. They cook it up in washtubs, using lime to filter out the impurities.

"The Mexicans convert pure opium into heroin differently than the French or Corsicans or Chinese or Vietnamese. The Mexicans are sloppy. They leave loads of impurities in the heroin, which is brown when it's finally processed. In France it's one hundred percent pure. The Mexican stuff is not even close. Ten years ago only ten percent of U.S. heroin came from Mexico; now it's ninety percent. The U.S. Drug Enforcement Administration did a study in East Coast cities which showed that one hundred percent of all samples taken was Mexican brown heroin. American junkies have become so used to brown that any white heroin filtered through Mexico is diluted with brown procaine. Otherwise, the wholesalers won't buy it for the junkies, who think brown is purer. You can't argue with a junkie about anything.

"There's really no way to stop the drug traffic out of Mexico. The border guards, the Narcotics Task Force and the Drug Enforcement Administration estimate they get only ten percent, and that's high. They use dogs; in fact, the most famous dog is a fifteen-year-old black Labrador who can sniff out anything. Soon as the dog hits he sticks his nose on the spot and rotates body around till he's sure. The dog's got arthritis, every disease known to dog, but he's a killer. He's one of the old-timers the narcotics guys made junkies of before sending them to the border. Now they put the mutts through Pavlov training. Shepherds are the best. Bloodhounds were once used but they were *too* sensitive. If a car simply *drove* through a poppy field the hounds went bananas. They've also got electronic devices, but they don't use them anymore. It was like putting the impossible question to a computer. The machine would self-destruct there was so much dope going through. Dope comes across in dune buggies, campers, trailer trucks, motorcycles, you name it. The border guards once snatched a gasoline tanker loaded with marijuana.

"As far as marijuana's concerned, it's like the Berlin Airlift. The planes flying across the border don't even worry about radar, there's so many of them. In the Southern Defense Zone some old master sergeant is up on a radar site watching them zip in. If he called in every plane, that's all he'd do all day. They come in low and fast—DC-3s, D-18s, Twin Beaches. The bigger the better. There was a story a few years back, during the Vietnamese War, where a U.S. Air Force Starduster landed on one of those small Mexican strips. The plane was loaded up with ten tons of weed—by Air Force personnel, in uniform—and took off across the border. I believe it.

"Another high profit goody is amphetamines. For years U.S. drug laboratories have sent amphetamine base down to Mexico where their subsidiaries produce mini-bennies and other kinds of speed. The Drug Enforcement Administration put a limit on what the companies could produce up here. There's no such ceiling in Mexico, so the base was shipped down, the Mexicans made the pills and shipped them back across the border to anybody who wanted them.

"The pills are easy to make. The base material—methamphetamine sulphate—arrives in the Mexican lab where they compress it into a capsule. They add some talc to give it body, get a sixteen-stage punch press, and turn out ten billion an hour. Of course, a lot of speed these days is no more than caffeine or cornstarch, but there's still a load of the real thing coming across the border every day.

"The Mexican officials do what they can to stop the flow but you have to understand it's all political down there. The police, the politicians, everybody, they all know the country would become insolvent if drug traffic stops. A few years ago they made a television documentary—the Mexican Connection. On the show a general was interviewed. He told the cameras hell no, he wouldn't take a two hundred thousand dollar bribe to let the farmers grow poppies in his military district. A week after the show aired two characters walked into the general's office and blew him away. The new general who took his place said yes, I will take bribes, you bet.

"Same with the politicians. In Mexico a politician has a six-year, one-shot deal to make his bundle and run. Nobody's re-elected, so a politician had better get what he can during his term of office. Chasing drug dealers would slow him down and probably get him killed. Stealing a car will get a Mexican national a much heavier sentence than running drugs to the U.S. Paco Carrera operated so smoothly down there because he bolstered the economy and he held a respectable job. He was an asset. The police would rather protect him than chase him down.

"Paco was a smart cookie. He was grabbing dope profit from both ends. He handled every facet of the business from the poppy field to the junkie in Detroit.

"As a wholesaler in this country he paid about sixty thousand bucks for a kilo of pure heroin. The heroin was 'stepped on'—further diluted—ten times before it reached the junkie. His original sixty grand investment returned four hundred twenty thousand—not a bad markup, and that's not including the street price.

"Wholesalers like Paco are the big profit-makers. Every top wholesaler, with very few exceptions, is known to the Drug Enforcement Administration. But the DEA can't touch them because the bigger they become the further away they get from direct dealing. Their flunkies handle the sticky end of the business. The only way to grab them is through conspiracy. That's how the government got Albert Anastasia, how they got Vito Genovese. Genovese was the biggest Mafia don in the world when he was busted, and the Feds got him on some junkie's statement that he talked dope with Genovese. Vito Genovese didn't know a junkie from a wheelbarrow, but this junkie said, yeah, he heard Genovese say he had the New York drug market locked up. He got thirty years. That was in the fifties. The Mafia, consequently, was a little leery of the Drug Administration. No more. The penalties aren't as stiff these days and the Mob is right back in the thick of it.

"Paco Carrera was no Mafia figure as far as I knew. I'm sure he was well-connected, though, and well-protected. The little scheme I cooked up was designed to avoid trouble of any sort. I thought it was flexible enough to let us adjust to whatever situation came up. We were traveling in style, and had an excellent cover. Everything seemed set to go smoothly. Seemed . . ."

Papa, Ramsey and Tommy Price checked into the Rosarita Beach Hotel, a magnificent structure overlooking the

Pacific. The hotel oozed with charm. Stucco verandas, courtyards, gardens, royal palms sprouting from smooth gray rocks, all contributed to the antique aura, and to the price. Papa's top-floor suite of rooms cost $145 a day, not including meals.

The trio unpacked their bags, showered, changed and two hours later were heading down the elevator in search of Paco Carrera, their target.

They learned from the desk clerk that Paco had a real-estate office not three blocks from the hotel.

Paco Carrera sat in his office. Beside him was Baez, his bodyguard, a short bowling ball of a man who said very little and listed as his main objective in life the maiming of his master's enemies. Paco Carrera was a slick little Mexican property salesman who profited by leasing parcels of land to rich Americans. According to the law, only Mexican nationals may own Mexican land. Foreigners may lease it. Paco Carrera managed and developed property for these foreign investors, which meant he stole them blind.

Paco's outstanding feature was a harelip meandering from the left nostril to the right side of his lip, yanking the lip up so that one huge tooth peeked through.

"Baez," he said to his bodyguard in Spanish, "how does taking a short vacation to Acapulco strike you?"

Baez grunted, meaning yes. Two grunts meant no.

"Very good," Paco exclaimed. "We leave this afternoon."

They were packed and ready to depart for the airport when they spotted a Cadillac limousine pulling up to the office. They watched the chauffeur emerge and hold open the rear door. A large man with a dark beard emerged first, followed by a smaller, ruddy-complected man. Both were excellently dressed in light-weight summer suits. The larger man wore a white, wide-brimmed hat. They climbed the steps and knocked on the office door.

Paco turned to Baez and said, "Acapulco may have to wait."

A few minutes later the four men sat around Paco's desk. Baez had served them coffee. Tommy Price waited by the limousine.

"In another half hour, gentlemen," Paco explained, "Baez and I would have been on our way to Acapulco. How fortunate you arrived when you did."

"How fortunate," Papa agreed, looking at Ramsey, who also agreed.

"Now," Paco continued, "if you will tell me what you are interested in . . ."

"Land, Mr. Carrera," said Papa, removing the hat and placing it on the desk.

Paco clasped his hands together. "Land! I have *land!* Land *so* magnificent, on a great cliff overlooking the blue Pacific. Stallions gallop along these cliffs which arch back towards the sea. The sea, with giant waves curling like serpents towards the shore."

"Very poetic, Mr. Carrera," Papa said with admiration.

"The words are mine. The inspiration comes from masters like Dylan Thomas, from Ezra Pound, from Joyce, Yeats. I have studied them all. I have absorbed them. They have become part of me. Shelley, Keats, Coleridge, Wordsworth, Blake—they all live in my brain. John Donne, Ben Jonson, even Shakespeare."

"Even Shakespeare," Ramsey said.

"It's such a pleasure to be in the company of men of letters," Paco explained.

"Even the unopened ones," said Papa.

"Even those." Paco had no idea what that meant, he was so lost in reverie. He floated back to earth and said, "I am pleased to see your interest in manifest destiny. This"—he swept his hand through the air—"is not the end of the frontier, gentlemen, but the beginning. Beyond is the sea, the unconquered sea. I have two hundred acres of frontier, two hundred acres of the most exquisite terra firma you have ever seen. Cortez stood upon it. Maximilian rode across it. Pancho Villa ravaged it. And the great Zapata"—Paco toasted Zapata with his coffee cup—"made love to beautiful women upon it."

"How much?" Ramsey inquired, cutting through. "How much do you want for the land?"

"For you, for your appreciation of the miraculous," Paco whispered, scratching his harelip, "three quarters of a million American dollars."

"Sounds reasonable," Papa said. "What's on it?"

Paco leaned closer to them and said with great confidentiality, "What's on it? Better to ask, what *is* it? A magnificent, supple brown and fertile virgin. As they say in your country—a cherry. Nothing! There is nothing on it. It is . . . pure."

"I haven't had a virgin in a long time," Papa smiled.

"Would you like to meet her?" Paco asked.

Papa's eyes grew wide. "Immediately," he murmured.

It looked like two hundred acres. The land *was* over-looking the sea. As far as being virgin soil, Papa wasn't exactly convinced. But what did it matter? He wasn't going to lease it anyway.

Tommy Price parked the car and they all climbed out. To their left a mountain range ran the length of the Baja peninsula. To their right the Pacific roared in. While Tommy stayed with the car—on Papa's orders because in Mexico no unattended car was safe for more than a few minutes—the four men strolled through the property.

"Whom do you represent?" Papa asked Carrera.

"Represent?"

"Yes. Who owns this property?"

Carrera thought that very funny and nudged Baez. "He asks me who owns it, Baez. Isn't that humorous?" Baez grunted. "I own it. This, along with seven hundred additional acres to the south, are mine. I own it all."

"Dope has been good to him," Ramsey whispered in Papa's ear.

"Maybe," Papa replied. "I wonder how many times he's leased the property."

"Isn't it magnificent?" Paco said with a sweeping gesture.

"Three quarters of a million is fairly steep," said Papa. "No electricity can be pulled in, except over the mountains. There's no real accessibility to the water, except by scaling those cliffs. There is no place for a landing strip for my airplanes."

"For your airplanes?" Paco asked.

"Only three," said Ramsey.

"I see."

"So you can understand, Mr. Carrera . . . why I am only willing to pay you five hundred thousand."

"Five hundred thousand. Why, that's . . . that's . . ."

"Half a million."

"Yes, of course. One moment. Excuse me." Paco took Baez aside and the two of them jabbered in Spanish for a few minutes.

Papa and Ramsey drifted down towards the edge of the cliff.

"We could snatch Carrera now," said Ramsey.

"But?"

"Baez."

"I know. He's carrying a gun."

Ramsey nodded. "He makes me nervous."

"A stone killer."

"He reminds me of Diez Laredo," Papa commented.

"And looks just as mean."

Diez Laredo was the 1st Commandante of the Mexican Federal Judicial Police in Mexico City. Papa had met him twice when Laredo had been present on drug busts on the Mexican side of the border. Laredo was younger than Baez, about thirty, with an ugly scar on his right cheek. They were both light-complected and small. Laredo, however, was in a much more respectable position, and his rise to power was legendary.

Twenty years ago he was a shoe-shine boy on the steps of the National Palace in Mexico City. The President came out one day, called Laredo over for a shine and asked the boy what he wanted to be when he grew up. A soldier, Laredo stated, I want to serve my country. The President snapped his fingers and said to his aide, 'Lieutenant, take this boy to the military barracks and make him a soldier.' Laredo was ten at the time. He later went to the military academy in Mexico City and, upon graduation, was sent to the Sorbonne in Paris for further education. He holds the rank of colonel now but has more power than any general. He is Mexico's number-two man; tough, rugged, intelligent, honest. He and Baez may have looked alike. They may have been as tough. They might have. . . .

"You sure that's *not* Laredo?" Ramsey asked.

"Laredo sweeps the floors with jerks like Baez," Papa said.

"So . . ."

"So we play it by ear."

Paco and Baez returned and said they would reluctantly agree to Papa's price, but only in cash.

"I always pay in cash," Papa announced. "Draw up the papers and I'll send them to my lawyers. It should take no more than a week for the money to arrive."

They shook hands and Paco said, "If you don't mind my asking, for what purpose do you want this land?"

"I envision a grand resort, winter homes and a

memorial park. Over there." Papa pointed to foothills at the base of the mountain range.

"Memorial park? In whose honor?"

Papa studied Paco's face for a moment, then said, "My own, of course."

Baez never let Paco out of his sight. Neither did he take more than one eye off Ramsey and Papa. For the next four days and nights Paco wined and dined them, including Tommy Price, upon Papa's insistence.

What prevented them from snatching Paco was not Baez alone but the dozen or so shady characters that followed them wherever they went. One false move and the shady characters would come out of the shade and put an end to Papa, Ramsey, Tommy and their rented limousine.

During that time Paco asked the nature of Papa's business.

"Thor-Ram," Papa told him. "You've heard of it?"

"No, I haven't."

"We manufacture arms."

"Limbs?"

"Guns."

"Oh."

"Sold both privately and to the military. Ramsey is my cousin. We started the business more than twenty years ago. That is, our fathers did. We inherited it."

"In California?"

"North Hollywood." Papa reached into his pocket. "My card," he said.

Paco took it and that night called the North Hollywood number for confirmation. Dotty answered the phone and gave them details. Dotty also assured them that the lawyers had the contracts and the money was forthcoming, by courier.

They met in Paco's office the following day. Paco was in high spirits after having gotten the confirmation from Dotty and sailed around the office.

"You know, Señor," Paco said in his reverie, "we Mexicans are of a unique sensibility. Land gives us, more than anything, the truth of our existence. You can do a lot of things to a Mexican. You can steal his beans. You can take his wife, his money. You can beat him. You can throw him in jail, wrest his job away. But if you try to take his land he will fight you till the end. Do not ever try to take away his land.

"There is much public land in this country. If a farmer wants to till the soil he may go out somewhere and find a piece of land belonging to the state. He does not have to pay. He simply has to farm it. That is all. No one will trespass on that land once he begins to farm it, for if someone does there will be a battle the likes of which you have never seen. Justice will prevail."

Papa and Ramsey nodded their agreement. Paco went on.

"The provincial people of this country, yes, that is where the heart of Mexico belongs. Not in Tijuana, not in Acapulco, not in Mexico City. The heart has been corrupted there. No, in the small towns of central Mexico, southern Mexico. Justice. The heart of justice."

While Paco paused to gather his thoughts Papa glanced over at Baez, who sat perfectly still in his chair, staring back at him.

"I tell you a story about Mexican justice," Paco continued. "Many years ago a small town in the Sierra Madres was besieged by banditos storming from the hills, getting drunk and shooting up the place. This happened many times. Finally, the people gathered and sent a small delegation to Mexico City to ask for military support. Soldiers were promised to ward off the banditos and the delegation returned. One week, two weeks passed. The banditos attacked. Finally, three weeks later, one soldier, *one*, a captain, arrived. We want many soldiers, not one, the people cried. What can one man do against all these banditos? Do not worry, the captain said, I will take care of everything. First, he said, we build a jail. Good idea, the people said. With one cell, the captain said, in the middle of the square. One cell! the people cried. What good will one cell do with all these banditos? Do not worry, the captain said, I will take care of everything.

"A week passes. One night a bandito comes into town, gets drunk, shoots up the place and leaves. The captain goes after him and brings him back. He places the bandito in the one cell and waits. Two weeks pass. Then, one night, another bandito comes to the small town. He too gets drunk and shoots up the place, and rides away. The captain gives chase and also brings this bandito back. Where will you put him, the people cried, there is only room for one in the cell.

"The captain says nothing. He goes to the cell and takes the first bandito out and puts the second bandito in his place. Then the captain places the first bandito against the wall and shoots him to death. I have to tell you, there was never a third bandito."

Papa and Ramsey were amused. Baez wasn't.

"So," Paco continued, "the captain's ingenuity and the people's desire to protect their land combined to make peace."

"Are you trying to tell me that banditos might attack from the mountains behind the land I'm interested in?" Papa asked.

"No, no, Mr. Thorson," Paco protested. "My point is once you have the land in your possession I will act as your captain. I will protect it, guard it, cultivate it, build your monument if you wish. I would like for you to see your virgin tonight perhaps, you and your friends, without me. Appreciate it, love it, as I do."

Which was exactly what Papa did. That evening just before dusk Papa, Ramsey and Tommy drove out to the property.

"Why?" Ramsey protested. "You're not going to lease the damn thing."

"You have something against sunsets?"

They stood on the precipice, Papa in his white linen suit looking more like Peter Ustinov than ever before. Ramsey wore a denim outfit, navy blue with gold stitching.

"Beautiful out here, isn't it?" Papa said in a dreamy voice, his head tilted up, gazing at the bright rusty sky.

"I could live here, Ramsey, I could. Build a small house, put in a generator, fish all day."

"Drink all night."

"Drink all night."

Papa's eyes swept the horizon where the colors folded round one another and the disappearing sun sent shafts of light darting through the clouds and over the black and blue sea.

"I think that's a good idea, Papa. But not this week."

Papa wasn't listening to Ramsey. The sea roared below. The wind hummed around him. A seagull squadron shuffled itself and made a flight pattern, lead bird and all, soaring high into the sunlight.

"No, I mean it, Ramsey. Out here."

"Are you drunk?"

"Absolutely."

"As Paco would say, 'drunk with the spirit of life!'" Ramsey chuckled.

"He's got some of the poet in him."

"Along with peyote buttons and cocaine, couple hits of speed and some green green grasseroo. Paco is a junkie. All junkies are poets . . . and most poets are junkies."

Papa walked away from Ramsey, moving slowly along the edge of the cliff. He felt the rocks beneath his feet and the dirt; soft, resilient.

"Was it something I said?" Ramsey asked, following along behind him. He spotted Tommy standing beside the car.

"Tommy," Ramsey called, "take a break, look at the ocean. Relax. Nobody's going to hurt the car."

Since they rented the limousine Tommy guarded it with his life. He wouldn't let the attendant drive it into the hotel's underground parking lot; he washed and waxed it himself; he talked to it.

Papa finally stopped.

"Does it look any better from over here?" Ramsey wanted to know.

Papa became slightly irritated and told Ramsey: "Can't you enjoy this? I know you want to go back and grab some broad; she'll be there. Take that advice you gave Tommy—relax."

"Sorry." Ramsey looked away to see what Papa was enjoying so much. After a moment he said: "You always do this!"

Papa was startled by the racket Ramsey made.

"Hey, I'm right here . . . I always do what?" he asked.

"I got a date at nine. It's eight-thirty. It takes at least a half hour to get back to the hotel. I'm never going to make it. Why? Because of your daydreaming. You get occupied with something and the universe goes on hold. We have completely different sensibilities."

"Mine is in the brain. Yours is in the groin."

"That's right. And I'll be goddamned if your brain is gonna keep my groin from having a good time."

"She'll be there," Papa assured him.

"You don't know these Mexican broads—of *course* you

know them—they get highly insulted if they're kept waiting."

"Mine always waited, Ramsey. What's your problem?" Papa said with a big smile.

"And you married every goddamn one of them."

"How else could I have gotten their best nights out of them? Getting married gives them inspiration. They don't care. Next time the moon comes up they're virgins again."

"Why don't we argue in the car, on the way back?"

"Why don't we."

They walked back to the car where Tommy held the door for them.

"Don't overdo it," Ramsey told Tommy.

On the ride back Papa pulled out a cigarette and shook it in front of Ramsey's face.

"A small house, nothing extravagant. I add on rooms as I need them . . ."

"And Dotty?"

With no more than a flicker of a pause, he said, "Dotty? Of course. I wouldn't move to this hunk of dirt alone."

Paco had made arrangements to meet them for dinner at eight o'clock the next evening. Papa, Ramsey and Tommy were dressing in their hotel suite.

"Think," Ramsey said. "What would Peter Graves have done in this situation?"

"A helluva lot more than we have. There has got to be a way to shake Paco's goons. But how?"

"I been thinkin' about that," Tommy said from the bed, still weaving rawhide. "We're near the water. Why not take them out fishing?"

"Tommy, you're a genius!" Papa said. "Take them out in a boat, get the drop on them and sail into an American port."

"What about my limousine?" Tommy asked.

Papa thought for a moment. "How's this? I'll call the dealer in San Diego, tell him to come down and pick it up. Leave it here in the hotel. I'll give the attendant a few bucks. Tell him the dealer will get it."

"Fishing," Ramsey mused. "That'll get rid of the goons . . . leaving only Baez."

"That's like saying *only* Hitler or *only* Rasputin."

"Now all we have to worry about is whether Paco likes to fish."

"For a half a million bucks Paco would like to do anything."

The waters off the Baja coast were the clearest Papa had ever seen. Long turquoise reefs jutted from the ocean floor, miniature mountain ranges riveted to the sand. He felt an odd sensation looking down into the water then back towards the vanishing coastline; from where he stood they appeared identical, of the same size and dimension. He remembered many years ago when he scuba dived off the northern California coast, when he'd strapped on the tanks and inserted the rubber mouthpiece and dropped backwards into the surf, and what an extraordinary sensation it was to have been transported from one element into another, and how the man who had taught him to scuba dive had said that so few people ever get to experience a sea change.

Papa raised his eyes towards the skipper, a burly Mexican, about fifty, with a closely cropped jet-black beard. He wore a skipper's cap and a skipper's outfit—a red and white horizontally striped pullover with white ducks and tennis shoes. He also chawed tobacco and spit it with remarkable accuracy into a bucket beside the wheel.

Baez and Paco wore recently bought sailor's clothes. So did Papa, Ramsey and Tommy. When they met at the dock and checked one another out, their expressions were similar to women who arrived at a party wearing the same dress.

"We look like the Peruvian Navy in drag," Ramsey remarked.

The forty-foot charter boat rumbled further out to sea. Aft were four lightweight aluminum poles dug into their cylindrical mounts. The mounts were attacked to swivel chairs fastened to the deck by steel runners. The skipper stood in the wheelhouse. Tommy Price played with his rawhide. The others drank beer on the lower deck, all except Ramsey who consumed enormous quantities of papaya juice from a plastic container.

"What kind of fish we going after?" Papa asked Paco.

"I have no idea, I do not enjoy fishing."

"Really? Then why are we here?"

"As a courtesy to you. Who knows, I may discover I like it after all."

"That's very nice of you. Had I known . . ."

Paco waved his hand in front of his face. "If I were opposed to fishing altogether, I would have objected." He smiled. "It's the least I can do."

Papa left Paco and moved over to where Ramsey squeezed the last of his juice from the container. "I'm dehydrated as hell," Ramsey said irritably.

"I'd like to get this over fairly soon," Papa informed him. "I'd like to reach U.S. waters before dark. I'll take Baez. You get Paco and Tommy can head up the stairs for the skipper."

Ramsey nodded. "I checked the gas situation. There's enough to get us to San Diego. The problem is, we're heading south right now. And the further we go the more gas we'll need."

"The way *I* figure," Papa explained, "when we stop the first time, that's when we'll hit. The signal will be when I get up from the chair for a beer. Give the message to Tommy. Make sure our bag is near the cooler. I'll pop the top, meaning get ready. I'll reach into the bag for the gun. *Then*."

Papa looked past Ramsey's shoulder at Baez, inside whose windbreaker was his revolver. Ramsey caught Papa staring.

"What?" he asked.

Papa shook his head slightly. "Baez."

"I haven't heard that idiot say one word the whole time we've been down here."

"Maybe he doesn't know any. It doesn't make any difference though. He's transmitting like mad. The message is all bad."

"That's the one problem on this caper."

"Uh? What's that?" Papa asked.

"Peter Lupas is on the wrong side."

Papa hooked a sailfish right away. He let out a hundred feet of line then snapped the reel. The fish shimmied into the air like a berserk belly dancer and plummeted down.

The skipper bounded down the stairs and rushed up behind Papa. The others kept one eye on the battle and the other on their own lines. Papa cursed out loud. This was the perfect time to make the snatch. All Ramsey had to do was get up and grab the gun, bash Baez over the skull and to hell with the fish. But Ramsey was too involved with what Papa was doing. Papa rocked back in his chair, and then dropped forward, reeling in, then back and forward until the fish drew to within fifty yards. The others had pulled in their lines. Tommy and the skipper stood behind him, shouting advice. Ramsey's chair was two away from Papa, which meant no signal could be given without Paco, seated between them, spotting it. Only Baez showed no emotion. His eyes drew a bead from Papa to the fish.

Sweat and salt water and beer coalesced on Papa's face. In the half hour since he'd snagged the fish his hands had gone numb.

"C'mon, you sonofabitch!" Papa snarled through gritted teeth.

The skipper was ready with a hook to pull the fish in. Papa wanted the battle to go on longer. Now he had forgotten about snatching Paco; this was war.

"Pool! Pool!" the skipper shouted. Papa pulled and yanked and thought he'd lost the bastard a dozen times. Each time the fish went under Papa thought it had broken the line, torn it away. But the fish came back harder and stronger.

The fish drew closer. The skipper leaned over the rail. The hook was down. One quick accurate gaff and it would be over. The boat tilted to one side with their weight.

"Oh, she's beautiful!" Papa heard Paco exclaim.

So are you, Paco, Papa said to himself. You're next. The gun, Ramsey, get the fucking gun.

With one looping swing the skipper gaffed the fish in the side and yanked. Ramsey got behind and pulled the skipper. Paco reached over the rail with another gaff and dug it into the fish. Baez did not move. Papa leaned back in his chair, breathing heavily. The sailfish was hauled into the boat and flapped on the deck. Blood spurted from the gaff holes.

"One hundred pounds," Paco said, impressed.

"That's how much *I* lost pulling it in," replied Papa. He pushed himself from the chair. "Now what I need is a beer." The signal.

Papa went to the cooler and drew out the can. He reached into the green carry-all bag for the weapon but couldn't locate it. He rummaged through the suntan oil and the extra shirts and the set of keys. Where's the gun?

"Mr. Thorson," he heard Paco say.

Paco smiled. "Baez has what you're looking for."

Papa shifted his gaze to Baez who held the .45.

Papa straightened up, casually, popped the beer can and took a long slug. He looked hard at Baez. "Just what the fuck are you doing in our things?"

From their expressions they expected some other comment. Paco changed from sly assuredness to embarrassment. "While you were pulling in the fish Baez removed the weapon, for safety reasons, you understand."

"No, I don't understand. I manufacture weapons. I carry them for protection. Your asshole over here," he said, pointing at Baez, "carries a gun cause he's a big fucking baby who wants to play tough. I don't like my possessions tampered with, Mr. Carrera. So you can tell the orangutan to put it back."

Paco didn't know what to think. He might have blown the land deal. What Papa said made considerable sense.

"Baez is a careful individual, Mr. Thorson," Paco said nervously.

"I think the word is 'stupid,' Mr. Carrera," Papa replied. "Do you normally let him blow half-million-dollar deals for you?"

Paco stammered and then, leering at Baez, chewed him out in Spanish. Baez answered in one short sentence.

"What's the verdict?" Papa finally asked.

"I am afraid I will have to bind your hands. I hope you understand."

Papa was not at all ready for that.

"Mr. Carrera, I am getting very mad."

"Yes, I can see that."

While Baez held the .45 Paco and the skipper went to tie their hands.

That's when Tommy Price made the biggest mistake of his life. Papa saw it coming but couldn't do a thing to stop it and Ramsey was too far away to ward the kid off.

Tommy was standing just behind the skipper. He lunged forward, pushing the skipper towards Baez. No more than five feet separated the three men. Baez jerked the .45 and fired three quick rounds. Two caught the skipper in the chest and the third made a large hole in Tommy's neck. Had Tommy been further from the rail he would have fallen under the skipper's weight. As it was, when the slug hit it lifted his body into the air and pushed him over the railing. He dropped into the clear sea and floated off.

Tommy's death stalled Papa, it shocked him. The moment for him was illusory, as if it happened in another time, a dark shadow moving through the sunlight. His body jerked as Tommy's did; he could almost feel the bullet himself. His feet left the ground, and the sound from the gun's detonation stayed with him for a long time.

Papa watched Tommy's body drift away. Baez re-entered his thoughts. He wanted to kill the man. Slowly. He wanted to drive a knife through his eyes, to carve the skin from his body and lay it in the sun to bake, to cut off his balls and hang them on a trophy board. Or even better: to shackle Baez against an upright piece of wood and fire the Prowler Fouler at him, over and over, until all life was pounded from him. But for now he would have to play his cards, weak as they were.

Papa sighed deeply and shook his head. "Dumb stupid kid."

Ramsey stood beside him rubbing both hands against his trousers. Paco's hands also moved, squeezing both palms together. The hands. As if they were partners in Tommy Price's death.

Papa turned to Paco. "You see what can happen when you let a maniac loose?" He gestured towards Baez.

"It was your chauffeur who . . ."

"It was my chauffeur—a kid, Mr. Carrera—who saw a punk with a gun." Papa stepped over the skipper's body, turned and started to kneel when he heard Baez grunt.

"What are you doing?" Paco asked.

"I'm going to bury the man. Do you mind?" Papa hefted the bloody body from the deck and carried it to the edge. He leaned over the rail and carefully dropped the skipper into the sea.

"Are you Catholic, Mr. Thorson?" Paco inquired.

"In my tastes, Mr. Carrera."

"Now," Paco said with a smile, "your hands please."

Papa raised his eyes to the small Mexican, and then to Ramsey. "Think. Martin Landau. What would *he* do?"

Three hours later they were back in Rosarita Beach, tied up in the cellar under Paco Carrera's office. They had been fed on frijoles and enchiladas, and given a bottle of thick sweet wine that tasted so grapy it must have been picked, squashed and bottled that morning.

"Paco's a smart little bastard," Papa was saying. "He figures the money'll be here tomorrow. He'll stash it in the bank, knock us off and that'll be the end of it."

"Wait'll he finds out there is no money."

"I figure we can stall him for a couple of days."

"And then?" Ramsey asked.

"I don't want to think about it."

But Papa did think about it. He thought about never leaving the cellar alive. He thought about Tommy Price. He thought about Dotty and the baby and wondered how they would get along without him if he didn't make it back. The cellar's dark mud walls reminded him of another place where the chances of him getting out alive had been even worse than this. Before drifting into the memory Papa checked on Ramsey, who sat wrapped in a large serape, shivering in the dampness. Earlier Ramsey had seen a rat scurrying across the dirt floor and pulled the blanket tightly around his body. A single overhead bulb flickered in the darkness. Papa watched Ramsey adjust his body against the wall.

DECEMBER 4, 1973. The Hotel Fenix, Guadalajara, Mexico. Papa sat in his room, knowing that somewhere in the hotel, possibly in the hallway outside his room, were two pistoleros waiting to kill him. The $50,000 in cash he carried was intended as pay-off money to get an American kid out of the Mexican jail where he had been incarcerated for drug dealing.

Before going out to confront the pistoleros Papa wrote a letter to Ramsey back in L.A.

Ramsey,

I am sitting in a hotel room in a foreign country under a 40 watt bulb at 1a.m. Friday.

I have "pulmonia" (pneumonia), the doctor says, and am out of tetracycline. I am a mile high, with breathing supremely difficult. The pollution here must be outrageous. The telephone wait to L.A. is four hours. The water has given me "little animals in my estomak" as the natives charmingly describe, and I am fighting puking constantly (between the runs).

What food I can get down tastes like burned soap. I have cashed a check for $50,000 (in pesos) and there are two pistoleros laying in wait for me. I arrived here Monday expecting to conclude business by Tuesday p.m. and spend no more than $300 in expenses. It is Friday 1 a.m. The lawyer has lied to me *repeatedly and can probably* not *do the job. Have spent over $700 in expenses so far.*

Nobody here speaks any fucking English. The girls smell like cheap perfume factories and worse—they let their hair grow (yuk!) on their legs. The TV worked for thirty minutes before breaking—everything was in Spanish anyway—and they have been going to fix it "manana" (since Monday).

Tried to get Jorge (the lawyer's brother in L.A.) but his phone is disconnected—no referral.

I am here trying to get an asshole junkie dope dealer out of jail—on a non-bailable offense.

You cannot believe what the Mexican coffee tastes like. I have developed a boil under my left arm (in the armpit) where it hurts to blink my eye.

My client is panicked—he's blown $10,000 American and lost his junkie son to Mexican penitentiaries for fifteen years. The attorney is screaming "what the hell am I doing and what is taking so long!" I sweat all day and am freezing my nuts off right now. There is no heat or air conditioning in this, one of Guadalajara's finest hotels. I am so fucking tired of mariachis. I could almost enjoy some of Dotty's shit-kicking cowboy moaning.

It looks very much like this mission will be a miserable failure. If I survive physically and don't get robbed or killed for the money, the American customs will detain me for two days or so to explain why I'm coming into the country with all this cash.

How about this for the exciting life and international intrigue of a bounty hunter.

                                                    Papa

There were two reasons why Papa ended his Guadalajara mission by pumping three slugs apiece into the bodies of the Mexican pistoleros. One had to do with the fact that not twenty minutes after posting the letter and returning to his room the pistoleros rushed through the door. Papa was sitting on the bed when he heard the door crash open. The .45 was beside him on the table. When the door crashed he fell forward, to the floor, taking the weapon with him.

The pistoleros opened fire the minute they entered the

room. The bullets flew around Papa who was on his stomach, aiming back at them. He squeezed off six rounds and the Mexicans slumped to the floor.

The second reason for shooting them had to do with honor. He had been doublecrossed by Guadalajara officials, the lawyers, the prison hierarchy, all of whom intended to steal the money he carried and bury his body in some ditch. Papa knew if he somehow got back to the States alive, and the news followed him that he got royally screwed over, his reputation would have been at an all time low. Which meant he would not be hired again, at least for some time, for any sort of Mexican assignment.

Papa left the pistoleros in the room and fled. Without saying goodbye to anyone he hired a private airplane to fly him out of the country, arriving at the border near Yuma, Arizona, late the following morning . . .

Papa's recollection of that experience, as he now sat in Paco Carrera's dungeon prison, made him shudder. The overhead light had flickered for the last time and the cellar was now bathed in darkness. The last sound he heard before dropping off to sleep was the patter of little feet racing across the cellar floor.

The following day Papa and Ramsey were brought upstairs to the chamber adjoining the main office. It was a Monday. The money, in the form of a bank draft, was due that day at two o'clock. It was a time Papa had arbitrarily dreamed up, never considering the possibility they would still be there.

At one forty-five Paco ordered Papa untied so that he might meet the courier. Ramsey's bindings remained intact.

"Do nothing foolish," Paco told him, "or your cousin will be killed."

"What do you think about that, cousin?" Papa asked Ramsey.

"Do nothing foolish. I'd appreciate it."

Papa felt a surge of energy when Paco untied his ropes. He figured it was the circulation returning to his hands. He sat directly opposite Ramsey. Baez was to his right, aiming the gun at him. Paco sat on Papa's left, unarmed. The time: one fifty-five.

"I hope that damn courier knows where . . ." Ramsey stopped talking. Something occurred to him. Papa caught it and watched Ramsey's eyes for some hint. Ramsey was staring off to Papa's right.

"You were saying, Ramsey?" Papa asked.

Ramsey shrugged. "The courier. I'm sure he'll know how to get here."

"Which, by the way, Mr. Carrera," Papa said, "I'd like to talk to you about. I think we should consider making an exchange—the money for our lives."

"That's impossible."

"That's *mission* impossible," Ramsey said.

"My favorite television show . . . until about a week ago. *Piñata, piñata.*" Ramsey began singing. "That thinga never won a race. *Piñata, piñata.*"

"That's *cucaracha*, Mr. Ramsey," Paco explained.

Papa noticed Ramsey's eyes again focused off to one side and dropped his head slightly to where he saw it, leaning against the wall. A *piñata* club, used by blind-folded South Americans to break open the *piñata* bag filled with prizes. The bag in this case would hopefully be the head of Baez.

Papa nodded casually, indicating he was for the idea.

It was time for a Ramsey performance. He continued singing his *piñata* song, rocking from side to side in his chair. Ten seconds later he rocked way to the left and toppled to the floor. To further charge the moment he let out a ballyhoo that reverberated through the office.

The fall drew Paco and Baez's attention while Papa made his move for the *piñata* stick. Before Baez could absorb what had happened Papa brought the stick around and slammed it against the side of his head. Baez went down, so did the gun, which Papa picked up and aimed at Paco.

"You can open your eyes," Papa said to Ramsey.

Ramsey did so, smiled, and continued singing.

"Get over there!" Papa scowled at Paco, who moved beside the semi-conscious Baez.

"Untie me and let's get the hell out of here," Ramsey insisted.

They ushered Paco outside to the big Chrysler, where they put him in the trunk in case the border guards got suspicious.

Forty miles of bad roads stood between them and the Mexican line. It would have been an easy drive, except for

three of Paco's men who happened to see them barreling
off in their boss's car. The three men gave chase.

"Now ain't that some shit," Papa said when he saw they
were being pursued. "Paco's in the trunk. They don't know
we have him."

"I've never had such a lousy time in my life," Ramsey
mumbled, and jammed down on the accelerator.

They couldn't chance going directly through Tijuana
where siesta was just ending and the traffic picking up.
They skirted the city by way of a miserable road that
snaked through the desert.

The crazy Mexicans behind them were playing Laven-
der Hill Mob as they struck their big white smiles out the
windows and took pot shots at the Chrysler. Ramsey
ducked down in the front seat, watching the road through
the steering wheel. Papa poked the .45 through the passenger window and squeezed off two shots. Neither connected. The road was too bumpy to take careful aim.

The pursuit car, an old Chevrolet, did not have the
stretch speed to catch the Chrysler. The Mexicans knew
these roads, however, and maneuvered closer on the turns.
Gunfire sprayed around them while Papa prayed that the
tires would remain intact.

Up ahead, the border. As a courtesy Ramsey would
normally have slowed down. Not this time. He split
right through the Mexican gate, spraying dust and puddle
water all over the guards' uniforms. He saw in the rear-
view mirror the guards chasing after him. The pursuit car
halted at the border. Ramsey pulled to the side, in the
U.S. sector. The American guards ran up.

"What the hell's going on here?" the guard captain
wanted to know.

Papa shrugged.

The captain looked at the Mexican license plate and
said, "You American citizens?"

"Yes."

"Whose car is this?"

"It belongs to the boss of those guys chasing us," Papa
replied, aiming his thumb to the rear where the Mexicans
were out of their car screaming and pointing at Papa.

By this time a half dozen guards encircled the Chrysler.
Passersby ambled over and stood behind the guards.

"Paper," the captain said.

Papa and Ramsey reached for their identification and

gave it to him. The captain inspected it and, seemingly satisfied, handed it back.

"Have you anything to declare?" he asked.

Just then a loud banging noise came from the rear. Papa and Ramsey turned their heads to the rear and saw the trunk pop up and down.

"*Nothing* to declare?" the captain repeated. "Pull over there."

Ramsey maneuvered the Chrysler to the other side of the guard station. They got out and Ramsey used the key to open the trunk. There was Paco Carrera with the tire iron in one hand, coughing and choking from the exhaust fumes.

"Who's that?" the captain wanted to know.

"The boss," said Papa, jamming both hands in his pockets.

"And what is he doing in the trunk?"

"Being punished," said Papa. He explained the situation to the captain, who started counting on his fingers.

"Stolen car. Kidnapping a Mexican national across the border, *running* the border."

"Running the border?" Papa objected. "No, no. We stopped. The Mexican guards don't care."

"Would you like to go back and find out how much they care?" the captain asked.

"Not particularly."

It took a few moments for Papa to realize that the captain was giving them no more than a hard time. Papa dropped a few names of Border Patrol and DEA honchos he knew, they got to bullshitting and laughing, and finally the captain warned them against this sort of thing and let them go. Papa thanked him, placed Paco in the seat between them, and headed north towards San Diego.

On the way Paco wanted to know what was going on, why was he now in California?

"Because, Mr. Carrera," Papa explained, "you jumped bail."

Papa watched realization dawn on Paco's face. "Oh, my God, you mean . . . ?" Then Paco wept. Who could blame him?

Half an hour later Papa escorted Paco into the San Diego Hall of Justice where he was handcuffed to a pillar while Papa filled out the necessary papers. When Papa returned he found Paco with his head buried in his hands.

"You all right?" Papa asked.

Paco slowly raised his head. "I was thinking."

"Good. You'll have a lot of time."

"I was thinking of a man named Mersault."

"Mersault."

"He is . . . the stranger of Camus' novel of the same name. I was thinking about how he stood at his prison window and gazed outside where freedom was, and how he thought: although they have incarcerated my body they can never incarcerate my mind. My mind will always be free."

"That's an excellent philosophy to carry to jail with you, Paco."

"Isn't it, though. I can still imagine Mexico. I can still imagine my property, the sea, all that I have ever known."

Paco's philosophical stance suddenly turned sour. His eyes saddened and his lips bent towards his chin.

"But I shall also imagine," he said, mournfully, "how beautiful, how . . . how exquisite, how satisfying it might have been"—his eyes fixed on Papa's—"to hold a half million dollars in cash? *That* my imagination will suffer."

"I know what you mean, Paco. For that one week I had a half million bucks. It's not easy."

"But you never really had it, Señor."

"Neither did you, Paco."

8

End of the Road

Papa returned to L.A. and dropped off Ramsey, promising to deliver his cut on the Paco Carrera snatch by the end of the week. In order to make the promise good he went directly to Richie Blumenthal's office on Bailbond Row.

When Papa entered the office Richie rose from his chair and walked briskly around the desk to shake his hand. Richie hardly ever did that. Papa wondered why this time; he hadn't called Richie with the good news.

"Papa, Papa, Papa," Richie said with great enthusiasm. "Come here, sit." He ushered Papa to the antique sofa and waited for him to get comfortable before returning to his chair behind the desk.

"What are you so happy about?" Papa wanted to know.

"I heard," Richie smiled, wagging a finger at him.

"Heard what?"

"Don't play coy with me," Richie admonished. "I got a call from San Diego. They told me. You got Carrera."

"And lost Tommy Price."

"I'm truly sorry about that," Richie said. "Now, about your fee."

"My fee."

"I wanted to talk to you about that," Richie said, his expression changing.

"I figured you would."

Richie rose again from his chair, straightening his suit coat, and clasped his hands behind his back. His old wrinkled face looked like a congested road map, and the fine silver white hair flared back from a receding widow's peak and fell over his collar.

"I can't pay you fifty percent," he announced.

"I won't take any less. That was the deal."

Richie shrugged.

"Twenty-five."

The ritual had begun.

"Forty."

"Thirty."

"Forty. I have the other . . ." He was going to say other *guys* but now there was only Ramsey to divide the pie.

"Thirty-five. You're getting such a deal. Minus . . ."

Papa cut him off. "Minus nothing. Thirty-five, bottom line." Wasn't it like the sonofabitch to bargain with his vulnerability.

Richie must have caught it and acquiesced.

"You got it."

With uncharacteristic swiftness Richie pulled out his massive ledger and wrote a check for $35,000, which he ripped from the page and carried to Papa, sitting beside him.

"That's the good news," Richie said sympathetically. "Now for the bad."

"If you don't think I want to hear it," Papa said, "don't tell me."

"If you don't hear it from me, somebody else will tell you."

"All right. I'm braced."

"Good boy." Richie patted Papa on the knee and stood. He walked towards the window and stood with his back to him. After a long pause he said in a voice that Papa could barely hear, "Jack Finnegan is dead."

A thousand-needle rush swept through Papa. The first word that came to him was "Why." He asked: "How?"

"It's a long story," Richie said, turning back to him.

"I've got time."

"I'll make it short." Richie returned to his desk, sat and folded his hands. "It happened yesterday morning, in his house, five slugs, right here." Richie tapped his chest, *mea culpa, mea culpa.*

"By?" Papa asked.

"Federal narcotics agents."

"On a bust?"

"A bust, yes. His own."

Papa churned his hands. "C'mon, tell me. His own?"

"Big case, Papa. Finnegan was—now this is what I heard, I don't know for sure—he was caught conspiring to sell one point seven million bucks' worth of cocaine to Federal narcotics agents."

"Sell! He was selling! Jack?"

Richie nodded. "Him and another cop. The other cop apparently blew the whistle on him. There was a battle. Finnegan got the worst of it."

"So it was his chart after all," Papa mumbled.

"What's that?"

"Nothing. Go ahead."

"The way I got it, the Federal narcos been working on the thing for months. In his house they found scales and dust. Talk about incriminating evidence. I never figured he was a bad cop."

"Bullshit!" Papa was yelling. "One thing he wasn't, was that! He was set up, he had to be?"

Richie shook his head. "No."

"Look, if a shoe salesman does a great job eight hours a day and goes out at night to steal hubcaps, that makes him a bad shoe salesman? For ten years his word was golden with me. He was set up. He—"

"I'm not gonna argue with you. I'm telling you what I know."

Papa's hands squeezed together. Sweat appeared on his brow. Jack Finnegan busted? Killed? By another cop? He focused the chart in his mind and remembered the details. They fit. Oh, they *fit.*

"The Federal narcs put the case together," Richie reiterated. "They had him cased. They caught him. They hit the place, his house. They got him."

"And they killed him."

"And they killed him."

"Doesn't that smell of setup to you, Richie? Did they

have to blow him away? Did he resist? Finnegan wasn't that dumb."

Richie again shrugged. "Believe what you want. I'm relaying information. I knew you'd be unhappy. I wish I never told you."

For Richie the topic had concluded.

"You want details? Use the phone—in the other office."

Papa left Richie and called Finnegan's unit. No information was available, he was told. He called the Federal building, where they ran him in circles. He finally contacted a friend in the Dicks bureau who filled him in. There wasn't much to add to what Richie told him: Names, times, locations. It was, said the friend, open and shut. The friend said he was as shook as anybody. It was unbelievable, the friend said. Everybody felt that way.

Papa left Richie's office in a stupor. First Tommy Price and now Jack and both were his responsibility; there was no doubt in his mind, and if he'd been just a little smarter, used his smarts just a little more, he could have touted them off. *Prevented!* Fuck the stars, they didn't pull the trigger. Constellations didn't fuse and light the sky with dead men's names, or spike their bodies, or single them out for a quick, painless end. It was haste that did them in, his own, and if he'd listened to those up-front warnings he was supposed to listen to, the ones that kept his own ass alive, he might have—that word—*prevented!* Call it guilt, call it dereliction, or the grand faux pas. In the end, *always* in the end, it came out stupidity. He should have known.

Why Finnegan did it, how he got caught and killed, also had to do with stupidity. Papa was convinced that Jack had started to believe his own publicity; his rising young star that everyone admired, his invulnerability. He no longer paid attention to that very requisite which brought him the stardom in the first place. Believing in your *vul*nerability made you careful, you covered yourself. It eased Papa's mind to know that, to some degree at least, Jack Finnegan killed himself.

Rocco Mason waited in a ten-year-old blue Mustang with the sides bashed in. Two mournful pouches sagged beneath his eyes, close together, small, concave, black buttons sewn into the red and white patchwork of his face. He was six years older now since Papa had pulled him, kicking and screaming, from his father's bar in Manhattan Beach. He was also crazier, but more deftly so. He had method to it.

In a queer way he had enjoyed spending time in prison. He found friends there, the only friends he'd ever made. They were still with him, protesting his revenge but understanding it. They ate bi-phetamines every day, just like the old days, Black Beauties that made him grind his teeth and talk a mile a minute and made him brave. Rocco Mason had eaten two before driving over to Papa's, where he now sat, down the street, watching the house. Waiting. He squeezed a small rubber ball in the palm of his right hand. He watched the rear-view mirror, the street ahead, the house, the people walking in and out, the cars passing by. His eyes were childlike the way they darted back and forth. The radio thumped out a country-western tune.

In the mirror Mason spotted the yellow Plymouth as it eased on by and pulled in front of the house. He watched Papa climb from the front seat, lock up and head up the steps. Mason waited another minute before putting the Mustang in gear, then he gripped the wheel and cruised by the house on down the street towards the bright yellow "LIQUOR" sign on Magnolia.

No one was in the house when Papa entered, though he heard someone pounding on something, out in the tool shed. He removed the .45 from its holster and carried it to the gun rack where he almost had a mild coronary. Every revolver, every rifle, the telescopic sights; all were covered with a thin coat of red rust.

"My-ron!" he screamed. No answer. He called again.

Myron bounded in through the kitchen door, a wide, proud smile plastered across his face.

"Hi, Papa," he clamored, but when he saw the fury on Papa's face he hunched his shoulders and fell back in retreat. "Have a good trip?" he said meekly.

"No."

"No?"

"Tommy Price was killed. Ramsey and I almost didn't come back alive. But I did get my man, and made some money, Myron." Myron smiled and grimaced according to the pitch of Papa's voice. "But not enough money to buy a whole new fucking set of guns."

"Why'd you wanna do that?"

"Because you ruined them. When you clean the guns and wipe off the oil, you have to rub more oil on. You didn't. They're caked with rust."

"Rust?"

"Rust."

Myron stood there like a big, cowering, bad-boy version of Jerry Lewis. He would have run away but he didn't want to turn his back on Papa.

"Papa, I'm sorry," he whimpered.

"You . . . are . . . sorry. You are the sorriest . . ."

Papa glowered at Myron. "Sit down. There," he ordered, pointing to the sofa, "until I figure what to do with you."

Seconds later the phone rang.

"Papa Thorson?" the voice asked.

"Who wants to know?"

"Is this Papa Thorson?"

"Who wants to know?" Papa repeated.

"Hello, Papa," said the voice. "This is Rocco Mason. Remember me?"

"Who could forget?"

"I'm outa jail."

"Congratulations. Still on speed, huh?"

Silence. Then: "How do you know?"

"I can hear your teeth gnashing."

"Didja get my letter?"

"What letter?" Papa said, pulling it from under the bar.

"You didn't get my letter!" Mason went into high speed. "You didn't get it!"

"What is this, a bad reception? I told you I didn't get it."

"Well, I sent it."

"Then call the post office. Don't bother me."

"I'm after you, Papa. I promised I'd get you. Remember that?"

"Mason, it's *your* memory that's fucked up, not mine. What do you want?"

"You, Papa. I want you. I'm gonna get you. I told you I was going to get you. That's exactly what I'm gonna do. Get you. You understand?"

"Five times. Listen, Mason, I don't want to hear your funny voice any more. No more phone calls or letters. Nothing. Do *you* understand?"

"I understand only one thing . . ."

"Mason?"

"Wha?"

"Byeeee."

Click. Papa hung up.

"Stay there," he told Myron and went off to the john where he found Fang drinking from the toilet bowl. He chased the dog away and sat, pulling a copy of *Argosy* from the stack.

Two additional calls interrupted him. One came from Richie Blumenthal wanting to know how he was coming on the Tony Bernardo case. Papa told Richie he was very close to finding the kid and would get back to him. The second caller was Winston Blue, who mouthed the same old promise to turn himself in.

"But how long, Winston?"

"Soon, Papa."

"I have twenty-five hundred bucks tied up in you, Winston. I want answers."

"Answers I got for you, baby."

"What are they?"

"Uh, uh, soon."

"Winston, I'm getting mad."

"Don't get mad, Papa."

"I can't help it."

"I'm too depressed to turn myself in right now, you know, and, uh, when I get better, yeah, that's when, uh huh."

Papa was too tired to argue so he threatened Winston and rang off.

Mr. and Mrs. Arnold Fish appeared at the front door.

Mrs. Fish was a big strapping mamma with a set of biceps as large as her son's. She lumbered rather than walked, sprinkled her sentences with Yiddish clichés and stood with her feet spread apart at a forty-five-degree angle. Mr. Fish resembled his name. Papa half expected him to be hiding gills under his yellow gabardine suit. Mr. Fish stood two paces behind his wife, bowed when she did, said, "Right, dear," many times and smoked a giant cigar.

When Papa answered the door in shorts with no shirt, Mr. Fish blanched. Mrs. Fish raised an eyebrow and gave him a disapproving once-over before marching into the room.

"Myron can't stay here anymore. He can't come over

here anymore. He breaks things. He's costing me too much money," Papa informed them.

"But he's so talented," Mrs. Fish protested.

"But not here. Mrs. Fish, his mind leaves him when he enters this house. He's terrific everywhere else. He's turned my home into a junk yard."

"Is that right, Myron?" Mrs. Fish said, glaring at her son.

Myron looked to Papa for help. Getting none, he looked to his father, who smiled sympathetically. Papa now understood where Myron got his facial expressions.

"Myron, I'm talking to you."

"Yes, Mama. I have trouble here. I, I have to admit that. And Papa is right. I can't ever come back here. Oh, God!" Myron sniveled.

"Myron!" his mother shouted.

Snap! Myron snapped out of it and stood to attention.

"You're also very talented, Mrs. Fish," Papa nodded.

"I know," she agreed.

"I want to do one thing before you take him away," Papa said.

"Go right ahead."

Papa walked up to the kid.

"I know why you brought Mama and Papa, Myron," Papa said. "So I wouldn't do this to you." Whack!

Papa's hand caught Myron dead on the chin and he went soaring towards the bar. The stools scattered first, and then the bar itself, unhinging from the floor bolts and stretching back towards the windows.

The surprise was still on Myron's face when he landed. His head bumped the foot rail and one leg was trapped beneath the paneling. Other men would have conked out, not Myron. He shook the dizziness out and climbed to his elbows, studying Papa's slowly crystalizing face.

Mr. Fish stepped around his wife and took Papa's hand.

"I should have done that twenty years ago," he said, pumping Papa's hand.

"Arnold!" Mrs. Fish said and Mr. Fish returned to his place behind her.

Mrs. Fish wagged a finger at her son and Myron struggled up and moved sheepishly to her, and then around her, where he stood beside his father. It was Jewish-American Renaissance, the three of them; Mama at the fore, fleshy-armed and severe, the stoic mistress; her wimpy troops taking up the rear. She ran her eyes over the huge, half naked, full-bearded male Gentile standing before her and expanded her massive chest. The impenetrable versus the unmovable.

"Goodbye, Mr. Thorson," she said, turning and moving between her children towards the door. Mr. Fish followed first. Myron paused by the door with a sidelong glance at Papa.

"I know you're unhappy with me, but I'll make it up to you. I'll prove myself. You'll see. I'll do it."

Myron bit his lip and scurried after his parents.

The three of them crossed the street and climbed into an old Cadillac. As they took off Mr. Fish waved to Papa from the passenger window.

Papa returned to his magazine.

A half hour later Dotty opened the bathroom door. Her face was drawn and her eyes were glazed, downturned and very sad.

"What's the matter?" Papa asked, drawing her down and kissing her on the forehead.

"Jack Finnegan."

"I know. Richie told me."

"So it really was his chart you read."

"Yes."

Dotty knelt beside him, taking his head in her arms. They remained that way for a time. On the wall hung a small, ornate mirror through which Papa watched their reflection. The mirror was old and the glass faded and through it they looked like subjects of some ancient photograph.

Papa focused on Dotty's soft auburn hair, the way it fell in gentle ringlets to her shoulders, and the way she cradled his head against her breast, the faded jeans she wore and the sweater that matched her eyes . . .

Los Angeles. June, 1965. Papa sat at a small corner table in Lombardi's, the murky basement restaurant of the L.A. County Law Building. At adjoining tables were judges and lawyers, bondsmen and their clients, cops and court stenographers, drinking and wolfing down excellent Italian food.

Papa said hello to them, most of whom he knew, but did not join them because he waited for a woman named

Dotty Barras, referred to him by bondsman Dell Hoey. The description given to him by Hoey read: tall, slim, red hair, quiet, twenty-five years old and good-looking. According to the bond certificate Papa had before him, Dotty Barras had posted bail on a male musician, Harold Platt, who had forfeited and left the state.

Papa had drunk three Jack Daniels and water in the hour he waited and was about to order another when he saw her come through the door.

"I was attracted to her right off. I've always been partial to tall lean women with red hair. I also had an iron-clad rule in the business: you don't shit where you eat. Which means if you sleep with the client you end up not getting paid by the client. I got in that bind a few times.

"So she sat down and told me about the musician and that he was in Seattle playing in some club. That was easy enough. All I had to do was call a Seattle buddy of mine and have the guy picked up and sent down here, which I did. The problem was how she would pay me off. She had already paid a thousand bucks to the bondsman, and owed me two, one of which I'd have to send to Seattle. Since she was broke, we made a deal. She'd pay off the debt by working for me. One out of every five pickups I had was a woman, which was a real hassle because all the broad had to do was scream rape and I was in trouble. With a matron along that problem was taken care of. In fact, I had a pickup that night and she went along. She was scared. I couldn't blame her. But she acted like a real pro, and little by little she paid me back.

"Dotty was living at the Evangeline Home for Women in Hollywood, where they locked the doors at ten p.m. So when it got to be two in the morning what else could she do but move in?

"She brought problems with her—mainly a three-year-old kid, Kenny—but she also brought a lot of strength. She worked, kept her end up, took care of her kid. She had responsibility and she took it. The musician ripped her off because she was good-natured and easy to take advantage of. With the kid and the job she never went out, and her ex-husband never gave her a cent. Vulnerability and character, she had them both.

"I wanted to help her. I wanted to protect her. I wanted to love her. She could cook, she was great in bed, didn't drink or take dope. She fit in with my own group of friends, very important. She had adaptability, and she wasn't phony like a lot of broads. She laid her cards on the table. What can I say, she was a woman."

With Papa's head still in her arms, Dotty asked, "Do you feel any better about me having the baby?"

"Should I?"

"It would make *me* feel better."

"What happened to the abortion you were getting while I was away?"

"I didn't have it."

"Obviously."

"Let's not fight, okay?" she said.

Papa nodded his head and placed one hand on her stomach, where he pressed gently.

"It's hard for me," he whispered, swallowing whatever else he was going to say.

9

The Branch Brothers

AUGUST 6.

They might have been the James Gang in another era, or
the Wild Bunch. They lived outside Lincoln, Nebraska,
and for years terrorized hell out of the region. But
throughout their career the Branch brothers itched from a
persistent burr in the rear. The Branch brothers were total
foul-balls. They never did anything right.

Papa knew about the brothers long before Richie
Blumenthal called him with the case. He knew, for instance, that they were all out of their minds and their craziness was a matter of public record. In order to fill in the
gaps Papa glanced over old bail-bond applications on the
brothers. He called a friend in the Law Enforcement Intelligence Unit (L.E.I.U.) of the LAPD, where he found the
most extensive information. The L.E.I.U. traded information with major cities throughout the country, dealing with
statistics on known criminals, with rumor and gossip, anything that might draw a more complete picture of the fugitive.

From the reports, Papa learned that the brothers—Matthew, Mark, Luke, John, Peter and Paul—had been arrested in four states for armed robbery, car theft, bad checks, assault and battery, assault with intent to kill, resisting arrest.

On April 14, 1971, according to L.E.I.U. files, five of the brothers had been cruising through Hastings, Nebraska. It was late at night and they were all loaded on rotgut. Matthew, the driver, spotted a jewelry store and announced what a good idea it would be to steal a cache of precious stones for their precious girl friends. Mark, reputedly the wildest of the Branches, agreed and grabbed a sledgehammer from the back seat and hopped out.

Since lock-picking was not in his repertoire, Mark decided to smash the front window, scoop up the jewels and take off. While the others waited in the 1953 Chevy, Mark stood before the window, spit into his palms, raised the hammer above his head and swung.

The hammer exploded against the impenetrable one-inch-thick safety glass and bounced back, bonking Mark on the skull and knocking him cold. Two Branches stormed from the Chevy and dragged their brother back. Twenty-two stitches later he was out of the hospital but was apprehended the next day because no one remembered to retrieve the sledgehammer with Mark Branch's fingerprints all over it.

Explosives held a fascination for the Branch brothers, especially nitroglycerine. Their first experience with nitro occurred June 21, 1972, when a friend instructed them how to make the explosive by simmering dynamite. Four of the brothers loaded an aluminum cauldron in their car and headed for the foothills at the base of the Ozark Plateau. They filled the cauldron with the dynamite, placing it on a pyramid of logs, and lit the fire. More beer was drunk.

"What the hell's the *matter* with this nitra glacereen?" Paul Branch asked impatiently.

"Damned if I know," Peter Branch said. "Let's go back to town for more beer."

They all piled into the car and headed for town, leaving the cauldron with Luke Branch to guard it. They returned an hour and a half later but couldn't locate the cauldron or their brother, or the foothills, for that matter. What they did find was a large smouldering crater and a lot of smoke. Luke Branch was buried in absentia the following day.

Now that the brothers had discovered the power and essence of nitro, they decided to make a profit from it. Their first target was a safe on the eighteenth floor of the Law Building in downtown Lincoln. The same friend who told them how to make nitro from dynamite explained how to open safes.

"When you blow a safe," he told them, "the safe always blows down. Straight down."

The Branches got all excited and one night broke into the building, riding the elevator to the eighteenth floor. They located the safe, waxed the nitro to it and stood back. Matthew Branch spread a mattress cover over the safe and sat on top of it. Since it blew down, what problem could arise? The safe blew—eighteen stories straight down—and ended up in the basement. Matthew Branch blew in the opposite direction. Matthew's body was buried in absentia the following day.

As Papa read these accounts he grew apprehensive about going after Peter and Paul Branch.

"These guys really *are* nuts," said Richie Blumenthal, to whom Papa passed the pages.

"That's supposed to be funny?"

The following case gave Papa the shudders.

In May, 1973, just north of the Platte River in Grand Island, Nebraska, John Branch tracked down a Grand Island police officer who had ordered the Branches out of town. John was the youngest of the Branches and wanted to impress his brothers by eliminating the cop whom he located in a Grand Island warehouse where the cop was inspecting the premises. John carried a double-ought buck, magnum load, 12-gauge double barrel sawed-off shotgun. He stalked the cop among the wooden crates and eventually spotted him. The cop's back was to him. John raised the shotgun and fired.

The blast caught the officer just above the kidneys and cut his body in half. He was driven to the coroner's in two cars.

Less than a week passed. Every Grand Island police officer was searching for John Branch. One of them found John in a downtown hotel room. The cop broke down the door and caught him napping in bed. The account of John Branch's apprehension read: The officer drew his .38.

BANG! BANG! Stop or I'll shoot! BANG! Halt! BANG!
BANG! BANG! Don't move! BANG! Put your hands
against the wall! BANG! BANG! As Papa read the passage he was reminded of the old S.I.S. team tactics.

John Branch never even opened his eyes, but he miracu-
lously lived, despite the nine slugs in his body. He lived,
that is, until he mysteriously died, en route from his hospital room to the operating table.

By 1973 only Peter, Paul and Mark Branch were still
living.

Papa listened to a taped interview between Mark Branch
and a Lincoln *Journal-Star* newspaper reporter. The interview had taken place at the Branch house and the only
reason it was granted was because this particular reporter
had gone easy on the Branches in his previous accounts.
He treated them as semi-folk heroes, or so someone told
the Branches. None of them had learned to read.

Part of the interview read as follows:

REPORTER: Why is it that you use so many explosives?

MARK BRANCH: For one, I like the way they sound.
They sound like somethin's happenin'. Somethin's been
done.

REPORTER: A lot of people have been hurt though.

MARK BRANCH: A lotta people ain't been hurt that
shoulda been.

REPORTER: What do you mean by that?

MARK BRANCH: That a lotta people ain't that shoulda
been.

REPORTER: Who, for instance?

MARK BRANCH: Cops.

REPORTER: You don't like cops.

MARK BRANCH: Hate 'em.

REPORTER: Why do you hate them?

MARK BRANCH: Cops' main job is to hurt you, throw
you in jail, make you ache. Cops is a gang that's legal.
They get away with murder. Nobody else does. Me and
my brothers is like illegal cops. We keep the legal cops on
their toes. We *keep* 'em legal, even though they're more illegal than we are. They protect the judges and the bank
presidents and themselves. They don't protect me. They
wanna hurt me. I hate 'em all.

REPORTER: You may hate the badge, what it represents.

But what about the man himself, the man behind the badge?

MARK BRANCH: Once that man puts the badge on he's a cop for life. Thinks he's somethin' special. The badge means he can get away with anything cause he's got the *law* behind him, whatever that is. The law. You know what the law is? The law is saying you want peace and killing to make sure you get what you want.

REPORTER: Aren't you doing the same thing with explosives?

MARK BRANCH: I told yuh, I like the way it looks and the way it sounds . . . and the way it makes cops jump.

Papa also read what happened to Mark Branch a few weeks after that interview.

The brothers, according to the account, raced along State Road 45 in the late afternoon, chased by three squad cars. Peter was driving. Paul and Mark were in the back seat with ten sticks of dynamite and 500 feet of rope cut into ten fifty-foot sections. Paul had tied one stick to each length of rope. The plan was to fire up the long wicks and when the squad cars got close drop them out the window one at a time. By using the rope they would be able to determine the distance needed so that the dynamite would explode under the squad cars.

"Light it, Mark," Paul said, watching a squad car draw closer.

Mark did and Paul lobbed the dynamite stick out the window, keeping one hand on the end of the rope. As the squad car pulled closer, Paul drew in the rope.

BOOM! The squad car rolled over and bit the dust.

Twice more the wicks were lit and twice more they were let out. The other squad cars held back though and the dynamite blew without affecting them.

Which was when disaster struck.

Rather than blowing out the next match Mark let it drop to the floorboard where it ignited another wick. The dynamite stick rolled under the front seat as Mark scrambled to the floor trying to reach it. He failed and began screaming at the top of his lungs. Peter wasn't able to understand the wild ramblings until Mark stuck his head over the front seat and told him, "Dynamite. Under your seat. Burning."

The car screeched to a halt. Two doors flew open and

Peter and Paul bailed out. Later they could only speculate why Mark took such a long time. The blast caught him full on the back and cut a crease from the top of his skull to the crack in his tail.

Papa closed the file and glanced at Richie Blumenthal. "Lovely family, the Branches."

"You want the case?"

"For the right money."

Richie ran his tongue over his lower lip and hunched forward. It was time for negotiations. "Ten thousand."

"Twenty."

"Twelve-five."

"Twenty."

"Thirteen-eight."

"Twenty."

"Fifteen."

"Twenty."

"Fifteen."

Papa felt the birth of a headache at his temples. "Fifteen," he said.

"See you when you get back."

"Ditto," said Papa.

Throughout his career Papa has encountered zany, outrageous men and women who broke the law because it was what they did best, and in a way they have given purpose and meaning to the occupation Papa has chosen for himself. Many of these criminals have killed, maimed, cheated, thus making life tougher on themselves. There is a recklessness among these people, and among those who hunt them down. They live close to the edge and seem to crave the danger there.

Living on the edge is a precarious existence, loaded with tension and anxiety, and the best way to reduce the tension and anxiety is to laugh out loud, howl till your lungs hurt, chuckle, guffaw or giggle. On-the-edge conversations consist of jokes and stories. The edge sounds of comedy, high and low. A person with no sense of humor spends a short life there because the misery and pain gets to him. Behind each joke and story is a horror so serious you *have* to laugh.

"I'm just about immune to it," Papa says. "I've been *just about* immune to it since the beginning and I'll be just about immune to it when I kick off. It's easy for me to sit back and laugh about the Branch brothers, but had I been there to see them in operation, or been on the wrong end from them, I would hardly be laughing.

"I would not, for instance, have wanted to be any of the victims the Enema Bandit operated on. He was particularly bizarre. He terrorized Los Angeles for months by stalking women and instead of behaving like an ordinary degenerate—rape, theft, beating—he gave his victims enemas. It takes a special mentality to work out aggressions *that* way.

"Crime is funny. Criminals are funny. Funny-grotesque, like the Three Stooges or Mack Sennett's Keystone Cops, the Marx Brothers. The gang that couldn't shoot straight is high comedy. We laugh at their failures. When I laugh at someone like the Enema Bandit it's out of nervousness, out of response to the bizarre, probably a fascination with it. I've run into my share of weirdos; most of them—I'm damned if I can say why—had a sense of humor.

"Consider this scene, which occurs I would say in half of all drug deals: a heroin dealer meets a heroin buyer in a hotel room. Half the time the heroin dealer is not selling heroin; he's selling milk sugar that looks like heroin. The other half of the time the heroin buyer has either counterfeit or easily traceable stolen money to pay for the heroin. Half of the time one of them is an undercover narcotics agent, and the other half of the time one of them is going to get hurt when the other discovers the shaft he's just been given. The game is: who finds out he's been shafted first. To me, that's black humor.

"Marc Fraser broke into Howard Hughes' secret files here in Los Angeles and found that the burglar alarm was broken—later found out to have been broken for two years.

Fraser steals all the top-secret papers, which turn out to have no secrets—except one, which he dropped on the way out. Fraser did find one file that had an interesting story to it.

"He called actor Leo Gordon with the story and how he got it. Why? Because Fraser figured it would make one hell of a movie. Gordon, whose attitude towards law and order rivals Jack Webb's, called the Feds, who had Fraser picked up in Tennessee, where he was hiding out.

"California wanted to extradite Fraser but there was Governor Brown who wanted to review personally each extradition—which automatically put that part of the legal system six months on hold. Months later Fraser's case had not come up and he was cut loose. Screw-ups—from a sleazo petty thief to the governor of California.

"The Branch brothers were considerably more dangerous. They created havoc, killed people, ripped off others, but they were also theater of the absurd. I was not wild about going after them because whenever they fouled up they dragged everyone else in the vicinity down with them."

Papa left Richie's and the next morning boarded a United Airlines flight at L.A. airport, arrived in Denver at noon, changed planes and flew into Lincoln at three-eleven. The mid-afternoon sky reflected the vast blanket of wheat fields and gun-metal gray mountains. Swathes of yellow ocher and lilac-colored cloud formations drifted low in the crisp, immaculate air. Squadrons of black crows sailed above the treetops and glided down towards wheat stalks bending in the wind.

Compared to Los Angeles, Lincoln was so clean. The airport, the cab, the sheriff's office, the streets, the people, were spotless. The air was clean, and the language and the attitude. There was a purity of spirit that reminded Papa of Montana. The land had something to do with it; how it spread like a loving woman and made you think good thoughts, and how when you were talking to somebody there wasn't a building in the background. The cab driver opened the door for him, twice, and thanked him with a smile over white teeth. It was a crisp city with a newly laundered look. And very, very slow.

The desk sergeant turned pages with deliberation. All of Nebraska seemed in a state of quiet, steady repose.

"The Branch brothers, hmmm?" said the sergeant. "I don't envy you, Mr. Thorson." Papa could tell by the way the sergeant sized him up that nobody, not even a man of Papa's size, would have an easy time bringing in the Branch boys.

"I got some recent mug shots on them," the sergeant informed him. "Lemme get 'em for you."

The sergeant returned with the mug shots and handed them to Papa. There were two, of Peter and Paul, and a third, Abel.

"Abel Branch?" Papa said. "Where's he?" He'd not read about a seventh brother.

"Abel? Oh, Abel. He's gone."

"Gone? Gone where? Out of town?"

"Nooo." The sergeant shook his head and smiled. "He died."

"Died?"

"Car fell on him. Cadillac. You see, up till about a month ago the brothers had this here hot automobile ring where they'd take two new Cadillacs over the Mexican border . . ."

Which was why they were in Los Angeles, Papa figured.

". . . but you know what happened?" The sergeant chuckled through his broken teeth. "They took down two Cadillacs at a time and came back with one. That was their payment. But the funny thing was they thought they were gettin' a clean car back when all them Mexicans did was repaint one of them, change the tags and hand it back to them the next day."

"What exactly happened to Abel?"

"Oh, he had the car up on a lift and it fell on him. One down, two to go. That's how we feel round here. You'll be doin' us a favor, Mr. Thorson, pickin' up Peter and Paul."

"All I need is a little help, Sergeant. Couple of men to go with me."

"Yeah, well, I surely wish I could help you out, but I can't rightly say any man would go with you. Them Branches is crazy."

"Just a couple of back-up men. I'll go in myself."

"Not out there at the house, uh uh."

"What if I draw them out somehow? Then . . ."

The sergeant shook his head. "Can't be done. They're meditatin' out there right now."

"Meditating?"

"I don't know what the hell that is but they spend two, three months a year on the farm. Don't leave it. Grow their own food. Send out for their women. Ain't nobody goin' in there, Mr. Thorson."

"Except me, I guess," Papa said.

" 'Fore you go, Mr. Thorson, you wanna leave me a name?"

"Name?"

"Your next of kin."

Papa rented the biggest car he could find because Peter and Paul Branch were huge. Papa read that Paul Branch was the smallest at six-four, two hundred fifty-five pounds.

Beside him on the seat was the Prowler Fouler, mace, the police flashlight and a .45. By now it was close to five and a wind had whipped up over the fields.

Far off to the west toward Colorado and Wyoming the sun sprayed its last colors across the sky. Along the roadside, standing taller than the car, cornfields mingled with wheat. He pulled out the rough map drawn up by the sergeant and studied it. He'd been on the road a half hour and was now deep into the farmlands. There were no road signs. He passed an occasional barn, a few silos, one country store. The sergeant told him to look for *indicators*, to indicate which way to turn. A horse farm, turn left; down three miles to a freshly painted dairy barn, turn right; past three dirt roads, turn on the fourth, left; up a half mile and there you are: run-down white house with a big front porch. Two cow barns on the left; one on the right. A shed. And a twenty-five-foot red cross stuck into the front lawn.

Papa pulled to a halt a hundred yards from the house. A new Cadillac with the right side smashed in lay behind the shed.

Papa climbed out and walked up the road to the shed behind which he took a quick leak and continued on to the house.

He saw the rear ends of cows inside the barn. An old, battered Chevrolet was parked on an incline, nose facing downhill. The incline looked man-made; a single mound of dirt on the north side of the house. Papa heard hens cackle. Two hounds slept on the front porch. He would have to avoid them.

It took him less than a minute to sneak around to the back of the house and as he neared the porch he heard grunting sounds from inside.

He pushed open the screen door and once inside listened for the direction of the sounds. From the right, he decided, and moved quietly along the hallway.

He peeked in the first room he came to and saw the huge white backside of a man pumping. The girl beneath him had her legs wrapped around his waist. Her long red hair fanned off to one side. Papa was able to see one half of her face. She looked bored. The man was making all the noise.

They were on a single dirty mattress, the room's only piece of furniture.

The girl was skinny. Her head was dropped off to one side and her mouth hung open. Her eyes were glazed over and nearly closed. She breathed quickly. And she synchronized her buttocks to the man's action above her. Papa thought it refreshing to see the old missionary position in operation again. Back in L.A. they did it from the chandeliers.

Papa left them to look for brother number two. The next room he came to was bathed in red—posters of Hitler speaking, Hitler marching and Hitler inspecting the troops made up the wallpaper. A swastika mobile hung from the low ceiling and, in the far corner, four carpeted steps led to an elevated, black-oak throne. Etched into the throne's seat: *"Lebensraum,"* living room, Hitler's word for Germany's supposed need for expansion, the Reich's manifest destiny. Nazi artifacts—lugers, swords, ornate daggers, pennants—were on display around the room and an ancient Victrola actually played a scratched up version of "Deutschland Uber Alles," the German national anthem.

He parted the beaded curtain and entered the room. Halfway across the floor he heard faint mumblings from an adjoining chamber.

"Sturm und Drang . . . Mein Kampf . . . mein kämpfen . . . mein Sieg." The words came in a low chant. He slowly parted the curtains and discovered big, blond Peter Branch sitting cross-legged on a rug in the center of a small chamber. Before Peter, on the wall, hung a dark bronze medallion the size of a Viking's shield with Hitler's face adorning the center. The sergeant had been right. This was meditation.

Papa knew the only way to take Peter Branch was to bang him over the head. He slipped through the curtain and, approaching from behind, raised the heavy flashlight and brought it down behind Peter Branch's ear.

Peter jerked his head up as the flashlight bent. He stared at Papa, dazed. Both hands remained on his knees. His head shook, attempting to focus his vision, and his head spun back and forth on its axis.

Peter's head stopped spinning and snapped up in Papa's direction. His eyes bulged from their sockets, and his lips moved back from his teeth. Papa braced himself. Peter toppled over, the fallen Buddha, everything in place but his hands, which lay atop one another near his knees.

"Hi, ther," a voice said from behind Papa, who turned around and saw the skinny girl in the doorway, naked. "How come you done that?"

"Where's your friend?"

"Ma free-und?"

"Right. The guy you were just with. Where is he?"

"Paw-ool?"

"The very one."

"Rot he-ah," she purred, swinging one arm behind her as she fell forward, flat on the floor, pushed from behind by Paul, who now filled the doorway. Paul Branch wore a nightshirt that came to his knees, his hair was tousled and his body loomed. He was Steinbeck's Lenny, a Cyclops, King Kong before the fall.

"Paw-ool!" the girl squeaked from the floor. "Don do tha-it!" She looked up, from Paw-ool to Papa and back, and crawled to a neutral corner for a ringside seat.

Papa drew the Prowler Fouler from his belt, quickly cocked it and took aim. Then it occurred to him if it took a metal flashlight on the skull to deck one brother, would a shot from the Prowler Fouler . . . He didn't want to use the .45. And then remembered the brother who took nine .38 slugs and lived.

Nobody moved. They stood glaring at each other. Papa had the Fouler trained on Paul's stomach, then lowered it a few inches towards his genitals.

"Ca-mawn!" the girl insisted, bouncing up and down and pounding her hands on her knees.

Don't provoke him, Papa pleaded silently.

Paul spoke first. "You done that to my brother?"

"Co-orse he day-id," said the girl.

"Shut up. You did that?"

"I did it," Papa said.

"Why?"

"Because I have to bring him back to Los Angeles. You, too."

Paul Branch stuck his face forward. "Ha!" and took off in the opposite direction.

"She-yit!" the girl said disgustedly. Then, turning to Papa and smiling, she cooed, "What's yo-uh name?"

"Joe Palooka," Papa said, and rushed after Paul.

The girl called after him. "Whay-ya goin? Ah'm Lorine. Ah thank yore cute. Ah thank . . ."

Papa spotted Paul Branch moving across the front yard

toward the Chevrolet. The nightshirt struggled against his knees as he pulled it up over his thighs and raced on. The hounds woke and raced after him, howling in the twilight.

Papa gave chase.

Paul reached the Chevrolet, leapt behind the wheel and turned the ignition key. The engine churned and churned. It sounded like the battery.

Papa had the .45 out by the time he reached the Chevy, and the moment he placed his foot on the runningboard the engine kicked over. He shoved the .45 against Paul Branch's temple.

"Don't do anything stupid," Papa told him.

Paul slammed one arm against Papa's chest. The .45 went off, sending the bullet through the windshield and knocking Papa off the runningboard. He managed to keep one hand wrapped around the window divider, and pulled himself back. With his balance regained, he clipped Paul behind the ear; Paul retaliated by striking back at Papa with his free arm. The movement also put the car in gear.

The Chevy lunged forward and bumped its way down the hill. They exchanged blows as the car picked up speed. Papa's right foot was on the runningboard; his left hopped along the ground.

Neither of them saw the maple tree ahead. The Chevy crashed headlong into the massive trunk, the radiator exploded, sending a water geyser spouting into the air as Papa flew off the runningboard and landed, belly down, on the hard dirt. The impact stunned him. The revolver squirted from his hand and he felt as if he'd been thrown into an undug grave. He didn't feel like getting up. There was no pain particularly. He was impacted. It took Paul Branch to get him on the move, the notion of Paul sneaking up behind. Papa didn't know how that could be possible but . . .

He placed his palms flat against the ground and pushed. He reached his knees and slowly rotated his body until he was able to bring the car into view. There, with his skull deeply imbedded into the dashboard, was Paul. The steering wheel was wrapped around his head like a sweatband.

Papa climbed to his feet and walked to the car, where he expected to find the man dead. Despite the collision Paul was still alive, and moving, trying to pull his head from the steering wheel.

"Mistuh Palooka?"

Papa turned and saw Lo-rine leaning against the Chevy's rear fender. She swept the hair from her face and tilted her head off to one side.

"Call me Joe."

"Jo-wo," she murmured, shoving forward her skinny naked bushy pelvis. "I seen you," she smiled. "You were good."

Papa bowed his head. "Thank you."

She ran her eyes up and down and around his body.

"It's gon be fun."

"Oh? What is?"

She ran her tongue over her lips the way they used to do in the movies and said, "I ain't never bee-in to Los Angeles befo-uh."

In under an hour Papa had the Branch brothers bound and gagged and loaded in the back seat of his car. Lo-rine helped. She also rubbed against him, said she *loved* older men, told him she was the best lay north of the Republican River, promised to do things he liked to have done, and went into the house to dress, only to return and take everything off again.

"How old are you?" Papa asked her.

"Mistuh Palooka, I ain't been ay-ast that in yee-aws."

"It slipped your mind?"

"Oh, Mistuh Palooka, you-ah so funny!"

"You're twelve, right?"

"Ah ay-um not! Ah'm fifteen and a hay-uf."

"And *I'm* too old to go to jail."

"Go to jay-ull. Whatevuh fo-uh?"

Papa went back to the Branch brothers. Lo-rine followed.

"Whatevuh fo-uh? Tell me tha-yet?"

"I could get ten years for just *talking* to you, Lorine. Go away."

"I we-ull not!"

He fretted because it was night and he wouldn't be able to catch the flight till the next day; but what he suffered from was a singular agonizing ache. He wished for it to go away but it would not. She stood there in front of him.

"You know what's gonna happen, Mistuh Palooka, don-cha? If you don't *do* it to me, I'll still tell the po-lice yuh did."

"No," Papa said, shaking his head. "I won't and you won't, because if you go to the police you'll be arrested

for consorting with these here good ol' boys. You'll go to
jail. I'll make sure of it. And jail's no fun. Next time your
boy here is in town, ask him."

While Lo-rine thought about that Papa climbed into the
car and leaned his head out the window.

"Goodbye, Lorine," Papa said, nodding to her. "I appreciate the help."

Lo-rine shifted her weight to one foot and stuck out her
thigh. "Fuck owff!" she said with a pout, "*Mis*tuh Palooka."

After Papa deposited the Branches with the sheriff's office he called United and was told that the only direct
flight from Lincoln to Los Angeles departed at 3:33 the
next afternoon.

Papa called home, went out to dinner, got loaded at the
hotel bar with jewelry salesmen from St. Louis and was
dead asleep by four a.m.

The sheriff's men placed leg irons on the Branch brothers because their wrists were too big for Papa's handcuffs.
They drove in squad cars to the airport where they
avoided a large crowd reaction.

On the way the sheriff's men asked Papa how he managed to capture the Branch brothers.

"Nothing to it," he said. "Drove a tank in, told them to
give up or get killed. They climbed in the car, knocked
themselves out, and there ya go."

Papa's immediate problem was taking the brothers
aboard the airplane without disturbing the passengers. Air-
line policy requires that prisoners not be handcuffed or
bound up in any way while the plane is in flight—the the-
ory is that the passengers may become upset if they see
shackled prisoners. To Papa's way of thinking, prisoners
without handcuffs are considerably more upsetting—or
likely to be. Papa sits at least two seats away from his
prisoners, in case they do get out of hand.

Papa and the brothers took their seats in First Class.
Papa sat across the aisle and back a couple of seats.

As they passed over the San Juan River on the Utah/
Arizona border, Paul drew close to his brother. "I got an
idea," he confided.

"You always get ideas. None of 'em's ever worked."

"That's a helluva thang to say to your own brother."

"I can say whatever the fuck I wont."

"You wanna hear my idea?"

"Is it long?"

"Short."

"Go ahead."

"See that stewardess up there?"

"Not like I want to."

"Two people go after one guy, right?"

"What?"

"Two people," Paul repeated. "Two cops always go after one crook. Takes two of them."

"So?"

"So, we got one cop going after two guys. That's what
we got, right?"

"So?"

"Let's say I tell the stewardess there that *we* are bringing *him* in, 'stead of *him* bringing *us* in, right?"

"Gawd-damn, that's the rightest thing you ever said."

"Ain't it."

"Go ahead."

"I will."

Paul struggled to his feet, fell back, struggled again and
finally made it up. Papa watched Paul stumble up to the
stewardess.

"I got somein to tell yuh," he said.

The stewardess gave him an ear.

"Me and him," Paul said, pointing to his brother, "we're
taking *him* in," he said, pointing to Papa. "We wancha to
let us off first. Hole the rest for three minutes. Don't want
no trouble."

"I'm sorry sir, but . . ."

"Hey!" Paul rolled up his pants leg. "See that mark
around muh ankle?"

The stewardess looked at the red ring left by the leg
irons. "Yes."

"Leg irons. We just brought him in. Headin' for L.A.,
throw his butt in jail. Need croperation."

When the stewardess showed hesitation, Paul said, "Put
it this way. We're private detectives. This guy's dangerous.
Kilt five cops last week in L.A., jumped bail. What 'bout
the innocent people here? Tell the captain."

"Tell him what?"

"Let us off first, so's nobody gets hurt."

"We'll let you off first, sir," the stewardess agreed.

"You will?" Paul exclaimed.

"Yes, sir."

"Well, gawd-damn," he said, slapping her on the arm. "What're ya doing right now? How *'bout* that?"

"I beg your pardon?"

"Now," he said, "doin' now. What say we slip in the toilet together?"

She walked away quickly.

Paul returned to his seat and whispered to his brother, "It's all set."

Papa not only watched the conversation, he heard it, Paul was talking so loud.

"What're you boys up to?" Papa asked.

Paul shrugged. "Tried to get laid quick. Stewardesses is tough in the air. You know what I mean?"

"In the air," Papa agreed, "they're very tough."

The brothers dozed off for a while.

Peter Branch woke up first and asked Papa what time it was.

"Six forty-five."

"Jesus, Paul," Peter said, shaking his brother. "Wake up. We're landin' in fifteen minutes."

The NO SMOKING and FASTEN SEAT BELTS signs flashed on and the pilot announced the weather and ETA. The plane lost altitude and everyone's ears popped and they all swallowed and sneezed to get rid of the feeling.

It was time for the stewardesses to take their seats. Paul caught his girl's attention and winked a signal. She winked back and Paul shed a crafty smile.

"Mr. Thorson," Paul said, "I do believe yore gonna have some trouble takin' us in."

"Yeah? How's that?"

The Branches chuckled together.

"We made an ar*range*ment," Peter said.

"No kidding. How so?"

"Never you mind," Paul interrupted. "Let's jest say we're ahead of the game."

"Trouble taking you in, huh?" Papa repeated, looking concerned.

The brothers looked at one another with secret grins.

"It's like this," Paul said. "We told a stewardess that we—me and Peter—was private eyes. We's takin' *you* in."

Papa waited for something else, didn't get it, and said, "That's all?"

"That's all!" Paul said angrily.

Peter nudged him. "Paul, tell him the rest."

"Rest?"

"About the gittin off first."

"Oh, yeah!" Paul sat straighter in his seat and continued. "We're gittin off first."

"First."

"Uh huh. We're gonna dispear in the airport. Nobody'll ever find us."

Papa considered that for a moment and shook his head. "You boys might just have somethin' there."

"So, Mr. Thorson," Paul said, "looks like yore plain outa luck."

"Looks that way," Papa replied, snuggling into his seat.

The plane landed. The brothers rose and pressed by the stewardesses, who signaled for the other passengers to wait. On the way Paul went to grab Papa.

"Don't worry about me," he told them. "Just get the hell out of here. I never want to see you again."

"You ain't too swift, Mr. Thorson." Paul laughed and turned away and the brothers walked from the plane.

They marched through the chute leading into the terminal, where they were confronted by a dozen LAPD and sheriff's men Papa had called from the Lincoln airport.

Papa walked from the plane just a few seconds later. He passed the Branches and smiled over at them. "Well, shake my ass, if it isn't the Branch brothers. How are you, boys?"

They scowled back at him.

"If it's any consolation," Papa said, "Lo-rine said she'll keep the place going while you're away."

Paul huffed. "Lo-rine cain't do nothin right."

"That," Papa said, "she must have learned from *you.*"

10

The Homecoming

A dozen people were gathered in the house when Papa walked through the front door. They ate peanuts from the penny machine on the television set Myron Fish had ruined; they gobbled crackers and chips and dip Dotty had placed in large plastic bowls on the counter; a young girl with long blonde hair played the out-of-tune piano. They all looked as if they'd been there for days, drinking, arguing. Some sat glassy eyed, slurring their words, on stools in front of the circular bar. The pagan strains of an African jungle concerto razored through the room.

Papa paused in the entraceway; he carried an overnight bag in one hand and groceries in the other. He spotted Dotty wading through the crowd towards him.

"Hi," she said, pecking him on the cheek.

"What's the occasion?" Papa asked.

Dotty shrugged.

"It started an hour ago, that's all I know. People began arriving. I'll chase them out if you want me to."

"No, no. I'll clean up, be back in a minute."

Papa pushed his way through the uninvited guests until

he vanished into his rear bedroom. Staying up most of last night and drinking on the plane had given him a headache. He would have preferred going to bed, and would have if some of those in the living room weren't old friends he hadn't seen in a long time.

One of them was Captain Harry Belinda of the LAPD who lived in a plush house in Beverly Hills. Belinda was talking to big-time cocaine dealer Buddy Tibari, who also lived in Beverly Hills. Buddy's house stood on a hill overlooking Captain Belinda's and was grander, more expensive, higher up, and a much better place for entertaining. Captain Belinda didn't much like the idea of Buddy standing on his balcony snorting coke and leering down into his back yard. The Captain had busted Buddy twice and both times Buddy got off and went back to his house in his Silver Cloud. Captain Belinda drove a Mercedes. Buddy came up from the streets of Chicago. Captain Belinda inherited his house when his parents died. The single thing both men held in common was a healthy respect for the law. Captain Belinda enforced it. Buddy Tibari circumvented it.

Buddy and Captain Belinda had often been to Papa's where they exchanged points of view and traded information. Buddy was not an informant but he occasionally steered Captain Belinda towards mutual enemies, in return for which Belinda did not lean heavily on him.

"But the day I catch your ass dealing smack," Belinda was saying, "there'll be a bulldozer on your front lawn."

"You know I don't play with that shit," Buddy protested, brushing ashes from his $150 jeans outfit. Buddy was about thirty-five, tall, with dark manicured hair. Papa said he looked like Vic Damone and since that time people called him Vic. Buddy didn't care. Buddy wasn't his real name anyway.

"I'll tell you what you guys oughta do," Buddy was saying. "Put heroin booths on every street corner. Let anybody who wants to shoot up get all the shit they want. The L.A. crime rate'd drop in half in one day."

"Because half the population would be too stoned to move," Captain Belinda pointed out.

"That's the way you cops always look at it. Make dope free and you'd lose your job."

Papa listened to them for a while and knew after a couple more drinks they'd be passing names back and forth.

There would be arrests made and deals consummated. Captain Belinda would head home at midnight, take two Excedrin for his splitting headache and climb into bed beside his snoring wife. Buddy Tibari would go home and blow coke with the two women he lived with. They'd go out to the rear balcony and cast small pebbles over the cliff into Captain Belinda's small kidney-shaped pool.

Papa drifted over towards the bar where Catherine Smithers sat on a stool. Even in her fifties Papa thought she was a considerable broad. Bleached blonde hair swept over her shoulders and the low-cut saffron crepe dress hugged her athletic body. Catherine Smithers spent four hours every day at the health spa, taught night classes in sociology at Santa Monica College and owned five apartment buildings, bequeathed to her by her late husband. Her late fourth husband. The other three had also died. The popular explanation for their deaths was that Catherine had worn them out.

Hovering by her were two ex-cons Papa hadn't seen in years. Both men—Marion Balm and Mario de la Fuente—had just gotten out of Soledad prison.

Catherine plied them with questions and drinks because they were masculine, rugged, intelligent men.

"I read five books a week," Marion told her. "Right, partner?" he asked Mario.

"Right. Not much else you can do in the joint."

Everybody was everybody else's partner. There were partners, ex-partners, ex-old lady's ex-partners, ex-old lady's ex-old man's brother's ex-partners. Papa had partners. Cops had partners. Dope dealers had partners. Partners in crime. Ex-partners in crime. Everybody in the room had a partner. Except the women. They operated solo. Women's partners were men.

Tonight Catherine Smithers wanted two bed partners, Marion and Mario, since they were partners anyway. She got her wish at eleven o'clock when the partners asked her where she lived. She smiled, she blushed, she grabbed her handbag and her drink and led them through the front door without saying goodbye to Papa who watched them go.

"Now I know why Catherine comes over here," Dotty said.

"And a very good reason it is," Papa agreed.

The major topic of the evening was the attempted assas-

sination of President Ford by ex-Manson groupie Squeaky
Fromme. An argument developed among Robert Louis
Stevenson, M.D., Ph.D., J.D. and four other Ph.D.'s, and
Dominick Chesi, a San Fernando Valley laundry chain
owner with excellent mob connections. Robert Louis Stevenson was a local doctor who tended to be rather free
with pills. He was too smart for his own sanity and period-
ically committed himself to a private sanitarium "rubber
room" for the mentally strange. There Robert Louis Stevenson threw his body against the padded walls, trying to
shake his brain back into place. He never totally
succeeded but he calmed down enough till next time. Dr.
Stevenson was forty-seven, tall, graying, extraordinarily
good-looking and almost totally whacked out from too
much education and eating too many of his own pills.
Dominick Chesi had to look almost straight up to see the
doctor's face. Dominick not only looked like Edward G.
Robinson, he wanted to play his life story in the movies,
and boasted to Papa that he *would* play Edward G.
Robinson. "I fixed it," he explained.

Papa was standing with them when Dr. Robert Louis
Stevenson pointed out: "Charles Manson has a socio-psy-
chic stronghold on those women. He transmitted the order
to kill Ford."

"Hey, Doc, listen," Dominick Chesi disagreed. His arms
flailed. His voice rose into a higher pitch. "You can socio-
psycho yourself to death. Charlie Manson has no control.
That Squeaky broad is flipped."

Papa interrupted. "I picked up Squeaky Fromme once.
She's a smart little tiger. She was number-two honcho in
the Manson clan."

"Two, shmoo," said Dominick Chesi. "No broad is
number two in an outfit like that."

"Dominick," Papa said, "who do you think ran the SLA
for instance? Not Field Marshall Cinque. He was an idiot.
He couldn't read. He couldn't write with a Crayola. The
proclamations they came out with were written by the
women, who had Masters degrees in English. Cinque was
a symbol—a black guy who was having a great time ball-
ing white chicks. For all he knew SLA mean Suck Lotta
Ass."

Dr. Robert Louis Stevenson lifted his head and cupped
one hand over his throat. "As far as I am concerned," he
said in crisp Bostonian vernacular, "Manson and Cinque,

and that crowd, played Iago to an already perforated social structure badly in need of repair. They saw holes through which they could shimmy, and did so. But rather than climbing the social ladder they drew the upper class down to them so that they might mingle with it."

Dr. Stevenson cleared his throat and continued. "You see, this type of individual must be socially motivated. He must also be able to gain control of each level as he reaches it, then quickly move to the next. Yet he is never satisfied with any of them, any of the levels. He thus becomes a *Zeitgeist*, a time spirit, an outcast who wanders through—or plows through or manipulates his way through—the various stratas, on his way to the zenith, or where he thinks is the zenith."

"Listen, Doc," Chesi said. "I'm sure what you just said is very heavy. I mean, it *sounds* heavy, the way you say it, but I think them stratas up there is making you dizzy."

"Dear man, I am referring to an element with which you are extremely familiar: the criminal element," the doctor pointed out.

"Criminal element?" Chesi replied, but was cut off by Stevenson, who raised his right index finger.

"And their reform. Do you realize there is an eighty percent recidivism rate in this state—eighty percent of all convicts leaving an institution return there. What are you doing about that?"

"Me? What am *I* doing about it?"

"Precisely."

"I'm trying not to be one of them."

"Legislation must be passed allowing certain men who leave the institution to be employed in a job where they would do the most good—as police officers. That is true rehabilitation."

"An ex-con a cop! Back to the rubber room, doc, you just slipped over the border."

"Mr. Chesi," Doctor Robert Louis Stevenson said with great formality. "Let me explain . . ."

At that point Papa slipped away and joined another conversation in progress, which turned out to be an extension of the one he just left. The subject: cops.

Captain Belinda had departed Buddy Tibari and was now huddled with Mad Dog Donovan, the ex-con and part-time bounty hunter who occasionally worked with Papa.

Mad Dog, who had served as a consultant for the LAPD in 1971, was well along into his cups.

"Listen," Mad Dog was saying, "I would never be a cop; it's too much like being in the army. The schedule would kill me. For a guy to be a cop he's gotta be an authoritarian, he has to fear and respect authority."

"Which you do," Belinda added.

"Which I do, yes, but screw it, it's hard work, too hard for me."

Papa entered the conversation with: "A lot of retired cops come to me looking for a job. After twenty years on the force they think they know everything they need to know about snatching a guy. They don't. I had one applicant who sent me his résumé. Up top was his name and age, then for two solid pages he listed every weapon known to man. That was it. How can I hire a guy like that? Just because he could fire a bazooka he thought he was in. Richie Blumenthal has advice for retired cops who want to get in this line of business: he tells them to follow me around for two years. Richie says they should pay *me* a hundred a week to let them tail behind and hold my briefcase. And after two years they *might* be ready to do the job the way it should be done."

Captain Belinda jutted forth his round, delicate face and said to Papa, "You know what happens when cops retire."

"Yeah, same thing that happens to psychiatrists—suicide."

"Happens all the time," Belinda agreed.

"Look at it this way," Papa said. "A cop's life expectancy after retiring is, what, two and a half years, that's it. Most of them have no family when they retire. Family life's murder on a cop. When he's active he gets a lot of ass on the side, he works weird hours, he gets divorced. When he retires he's cut off from his buddies. He might have dinner with them once in a while but all they talk about is the past, old cases. There's nothing new in his life, nothing current. The man is lost. He's like the guy who comes out of combat; nothing can match the excitement. So what does he do? He scouts around for a job, security guard, private dick. He's not fit anymore. So, he takes his life. Life has lost its meaning. The whole world for him is criminal, sick. I don't want a guy like that working for me, somebody who for twenty, thirty years has checked in his brains for a badge and a gun. Forget it. You'd do the same thing. You *do* do the same thing. You *make* him retire."

Belinda shrugged. Papa went on.

"Now, I'm not talking about you. You're captain, you'll make a commander, then deputy chief, maybe chief. You're administration. You used your brains. You'll get snapped up by some hot-shot organization. But how 'bout the poor slob of a twenty-five-year patrolman?"

"I see your point," Belinda said, "and it's depressing."

"Then let's drop it."

The party noise grew louder as others filtered into the house. By one in the morning two dozen bellowing drunks filled the living room. A neighbor complained and at one thirty a squad car pulled up front to check out the complaint. When the policeman appeared at the door and spotted three senior officers inside he bowed and back-stepped down the sidewalk.

Papa was as loaded as the rest of them and when he was asked to play gin he begged off, saying he wouldn't be able to see the cards. He felt tired. He needed sleep. Dotty told him to go to bed but he said no; he'd never been one to leave a party, especially his own, until the very end.

Dialogue became monologue as the guests took turns telling stories. Someone, Papa couldn't remember who, mentioned the case to which Papa had earlier referred, which led to the arrest of Charles Manson. Papa had gone after a clan member who he traced to Manson's desert hideout and later to the Spahn Ranch where the clan spent much of their time. He had taken the county sheriff with him. Just a week later, freaked out on LSD, and perhaps in partial, irrational retaliation against the sheriff's pressure, the Mansonites brutally murdered Sharon Tate, Jay Sebring and the LaBiancas.

In Papa's estimation, Charlie Manson possessed a classic Napoleonic complex: short man feels cheated, inadequate, will take over world to show he is really big man. For this reason and because Manson spent more than half his life in prison, Papa in part attributes Manson's power over women to his hatred of them. He operated like a pimp. He fed them drugs and offered them the security of a family and in return they did his bidding. He was a sexual overseer rather than participant. Manson didn't like sex with women but he used the psychic power inherent in sex to control his women. He decided in prison that, for what-

ever reasons, women were responsible for sending their
men there and consequently he didn't trust them. If you
can't love women what else can you do with them: ignore
them or control them, use them. Little Charlie Manson
found young, susceptible women for this purpose.

Papa was the subject of another monologue in which
Ahmed Sullivan, an astrologer from Malibu, explained
Papa astrologically.

"Papa's like a big, nice kid," Ahmed said. "He's sensitive, receptive to others, but he's the last person to see his
own problems. He has a subconscious fear of success. He
hates to lose control. Look at all those guns. He's a
Cancer. Cancers go through life acting brave, but they
also hide a fear inside. Papa is violence-oriented but not
violent. Why does he back down killers? Because he needs
to fit the self-image he's created. But at the same time he's
benevolent, fatherlike, and also threatening and sinister
and scary—all of them. Underneath all that he's got a
heart of gold.

"He seldom preaches or uses the words God or religion.
People don't realize it but the people here in this room,
and the hundreds of others who pass through here, eating
his food and drinking his liquor, are his ministry. He has
become, for all practical and spiritual purposes, our
Papa."

"All of that?" Papa said aloud.

Ahmed Sullivan turned towards him, a startled expression on his face. He didn't know Papa had been listening.

"That's what your chart says," Ahmed told him.

"Hyper-sensitive, psychic, generous, egocentric, mater-
nal, how 'bout those?"

"All of the above," Ahmed agreed.

"In other words . . ."

"Papa, you're living in the wrong time."

One after the other the bits and pieces of conversation
swept over Papa. He caught snatches of this and that,
faces parading by, drinks poured from fresh bottles Dotty
carried in from their bedroom.

He listened to the late Jack Finnegan's favorite informant Danny Krebs talking about the concept of class,
which Krebs had plagiarized almost word for word from
Papa.

"This is something I been thinking about for years,"

Krebs told his audience. "Class criminals, criminals with class. A guy who screws little boys in the ass—no class. A guy who pulls a job with his partner and on the way out the partner falls down and the guy helps him up—that's class. Beating up and robbing an old man in a sleazo motel—no class. Pulling a big jewel heist at a giant hotel—class. Al Pacino blasting into that Brooklyn bank in *Dog Day Afternoon*—no good. The guy who took out ten accounts in different banks, dropped his new magnetized deposit slips in the blank deposit-slip drawers, waited a week while all the money deposited went into his account by magnetic computor and then withdrew a hundred thousand bucks—class. No muscle. No brutality, slick, sophisticated, little imagination here and there. Murph the Surf. Loads of class. Nobody gets hurt.

"Couple weeks ago, right down the street here, a guy leaves his house and finds his car missing, right? Calls the cops, nothing for two days. Then one morning he goes out and there's his car, in the same spot. On the front seat is a note: 'I'm sorry I took your car. It was an emergency. Please accept my apologies and this forty bucks to fix the broken window.' Also with the money are four choice tickets to the Rams game. That's beautiful. The guy takes his wife and kids to the game. When he gets home his house has been totally cleaned out, furniture and all, by a moving van. That's class."

Danny Krebs could have gone on for hours.

The phone rang, pulling Papa away from Danny. Dotty handed the receiver to him. On the line was Winston Blue.

"Papa, uh, uh I'm glad to see you made it back, that's right, I am."

"Winston, your time's run out," Papa said.

"Hey, don' you know it. Uh, I'm ready to turn myself in."

"You've been ready for months, Winston. Where are you? I'm ready to pick you up."

"Uh, Papa, not yet."

"What about my twenty-five hundred bucks?"

"It's safe."

Just then the operator came on the line with an emergency call for 345-8876.

"That's interesting," said Papa. It wasn't *his* number.

Winston screamed at the operator to forget about it, he didn't want to talk to nobody.

"Uh, you hear that number, Papa?"

"Yes I did."

"Which means what?"

"Which means I'm coming after you."

"Hmm, looks like I better get ready for real, don't it?"

"I would recommend it, Winston. Otherwise, I'll track you down and crack your head open."

"You'd do that, Papa, to me?"

"I wouldn't be able to control myself."

"Uh huh." Papa could almost hear Winston's wheels turning. "When?"

"Pick a time. Tomorrow morning."

"So soon?" Winston sounded honestly surprised.

"See you Winston."

"Oh, Papa," Winston sighed, "what *am* I gonna do?"

"Wait for me."

Papa hung up. He'd check in the morning and get the address belonging to the phone number.

In groups of twos and threes the guests began wading out through the front door. Car engines sputtered into action, doors opened and slammed shut. Loud boisterous laughing jangled in the street. Finally, by four a.m., only Dotty and Papa remained. Even Fang was out cold, curled upon the living room sofa.

Before going to bed Papa took a massive dose of vitamin B to help restore the juices all the booze had taken away. When he finally crawled under the covers he glanced over at Dotty who was already asleep. Her round stomach made a small mountain in the blanket. As the morning light filtered through the blinds Papa thought about the baby. It meant a lot of things to him: another mouth to feed: a pain in the ass; of Dotty's, not his, design; a lot of noise and diaper changing. It also meant an extension of himself, something of his own making. A creation. He knew this would be the first child he'd ever admit to fathering.

11

The Taking of Winston Blue

Winston Blue was black as the number-nine coal. Exceptionally long eyelashes shaded Winston's eyes. His body was long, lanky and bony, and when he walked he actually shuffled, as if every limb were part of a grand choreographic swish. He glided from place to place on his toes, and when he came to rest it took his arms a few moments to catch up with the rest of his body.

He posed, he gestured flamboyantly, he held a profound sense of himself and the reaction he created in those who scrutinized his movements. There was something regal about him, perhaps the way his head tilted back and off to one side, perhaps the way he talked *at* rather than *with* the people he knew. Whatever the case, he demanded undivided attention, and got it.

What gave away his meager origins was the way he spoke. Nothing he said could mask the street jargon of his Detroit neighborhood. Winston was a Motown boy who fought his way out of the ghetto by watching Bette Davis movies and escaping to Los Angeles at age sixteen. He tried shielding his background by saying he was from Boston because being from Boston sounded sophisticated. No one from Boston ever sounded like Winston, so he found himself admitting the lie. As it turned out he gained far more respect being from Motown. It seemed Detroit blacks were supposed to be the meanest men alive, meaner than New York blacks or Chicago blacks. Motown blacks fought dirtier, so their reputation went. They killed dirtier, swore dirtier, ate, drank and slept dirtier.

Not Winston, however, who deplored dirt of any sort. He had unfortunately inherited the Motown reputation through no fault of his own; he was born into it. Yet he was the antithesis of all that was Motown. He was gentle, he avoided all physical confrontation, including sex, which he considered unhealthy for the way sex divided his attention. Sex, for Winston, was the enemy of narcissism, a condition to which he devoted a great deal of his energy.

These things Papa knew from past bouts with Winston. Papa further knew that this tall, statuesque man was clever and crafty and would, at the drop of his wide-brimmed, sable-belted hat, slide the rug out from anyone with a few dollars in his pocket.

It was not beyond Winston's code to lie, cheat, steal or misrepresent his intentions in any way he could. Living meant warring; Winston's weapons were his wits. Papa personally knew or had heard about dozens of unsuspecting souls relieved of their funds by the smooth-talking man, including Papa himself, who meant to do something about it.

While Winston waited for Papa's familiar yellow Plymouth to cruise into the neighborhood, he chatted with his recently acquired partner, a young Chicano he discovered in the Thrifty Discount Drug store on Sunset Boulevard. The Chicano's name was Real.

"Real?" Winston asked the kid. "As in deal?"

No, as in Ray-Al but the kid was so impressed by Winston's cool demeanor that he didn't want to disagree with him. Real it would be. Yet Real wasn't strictly Winston's partner, not the way Winston saw it. More accurate would be valet, slave, peon, vassal.

"Real, that's me," the kid replied.

Winston stood at his apartment window gazing out to the street below. The powder-blue velour robe contouring his body fell to the tops of two expertly crafted lambskin slippers. He lifted a King Sano to his lips and slowly inhaled the smoke into his lungs. Behind him, seated on an

oversized Indian pillow, was Real, in a caftan Winston had
given him. Surrounding the pillow were heavy Dansk
pieces, and beyond, gracing the bedroom, a canopied
water bed with a tiger-skin mat. Chain lamps hung in four
locations, stained glass Tiffany imports that Winston had
purchased with a stolen BankAmericard. The only legiti-
mately bought items—the bed, the sofa and chairs—were
so heavy they had to be delivered. Even so, Winston had
placed only a deposit on them, never planning to honor
the balance. He rather enjoyed the $400 a month flat. He
enjoyed the spaciousness and the accessibility to neighborhood shops. But Winston moved a lot, having spent no
more than four months in any one place. It was the nature
of his life-style to remain one step ahead of the flock of
collectors always on his trail.

"Yellow. Yellow," he said aloud. "What goes with yellow?" Meaning that Winston could coordinate the outfit he
wore with the color of Papa's car. Color coordination was
essential to him; on a sunny day he wore bright colors; on
a bleak day, muted shades. His wardrobe filled two walk-
in closets: $300 Cardin suits; $85 Gucci shoes; $150
specially made Stetsons; scarves; gold ring to go with the
gold tooth in his mouth. Winston dressed splendidly.

"Real," he called.

Real leapt from the pillow. "Yessir?"

"A Kleenex, please."

Real went to the Kleenex box, which Winston could
have reached by dipping two inches to his right, and
handed a napkin to his master.

Winston dabbed the perspiration from his brow and
gracefully dropped the Kleenex, which Real caught and
deposited in the wastebasket.

Winston had already rubbed a gob of pomade into his
scalp, combed his hair with the small rake he carried in a
rear pocket, and was ready for application number two.
But not quite yet. He would begin the long, exquisite
process of readying himself when he saw Papa's approach.

The headache Papa suffered was no small pain. Old
Jack Daniels swam through his brain and agitated the
walls of his stomach. His bloodshot eyes looked like road
maps, and his face carried the vacant, lost-in-the-shuffle
helplessness of a Stan Laurel. He drove towards Winston
Blue's by instinct alone.

After checking with the telephone company's trace operator he called the Van Nuys police department for a squad car to meet him at the address, just in case, for among Winston's characteristics unpredictability was high on the list. Papa knew, for instance, that Winston traveled with a partner, usually someone who protected him and did his violent bidding. Two of Winston's former partners were now serving time in the joint for aggravated assault, about which Winston testified his ignorance.

An F-car (felony undercover) was already parked when Papa pulled up to the apartment building. He struggled from the front seat, taking his sunglasses with him, and strolled over to the young officer.

Just then a high-pitched voice sailed down from the second floor.

"Yoo hoo, Papa. It's me, Winston."

Papa squinted then fixed his eyes on Winston's skinny frame leaning out the window.

"You coming down!" he shouted.

"Hey! You bet!" Winston called back. "One jiffy."

With that, Winston disappeared.

Papa greeted the officer who told him his partner was covering the rear exit.

"Name?" the officer said.

"What?"

"Your name. What is it?"

"I gave all that to the desk sergeant."

"I need it for my own records."

It always happened. Cops had to do everything in duplicate or triplicate. Papa had delivered the same information so many times to so many people he considered carrying printouts with him.

The officer spent fifteen minutes meticulously jotting down the particulars. Good thing there's somebody on the back door, Papa thought, Winston could have been out of the state by now.

Finally, the officer picked up his walkie-talkie to call his buddy out back who told him the coast was clear, no one had passed in or out. Papa asked the cop to borrow his bullhorn, and carried it to the side of the building.

"Winston!" he shouted. "Where are you?"

Real's head appeared at the window. "He's in the shower, said to tell you he'd be right down."

"In the shower!" the detective exclaimed. "Let's take that bastard!"

"Whoa, whoa." Papa calmed him down. "He's got somebody else with him up there. We might have trouble."

"You going to let him get away with that! A shower!"

"Yup."

"Man, I wouldn't."

"Why not?" Papa asked.

"Why not? Cause that sonofabitch is taking *my* sweet time. He's resisting arrest."

"But he will be down."

"How do you know? He may never come down."

"Oh, I think he will. He can't live without clean clothes."

Clothes. Winston had the most difficult time selecting an outfit appropriate for going to jail. It was a choice between flamboyant assertion and conservative repose. Manic or mute. He called for a second opinion.

"Real! Come over here." Real did. "I'm ready for the wardrobe but I just can't find what I'm looking for. Help me out."

"Yeah? Help you out?"

"Would you?"

"Would I! Lemme see what you got." Real shuffled through the rack and selected three ensembles.

"Mmm!" Winston stood back to inspect them. He chose light beige because it matched the car and because, as he admitted to Real, "I feel awfully airy today."

And beige shoes and a beige vest, and a darker beige shirt to go with his beige silk underwear monogrammed on the lower right side. He chose a beige felt hat and beige gloves.

"Winston! Get your butt down here!" the bullhorn barked from outside.

Winston checked himself one last time in the mirror and strode to the window where he called pontifically, "I am ready."

"Hands high. Coat open."

"I *know* the procedure." Winston disappeared inside.

The Van Nuys cop crouched behind one bush guarding the entrance. Papa stood behind the other. The officer's .38 was out.

The front door swung open and there stood Winston, posing, hands on his hips and the beige felt hat drawn low over his eyelids.

"Very nice, Winston. Try it with your hands up."

"Oh," Winston moaned, "though you was Avedon and I the study in your immortal pose."

"Miss America, Winston. Down the ramp."

Winston curled both hands in the air and sashayed down the sidewalk, a wide smile on his face and the gold tooth sparkling below his upper lip.

"Where're them flashbulbs poppin'?" he asked.

Winston halted halfway when he saw the cop step from the bushes with the .38 in his hand.

"You can shed the iron, Mr. Policeman," Winston told him. "I am not considered dangerous, tell him, Papa."

Papa raised his eyebrows and nodded to the young cop, who lowered the weapon but would not put it away.

"And another thing," Winston said, staring at the officer's feet. "Never wear brown shoes with blue trousers."

An hour later Papa pulled into the parking lot outside the basement booking station of the New County jail. He led the tall, lanky clotheshorse through the construction work which had been going on for as long as Papa could remember and held the glass double doors for him.

Directly before them was a horseshoe desk, behind which sat two uniformed cops filling out forms. Papa said hello to a couple of bondsmen he knew from the Row. Off to their right, seated on benches, lingering against the walls and huddled inside the bank of phone booths, were relatives and friends of prisoners, prisoners themselves, children, Chicanos, housewives, all waiting. Some were defined by the clothes they wore—pimps and hookers and bikers and construction workers and businessmen. Many looked as if they'd been there all night. Sleeping children nestled against their mothers. Dead, vacant glances followed Papa and Winston to the desk; the only life in the room belonged to the bondsmen who scurried in and out as quickly as they could. Everyone else was stuck; the cops for the duration of their beat, the citizens for God only knew how long.

Papa hated the booking station and the deadening effect it produced in him. He had spent almost as much time in this place as he had anywhere else, thousands of long tedious hours waiting for waiting. He led the handcuffed Winston Blue around the desk where he presented the officer with a certified copy of the bailbond on Winston and the power of attorney authorizing him to bring him in. The officer inspected the papers and handed Papa a booking slip and arrest form, which he quickly filled out and carried to a glass-enclosed office in the back. Here the forms were folded and inserted into a glass tube, which was shot upstairs to the records section. There the data was checked for the right case and bond number, whether the fugitive was brought in on time and whether he was the right fugitive at all. Fingerprints determined that. No police department wanted a slew of false arrest suits on its hands. Bondsmen were capable of dragging in prisoners who *might* have been the ones they were after.

This part of the booking procedure took anywhere from ten minutes to two hours, depending upon the case load. Papa showed Winston to a seat on one of the benches where they settled in for the wait.

Their seat provided an excellent view of the frisk area, a small, five-by-five room where the prisoners were checked for weapons and shoved around by the officers in charge. Papa understood why the cops humiliated the hell out of the people they jammed against the wall, in full view of those in the waiting room. It served as a warning to anyone who might consider giving the cops trouble.

Winston Blue blanched at the treatment he saw.

"That's me in no time at all," he said to Papa.

"If you hassle them," Papa agreed.

"Don't make no difference. You smile, you shit, you jump, pain's the same. I been this route."

"I know, and I wanted to ask you about that. Where'd they send you before—the Queen Tank?"

Winston was highly insulted. "I ain't no nelly faggot, Papa, you know that."

"Then, in the main cells, what happened to you?"

"More of the same."

"I'll tell you, Winston, it's been a while for you. It's not the same anymore. I'd strongly suggest you tell the coppers to put you in the Queen Tank. You know what the gorillas in the main cell will do to you. At least in the Queen Tank you'll have a chance."

"I can take care of myself," Winston said in his best basso profundo.

Papa knew better. It often took the cops sixteen hours to book a guy. First they stripped and searched him. They made him bend over and spread his cheeks, after which they sprayed DDT up his rear and in his hair. He would then have to wait sometimes as much as four hours seated naked on a cold bench. The police put up with nothing at all in these barren rooms filled with raw freezing bodies. If the prisoner didn't answer quickly enough, or if he backtalked, the cops dragged him by the hair across the iron floor. He was kicked and punched. It didn't matter what offense he was in for, traffic tickets or grand larceny or manslaughter, he was treated the same as everyone else. It was a jungle of corrugated steel. When he breathed it sounded metallic.

It was always the most humiliating, dehumanizing experience Papa ever witnessed. The only law operating was force, survival of the strongest, and meanest, the most brutal. Men mysteriously died, others went crazy, and the most unbelievable thing of all was that no one had been to trial for the alleged crime. This was a detention center where they *awaited* trial. Close to a third of the men would later be found innocent . . .

"So I'm telling you," Papa was saying, "the Queen Tank's your only shot."

Winston wasn't listening. "You know," he told Papa, "the reason I waited so long to turn myself in—"

"You didn't turn yourself in, Winston, the phone call did."

"—was because I hate this place. You know they're goin' to ruin my clothes."

"Why didn't you wear rags?"

"Papa! You *know* I got no rags. Rags is for other people." Winston shuddered as he watched the booking cops ram another guy against the walls in the boxlike room. "God, look at that."

"You wouldn't have to go through it if you got a job and bought your own cars, instead of stealing them."

"I ain't qualified for a *job*."

This was Winston's fifth grand theft-auto beef. He was a sucker for a good-looking Cadillac.

"Besides," Winston added, "it ain't stealing them that I like, it's driving around in them. It's in my nigger blood to drive around in big cars, you know that. Part of my inheritance, unnerstand? I mean, I'm from De-troit."

"Come see me when you get out. I'll get you some work," Papa told him, knowing the idea had been erased from Winston's mind forever.

"I have erased that from my mind forever," he announced and turned the other way. A moment later: "You hurt me, Papa, s'gestin' somethin' like that. Cruel, just cruel."

Winston's records came back a few minutes later and Papa's cuffs were replaced by a pair from the officer's belt. The cop, a mean little guy with a squinty face, grabbed Winston's skinny arms and hustled him into the padded room.

"Stomach to the wall," he barked, jamming Winston in the small of his back. "To the wall, spook, you hear me!"

Papa watched from the hallway.

"Spread 'em!" the cop said, separating Winston's legs with the nightstick he carried.

When Winston began to protest Papa shook his head, don't do it.

"Take it easy, man!" Winston intoned. For that the squinty one elbowed him just above the kidneys, and he fell to his knees.

"Up!" ordered the cop, yanking him to his feet.

A smile appeared on the cop's face as he throttled Winston, whose screams reverberated off the outside walls. His shoes were taken off and thrown in a corner. The cop took hold of his suitcoat and with a swift jerking motion tore it from his body. Winston's belt was taken away. His shirt was ripped open down the front, buttons popping to the floor. All the while, expert knuckles worked on his body. Bruises didn't show as well on black men.

Papa understood the frustration booking officers felt at having to frisk every prisoner brought in, but the methods some used were well beyond the call of duty. Knowing that Winston was brought in by a bounty hunter, and not one of their own kind, seemed to give them the pleasure of demonstrating the first *official* punishment. Cops resented bounty hunters and their bondsmen. After spending miserable hours bringing a man in, the bondsman could bail him out within minutes. But as far as Papa was concerned that was no excuse for delivering so much pain here in the concrete room.

Papa knew he would never become totally immune to the treatment he witnessed. It mattered some that Winston

was an acquaintance, but Papa found himself wincing at
the scene regardless of who it was. Here lay the essential
difference between himself and too many police officers.
The law made it possible for them to torture, and they
worked it to the limit. They had to be tough, to play soldier. They had to take a guy in handcuffs and treat him as
if his hands were free.

It was this part of the business that Papa most despised;
when a prisoner of his had come peacefully and was transferred into the custody of law officers who made an animal of him. Those cops didn't care whether the man was
docile or dangerous, whether he put up a fight or not, he
was just another asshole on whom to take out their aggressions. In their mentality, guilty or no, he deserved everything he got, the more the better.

It was this behavior that gave cops a bad name, and
from which they derived their holier-than-thou attitude
toward the public in general. For Papa it was a damning
statement on a society that put a club in the hand of a
half-wit to administer its law.

The last thing he saw before leaving was the squinty-
eyed policeman wrapping one hand around the back of
Winston's neck and pushing his skull against the wall.

*Elmo Sellers, a twenty-six-year-old man with facial blem-
ishes and a thin hairy body, entered the L.A. County
courtroom and sat beside his lawyer. In the same courtroom, also with a lawyer, was Sellers' wife, Janet, from
whom he was separated. The case in question was custody
of their eight-month-old son.*

*Judge Carroll Blackwell entered the courtroom and took
his place at the bench. Judge Blackwell had made his decision and called the participating parties forward. Elmo
and Janet Sellers and their attorneys approached the
bench.*

*Despite the state's usual practice of awarding custody of
a child to the woman, Elmo Sellers claimed that his wife
was a prostitute and should not be awarded custody. Judge
Blackwell decided otherwise, awarding custody to Janet
Sellers, and to Elmo Sellers limited visitation rights. An
explosion occurred inside Elmo Sellers' mind when he
heard the verdict. At that moment he made the decision,
no matter what the verdict, that he would have the child,
at any cost.*

12

The Two-Step Aisle

SEPTEMBER 15.

At three o'clock in the afternoon Papa turned right off Highland and merged with the frenzied traffic of Sunset Boulevard. Dotty sat beside him, looking out her window. Papa automatically glanced towards the white, graffiti-stained buildings of Hollywood High standing off to the right. It had long been a habit with him—checking out Hollywood High. On any given schoolday, at the *very* least twenty-five nubile girls decorated the sidewalk. They might have been only sixteen. They looked twenty and brought a wistful smile to Papa's face. To his mind there was no better way to approach Sunset.

Positioned along both sides of Sunset were billboards announcing an Elton John concert, War's new album, Tom Laughlin's beefy frame with the film logo "The Master Gunfighter." Women in tight jeans and loose-fitting halters trudged along the sidewalks in their platform heels. Down below, towards the west, the city sprawled in magnificent disarray. The Santa Monica mountains loomed in

the distance. Beyond was the Pacific. To the right, climbing up the hills towards Laurel Canyon, houses were
piled one atop the other. Passing Papa on the Strip were
Bentleys, Rollses, antique Fords, Stingrays and a thousand
Mustangs. No Volkswagens. Hollywood is not a small-car
city.

The Strip used to be Papa's stomping ground before he
set up housekeeping in the Valley. He spotted the apartment building where he had lived for years. For him the
Strip would always mean action. Every hustle in the world
had gone down on Sunset. Hookers and gay boys hawked
their bodies here. Businesses began and folded. Would-be
actors and actresses hounded their agents by day and
waited tables by night. Dream Street. Sunset Boulevard.

They turned left on Doheny, the border between Hollywood and Beverly Hills. For Papa Beverly Hills was more
myth than reality. He knew Hollywood residents whose
premier ambition in life was to cross the border into Beverly
Hills, to mingle with the filthy rich. BEVERLY HILLS,
they clamored, HERE WE COME! Yet, oddly enough,
when it came time for the move, few made the cross-over.
Instead they migrated to Malibu or Topanga Canyon, to
the skinny hills of Laurel Canyon or over breakheart
pass on Mulholland Drive. Only a handful shifted to Beverly Hills. The reason, in Papa's estimation, had to do with
class, or rather the lack of it. Beverly Hills is a lovely section of Los Angeles; big, expensive homes line the ave-
nues; the lawns are manicured; swimming pools and tennis
courts are *de rigueur*. The entire area is a showcase for
opulence. Unfortunately, in Papa's view, the people who
house themselves there know very little about what happens beyond the Beverly Hills borders, except what they
read in newspapers. The exclusivity of the place has only
in small part to do with location. There is mental exclusivity, social exclusivity and even moral exclusivity. For those
living in Beverly Hills the pinnacle has been reached, leaving the rest of the world behind. Beverly Hills has one of
the highest crime rates in the country, committed by the
people who live there. All the crime is on paper, behind
the scenes, million-dollar swindles, neighbors pulling fast
ones on each other. All in beautiful, exclusive Beverly
Hills.

A dozen blocks down Doheny Papa turned onto Norma
Place and drove carefully down the narrow street where

dogs and children darted from behind cars. Bright green artificial grass decorated the small patches of lawn. Frisbies flew everywhere.

It took Papa fifteen minutes to find a parking space. He squeezed the Plymouth into the slot and got out. Cars slowed down as they passed. Passengers gawked at Papa, kids pointed fingers at him through rear windows. Papa usually received stares. He knew he looked unusual. His bulk. The thick beard. The menace. But they weren't the main reasons why people stared now. Papa wore a black suit, and around his neck was a clerical collar of the sort worn by priests and ministers, and on his head was a Homburg. It was the outfit he wore when he performed a marriage ceremony.

When Dotty rounded the car Papa held out his hand, she took it and they walked towards the house, passing beneath bottlegreen bowers sprinkled with hyacinth. A half dozen cats sat on their stone perches, watching them pass. White latticework formed Italian garden walls on either side of the path while sunlight sprayed through the slats and made tiny square patches on the cobblestones.

They continued through the maze of flowers. Ahead stood the tiny cottage, from which rock music thumped a melodic beat. A large wooden door hung lazily against a row of bushes. They passed through the doorway and into the small garden entrance where they were met by Jollie, one of the world's beautiful women, blonde and soft in the perpetual halo surrounding her head.

"Hiya," Jollie smiled, kissing them both.

Dotty opened the folder she carried and handed Jollie an LP, Strauss' "Thus Spake Zarathustra."

"The wedding music," Dotty told her.

Bounding in from the living room and posing magnificently under the archway was Herman, the groom. Herman got a load of Papa's outfit and said, "The bigger half of the Smith Brothers. The Messiah? The Messiah's grandmother. How are you?" Herman strutted across the patio and shook Papa's hand. He also took Dotty's hand and pulled her close.

"I'm not married *yet*, sweetheart," he said.

The ceremony wasn't for another hour and a half so Papa grabbed some wine and sat in the swinging wicker chair. Herman dashed around arranging glasses and napkins, moving furniture and dropping one-liners as he passed.

Herman trained racehorses. He also bet on racehorses. And he never lost. Papa had done Herman's astrological chart which indicated luck. It also spelled financial brain torture, showing huge sums of cash floating into Herman's hands, and floating out again. He would win $500 at the track, spend it on a magnificent suit and then somehow ruin the suit on the way home. Cash worked for Herman but once he traded it away for something tangible it lost its power.

"Financially you're like the millionaire shipwrecked on a small desert island," Papa said.

"Profound! That is *profound!* This man is so unbelievably profound that . . ." Herman turned and marched off into the other room.

Herman wasn't normally this frantic. Neither did he get married every day.

Other guests began arriving, couples already married, some about to be, some with no shot in the world. They were ushered through the cottage towards the rear garden where they were seated around a picnic table. Everyone began drinking and Papa vaguely wondered why ceremonies he performed always got reversed. Receptions proceeded ceremonies and continued after the vows were exchanged.

Among the guests, the only solo member was a thirty-year-old man who had just flown into Los Angeles from the East Coast. His name was Logan and he had known Herman and Jollie for two years.

Papa was still in his swinging chair when Logan, who wrote books for a living, was introduced to him and began asking questions. During their conversation guests filtered in and out but generally left them alone.

"Are you authorized to perform wedding ceremonies? Is it legal?" Logan asked Papa.

Herman heard the question. "Papa's a bishop. The Temple of Inspired Loving."

"Inspired *Living,*" Papa corrected him.

"It's not one of those churches you pay twenty-five to join and every twenty-five thereafter you're promoted?" Logan asked.

Papa shook his head. "No. It's for real, sanctioned by

the state and the I.R.S. Been a bishop for . . . Dotty, how many years've I been bishop?"

Dotty thought for a moment. "Five."

"Five," he repeated. "The church has got fifteen, twenty thousand members throughout the world."

"You saw the light, that's why you joined? Or didn't see the light, or wanted to see it?"

"None of them. It started as a business arrangement. Dr. Frank Winston is a former deputy Real Estate Commissioner. He began the church, oh, ten years ago. One day he called me and asked me to investigate some property in Riverside County, for the church. I did. He liked it. He also wanted me as a member of the church. I didn't have a real estate license, but later, as a bishop and church officer, I was authorized to negotiate in all matters, civil or religious, on behalf of the Temple. There are only six of us, six bishops in the United States.

"In certain ways it's completely understandable why I joined the Temple of Inspired Living. I was brought up going to a lot of different churches. I lived in a town up in Montana, Anaconda. Just a plain old German, Swedish, Norwegian, Lutheran, Presbyterian, Methodist, Catholic town. I went to all of them. Got five silver stars and a gold one for never missing Sunday School five years in a row. I came out a heathen.

"All that Christian upbringing killed a lot of the meanness in me, which isn't so good for the business I'm in." Papa waved his hand in the air. "Example. My father did some of his business over the phone. Many times I listened to him haggling over the price of something. When no agreement was reached he'd take a coin from his pocket and say into the receiver, 'Heads or tails?' The guy on the other end made his choice and my dad flipped the coin. Didn't make any difference whether it went *for* him or *against* him. He called it the way it fell. There was never, ever, any question that he might have called it his own way. That's *integrity*. Can't find much of it these days."

By this time many of the guests had wandered over and stood by listening to Papa.

"Far as organized religion went, it never did make me a believer. It made me a skeptic. Especially when churches pay no taxes and own so damn much land it makes my head spin. Catholic Church, Mormon Church, all of them, lobby like mad in Washington and cry poverty any time they can—all in the name of God, of course. Hell, everything *I* do and make is in the name of God.

"The Utah Construction Company, heard of it? Multibillion dollar Mormon tax shelter. They own so much tax-free land it looks like the Louisiana Purchase.

"Organized religion's biggest sin—the biggest sin for anyone—is the loss of spirit. It got all tangled up in negotiations, power plays and deals. The spirit's gone now. All that's left are a few rituals, reminders of the way things were and should still be. A front.

"At least in my church everything's on the line. It's straight-away. It applies to living today. What it promotes is the Golden Rule without all those complex philosophical overtones. I like it. It's immediate. It's pertinent to me."

Moments later, when the sun had reached a point where it shone through the overhead skylight, Logan rose and thanked Papa for his company and strolled into the garden, followed by the other guests.

Papa continued swinging. He felt cool in the yellow-green atmosphere of the cottage. The chatter seemed far off now. Beyond the double glass doors the bower formed a tunnel encased by overhanging leaves. His eyelids dropped. A haze settled in. And he wandered. Back. To Anaconda. To the railroad cars lumbering into town with mountains of hardrock ore in the open bins, and further down the tracks the smeltering plants pumping dark gritty black clouds into the sky. Faces of those who had raised him as a child appeared and vanished. His grandfather, the wizened Grand Cyclop of the Arizona Chapter's Ku Klux Klan, who had brought him Indian blankets from Nogales and Silver City. His mother, Eastern Star chairwoman and member of the D.A.R. and Ladies Aid, who wore fancy yellow dresses and gave him a sister when he was seven. His father, the Exalted Ruler of the Fraternal Order of Elks, who ran the family's 160-acre ranch, the grocery store and the town as its mayor. And his aunt, Challie Forsman, mystic, astrologer, and Aunt Jessie Williams, Broadway actress whose portrait hangs from fifteen pegs on the walls of the magnificent Utah Hotel in Salt Lake City, the soprano soloist who delivered the first radio broadcast for the Mormon Tabernacle Choir.

Papa's eyes remained half closed when he spotted the diaphanous figure of a woman standing in the garden with a small wine glass in her hand. Sunlight glistened off the brim. She seemed the spitting image of Big Annie Harding, Anaconda's one and only madam. Big Annie had between six and twelve girls working for her in the two-story duplex on East Park Street. Papa used to deliver groceries to her place but never got the kind of tip he really wanted—one of the girls. Big Annie told him he never would either, because if his father ever found out it would mean the end of Big Annie's career. Papa was fourteen at the time and got the jitters when he carried the bags to Big Annie's front door. He'd step inside and glance around at the women, none of whom he'd call a striking beauty, but at fourteen he wasn't looking for striking beauties. The best-looking girl in the house—best by a long, long shot—was a cute little black girl from Salem, Oregon. Seeing her for the first time sent ecstatic shudders through him; seeing *any* black brought a reaction. There were only two in all of Anaconda. Papa was sad to see her finally go. In that whole time, despite her looks and body, she turned not one trick. The men all wanted her; they must have, to Papa's mind. What the men didn't want was the word to get out about their "dark" desires . . .

Anaconda, Montana, 1939. It was the wild northwest then with wide open spaces and rabbits and field mice racing along trout stream banks, wily coyotes and speckled dogwoods rising out of flower beds, and trails meandering through trees that grew and lost their leaves, and bright crackling days with hunters tracking through the fallen leaves, hibernation and death and mountain peaks that never lost their snow.

"It was winter. I was ten and I'd been stalking rabbits about two miles from home up along Sheep Gulch, when a flash blizzard came up. I hauled ass into the mouth of a small cave and started piling rocks one by one into the opening because it was so damn cold and my hands felt like they were going to fall off they were so numb.

"The cave was an old mine shaft with overhead beams criss-crossing the ceiling. About the time I got the last rock in place the gale must have jarred the beams and one of them fell on me and drove a spike through my hand. I hardly felt it but the blood gushed out and froze on my skin. It was a big six-inch diameter beam and it had my arm pinned to the ground. I didn't panic but I knew I'd have to do something pretty damn fast. You never knew

how long those blizzards lasted and there wasn't anybody
who knew where I was, so I wrapped my free arm around
the beam and with more strength than I knew I had I
slowly pulled the spike out. I packed snow into the wound
and it was about that time when the pain started up. It
stung! But it wasn't until later on, after the blizzard blew
on by and I was halfway home, that the real pain went
through me. But I didn't cry. A man wasn't supposed to
cry, not then, not in town, not in fights or when you got
the hell beat out of you. You took it; it was part of the
code.

"It wasn't nearly so rough out in the storms as it was in
town though. As I got older the idea of having fun was
getting drunk and having a beef. I've been drinking since
twelve. Up there didn't make any difference how old you
were, if you were big enough to reach the bar you were
big enough to drink whiskey. One of my best friends, the
gang I ran with, was much older than I was. My best
friend was Shipwreck Kelly, who used to babysit for me
till I got old enough to travel with him. He and I used to
take off for Butte on weekends, to this place called Mer-
cury Alley. Cops were stationed on each end of the alley
which was boarded up on both ends, and all the way down
the sides were whores you could get for a buck a throw.
We used silver dollars then and used to flip the coins at
the whores and got a real messy piece of ass.

"Ship loved to fight and one night he got into it with
Orin Eckleson. My father had made Orin a cop so he was
a natural target for Ship and me. They had a bloody battle
and Ship went to jail. He was out the next day. If you so
much as breathe on a cop today you get sent to the joint
on an assault with a deadly weapon beef, makes no difference if the cop eggs you on or not. Then it was a fight between two men.

"My problem was my size. I was the most natural target
in the world for any drunk who wanted a beef. A man
gets drunk his confidence grows and he's looking for the
biggest guy in the bar, which almost always happened to
be me. I liked to drink and whore and fight as much as
anybody but I never went looking for brawls. Sometimes
I'd be leaning on the bar and all of a sudden some lush'd
stroll up and clip me on the chin. Just like that. No provocation, nothing said between us. He just spotted a big body
and wanted to beat on it. I beat back and broke jaws and

knocked out teeth and of course the rest of the gang was there to help me out since I was the baby of the outfit. So it was really dumb of these drunks to pick on me. But they never learned, they kept coming back for more.

"I had a hell of a lot of brawls under my belt by seventeen and I wanted to leave Anaconda, not because of the fights but I guess you could call it wanderlust. I joined the Navy and went into flight training. Logged lots of flying hours until somebody at the Pentagon figured out the war was winding down and every last one of us was yanked out of flight school and told we should have some real live wartime experience. I shipped out on the USS *Ingersoll*, off to the South Pacific.

"To get on that ship I first had to go down to New Orleans where it was docked at the Naval base at Gulfport, on the Mississippi. New Orleans was just a few hours away so every weekend my buddies and I took off for Bourbon Street, in the French Quarter.

"That's where I killed my first man, a big old sailor, in a Puerto Rican bar. He was drunk and bragging and ballyhooing and calling everybody a sonofabitch. I wasn't paying attention. I *was* paying attention rather but not doing anything about it. Well, the same old damn thing happened. He lit on me 'cause maybe I wasn't paying the attention to him he thought I should have been paying. It was old times—broken bottles and throwing chairs, except he was getting dangerous all of a sudden. He came at me once, twice, three times. I was getting tired and irritated and I knew I either had to get out of the bar or cold-cock him.

"Figuring he would have chased me out to the street if I did decide to leave, I stayed. I remember when he came at me for the last time. His arms were chugging at me. I was bleeding from the nose from a cut he gave me off the bottle. I hit him three or four times, once in the Adam's apple, he fell off to the side and his head hit against the bar rail. The Adam's apple did him in. He choked to death. I wasn't even booked when everyone in the joint swore it was self-defense.

"It was a helluva feeling when he died. I was scared and excited as a sissy, both, and I sure as hell was a big man around campus on the Naval base.

"So, a few months later on the *Ingersoll* the war was over and I went to Boston for discharge. I'd never been to

Boston before. From there I went to New York with a couple of the boys and stopped by the nearest whorehouse because I hadn't been laid in months and, I couldn't believe it, but who owned the whorehouse but Big Annie Harding. We threw our arms around each other and talked about old times. I found out that Annie not only ran whores in Anaconda and New York but she owned the largest chain of cathouses in the country, from Seattle to Boston. Her daughter, who I was told never knew what her mother did, got a Ph.D. in music from Juilliard.

"It was time to go home. I went back to the ranch. Montana hadn't changed a bit. I never did really know my dad, he was so busy with the ranch and running Anaconda and the Elks meetings and all that. He was like the invisible man around the house when I was a kid, but I loved him. He instilled in me a deep sense of what an honest man should be. I read and absorbed a poem he gave to me, Kipling's 'To Be a Man.' Honor, morals and principles, that's when I learned from my father. He died long before his time.

"My father never made the mistake of trying to be a buddy like so many fathers did. He accepted the responsibility of being a parent. Sure we were buddies—hunted and fished together and all that—but when push came to shove he was a disciplinarian and took that responsibility seriously.

"After Dad's death my mother moved to San Rafael, California, and after the war I followed her. With the D.A.R. and the Ladies Aid she was steeped in tradition. She even had her family genealogy done and traced her ancestors back to the Norman invasion of England in 1066. It turns out that one of William the Conqueror's right-hand men was the first Earl of Hereford; her maiden name was Hayford, and there you go.

"I'll tell you, I was scared of that woman. When I was a kid I would rather have been beaten with a club than have her raise an eyebrow at me. She might have come from genteel stock but in the midst of all that, or because of it, she was one tough woman. Talk about being raised by the iron fist. Even when I got to California and started in at the university, I paid my own way with jobs and the G.I. Bill. Wouldn't take a cent from her because that would have given her too much control. That didn't stop her though. She still tried to run my life.

"The first thing I did was give her a copy of Philip Wylie's *Generation of Vipers*, particularly the sections on Momism and how Moms can ruin their kids. When that didn't work I told her straight out to get off my mother-fucking back. I was a grown boy now. 'What did I do, my dear son? What did I do to ever hurt you?' she cried over and over. As far as she was concerned the umbilical cord was still hanging there solid between us.

"Being brought up by women, and with a mother as strong as she was, I can sort of understand my lack of success with them on any long term basis. Way down deep I must have believed they were all tyrants out to rule me.

"I do believe teamwork is the soul of any relationship with a woman. But every team has a captain. And that has to be me . . ."

Papa awakened with a start and looked up to see Dotty standing over him.

"Ready?" she said.

Papa struggled from the swing chair and stretched. The wedding guests were already waiting for him in the garden. He removed a piece of paper from inside his suitcoat. On it was a prayer he had composed from various sources the night before. This was his thirteenth wedding and he wondered if *that* meant anything. He had refused to marry some couples because after doing their astrological charts he saw too many conflicts. Some of the couples went elsewhere and got married.

On his way to the garden he placed *Thus Spake Zarathustra* on the turntable.

The garden was too small for the crowd, who stood bunched together, some carrying drinks. Papa walked in and frowned at them. They placed their glasses on the table and Papa went to his position in front of Jollie and Herman. Dotty took pictures. The ethereal strains from *Thus Spake Zarathustra* filled the room. Papa paused to listen and felt goosebumps sprouting on his forearms. He began.

"We are gathered here in the presence of this company to join together this man and this woman in marriage, which is an honorable estate, not to be entered into inadvisedly or lightly, but reverently, discreetly and soberly. Although we are of varied religious persuasions we all pray in our own fashion for whatever we individually perceive to be a deity."

Papa hesitated for a moment to look at the couple. Both were glassy-eyed. Their heads were cocked to one side. They stared up at him.

"Keep us, O Lord, from pettiness, let us be great-minded in thought, word and act. Help us put away pre-tense and face each other in deep trust without fear or self-pity. Let us be done with fault-finding and be quick to discover the best of every situation. Guard us from ill tem-per and hasty judgment so that we may take time for all things, and may we always be kind and gentle. May we suppress every impulse to strike back, even under the guise of humor.

"Lead us to be swift with kind words. Prevent us from ever resorting to the icy barrier of silence. Let the heat of love reduce pride to ashes. Teach us never to ignore, never to hurt, never to take for granted.

"Herman, will thou have this woman for thy wedded wife . . . ?"

Herman and Jollie placed rings on one another's fingers and Papa went on. "In the words of the Apache and the Prophet. Now you will feel no rain, for each of you will be sheltered to the other. Now each of you will feel no cold, for each of you will be warmth to the other. Now there is no loneliness for you. Now you are two bodies with only one life before you. But let there be space in your togetherness, and let the winds of the heavens dance between you. Love one another but make not a bond of love. Let it rather be a moving sea between the shores of your souls. Fill each other's cups but drink not from one cup. Give one another of your bread but eat not of the same loaf."

Papa's voice swelled with the music. Something near-magical was happening. The guests had stopped fidgeting. They listened and felt a new power enter the room, as if they too were partners in this wedding. Papa noted their expressions, and their stillness and the leaves rustling as the breeze swept among them.

"Give your hearts but not into one another's keeping, for only the hand of life can contain your hearts. Stand together but not too near together. Go now to your dwell-ing place and enter into the days of your togetherness, and may your days upon the earth be peaceful and good . . ."

The music climaxed with Herman claiming his bride, and the whole company congratulated them both.

It was a two-step aisle from the ceremony to the kitchen where Herman had waiting a tray filled with tuna salad, deviled eggs and fruit. Champagne corks popped. Papa was famished and ate his portion, along with five others. He saw Jollie and Herman watching each other through the crowd. They exchanged secret glances and smiled at one another.

It was a day for memories as Papa went back to his own first marriage. He had been at the Berkeley campus of the University of California where he had been taking twenty-one semester hours, working eight hours a day, six days a week as a Juvenile Hall counselor, and in his spare time, what there was of it, he built a house.

His wife Samantha was a rich girl who had moved from her father's home into Papa's. She was bored. She hardly saw her husband. She couldn't stand being cooped up in the house. She bitched and moaned about the situation. Papa could understand why but he could not bear to listen to her complain all the time. He explained to her that she had to live her own life *with* him, not *for* him. She took a job in a lawyer's office.

She complained about his working so much, but at twenty-two his adolescent pride prevented him from spending one cent of the money her father offered every month.

The marriage ended one day when he picked her up from the office. He hadn't slept for forty hours between school and work. From the moment she got into the car she whined about the condition of their relationship. She wailed and repined and grumbled and fretted and he listened to her for half an hour until he could take it no longer. Her last words were: "We never go anyplace." He released both hands from the steering wheel and took hold of her shoulders. The car inched along at barely five miles an hour. He said: "You are now going someplace. Out!" Papa picked her off the seat and pushed her out onto the soft shoulders by the road. Papa kept going.

He got a call the next morning from her lawyer, who told him that Samantha had filed for divorce. Papa didn't contest it.

But that was a long time ago, when he was young, when he wanted to make some mark in the world. As he thought about it, now, in Herman's kitchen, he realized that things had not really changed all that much. He still had the same desires, the same motivations. He looked and felt older but he had not calmed down. If anything, life was more intense. There were more responsibilities. One of them stood across the room—Dotty—and another was growing in her belly.

Papa mingled with the crowd, thanking people for their compliments on the ceremony. He knew he was getting bombed on the wine and wished he had brought his own bottle of Jack Daniels. Liquor stores were close by but he didn't feel like making the trip. Dotty would have gone if he asked her but she seemed to be having too good a time and he didn't want to interrupt her.

He checked his watch. It read: 5:30. He picked up the phone and called his answering service. Of the eight messages three seemed in need of immediate attention.

His first call went to Ramsey, who informed him that United Insurance had gotten in touch.

"Bobby Ching," Ramsey said. "You know about him?"

"No."

"Jumped bail. Seventy-five grand."

"Where is he? Forget it. I can guess. Mexico."

"Wrong. Canada."

"What the hell's a Chinaman doing in Canada?" Papa asked, slurring his words.

"Are you drunk?"

"Yup. What the hell's a Chinaman doing in Canada?"

"You shouldn't drink so damn much."

"I know. My liver is five hundred years old. What's a Chinaman doing in Canada?"

"How do I know. He made a wrong turn. Here's the deal: Ching's father owns a San Francisco restaurant, which he won't own for long if his kid isn't picked up. United will pay us thirty-five grand to bring him back."

Papa paused on that one. United will pay $35,000, he thought to himself. $35,000! United wouldn't pay $35,000 to get its own president back. "What's so special about Bobby Ching?"

"Oh . . ."

"Ramsey?"

"What?"

"What's so special about Bobby Ching?"

"He jumped on a second-degree murder rap."

"What else?"

"He's been in Canada for almost five months."

"Almost . . . For crissakes, why has United waited so long to get him?"

"Well, that's the sticky part. They haven't. Two guys have already gone after him."

"And?"

"They haven't come back."

"That's encouraging. Let's make reservations at Forest Lawn. You're out of your mind. What could *we* do that they couldn't?"

"Ching's father will go with us. He knows where the kid is. He'll take us to him. I think we can snatch him."

"With what, a tank?"

"Yes or no?"

"No."

"That's your final word?"

"It is," Papa declared.

"Fine. I'll pick you up at eight in the morning. Bring warm clothes."

"Ramsey!" It was too late. Ramsey had hung up.

The next call went to Richie Blumenthal, who was curious to know how far along Papa was on the Tony Bernardo case.

"Tony Bernardo?" Papa asked, trying to crystallize the name from the booze-clouded catalog.

"Tony Bernardo! The kid I been calling you about for months."

"Oh, right. I'm still on it."

"I hope to Christ you are. I got, as you damn well know, twenty-five hundred of my own dough on that little fucker."

"Twenty-five hundred! Richie, that's like stealing a bucket of sand from the beach."

"Tell me you're not interested anymore and I'll get somebody else . . . and you can find another bondsman."

Papa had delayed snatching Bernardo because, in part, he loved to listen to Richie's suffering. It was a rare occasion when Richie invested his own money in a client and Papa loved to see him sweat—for all the times he made Papa sweat himself.

He teetered on the border between telling Richie to stay calm or fuck off. Of the 5,000 cases Papa had worked on over the years Richie Blumenthal had provided about 1,-500. Telling a bondsman with that much clout to fuck off would be crazy.

"Fuck off, Richie," Papa said.

"What's that supposed to mean?"

"It means I'll bring Tony Bernardo in before the deadline."

"For sure?"

"You want an affidavit? You have my word."

Papa hung up and made one final call to somebody named Franco Disi. The answering-service girl could tell him nothing other than Franco Disi was in a great rush to contact him. Papa couldn't place the name. From the exchange he knew the location was somewhere in San Fernando Valley.

The man who answered the phone told Papa to hang on and Franco Disi came on the line.

"Listen, Mr. Thorson," Disi said in his gruff Brooklynese, "our mutual friend, Robby Dolan. Robby Dolan?"

"Robby Dolan," Papa repeated. "I know him."

"Robby said I should get hold of you on this problem I'm having." Franco Disi wheezed and coughed and went on. "I got a coupla nightclubs here in the Valley and for the last coupla weeks I been getting a lot of heat from this one guy. Protection heat."

"Who's behind it?"

"Who knows? This gorilla's been here twice, says unless I pay up he's gonna burn me bad. I got guys on the street trying to find out who's fronting him. Nothing. And I'm worried. Who can tell what this weirdo might do? He could hit me, bomb my joints. I got a family. So, Robby tells me to call you."

"What's wrong with the cops?"

"You want a list?"

Papa drained his glass and passed it to Herman, who was walking by. Herman refilled it for him. "What do you want me to do?"

"Find him and cool him off. Robby says you got a knack for that kind of thing."

"Sure, but just because your people can't find out who's behind him doesn't mean he's alone."

"Believe me. By now I woulda known."

"Why don't you get one of your own people after him?"

"I, uh, can't afford to get involved, Mr. Thorson, if you know what I mean."

Whatever he meant, Franco Disi couldn't afford to get involved.

"Have you got an address on this guy?" Papa asked.

"I got a name."

"What is it?"

"Myron Fish."

Papa sat down. He took a quick slug of wine and lit a cigarette.

"You still there?" Disi asked.

"Myron Fish? Big, short black hair, mean-looking, squeaks when he talks?"

"That's the guy!" Disi exclaimed. "You know him?"

"Well."

"He's coming over tonight, over to the club on Ventura. He packs a forty-five."

"Covered with rust, no doubt."

"How's that?"

"What time?" Papa asked.

"Nine sharp. That's what he said."

"Myron is punctual. Okay, Mr. Disi. I'll take care of it."

"Oh, thank you, Mr. Thorson. I really appreciate this. Whatever the fee is, I'll pay you anything . . ."

Papa cut him off. "This one's on the cuff. Just being there will make it priceless."

Papa hung up and went to look for Dotty. He found her in the garden talking to Jollie about childbirth. Papa told her about Myron's new occupation.

"He's finally gone insane," Dotty said.

"I wouldn't doubt it. You want to come along?"

"I wouldn't miss it."

Papa and Dotty left a half hour later. Herman and Jollie by this time had gotten very smashed and were arguing about their need for independence. Papa wasn't exactly sober either. He drove home very slowly and still made two wrong turns.

It was just after midnight when Elmo Sellers quietly climbed the steps to the apartment he once shared with his wife. Outside the door he listened for the sound of his eight-month-old son but could hear nothing. He paused for a moment, the thoughts of yesterday's custody trial reeling through him, then he inserted a key in the lock. The door eased open and Sellers went in.

A single light showed from beneath the door to the large bedroom. The baby's room next door was dark. Sel-

lers tried to block from his mind what he suspected was taking place in the large bedroom. He continued into the next room, where he wrapped the child in its blanket, then left the apartment, descended the stairs and climbed into his car. A half hour later he and the baby arrived at the L.A. airport to board a plane for Hawaii. Surely, he thought, his act would bring his wife to her senses. She would relent, give up her prostitution and come back to him. But he would need to be on his guard against the law. They would never understand . . .

13

The Enforcer Fish

Papa and Dotty arrived at Franco Disi's at eight-thirty. The building sat way back from the road surrounded by a parking lot with a wooden fence running along the perimeter. A valet parked the car and they went inside where it was dark and subtle with tables up front and cavern-like booths in the back. Waiters in gray shortie jackets and bow ties hurried down the aisles. There was a wine steward and a maitre d' for added class.

Franco Disi met them at the door and ushered them to his office. They passed dinner guests who had begun a steady exodus to the nightclub where a five-piece band played popular dance music.

Franco closed the door behind him and moved around his desk. A waiter entered with a Lazy Susan filled with sandwich meats and a relish tray which he placed on a stand.

Dotty sat in the leather chair that faced the desk. Papa stood behind her.

"Fish called a little while ago," Franco told them, "said he'd definitely be here at nine."

Franco Disi was a scratcher. He continually scratched his face and arms and neck. One hand scratched the other hand. When he wasn't scratching he was gesturing; grand, sweeping circles that never came to rest. Papa figured he was naturally hyper. He had known guys like Franco Disi before. Little guys, ex-hoods with barely visible IQ's, who had climbed out of the bush leagues by either taking a small rap for a big guy or remaining loyal to the big guy who played his cards right and pulled the little guy along with him. Papa saw one thing common to all of them—an exaggerated sense of importance. In their own minds they'd become quintessential men. Their possessions had become vulnerable. They had become vulnerable. Anything out of the ordinary was a threat. It threatened what they considered a territorial imperative. Franco Disi didn't know that Myron Fish broke Papa's television. He didn't know about the ruined flashlight in Watts. He didn't know anything about Myron, except that he might somehow scatter the territory and weaken the imperative.

At two minutes to nine Franco's door opened and one of his henchmen, a shorter replica of Franco, announced the arrival of Myron Fish.

"Tell him I'll be right out," Franco told him, and then looked over to Papa with a hopeful expression.

Papa nodded. "Go out and meet him. Bring him back in. I'll be ready."

Franco jerked his head up and down and went from the room. Dotty moved to a leather armchair in the far corner of the room while Papa dimmed the light a few degrees to give the room a murky, sinister cast. He walked to Franco's desk where he leaned against the mahogany. He inserted a cigarette into the Aqua-filter and lit up.

A moment later the door opened. Franco held it open for Myron Fish. Myron looked like a character straight out of a George Raft movie. A tight-fitting double-breasted blue pinstriped suit hugged his body. He wore a fedora with the brim flipped down over his brow. A shadow of a moustache grew on his lip. Patent leather or spit-shined shoes—Papa couldn't tell which in the darkness —sparkled beneath his pegged trousers. There was a bulge over his left breast where the big .45 Franco mentioned nested in its shoulder holster.

Myron's head swiveled back and forth, trying to focus his eyes which were hidden behind dark glasses.

"Hello, Myron," Papa said casually.

Myron froze. He knew the voice but couldn't tell where it came from. He removed the glasses. His eyes popped open and shut until he recognized Papa's bulk at the desk. His composure collapsed. Short audible bursts escaped from his mouth.

"Sit down," Papa commanded.

Myron stumbled towards the nearest chair and sat, trembling. Papa peered down at him. "Mr. Disi tells me you're putting protection heat on him. Is that true?"

"Pro . . . pro. . . ?"

". . . tection heat. Protection heat," Papa said. "That's a no-no, Myron."

"No-no."

"That's right."

Myron wilted, folding like a dying flower. Both arms squeezed closer to his sides and both his knees pressed together. His body seemed to shrink as he drew himself into a fetal position. He looked as if he might suddenly disappear, leaving only the suit, hat and shoes in a rumpled pile on the chair.

Papa pushed himself from the desk and loomed over him. He reached down and removed the fedora. Myron's eyes leaked down his cheeks and into the corners of his mouth. His olive skin had turned pasty white.

Papa now carefully extracted the .45 from inside Myron's jacket and pointed the muzzle directly at his nose.

Papa then dropped the .45 into his own pocket and returned to the desk. "I hate giving lectures," he said, "but, Myron, I want you to listen carefully. Some guys are no good fooling around with the law, whichever side they're on. You're one of those guys. You failed as a bounty hunter. You'd make a terrible cop. Bury this fantasy trip you're on. It's no good for you. You want me to be proud of you? Do you? You want me to respect you?"

Myron's head pumped up and down.

"Then don't try to be something you can't handle. Work with your computers. You're a genius with them. How many people are a genius with anything? Go with your talent. It could make you rich and famous, a hell of a lot more rich and famous than this cops and robbers crap. You want power? You want respect? You can have it. It's waiting for you."

Light seemed to spread over Myron's face. This is what

Myron has been longing for—here was the father he always wanted telling him what to do, paying some tribute to him, being concerned.

"So be a good boy—be a *man*—go out there and do it. Right?"

"Right!" Myron was half out of his seat.

"Okay, Myron, shove off," Papa said, "and don't come back."

Myron marched from the room. He passed Franco Disi, who stood transfixed by the door. Dotty rose from her seat and joined Papa. They started out together and paused at the door, where Franco had his hand extended.

"I don't know how to thank you, Mr. Thorson," Franco said earnestly. "You ever want a good meal, see a show—I got some top entertainment out there—lemme know. Or don't lemme know. Just show up. The place is yours."

"That I may take you up on—the meal."

"How 'bout now?" Franco insisted.

"Not tonight," Papa explained. "Gotta go to Canada tomorrow morning."

Dotty looked up at him with surprise. "Canada?"

"I'll tell you about it," Papa said, shaking Franco's hand.

While they waited for the car to be brought around a smile crossed Papa's face. He winked at Dotty. "I think I missed my calling."

The argument began quietly on the ride home. Nothing in particular touched it off. It started like always, with a comment taken the wrong way. Dotty began the ride seated close to Papa. Halfway home she was pressed against the passenger door delivering her comments out the window.

"You don't *have* to go to Canada," she said.

"No, you're right, I don't. Why don't you go? You can pay the bills."

"That's not what I meant."

"What, then?"

"It's a long drive. You haven't been feeling good lately, have you? You haven't, have you?"

"I've been feeling all right."

"That's not what you said."

"I am fine," he said emphatically.

"You don't look it."

"Thanks a lot."

"That's not what I meant."

"That's the second thing you didn't mean. What *do* you mean?"

Dotty paused and refolded her hands in her lap.

"I'm worried about you," she muttered.

"I'll be all right."

"I mean it."

Papa squashed one cigarette, lit another one, and followed the arrow pointing to the Hollywood Freeway.

"Know what I mean?" she asked.

"Yes, I know what you mean."

"What about Canada?"

"What about it?"

"You won't go?"

"I will go."

"But . . ."

He looked over at her.

"Get off my back, okay? I'm going, with Ramsey, for thirty-five thousand dollars, of which I'll hopefully make three thousand, which will pay for your baby."

"Our baby," said Dotty, by now having moved to the window. "I don't want you to go to Canada. The baby is due in less than two weeks. What if you're not here?"

"What if I'm not?"

"You don't want to see your own child!"

"It won't go anywhere."

Dotty grunted in disgust.

"What do you want me to say!" Papa said. "I didn't ask for the kid in the first place . . . coming into a society like this—crime and poverty and—"

"Oh, bullshit. Those are stupid reasons. Don't blame it on society. It's you."

"Of course it's me. I'm telling you what bad timing it is to have a kid—"

"You *like* having one. How many forty-nine-year-old men have kids?"

"The stupid ones . . . or the ones who were fooled into it."

"I've heard *that* enough."

"You're goddamn right you have."

Dotty did not stay with Papa that night. She took

Kenny and slept at the apartment she maintained down the street. Papa packed the warm clothes Ramsey suggested, watched the local news and "The Best of Groucho" rerun and, finally, fell asleep during a late movie.

14

Ching and Faust:
Lose One, Win One

The coast highway between Los Angeles and San Francisco is California's Road to Bali. Ramsey and Papa did not have to meet Robert Ching, Sr., until five in the afternoon. It was now seven in the morning and they decided to take the scenic route. They drove through southern highlands, along the shore, and into the muddy flatlands until they reached the winding mountainous road that would take them to San Francisco, ten hours away.

Ramsey drove the first leg through Santa Barbara and San Luis Obispo and watched the coniferous and broadleaf forests on the distant hills. Diesel cabs rumbled south at great speed and sent powerful gusts against the car.

Papa pulled a map of Canada from the glove compartment and with a red pencil traced a route to the British Columbian town of Lytton, on the Fraser River, their ultimate destination. Bobby Ching, Jr., was somewhere in that vicinity, according to Ching's father, who would accompany them in the search.

Canada was an excellent stomping ground for bounty

hunters because Canadian extradition law made it almost impossible to legally bring back a fugitive. Canada would only extradite on a matter which was also a crime in Canada. It also charged the U.S. bondsman or insurance company with paying the Canadian Queen's Counsel, all court costs and the defense attorney. The tab normally fell between $5,000 and $10,000 and there was still a very good chance that the fugitive would get off. Bounty hunters were a cheaper bet.

Bobby Ching, Jr., skipped bail in Los Angeles after he allegedly killed a man in a West Hollywood apartment. His father had put up the mandatory 10 percent of the $75,000 bail.

"I ran a check on the old man," Ramsey told Papa. "He is not exactly poverty stricken, and won't be, even if his kid never comes back."

"What? He owns the Forty-niners?"

"Better than that. On Revolution Boulevard in Tijuana . . ."

"Uh huh."

"Where us Jews own two-thirds of the shops and the Chinese own the rest . . ."

"I can see it clearly."

"Mr. Ching owns *most* of the rest."

"Which means he's got more dough than Richie Blumenthal."

"Makes Richie look like a pauper. But," Ramsey pointed out, "he had to put his San Francisco restaurant up for bail because no insurance company wants Mexican cigar stores for collateral."

"If he used his magic oriental brain he would have left his kid in jail."

They drove the Big Sur among pine forests and shrouded log cabin restaurants with cottages in back and animals in the road. Then they pushed into high country chaperoned by nipple brown hills and horse fences, and down below low-slung cliff homes perched elegantly on their small plateaus. A thousand feet down, the Pacific thundered in.

They reached San Francisco at four thirty and headed for Ching's place, the Pagoda.

"The Pagoda," Papa said. "Isn't that Japanese?"

"Yes, it is."

"And Ching's Chinese. Where do you find these people?"

As usual Chinatown traffic was backed up for blocks. People in colored silk pajamas and business suits milled in the street. Food odors wafted out from restaurants and portable radios blared. Beautiful oriental children bounced along in their parents' backpacks and wizened old women with dark slanted eyes and black dresses gathered on street corners in threes and fours. Papa heard oriental music drifting down from second-floor windows where men and women stood watching the scene below.

Thirty minutes later Ramsey pulled in front of the Pagoda, a garish building with light treated wood and palm trees and small huts where intimate couples ate their meals. The Pagoda was in a class of its own. Namely, the tourist class.

They found Robert Ching, Sr., eating alone in the back room. Ching welcomed them and told his man to bring food for his guests. Ching was small and bald, about fifty-five, with skin the color of dried mustard. He wore a dull cotton shirt and brown pants and a cluster of diamonds on his right pinky. One of his eyes was larger and more bloodshot than the other and the eyebrow above it made a wide black arch. He had no lashes or lips and when he talked his mouth barely moved.

"What I want you to do," Ching told them, "is talk to my son. Talk to him. Make him come back. Tell him what I will lose. Tell him how he hurts me. Tell him that no harm will come to him."

"That he won't believe," Papa said. "He already knows. That's why he's in Canada." Papa paused for a moment, staring down at him. "Mr. Ching, have you talked to your son recently?"

"Two day back."

"Did he mention two other men who went up there looking for him?"

The expression on Ching's face confirmed it.

"Did he tell you what happened to them?" Papa asked.

There it was again.

"*What* happened to them?"

Ching shrugged. Papa looked him in the eye. "I didn't hear you."

"They meet with . . . ill health."

"And you think we can talk sonny boy into coming

back?" Papa pushed the food away. "Do you realize that two guys have already died, in addition to the one he killed in the first place. What makes you think he won't do us in?"

"He gave his word."

"I'll bet he did."

"I give you fifteen thousand dollar more. That make fifty. Twen'-five one. Twen'-five other. You be rich."

Papa now understood how Ching made good on Revolution Boulevard.

"Talk him back," Ching insisted. "No guns. He not want to fight. He tell me that."

"Did he also tell you how many people were with him?"

"None. He is alone."

"Excuse me, Mr. Ching. I want to talk with my partner." Papa led Ramsey back towards the entrance.

"That's fifty grand, twenty-five apiece," Ramsey said. "We could do worse."

"Something's wrong."

"Like your attitude. I need the money. I have expenses. I admit things are weird but we've been in worse binds. Let's play it out and if it looks ridiculous we can split."

"Whoa!" Papa presented a palm to the front of Ramsey's face. "Two guys dead already. Ching dresses the deal with fifteen thousand dollars and . . ."

"You 'whoa,' " Ramsey said, cutting him off. "This is *my* case . . ."

"Then take it. It's all yours."

"Wait a minute! I got the call and called you. You obligated yourself when you said 'yes.' Now you want to renege."

"Go ahead."

"And if anything happens to me you will be partially to blame."

"Just a—"

"That's a *fact!*" Ramsey waited. "You talk about honor, an honorable man."

Papa's face grew still. "Am I not?"

"You are, and I can't understand why you're arguing with me. There should be no question. You *have* to come. You gave me your word."

"Ramsey."

"What?"

"How scared are you?"

"I'm terrified."

"Then why go on?"

"I told you, I'm *broke!* I have to pay alimony."

"Even my wife loved me more than that."

"Are you in or out?"

They walked back to the table and told Ching to be ready in half an hour. He was at the car in ten minutes and his bag was loaded in the trunk. Ching sat alone in the back. Papa drove, turning the radio knob until he discovered a station playing Ravel's *Bolero.* Ramsey stared out the window at the swamps and steppe grass irrigated by the San Francisco Bay.

Back in North Hollywood Rocco Mason sat behind the wheel of his old Chevrolet. He'd been watching Papa's house for over an hour. Before that he had called Papa's number and Dotty answered. Mason identified himself as Sergeant Jacks of the LAPD and said he was trying to locate Papa. Dotty told him that Papa would be out of town for two or three days.

It was not Papa who Rocco Mason sought. He wanted Dotty, which would be the first step in an elaborate plan Mason and his two buddies had concocted to make Papa come to them.

Mason watched the house, his teeth grinding from the amphetamine he took. He sweated profusely. He ran a hand through his hair that he hadn't washed in days and nervously rubbed the grime and sweat on his pants. He smoked cigarette after cigarette and threw the butts out the window when the ashtray overflowed. He unconsciously fingered the red blotches on his face, which the speed brought on. Mason once had a young face before the speed made it old; now he looked forty, though actually he wasn't yet thirty.

When he reached for another cigarette and found the pack empty he opened the car door and got out. A kid raced by on a bike. Two cars passed him and an old man watered his lawn two doors down from Papa's.

Mason didn't expect any trouble, but just in case carried a .357 Magnum, given to him by one of his buddies waiting for him back at his place. Mason had decided to grab Dotty alone, figuring one man would be less conspicuous.

He wore a gray suit that shone metallic in the sunlight and a light blue shirt open at the collar. His teeth contin-

ued grinding and he kept his right forearm tucked close to
feel the revolver tucked in his belt. He had to walk out of
the shadows to cross the street, and the sunlight blinded
him. A third car appeared, and disappeared into its garage.

Mason scaled the steps and heard a dog growl from inside the front door. He slowly withdrew the Magnum but
kept it out of sight within the jacket flap. The dog inside
began to bark.

Mason wasn't sure where Dotty was in the house but he
knew he had to act quickly. He tried the knob and found
it locked. He pulled a thin piece of wire from his pocket
and inserted it in the keyhole.

"Canada!" Ramsey sighed when they crossed the border.
"It's about time," Papa replied.

When no reaction came from Ching, Papa shot a look
to the back seat, where he saw the Chinaman's eyes closed
and his body curled up in the corner.

Papa followed the Fraser River through Chilliwack and
Hope and remembered the hunting trips with his father
into Alberta and Saskatchewan, and how they used to
drive back into Anaconda with two bucks strapped over
the front fenders.

Ramsey leaned back over the seat. "Ching?" he said.

Ching's eyes popped open.

"Wake up. We're getting close."

Ching sat up and looked out the window. "Canada?"

"That's what the sign said."

The main road traveled high above the river. Papa
looked over the edge and watched the rapids surge over
smooth brown rocks jutting from the surf and small bub-
bling waterfalls cascading to a lower level. He spotted
single-man kayaks and canoes pitching and rolling in the
downstream current.

They passed logging camps and log jams and fir and
redwood trees and dairy farms dotting the countryside.
Fur trappers passed them, moving south. They watched
nickel being mined and spotted hydro-electric plants beside
the river, along with pulp and paper mills.

"Goddamn, this place is busy," Ramsey commented. "I
thought we were in the wilderness."

They'd been on the road a good 800 miles since leaving
San Francisco and decided to spend the night in a roadside hotel that looked like a castle. Their meal was extrav-

agant—huge slabs of dark juicy venison soaked in
béarnaise sauce, two bottles of 1964 Château Haut-Brion,
from which Ramsey reluctantly drank one glass. Ching
was a vegetarian and when his food came he pulled a bag
of noodles from his jacket and spinkled them over the top.
Later they all slept in four-poster beds with down-filled
mattresses.

It was after nine the following evening when they pulled
into Lytton. The town was dark and noiseless except for
music from scattered neighborhood bars. Papa parked in
front of the Excelsior Hotel.

They checked in, Ching having called in reservations
from San Francisco, and went to the coffee shop, where
battle plans were drawn.

"What time are we supposed to see your son?" Papa
asked.

Ching checked his watch. "One o'clock."

"In the morning? You mean three hours from now?"

Ching nodded.

"Why?" Papa wanted to know.

"Why?"

"Why one in the morning. Why not one in the afternoon?"

Ching shrugged.

"Bobby sleep during day."

"We drive all day while sonny sleeps. That's great. Anything else we should know about?"

"You must promise not to force him to come with you,"
Ching insisted.

"I wouldn't think of it," Papa said. "You, Ramsey?"

"Never crossed my mind."

"Well," Papa said, picking stray bits of egg salad from
his beard, "we've got a couple hours to kill. Whaddya
want to do? How 'bout one of those bars we passed?"

Before Ramsey could agree, Ching held up one finger
and said, "One moment, prease."

Ching had an announcement for them. "Two hour. It
take two hour to find my son."

"What do you mean?" Ramsey asked, looking over at
Papa.

"I mean he's not here."

"Not here?" Papa asked.

"No."

"Where, then?"

"Somewhere else."

"That's logical. You wanna give us a hint or should we guess?"

"I take you to him." Ching smiled. "Bobby said I should do that so you not call cops."

"Smart cookie, your son."

"Cookie," Ching replied, holding the smile.

Ramsey pushed himself from the table. "Why don't we go up and change and meet in the lobby in half an hour." He reached into his pocket for cash to pay the bill. Ching stopped him. "You pay last meal. I pay this."

Ramsey looked at him. "That's white of you, Ching," Ramsey said straight-faced. He'd picked up the meal tab back at the castle—sixty bucks. Ching drew three singles from his wallet and placed them on the table. The sixty went on the expense voucher but that wasn't the principle as far as Ramsey and Papa were concerned. Here they were about to save the old man's restaurant and he's playing chutes and ladders with the meal checks.

A few minutes later Ramsey went to Papa's room to device strategy. No weapons, Ching had said.

"Mace," said Papa.

"It'll have to do," Ramsey agreed.

"The rest we'll hide under the seat."

"Ching's not as dumb as he looks, is he?" Ramsey said.

"Not even close."

"Which means his kid is probably no slouch either."

"I have that feeling." Ramsey held the leather jacket for Papa to slide his arms through.

"Just had a bad thought," Papa said. "What if this is a set-up, what if Little Ching blasts us as a warning to anybody else coming after him?"

"What if you stop worrying so much and think about the money."

"I try."

"And?"

"I'll try again."

Ching was waiting in the front seat when they got to the car and Papa told him to get in the back. Ramsey hid the Prowler Fouler and two .45s under his seat.

"Okay, Mr. Ching," Papa said. "Navigate."

"Turn around, go five miles east, turn right."

Ramsey leaned back over the seat and smiled. "Got any Chinese proverbs you want to pass the time with?"

"I don't know Chinese proverbs," Ching said.

They drove the five miles in silence and turned right.

The road was horrible. Mud puddles from a recent rain filled large potholes and played havoc on the Plymouth's shocks. The heavy mist made it impossible for Papa to see more than a few feet ahead. There was no moon.

"Mr. Ching, how much further?" Papa asked.

"Thirty mile."

"What!"

"He said thirty," Ramsey replied.

"I'll need a new car after this," Papa mumbled.

They bumped along the road at fifteen miles an hour. A squeak developed at the right front wheel. Papa could find no music on the radio. Ramsey squirmed in the front seat until he fell asleep. Papa looked through the rear-view mirror and saw Ching who sat upright, eyes wide.

The night was pitch black. Ferrets and field mice and rabbits scurried across the headlight beams. The road grew more treacherous as asphalt turned to gravel and then to dirt, all of it marked by holes deep as craters. Papa stayed awake by trying to avoid them. His eyes burned and he kept turning the heater up and down looking for the right temperature. Outside it had dropped to below freezing.

"Here!" Ching cried out suddenly. Ramsey bolted. Papa pressed the brake.

"Where?"

"Here," Ching repeated, pointing to the left. "Go here."

Papa turned and found himself on a side road as bad as the road he'd just left. The terrain looked the same, what he could see of it, a few trees sprinkled along the roadside, flatland beyond. It seemed a desert.

Two hundred yards along Ching again called out: "Here!"

"Here, what!"

"Here. We are here."

Papa looked out the window. He squinted his eyes and saw the faint glow from . . . inside a house. He was parked on somebody's front lawn.

"I love to come in like this," Papa said. "Right up to the front door. How do you do? We're here to take you to jail." He looked over at Ramsey. "United Insurance, huh? You sure know how to pick 'em."

When Papa climbed out he saw another surprise seated in a chair on the front porch. A young Chinaman with a

Winchester across his lap and criss-crossed bandoliers on his chest. The Chinaman rocked gently, paying them no attention.

"What the hell is *that?*" Papa said. Ching shrugged. Ramsey felt for the mace cannisters inside his jacket.

What Papa could see of it the house was a large, rambling structure that extended into the darkness behind. To their surprise, the Chinaman made no move to stop them as they entered through the front door. The glow came from a single lantern burning on a table in the center of the large room. Four straight-backed chairs sat around the table. In the chair that faced the door was Bobby Ching, who rose to greet his father to whom he bowed ceremoniously. Little Ching nodded to Papa and Ramsey, came around the table and led his father to a chair.

There was little similarity between father and son. Bobby was taller and had a full head of black hair, parted in the center, that fell over his shoulders. He wore a heavy white parka with a gray fur collar, jeans and climbing boots. When he moved he took short, direct strides and seemed to Papa a very deliberate young man. The glow from the lantern gave Ching's face a demonic quality, with the shadows rising high over his cheekbones and eyes. The Chings began speaking quietly to each other in Chinese. The father did most of the talking, every so often gesturing towards Papa and Ramsey who remained by the door.

Papa inspected the room: gray cement walls with paint peeling away; gutted out windows that made the place look as if it had been the victim of a bombing attack. Apparently no one had lived here for years. Papa had no idea what lay beyond the room, in the back, except that he made out the side of a distant wall as the light flickered against it. Beyond the gutted out windows, total blackness. The floor, also of cement, held two piles of wood shavings tucked in one corner and a small rickety table on which a coffee urn and a half dozen metal cups sat. What were a half dozen cups doing there when Ching was supposed to be alone? And who was the Chinaman with the Winchester?

"Alone? Is that what Ching said?" Ramsey asked.

"Twice."

"And how 'bout those other cars outside?"

"What cars?"

"You didn't see them?"

"No."

Ramsey tweaked his nose. "Three of them, over near the barn."

"Barn?"

"Yeah, there's one of those, and who in hell is the guy on the front porch?"

"Must be one of those Chinacanadians we heard so much about."

Papa glanced around the room and back to Ramsey. "One Chinaman, three cars, and all those black holes in the wall. What's behind all those black holes?"

"Another thing to make me paranoid."

"I've seen ten Chinamen stuff themselves into one car. Three times ten means there might be a lot of people watching us right now."

"And aiming at us."

"That, too."

"Hello there?" Ching called to them. Ramsey and Papa ambled over to the table.

"You tell my son why best to go back," Ching said to Papa.

"You tell him, Ramsey," Papa said with encouragement.

"Oh, let's see. Indian summer. The football season. American women."

"Cool the jokes," said Little Ching with a disdainful look.

"Right. Then how 'bout if I ask you a couple of questions so we can *really* find out why you should go back. Question one: Papa?"

Papa reached out and pulled the lantern closer. "This guy you killed . . ." he said.

"Allegedly killed," said Little Ching.

"Mmm hmm. Why did you allegedly kill him?"

"Stole my drugs."

"He stole your drugs. That's too bad. What about pleading temporary insanity."

"More jokes?"

"No, I'm serious. Maybe you were slightly crazy at the time, didn't know what you were doing."

"I knew."

"What about self-defense?"

Little Ching laughed at that.

Papa figured it was time to use the only ace available in this ridiculous case. He gestured towards the old man. "You want your own father to go broke?"

"Will you go broke, father?" Little Ching asked.

Big Ching paused. "In San Francisco," he said.

"His pride and joy gobbled up by an insurance company?"

"He can build another."

"A restaurant he's had for—how many years, Mr. Ching?"

"Thirty-eight."

"Thirty-eight years in the same place," Papa declared. "It's like losing one of his arms. A new restaurant, in a new place. It's not the same."

Little Ching began talking in Chinese all over again. In the midst of it Big Ching said to Papa, "Excuse, please. Be with you."

They returned to their corner. Ramsey pulled a chair over, sat down and looked up at Papa. "You gave it your best shot."

"What are we doing here?"

Papa stuck his hands in his pockets and moved away from Ramsey. He paused by the door, glanced into the darkness and walked outside. The Chinaman was still there. Rocking.

"Hello," Papa said to him.

"Hello."

"Cold, eh?"

The Chinaman nodded.

Papa lifted his head and stared out over the dark expanse. "Beautiful night, clear."

The Chinaman nodded.

Papa turned to the Chinaman and looked at his weapon. "Winchester. Old, huh?"

"Old."

Papa extended his arm. "Mind if I take a look?"

The Chinaman grunted and handed over the rifle. Papa pumped it once and checked for cartridges. It was loaded. The Chinaman gave him a large toothy grin.

"Mind if I show it to my friend?"

The Chinaman waved his okay and Papa carried the weapon back inside. When Ramsey saw the rifle he stiffened. The Chings glanced casually at Papa and went back to their conversation. Somewhere off in the distance a wolf howled. Papa stood near the door wondering what to do next. Little Ching had given no sign of concern and that worried him most of all. His eyes once more scanned the black holes.

"Ramsey?"

"What?"

"This is a *lousy* situation."

"Amen."

Papa cocked the Winchester once more. The sound crackled through the room. Little Ching looked up and smiled. "Very old gun."

"Got one myself," Papa replied.

Now that Papa had the rifle he could put the plan into action. It would be a simple matter to aim the Winchester at Little Ching and order him to rise and walk through the door to the car. Ramsey would drop mace on the floor, over by the black holes, to shield their exit. They would move out slowly, keeping the barrel against Little Ching's head. Then they would haul ass out of there, making sure to put slugs in the tires of the cars outside. That was the plan. Papa knew it. Ramsey knew it.

Papa slowly raised the rifle. Ramsey's hands were locked on the mace cannisters. He was half out of the chair ready to lob the cannisters to the floor. The Chings talked on in Chinese. The Chinaman's rocking chair squeaked outside the door. Black holes surrounded the room. The lantern flickered.

Then it started, the laugh, from deep in Papa's throat. It rolled from his mouth, high-pitched and nervous, and it filled the room. He couldn't stop. The rifle lowered and Papa bent over with the pain the laughter brought to his stomach.

The Chings looked at him, startled. Then it was Ramsey's turn to see the light, or understand the lack of it . . . black holes. His rattled laugh erupted and matched Papa's. They made a symphony together. Ramsey pitched and rolled in the chair. Papa rocked on the balls of his feet. They laughed, they guffawed. Tears were in their eyes when they finally settled down, breathing heavily, their lips cracking in the freezing air.

"Hey, you know what?" Papa said, laughing harder.

"Wh . . . what!"

"We . . . we just blew . . . ha, ha, ha . . . we just blew thirty-five grand!"

"So . . . so how come you're laughing?"

"What *else* can I do?"

Papa turned and walked out through the door to the

porch where he handed the Winchester to the Chinaman, thanking him, and returned inside.

Little Ching rose and walked to the small table where he filled four cups with coffee and carried them back to his seat. Papa and Ramsey joined them.

Papa took a swallow and almost threw up. It was the worst coffee he ever had. It wasn't *even* coffee. He had no idea what it was. He checked to see if Little Ching was drinking. He was. At least it wasn't poison, although to Papa's mind poison had to taste a hell of a lot better than this.

"You're actually drinking?" Papa could hardly believe Ramsey was doing it.

"It's not bad."

Big Ching called them over. "My son," he told them, "will go back with us."

"You will?" Papa asked, trying to cover his astonishment.

"Yes."

"When?"

"Tomorrow morning."

"Why not now?"

"I have things to do. You go back to the hotel and return tomorrow morning. Nine o'clock. I will be here."

Another one of Little Ching's famous promises, Papa thought. "That's two hours in, two back, and it's three now. Why don't we wait? Couple more hours won't kill us."

"Can you be sure?" Ramsey said from the corner of his mouth.

"No, no," said Little Ching. "It is better my way."

"It certainly is," Ramsey said in another aside.

Papa cocked his head. "I'd sure hate to drive all the way out here again and find you gone."

"I give you my word," Little Ching promised.

There you go again, Papa said to himself. My Word I'll come back. My Word I'm alone. Way too many holes in Little Ching's Words.

Papa was still pushing. "Wouldn't you like to sleep in a comfortable bed in a nice hotel. Have breakfast. We bring you back in the morning. Do your thing. There's no rush."

"We do it my way. Best for everyone." Little Ching was just insistent enough for Papa to not push him further.

"Okay, Mr. Ching, we have to go now. We'll come back for your son in the morning."

The old man took Junior's hands and thanked him in Chinese. They embraced. More words were spoken. On his way out Papa nodded to the Chinaman on the porch. "See you later." See you later? he thought. When hell freezes over.

Little Ching walked them out and Papa spotted the three cars Ramsey had mentioned. All late-model Buicks.

Little Ching shook Papa's hand goodbye and said, "I want to congratulate you on your good sense. You must be very successful in your business."

Papa stared him in the eye. "Most of the time," he said.

"Understand, Mr. Thorson. All this I do for my father. My father would give up everything he has to get me back. The restaurant? It does not live without me there, just as my father does not understand what I must do."

Little Ching talked straight. He explained the situation. No hard feelings but that's the way it goes.

Papa got in the car, backed onto the road and drove slowly away.

They had gone a half mile when Papa turned to Ramsey and said, "Three things are for certain. Bobby Ching, Jr., will not be there tomorrow morning, that's one. And number two—we are driving out alive."

"And the third . . . ?"

"Those two other guys who went after Ching . . ."

"What about them?"

"They *tried* to snatch him. No wonder they're dead."

"My son," Ching said from the back seat, "he will be there."

"You bet."

"He-will-be-there!" Ching pounded the seat with each word. "You must go back tomorrow."

"Oh, I'll go back," Papa said.

Ramsey jerked upright. "You will!"

"Oh, yeah. I've got to check something out."

At seven thirty the next morning they were bouncing over the potholes once again as Papa cursed every miserable crunch of the tires.

The land was different during the day. There were mountains in the distance and flocks of mallards winging through the sky and farmers with big hats driving antique red tractors along the road. Leaves fell from the trees and made a patchwork of colors on the land. Autumn had made its appearance and with it a constant wind that rustled through the birch and maple and blew the leaves across the road.

They came upon the house which in the light was far different than Papa had envisioned it in the dark of last night. The desert that he imagined surrounded the house was instead a garden and the foot of a mountain that climbed a thousand feet behind the house. Tall sycamores guarded the barn where the Buicks had been parked, and the porch where the Chinaman sat was termite infested and ready to fall away from the main building. The rocking chair remained, rocking in the wind. Some of the gutted out windows still had frames and from one of them a chicken jumped to the ground and raced across the hard dirt towards the barn.

Papa pulled in front of the porch and the three of them got out. Inside the house nothing was different; the lantern sat on the table; the coffee urn and cups were in the same place.

What Papa was looking for would not be inside but outside near the windows. He found them. Scattered on the ground were empty shotgun shells, a set of sterling silver .38 caliber grips with gold inlay, three 12-gauge shotguns, and the Chinaman's Winchester.

Papa and Ramsey stood silently over the paraphernalia. There wasn't much to be said. It was only what they'd suspected. Had either of them made a false move the previous night they would have been caught in a massive cross-fire. Here in the bright morning the strong potentiality of death struck them as something other than a laughing matter. Absolute certainty. Ironically it was laughter that had saved their lives. But there was no laughter now as they reconstructed, in their minds, the small Chinese army who had trained their guns through the black holes, waiting, probably hoping, for the moment to open fire.

Papa reached down and picked up the .38 with the silver grips.

"Not a bad set," he said. The grip was the most valuable part of the gun. "Worth slightly less than thirty-five grand."

Papa knew why Ching had left the artillery; the kid and his bandits were most likely across the border by now and the border was no place to be caught with stolen weapons, which these had to be.

Old man Ching came up behind them with a paper in his hand. The script was in Chinese and, said Ching, addressed to him. He read it to them.

"Dear Father.

Understand. I cannot go to jail which these men would have me do. I am still young and do not want . . to spend my life without freedom. My friends and I are going to another place to find freedom. You understand. I am sorry about your restaurant. I love you for releasing me with the bail money, which I know was a great sum, but for no sum can I submit myself to the police. They will destroy me. You can tell your friends, who are police, to thank you for being alive. In your presence I would kill no one. Unless they forced me to. They were smart enough to see that. I love you and will contact you soon.

Bobby."

Ching lowered the letter and glared at them.

"You are police?" he asked.

"No."

"My son says you are police."

"Your son thinks everyone is police." Papa said.

Ching lowered his head and walked to the car. Papa and Ramsey followed and they drove away from the house with the black holes.

On the way back to Lytton, Ching fretted in the back, Papa considered ways to salvage the trip. Knowing United Insurance as he did it would be hell collecting expense money from them. The Plymouth was about ruined and between him and Ramsey over $300 had already been spent.

"Got any ideas?" he asked Ramsey.

"About what?"

"How to salvage something from this fiasco."

"We could rob a gold mine."

"Forget I asked."

"I already have . . ."

Papa estimates that on between 20 and 25 percent of his cases he never got his man.

"The Ching thing was a good example of what happens

when you wade through tons of crap and then when you finally come out, what do you find? More of the same.

"Ramsey and I were never closer to death than up in that house with those shotguns trained on us. I could almost feel fingers squeezing triggers when I cocked the Winchester. That's part of the business, knowing when to pull back, knowing when your ass is in a sling. I took it as far as I could, as far as I was *willing* to take it. In that way I was in charge of the situation; I had the choice. But the odds were so damn bad there was no *way* we could have come out alive. There's a small governor in my head that goes off, a signal that nearly thirty years of chasing these characters has made very sharp. And out there, through those black holes, the signal was coming in loud and clear: Back Off . . .

Two hours later they pulled into Lytton, at the junction of the Fraser and Thompson rivers, where Papa called two Seattle bondsmen, neither of whom had anyone they wanted snatched. On an outside chance he called San Francisco for Manny Tiger.

"Papa!" Manny exclaimed. "How the hell are you?"

"Tired. Listen, Manny, I'm up here in British Columbia and—"

Manny interrupted. "Hey, hunting or fishing?"

"Both. I just lost a big one. Took off like a bolt out of hell and—"

Manny broke in again. "And you wanna know if I got somebody, so it shouldn't be a total loss."

"That's right."

"You're in luck."

"Whaddya got?"

Papa could hear Manny Tiger rustling through papers.

"Faust," Manny said. "Helmut Faust. Let's see. Jumped three months ago. Ten thousand forfeiture. Oral copulation and sodomy."

"Wonderful."

"I got an address on Faust. Where are you?"

"One hundred miles north of the Washington border."

"Anywhere near Hope?"

"Hope?" Papa thought for a second. "We passed it on the way up."

"Two-oh-three Summerland Avenue in Hope."

Papa repeated the address and wrote it in his notebook. "Description?" Papa asked.

"Five ten. Hundred and seventy. Black hair, gray at the temples. No distinguishing marks."

"That sounds like you, Manny."

Manny ignored that. "Slight German accent."

"Armed?"

"And considered dangerous. Ten thousand bail."

"And my commission?"

"Twenty percent."

"Twenty percent!"

"Plus expenses."

"Expenses? I'm already here. Manny, armed and considered dangerous. This is no paperhanger I'm going after."

"All right. Thirty. That's the best I can do. Take it or leave it."

Papa mentally tallied the figures. Thirty percent of ten grand was three thousand, split two ways, gave him fifteen hundred. "Plus expenses," Papa added.

He listened to the silence on the other end.

"Done," Manny finally said. "But," he warned, "the expenses . . . keep it under five hundred, okay?"

"Under five hundred."

"*Way* under. See you in a coupla days, Papa." Manny rang off.

It was after two when they reached Hope and checked into a hotel. Ching called the local airport and chartered a plane back to San Francisco. Before Ching took off Papa remembered something.

"Mr. Ching," he said. "Didn't you promise fifteen thousand dollars whether we took your son or not? Didn't he do that, Ramsey?"

"He sure as hell did!" Ramsey's spirits soared. "What about that fifteen thousand, Mr. Ching?"

"Don't remember nothing."

"Wait a minute!" Ramsey protested. "In your restaurant, you promised to pay us, goddammit."

"No, no." Ching tried to leave. Ramsey blocked his way.

"Yes, yes," said Ramsey.

"Do not touch me. I have you arrested."

"Listen, *punk*," Ramsey hoisted him up by the shoulders. "You ain't leaving till you pay off."

"I have no cash."

"We'll take a check," said Papa. "Forget it, we won't take a check." Ching would stop payment on it. "Let him go, Ramsey. We'll get to him later."

Before releasing him Ramsey pulled Ching so close their noses touched. "Ching," Ramsey scowled, breathing up the Chinaman's nostrils. "I hope your kid never comes back. I hope your crummy restaurant burns to the ground, with you in it. And when they bury you I hope it's under a mountain of egg foo young. You're a pissant excuse for a man. A liar. A total fucking asshole. I'm gonna have the Frisco cops tail you. I'm gonna have the IRS check your books. And I'm gonna have the Chinese Mafia put the squeeze on you, *so tight*, that your squinty fucking eyes are gonna turn straight up and down. Don't *ever* cross my path, 'cause I'll run your ass into the ground. Now, get outa here!" Ramsey dropped him. Ching's legs buckled when he hit the floor and he fell over.

"Out!" Ramsey screeched.

Ching crawled from the room, clutching his small overnight bag to his chest.

"You sure told him," Papa said after Ching had gone.

"I'd forgotten all about the fifteen grand. If I didn't know the creep had so much money . . ." Ramsey stopped in midsentence. "Screw it, I would have done the same thing."

"Now what do we do about Helmut Faust," Papa said.

Papa and Ramsey drove to the outskirts of Hope, where they found two-oh-three Summerland Avenue, a two-story frame house nestled among giant fir trees. The house sat a good hundred yards back from the road. A driveway led to an adjacent garage where an old Mercedes was parked. By this time Papa's car was really acting up. It badly needed a new set of shocks and probably front- and rear-end work. As they sat watching the house Papa wondered how he might write off the repairs to Manny Tiger's expense account.

"Let's use our imaginations for a change," Papa suggested.

"All right," Ramsey agreed. "Let's."

They spent the next twenty minutes using their imaginations.

"Well?" said Ramsey, shaking dandruff from his sandy hair.

"Not on the seat," Papa scolded him.

"I've used my imagination," Ramsey announced.

"And?"

"It's blank."

"So is mine."

"Good. Now let's figure out how to snatch this guy."

"Helmut Faust is probably not alone," Papa said.

"After Little Ching nobody will ever be alone again."
Papa smacked his lips.

"Anybody ever tell you about that?" Ramsey asked.

"What?"

"Smacking your lips. You do it all the time."

"No, you're the first."

"You *do* do it all the time. How long have we known
each other?"

"I don't know, six years."

"You've always done that, smacking your lips."

"I know."

"Hmm," Ramsey said, staring at the lips.

Papa looked over at him. "Do you mind?"

"I bet if you got that cured you'd lose weight, no shit,
you would." Ramsey imitated the smacking. "It's like—
smack, smack—calling out for food. You know—smack,
smack—telling it to hurry up and climb in your mouth."

Papa didn't mind jokes about his weight from Ramsey.

"What'll it be," Ramsey said, changing the subject.
"Rush in or sneak in?"

"Neither one."

"Fly in or tunnel in?"

"Nope."

"Walk in?"

Papa shook his head. "Plow in."

"Plow in?"

They remained down the road for another hour. No one
came or went. The house lights flickered on as darkness
blanketed the area. A few minutes later Papa started the
car and drove back to Hope.

Early the next morning Papa went hunting for a
mechanic with an old truck to sell, and shortly found one.

"You can't fix my car for less than two hundred dollars?" Papa asked the mechanic.

"No way."

"And you want how much for the truck?" Papa ges-

tured towards the '52 Ford pickup parked alongside the
garage.

"Runs like a top."

"I need it for two miles."

The mechanic thought that was funny. "Two hundred."

"Two hundred for that wreck?"

"I put a lot of muscle in that wreck, I'll have you
know."

"Tell you what," Papa told him. "I'll give you three
hundred for the truck *and* the repairs."

When the man hesitated Papa added, "Or I'll take my
business down the street. I'm sure there's a lot of trucks in
this town."

"All right, three hundred, but you're getting a helluva
bargain."

"So are you," Papa assured him, and then said, "All I
want on the receipt is: One Truck—three hundred dollars.
No repairs, nothing. Just the truck. Got it?"

The reason for this was that Manny Tiger would not
pay for car repairs but he would pay for the truck as a
necessary item for the capture of Helmut Faust.

Papa said he wanted the Plymouth ready by the following afternoon. He got in the truck and started back for the
hotel where Ramsey was probably still sleeping.

Ramsey surprised him by being up and dressed and they
ate breakfast downstairs. Later, in the street outside the
hotel, Papa pointed to their new machine.

"Elegant," Ramsey said. "Where's the car?"

"Getting patched up."

"Are you going to tell me what the plan is?"

"Yup."

Ramsey waited, then said, "When?"

"Soon as I can figure out what it is," he said, and
started out for Helmut Faust's.

Papa parked where he had the previous evening. Here
in the early morning the area was greener and perfectly
matched the color of the truck.

"True environmental protection," he told Ramsey, who
said what a bad pun that was and took a look at the
house. It was mostly hidden by the trees around it but he
was able to spot the Mercedes parked by the front door.

Papa smacked his lips and blew his nose and said to
Ramsey, "Here's what we're going to do." He pointed his
finger up ahead toward a cluster of bushes. "You're going

to hide behind that bush. I'm going to stay in the truck. When you see that Mercedes coming down the drive, signal me," Papa said, and then warned, "There may be a half dozen guys in there with Faust."

"Sodomizing all over the place."

"So when we move it's gotta be real fast. You make your break when I take this thing off." Papa reached in the boot behind the seat and pulled out an orange and brown hunting cap with ear flaps. He clamped it over his head and popped up the visor.

"Marjorie Main?" Ramsey said.

"Zazu Pitts," replied Papa. "Let's get this show on the road."

Ramsey stepped from the truck, felt with his upper arm for the .45 sheathed in the shoulder holster and, crouching low with his fingertips skimming the grass before him, lumbered toward his hideout up ahead. He kept one eye on the house for movement. Papa watched him maneuvering through the trees, the lambskin collar weaving in and out of view. For Papa, Ramsey had always been the warrior. If it wasn't bounty hunting, Ramsey would have been a soldier of fortune. Ramsey's enemies were all big—governments, armies, nations. And their injustices were even bigger. When Ramsey defended he defended for everybody and became both the spokesman and the lawyer. The world was his client. He was also one hell of a bounty hunter. Each time they went on a case together Papa became more convinced that Ramsey was the best partner he'd ever had.

Papa saw Ramsey reach his spot and wave, to which he flashed the headlights. They waited. For three hours. With nothing to study but the scenery which in time they knew by heart. This was the worst part of the job—the stakeout. It was boring and time consuming and it hurt your eyes. It was lonely. And it made you think negative thoughts. A stake-out, as far as Papa was concerned, was the last step before hell.

It was noon when Papa saw Ramsey's signal. He peeked around the trees and saw the Mercedes backing up and starting down the drive. He cranked up the truck and put it in gear.

The truck eased slowly forward and he could hear the gravel crunch beneath the tires. A high log fence stretched from the tree line across the length of the property. Over the top log Papa could see the black automobile and up ahead, the break in the fence where it would soon appear. Papa slowed down, waiting for the Mercedes to get beyond the fence. He watched it approach the gate. "Goddammit, don't stop," he said aloud. The driver lost no speed in turning the corner but he never completed the turn because Papa plowed the truck into him. The car spun completely around and came to rest in exactly the same position.

Both doors flew open and out leaped Helmut Faust himself and his young driver. Papa was already on the road, barreling toward the car screaming like a banshee, the cap pulled way down over his eyes.

"Where the hell you goin'! What the hell's the *matter* with you! You're supposed to stop over there. Look what you done to my truck!"

Papa noticed that both Helmut and the driver were packing.

He ranted on. "This is my only truck. You ruined it. *I'm* ruined. What are you gonna do!"

Helmut looked more confused than angry when he said, in his smooth Bavarian accent, "Look here, I'm sorry about this. What shall we do?"

"Well," said Papa, removing the cap. "I don't know." Ramsey crept toward the driver. "I have a paper here," Papa continued, patting his chest pockets and moving closer to them. From the corner of his eye he saw Ramsey directly behind the driver.

"You got a license?"

It was a bad question because Helmut turned toward the driver whom he watched get clipped behind the neck by Ramsey's gun.

Faust went inside his jacket. Papa was a split second behind him. Faust was quick and he had the weapon out and raised by the time Papa got the handle on his own.

Faust pulled the trigger and the bullet slammed into his own man. Ramsey hit the dirt before he could fire another.

Papa's right arm swung high from his hip. The .45 was in his fist. He caught Faust with his forearm, on the jaw, and he heard bone crack. Faust's head shifted into an unnatural position and he seemed to freeze in mid-air before sinking to the ground.

Ramsey stuck his head over the fender.

"I'm proud of you," he said.

The truck was a total wreck, so they drove Helmut's Mercedes into Hope where they found the Plymouth ready. They had left Helmut's young driver back at the house; as far as they knew there was no price on his head. They had no authorization to bring him in.

They inspected Helmut's identification and found that he was a German citizen on an extended U.S. visa and therefore not the type of fugitive you wanted to try out on the border patrol, whose interest might supersede their own.

They managed by keeping to the river until Rosedale, then headed south through Sardis and Vedder Crossing and over a dirt road that cut the border just north of Glacier in Washington State. Homeward bound. This trip would not be a total loss.

15

Where's Dotty?

Papa left Helmut Faust with Manny Tiger in San Francisco and drove straight through to Los Angeles. He rode the quick route down 101, an eight-hour shot through wine country and roadside stands stocked with vegetables and farmlands undulating towards the mountains to the east. He was working on adrenalin overdrive now, just past midnight, and looked forward to falling asleep sometime late the next morning.

At nine thirty a.m. he dropped Ramsey at his house on La Brea and started for North Hollywood.

He parked the car in front of the house and climbed the steps to the front door. He inserted the key in the lock and pushed open the door. The first thing he saw was the blood on the rug, two spots the size of silver dollars. The house was quiet and exceptionally clean.

"Dotty!" he called out. Silence. He went out back to the shed to look for Kenny, who wasn't there. Back inside he called the answering service. The girl asked him what was going on.

"What do you mean?"

"People all over have been looking for you. Something about Dotty."

Papa hung up and sped across the street. He was intercepted by Jimmy Webb running down the sidewalk at him. Jimmy came up huffing and puffing and told him the bad news.

". . . and I got in the house. The door was wide open and there was Fang on the rug, a gash in his head. He's down at the vet's, he's okay."

"Where's Dotty?"

"Nobody's seen her, Papa. Her apartment's empty. Kenny don't know where she is. I got people looking everywhere. Missing Person's on it. There's an APB out. I mean, it was two days and nobody saw her, you know. And we couldn't get you—"

"Who hit Fang?"

Jimmy shrugged.

"What about the house? Anything missing?"

"Well, like I said, just Dotty far as I can tell. I checked through but I didn't know what I was looking for."

Just Dotty . . . Papa hurried back across the street and into the house. He checked the bedrooms and his office and the papers behind the bar, the four cases of booze kept in the back room and the refrigerator. Nothing had been touched. He called LAPD Missing Persons and talked with his friend Sergeant Sain who told him a state-wide APB was out on Dotty and cops in four states were on the lookout for her.

Jimmy was close behind him. "I mean, Dotty goes off sometimes but there was Fang with a concussion. I figure . . ."

Papa spent the next half hour with a phone receiver on each ear. He called all the hospitals and Dr. Furey, Dotty's gynecologist. Nothing. Jimmy said he already contacted everybody he knew but no one had reported in. Papa figured there were two hundred bodies searching for Dotty on the street, not counting the police. He left the black phone open for incoming calls.

One came in a moment later and Jimmy answered it. "It's for you," he called from across the room.

Papa took it and said in a voice on edge, "Hello?"

"Well, now," the party said. "I never thought you'd get back."

"Who is this?"

"This is your buddy Rocco Mason, Papa. 'Member me?"

"I'm busy, Mason. Call back some other time."

"Don't hang up! Cause maybe it's me that's *making* you busy."

Oh, God, no, Papa thought, not Mason.

"What does that mean?"

"I got somebody here with me that you know."

"Mason . . ."

"Uh, uh, Papa, don't get riled. Your girl friend's going to be just fine."

"Put her on."

"Hey, no thankyuh. She might say where I am and I ain't quite ready to leave yet. I snatched her, Papa, just like you snatched me."

"Mason, I'll—"

"Now, now, Papa. I don't want to hear no threats. You ain't in a position to threaten me."

"You touch one hair, Mason, and I'll kill you."

"You hear what I jest said, I don't want no threats!" Mason answered in his high-pitched nasal voice.

"What *do* you want, Mason?" Papa said evenly.

"What I wanted all along—you! I'll make a trade. Your woman for you. That's a pretty good deal."

"Where are you?"

"Tokyo." Mason laughed. "Won't buy that? How 'bout Rome?" When Papa didn't answer, Mason continued. "I'm gonna let you stew in your own big fat coupla days. Don't come looking for me cause you'll never find me. Course if you do I hate to think what might happen to the little woman. Soon's I figure out how to make the trade I'll get back to you."

"Mason, when I get ahold of your sick fucking head—"

"Sick! I ain't sick. I never *been* sick. Don't *ever* call me sick. Know why?"

Papa's eyes swept the floor. He pressed the receiver closer to his ear. It sounded as if Mason had left the phone. Then he heard a slap and a woman's scream. Papa gripped the phone so tightly his knuckles turned white.

Mason came back on. *"That's* why," he said. "Be talkin' to you." Mason rang off.

Papa slowly replaced the receiver and caught Jimmy watching him from across the room. "Rocco Mason," he said quietly, his mind working at full tilt.

He glanced up at the wall calendar. September 29th was circled in red. It was the day Dotty was to give birth. Three days away.

Papa sat behind the bar and poured himself a magnum shot of bourbon. The room was dark, the draperies having been pulled across the windows. The air conditioner whirred behind him. Jimmy sat motionless on the sofa. The place felt like a mausoleum.

Papa closed his eyes. A pain grew in the pit of his stomach. He was helpless. He hated it. Hated himself. Dotty . . . the baby. Where was Rocco Mason; the words tumbled over and over in his mind. Where was—

And then finally it hit him. He picked up the phone and began dialing.

PART III

On the island of Maui in the Hawaiian Islands Elmo Sellers was running out of money and patience. His child, much as he loved him, had also become a burden. Sellers had to take him everywhere because he could not afford to hire a sitter. That was what he told himself. Actually he trusted no one and constantly feared that the law or an agent of his estranged wife was nearby waiting for the right moment to take the child back to the mainland.

His wife . . . Sellers still missed her. Despite what she had done to him he never stopped wanting to be with her, and the more he thought about it during the long lonely moments the more he reminded himself that the reconciliation he hoped for could only be possible if he made the first move . . . after all, how could his wife know where he and the baby were hiding?

Elmo Sellers knew that he had made a bad decision running to Maui. On September 28th, the baby in his arms, he boarded a Continental Airlines flight back to Los Angeles.

16

Mason

Papa rode the freeways swerving from lane to lane at seventy-five miles per hour. On the seat beside him was a piece of paper with a hastily scribbled name and address. Two mace cannisters lay on the floor and the Prowler Fouler on the back seat.

It had been a relatively simple but time-consuming matter to find out where Mason was staying, at least where he was supposed to be staying. A call to his parole officer provided the address on Olympic Boulevard. Papa was careful not to ask the parole officer himself because he would have wanted to get into the act. Instead he asked one of the girls he knew in the office to check the information for him. The address on Olympic belonged to a Rachel James.

The conversation was fresh in Papa's mind when he took the exit off the Ventura Freeway. He wondered whether Rocco Mason would be with Rachel James and considered the possibility that Mason might have a cohort or two with him.

Papa arrived at the address and followed the sign pointing to the manager's apartment. The building was white
stucco, set close to the street and surrounded by manicured hedgerows. It had once been a high-rent building
and still retained some of that flavor. Papa walked up the
bleached sidewalk and entered.

Inside the building he located the manager's office and
knocked. An older woman with snow-white hair answered
the door.

"Mrs. Rinaldi?" Papa said, having noticed the name on
the mailbox.

"Yes?" Mrs. Rinaldi replied cautiously.

"Ralph Thorson. I'm inquiring about Rachel James."

"You have identification?"

"Of course." Papa reached for his wallet and showed
her his ID card.

"What would you like to know?"

"What apartment she's in and if she's alone or not."

Mrs. Rinaldi cocked her head up the stairway. "Two
ten, around to the left. Alone?" She shrugged. "Miss
James is seldom alone."

Papa picked at his beard, wondering how to tell Mrs.
Rinaldi that her apartment building might suddenly become a shooting gallery.

"However," she continued. "She was out this morning, I
know that. She came in an hour ago. I was outside on the
lawn. No one was with her."

"In the last couple of days, have you noticed a thin
red-haired woman, pregnant, entering or leaving the
building?"

Mrs. Rinaldi thought for a minute. "No."

"No way she could have slipped by?"

Mrs. Rinaldi gave him a look that said nobody *ever*
slipped by.

"Thank you, Mrs. Rinaldi."

Mrs. Rinaldi stuck a white crooked finger in the air.
"Good hunting," she said.

Papa started up the stairs.

On the second-floor landing he moved quietly down the
corridor until he found 210. He stood outside the door for
a moment, listening. No sound came from inside the
apartment.

"Rachel?" Papa called through the door.

After a moment a voice replied, "What?"

"Rachel? Business."

"I'm sorry, she's not here."

Papa nodded his head. "If you don't open up I'll have to kick it down. You've got five seconds."

The latch flipped open and the lock disengaged. The door opened. The lady had Susan Hayward's red hair, Catherine Deneuve's eyes, Tuesday Weld's mouth, and when she turned back into the room, a backside that was high, round and tight. Rachel James' white cotton robe, ass-high with a tie around the waist, slipped here and fell away there. Papa concentrated very hard on looking her in the eye; he noticed a slight bruise appeared beside the left one.

His .45 was out as he slipped into the bedroom and kitchen—no Mason—and returned to the living room.

Rachel never stopped moving, even when she stood still. Her body swayed to the Temptations from a stereo perched on shelves against the opposite wall.

"I'm looking for Rocco Mason," he told her.

"I don't know Rocco Mason," she said without missing a beat.

"His parole officer says you do."

Rachel sat on a chair and crossed her legs. The robe parted, opening a V at her crotch.

"Where is he?" Papa demanded.

Rachel sighed. "I just don't know what you're talking about."

He leaned forward and placed both hands on Rachel's shoulders. He pulled her forward. "Listen," he said intently, "you'd better tell me where he is or you're going to meet with accidental bone damage."

As Rachel thought about that, Papa shifted his legs so that she couldn't kick him in the balls.

"Where?" he said, squeezing her shoulders.

"That *hurts*." Rachel tried to struggle free. Papa continued the pressure and said in the same even voice, "Hurry up, Rachel, or you'll be compacted. Your bones are giving. Feel them?"

Rachel's eyes widened and Papa saw the dilated pupils where amphetamine was working. He glanced at her bare arms and saw the tracks where she had shot the speed.

"Where?" Papa repeated.

"Mexico."

"Bullshit."

"He *is!* In Mexico. He left this morning, to buy drugs or something."

"Where in Mexico?"

"Mexicali."

"He called me three hours ago, Rachel. How how the hell could he be in Mexico?"

"He called on the way. How do I know?"

"Thanks for nothing," Papa said, and started toward the door.

"I have an address," she called after him.

Papa turned back.

"He gave you an address? How nice of him. What about the woman with him?" He watched her reaction closely.

She hesitated and her eyes closed slightly as if trying to remember something.

"The woman," Papa said, "red hair, pregnant."

"Pregnant?"

"What about her?"

"She . . . she was okay."

Something was very wrong with this entire situation. Somehow the vibes weren't right. Papa was confused.

"The address," he said.

"Yeah, sure." Rachel reached towards the end table and pulled a piece of paper from the stack.

"Twenty-eight Calle Ruiz. Mexicali."

Papa repeated the number and said, "I hope you're telling the truth, Rachel, because if you're not, when Mason's picked up for kidnapping you'll be an accessory. That's worth about twenty years. Now let me ask you again—where is he?"

"Honest! I don't want anything to do with that man. He's fucked up. He's . . ." Then she started to cry.

"I'm wasting my time," he grumbled.

He turned and started from the room. Behind him Rachel stopped crying and called after him.

"That's what he said! He's there! He's in Mexico! He told me!"

Papa could hear her all the way down the stairs and into the street, where he climbed into the car and squealed away from the curb.

At the first phone booth he found he made a call to Billy Whitelaw.

"Billy," he said, "what're you doing right now?"

"Watching a movie. Jimmy Stewart is—"

"Is your plane gassed up?"

"Yeah, but—"

"Van Nuys Airport?"

"Yeah. What's—"

"Meet me there in twenty minutes. We're going to Mexico."

17

End of a Life

Billy Whitelaw had his Twin Comanche ready by the time
Papa arrived at the airport. Papa hurried across the airstrip, climbed up and strapped himself into the co-pilot
seat. Billy checked his watch and shook his head.

"Twenty minutes?" he said. "Man, you're never on
time."

"Sorry."

"Should I ask you what's this sudden hard-on you got
for Mexico?"

"I'll tell you. Let's go."

Billy looked out the window and yelled, "Clear!" and
radioed in. "Tower, this is Twin Comanche Four Five
Yankee ready for takeoff."

"Roger, Four Five Yankee, taxi for takeoff."

Billy took the aircraft to the head of the runway where
he set the brakes and opened the power flaps, setting them
to fifteen degrees. He sent the throttle to 2200 rpms and
watched the engine gauges go into green. The magnetos
checked out, and the flaps, and he dropped the throttle

back to 1000 rpms. The feathering checked. He idled and reset the mixture.

"Twin Comanche Four Five Yankee, ready."

"Roger Four Five Yankee. Clear for immediate takeoff!"

The plane started down the runway's center line at 85 mph, at which point Billy pulled back the yolk and they were airborne.

When he felt the landing gear pull inside, Papa sat back and breathed deeply. The Comanche climbed to 5,500 feet and leveled off. Billy pushed the transponder which appeared on tower control's radioscope as a beeping white dot. Billy would fly IFR to Mexico, letting the towers along the way guide him in. It was the safest way with all the commercial and Air Force traffic in the sky.

Here was Billy Whitelaw—who looked like Andy Griffin's twin brother—in Papa's estimation a complete lunatic when it came to planes, motorcycles, cars, anything on wheels. Yet Billy's destinations were always reached, which made him the most reliable pilot Papa knew. They used to team up together on repossessed airplane snatches. Billy's main job was locating the plane, driving up to it and flying it back to whomever or whatever owned it. He took Papa along because Papa knew how to fly airplanes and Billy was a firm believer in co-pilots.

The case they had worked on together was down in Baja, not a repo job but just as hairy. It was a regular snatch where Papa grabbed the guy and brought him back to the beach where Billy had landed the lightweight Apache he was flying at the time.

Papa's prisoner had friends who were on his tail so he quickly got the guy into the plane and told Billy to take off. Billy taxied down the hard sand but couldn't get a liftoff. The problem was weight. Papa and Billy together hovered at the 550-pound mark and the prisoner upped it to 800.

The plane would never make it off the sand. Billy said get rid of the guy. They argued. Papa pleaded for one more try. With the friends bearing down and one failure already, Billy got the jitters. But his good sense took over and he started to believe he'd make it out.

He taxied back to the boulder formation, the takeoff point, gunned the engine and started down the runway. Papa spotted the friends scrambling from their car and heading down the beach.

Billy swore at the Apache and gripped the wheel. His profanity had a rhythm and it was by that rhythm that he planned to draw the plane off the sand and slide over the mountains that stood directly ahead. They were all silent, even the prisoner who pressed the handcuffs between his legs.

They stayed on the sand a long time but Billy didn't budge. He was looking for the lift spot somewhere on the beach, big finger-drawn letters that said "PULL!"

The mountains were on top of them and Papa could see no way . . .

"Now," Billy said, and eased back the wheel.

The bumps stopped and Papa felt the gear inhale. God, there was no way. The plane caught a 70-mph air cushion and floated higher.

Billy picked his second spot, a deep crevice between the peaks that only an exquisite left bank could maneuver. Billy had no business banking this soon but that's what it called for so he angled in. The mountain rock seemed so close you could almost pull a flower from it, and Papa could feel the belly brushing. Up. Sliding the wall. The Apache climbed. Until . . . the wall disappeared. And there was only sky.

Papa heard his prisoner regurgitating in the rear seat . . .

Past escapades with Billy Whitelaw occupied only a few moments of Papa's thoughts. He spent most of the flight with Dotty and Rocco Mason.

"I knew right away that Rocco Mason was setting me up. Rachel James was told by Mason to give me his location. Mexico? Perfect. All he had to do was blow me away and head across the border. No U.S. court would let Mexico extradite him and the Mexicans couldn't care less. One American citizen killing another is no big deal.

"Rachel James was too obvious, too hyper. She was like a million other junkie broads. Total masochists, every one of them. They get turned on by a fast-talking boy who deals crystal meth and she falls in love with both of them. Then he starts talking on her, do this, do that, turn a few tricks, lift a few coats, take a few raps for me. She does it, all with a smile. Then to keep her ass in line he cuts her off for a few days. By that time she's ready to eat through a half mile of Buffalo shit to get her candy. Thanks to Rachel, I knew more or less what was waiting for me.

"We flew over the desert down around Palm Springs, where I once saved a Detroit car manufacturer, who will have to remain nameless, a load of insurance money . . . One night a guy drove into the desert. He was drunk and parked on the road with the engine running and went to sleep. He was found dead the next morning. His relatives sued the manufacturer because of a hole in the exhaust system which that particular model was supposed to have. I took the car to a lab and checked it under simulated conditions. There was no hole. Turned out that the guy had left his window cracked and ordinary exhaust fumes seeped in to create a vacuum, and it killed him. I got a new car out of the deal.

"He died from the synergistic effect of two separate depressants, in his case alcohol and carbon monoxide. The more popular method is a combination of alcohol and depressant drugs, which did in Alan Ladd, Dorothy Kilgallen, Inger Stevens and Marilyn Monroe. If not proven otherwise, the deaths are ruled accidental, which means insurance companies are not left off the hook; in fact, they may have to pay double indemnity. For that reason insurance agents try to get to the coroner's office first, many times with—how should I say it—rewards for those coroners who do rule in favor of suicide.

"So much for death. Every goddamn thought I had—that was it. Billy stayed quiet. The radio moved us from tower to tower. Palm Springs to Imperial Valley and finally Calexico.

"I thought about Dotty dead and me without her anymore and about how old I was and could I get somebody to take her place and the answer was no I couldn't, not like her. Not ever. And while I was loving her I was hating Mason. I remembered his face, I couldn't help that. The more I thought about him, the pieces fitted in. He was the kind of loser you want to destroy totally. He started out as a sniveling little creep and that's the way he'd end up. And for what he did, I wanted to kill him. How romantic it would all be, one of us dying south of the border . . ."

Papa looked below and watched El Centro come into view.

"What about landing at Mexicali?" he asked Billy.

"Okay by me if you want four hours of red tape. You're paying for this."

Papa gave no reply and Billy Whitelaw added in his drowsy voice, "Since you're on tight time I figured you wanted to get in and out. Hell, we can mosey across the border, it's right there."

"Fine."

"Now," Billy said with more authority, "what is the plan for *me?* Do I sit with the airplane engine running? Do I march with yuh? What?"

"With me."

"And what's the plan in general, not tryin' to be nosey?"

"We'll have to play it by ear."

"By ear, yessuh, I play life by ear, so that's nothin' new. I 'member with the Third Yoo Ess Army, Second Infantry Division, with the Indian patch on their sleeve, down in the Congo, nineteen and sixty four . . . wait a minute, gotta get UNICOM."

Billy changed frequency to 122.8.

"Calexico UNICOM, this is Twin Comanche Four Five Yankee, request airport advisory."

"Four Five Yankee, roger. You'll have traffic at one o'clock in oh-five minutes. Verify."

"Roger UNICOM. One o'clock traffic, oh-five minutes. Will verify."

Billy turned back to Papa.

"What was I sayin'?"

"Congo."

"Congo. Jungle bunnies everywhere. Remember Dag Hammarskjöld, Secretary-General of the UN? I knew the guys who killed him. Southern Rhodesia, Ndola airfield, September, 1961. They were in the jets intercepted Hammarskjöld's airplane, knocked him outa the sky."

"That was no accident?"

"Not the way they tell it. They made twenty-five grand apiece for that job. They just played it by ear."

"You'd think they'd find out about that?"

"Who's they?"

"The government, somebody."

Billy Whitelaw let out a horselaugh. "They figure it ain't healthy to tell on themselves. And who's gonna blow the whistle? Who's got the clean hands? All they do is get the world on their ass."

Billy called UNICOM.

". . . Four Five Yankee. Traffic at one-o'clock, verify. Over."

"Four Five Yankee, roger. Advisory. Winds from two-three-zero radius at fifteen knots. Sky overcast."

From the air Mexicali was more invisible than L.A. Smog and soot blanketed the scattered city and even from 2,500 feet Papa could barely make out the city. Billy received landing instructions and dropped rapidly until he leveled off at 125 mph. The Calexico strip appeared in the distance. Billy lowered the landing gear, reduced manifold pressure and as he dropped air speed gradually opened the flaps to 45 degrees.

The dirt and black-top landing strip drew up to them. The single quonset hut appeared on their left and the border gate ran alongside the airstrip about a half mile on either side. The plane coasted in and backroared down the strip.

"Find something out of the way," Papa told Billy.

"Sure thing."

Billy taxied by the hut and parked the Comanche as close to the runway as he could. They climbed from the cabin, locked it up and started for town.

They walked the wide dusty street leading to the gate. Antique gritty signs suspended from hinges hung in the dry air. The signs advertised loans, rent-a-cars, cheap jewelry and cheap food and beneath the signs were shops with racks of clothes out front and shills who enticed them to buy, in two languages.

Papa turned into the EZ Rent-A-Car office and told the clerk he wanted something inexpensive for a couple of hours. The clerk asked for a credit card, Papa produced one and the deal was consummated.

They drove the '75 Comet across the border and asked the first *policia* they found for the location of 28 Calle Ruiz.

"Ain't it about time you tell me what the hell's goin' on?" Billy Whitelaw said as they headed towards the address.

"Dotty's been kidnapped."

Billy did a slight double-take.

"Holy Chi-rist!"

"That's what's going on."

"And we're supposed to get her back."

"From a guy named Rocco Mason."

"You know for a fact this Mason's got her?"

"Looks that way."

"And what do I do?"

"Keep the engine running."

"That's all?"

"That's a lot."

At 28 Calle Ruiz is a bar—Las Estrellas. The building walls are brown with soot but sturdy. A garden of dying plants lies in the courtyard between the buildings. At the front on street level Las Estrellas shares half of one floor with a shoemaker. The sign above the door is neon-lit, half the letters working, and the door wears a coat of chipped red paint. A small, square picture window peers into the street.

Papa drove by the bar and parked the Comet down the street.

"Sure you don't want some help?" Billy Whitelaw asked him.

"Not up front," he said, "but be ready to hightail it outa here. Soon as I get inside, back up to the door."

"How long you gonna be?"

"Half hour, at the most."

"And if you're longer?"

"Come on in and get me."

Papa climbed out and felt in the small of his back for the .45. It was intact. He waited till Billy slid behind the driver's seat before walking the fifty yards to Las Estrellas' entrance. Billy was already edging backward when Papa pushed open the door and went inside.

The bar was hot and dusty, with banditos seated three at a table playing cards and guzzling shots from a tequila bottle. They wore sombreros held by rawhide bands drawn under the chin. They were thick-mustachioed, dark-faced, with scowls and quick laughter from the bottom of the throat. Round wooden tables occupied half the long rectangular room with a hardwood bar running the length of one wall. Drinking among these cowboys were blue-collar workers with blue shirts and darker blue pants. Papa towered above the patrons as he strolled to the first stool and scanned the room. He spotted an American at the other end of the bar who had blondish straight hair that fell over one eyebrow and an angular face. The man at the bar did not immediately notice Papa, but when he did he threw down the rest of his drink and vanished into a rear alcove.

Papa moved along the bar to the far end, where he leaned forward and called to the bartender.

"*Comprende inglés?*"

"*No.*"

"*El hombre aqui, dos minutos pasados. Dónde?*"

The bartender shrugged.

"*Por favor, señor, dónde esta el hombre?*" Papa placed ten dollars American on the bar.

"*No sé,*" said the bartender.

Papa placed another ten dollars American on the bar.

"*Con pelo rubio, aquél hombre?*" he said.

"*Si?*"

The bartender contemplated.

"*Es muy dificil.*"

Papa rolled his eyes.

"*Si. Entiendo,*" Papa said and placed *another* ten on the bar.

"*Ah, requerdo!*" the bartender exclaimed.

"*Bien. Qué?*"

The bartender leaned forward. "*Treinta y dos.*"

"*Gracias, señor.*"

The staircase was narrow and painted green and the walls were bright yellow. Cheap reproductions of bad Mexican artists hung upon the walls. He started up. The stairs were sturdy which meant they hopefully didn't squeak.

On the first-floor landing Papa looked down the hallway to check the apartment numbers. Double digits—11, 12, 13—which meant the ground floor was the ground floor and this was the first. He had two more flights to go.

He braced himself against the handrail and peered up through the chute between the winding staircase. Nothing. He continued on.

On the second floor he again glanced up the chute. Movement. Something was up there, all the way up, on the top floor. Someone waiting or . . .

Papa's forehead was bathed with sweat. His throat was dry. He ran his tongue over parched lips and smacked twice.

Out came the .45. The weight of it felt good in his hand. On his way towards the third floor he hugged the wall. His head was raised and both eyes made sweeps of the space ahead.

Slowly, quietly, one step at a time, Papa ascended the

stairs to the third floor. Shafts of dusty light shone from under doorways, illuminating the red and black vinyl corridors. Metal and glass lamp fixtures were stationed at either end of the hallway and a blackened window overlooked the street.

He had difficulty making out the room number. *Treinta dos*, thirty-two. He found it and drew a bead from the floor above. There was a visible line. Thirty-two stood next door to a broom closet. Papa stepped inside. Behind him, an assortment of mops and pails and detergent, a length of rope and shammies. He rested his gun hand against the door frame and speculated how he might catch the attention of the guy upstairs, if there *was* a guy upstairs.

One solution came after he sank his free hand into his pocket and pulled out a coin which he held up for inspection.

He pressed the coin between his index finger and thumb and scraped it against the metal strip running down the door frame.

Twice he grated it against the metal. The shrillness made him wince. He pressed one ear against the door, listening. Then he heard it, footsteps on the stairs.

Papa backed away from the door and dropped his eyes to the floor. He replaced the coin in his pocket and gripped the knob.

His eyes had already adjusted to the darkness and he could hear himself breathing in the stifling heat. He slowed the respiration down, drawing air in through his mouth and allowing it to gradually escape through his nose.

The .45 was raised. He could feel the cool steel brush his cheek.

There it was, the first sign of a shadow intercepting the light and moving steadily by the door. He heard shoes scrape along the hallway. The shadow moved on by.

Papa pushed the door open, slightly, and saw not two feet from him the broad back of a fat man. He saw the man's head rotate from side to side and noticed his right arm extended in front of him and figured there was a weapon in his hand.

Papa pushed the door further open and stepped forward. The .45. From the rear the fat man had no neck. His rumpled suit coat slipped up under his ragged hair. To knock him out Papa had to connect just behind the right ear, the most vulnerable spot on his head.

The fat man apparently felt someone's presence behind him and started his turn. Papa brought the barrel down. The silent impact. The fat man jerked and grunted and stayed up long enough for Papa to slip one hand under an armpit to break the fall. He quickly reached around the fat man's body and fumbled for his weapon. He missed but the gun hit the man's thigh before dropping to the floor.

The fat man was heavy and Papa struggled dragging him to the closet, where he deposited him, on his back, head resting between two pails. The man bled some from his wound. Papa inspected it briefly and decided that he wouldn't be getting up for the time being.

When Papa returned to the hall he picked up the fat man's weapon and dropped it into his pocket. Now came the difficult part.

He stood by the faded yellow door to number 32 and decided there was only one way to break in—kick down the door. He checked the wood and found it standard two-inch thick, hinges on the right, knob on the left. He'd kicked in dozens just like it.

He stood to the right of the door so he wouldn't be spotted through the peephole. He rubbed the drowsiness from his eyes and took a couple of deep breaths. He picked his spot on the door, the hinge side, and kicked in. The sound roared through the hallway and the door blew down. Papa rushed in and came face to face with the blond-haired guy from the bar. He sat alone on the sofa. Papa scanned the room: tattered furniture and dirty lace curtains, a bedroom and bathroom door and a dozen places where Mason could be hiding.

"Where's Dotty?" he said to the blond man.

The man shrugged and Papa noticed his eyes momentarily shift over his left shoulder, and Papa started his turn.

Just then a sharp pain laced through his left side. He cried out. Nausea swept over him and he started to reel. But his motion continued and as he completed the revolution he came face to face with Mason. Papa's weapon was raised, the barrel crashed through Mason's teeth, and he pulled the trigger by reflex action.

The inside of Mason's mouth exploded with grayish-green gas which seeped from his nose, mouth and ears. Blood came from his eyes. His broken white teeth flew straight out of his mouth and pelted Papa's face. Then Mason's head detonated. Skin and hair and flesh blasted into the air. A smoky syrup oozed from the neck cavity and flowed over his shoulders. Mason's body banged against the wall and collapsed to the floor.

As Mason fell Papa heard a noise behind him. He turned around and saw the blond man reaching for his jacket.

"Don't," Papa said.

The blond man didn't and pulled back to his original position. Papa reached down and slowly pulled the blade from his side. It was four inches long and could have done real damage had it not struck bone. The severe pain would begin in a few hours.

"Where's Dotty?"

"I don't know."

Papa walked across the room and stuck the .45 into the blond man's face and asked him again.

The man's eyes widened and he said in a low voice, "She ain't here."

"Where is she?"

"I don't know, man. Mason never got her."

"What!"

"He never snatched her. She wasn't in the house when he went after her. He did this to, you know, he wanted you bad, so—"

"You . . . never . . . had . . . Dotty?" The idea was inconceivable.

"No, it was a plan, Mason's plan, to get you here. He waited around a couple days by your house. She never showed, so he figured he'd maybe luck out, she wouldn't show and, uh, you'd think he had her when you got home. Looks like you did, and like she never showed or this wouldn't have worked."

"I still don't believe you," Papa said.

"It's the truth."

Papa pulled the man up by the lapels and carried him into the bedroom and then the kitchen to look for Dotty. The knife wound throbbed.

"I'm *telling* you, I never seen her. Where's Ted?"

"Who?"

"Ted. The guy outside."

"In the closet. Listen," Papa said, "if you're bullshitting me I'll—"

"I'd get outa here. if I was you. The cops'll be here any minute."

Papa breathed deeply. The wound was getting worse and he had to patch it soon.

"You have two choices," Papa said. "First, it's going to cost me a twenty-seven-cent bullet to blow you away cause I don't want a witness."

The blond man waited with great expectation for choice number two.

"Or, I let you live. If you ever say anything about what happened here it's your word against mine. And what the hell were you doing in Mexico when you're on federal parole? Right back to the joint. Understand?"

"I won't say a thing," the blond man said, then added, "I seen what happened. It was self-defense."

"No, no. There was no self-defense. There was no shooting. There was nothing."

The man nodded his head.

"Fine. Now, this is going to hurt you more than it is me."

The blond man looked confused, but only for a second, because Papa swung his free hand from behind his back and caught the man's chin with a solid right cross. The man went down and Papa figured he'd at least be out for a while.

He heard voices outside the door, and nodded to four Mexicans when he walked into the hallway and headed for the window overlooking the street. The Comet sat directly below. Papa pulled a few coins from his pocket and one by one flipped them on top of the car. He heard them clink off the metal. Billy Whitelaw stuck his head through the window.

"Billy!" Papa called.

It took Billy a few seconds to realize the voice came from above.

"Papa! What's up?"

"Third floor. Gimme a hand. Take the keys with you."

The four Mexicans still waited outside Mason's room when Papa returned. Their eyes wandered over him. They saw the .45 in his hand and the patch of blood spreading down his pant leg. The pain was driving him crazy, and he thought about the first-aid kit in Billy's plane.

Billy appeared on the second landing and took three steps at a time on his way toward the third. "What's up?"

"It's a mess. I got a guy inside."

Papa turned inside and he heard Billy grunt.

"What happened to you?" Billy asked.

"Knife."

Mason's decapitated body lay on the floor, his viscera splashed against the wall.

"That one," Papa said, pointing to the blond man. Billy picked the man up and draped him over his shoulders.

On the way down Papa asked Billy what the bar was like.

"Packed. And the cops'll be here any minute."

With Papa in the lead they made their way down the stairs and through the crowd gathered by the alcove. The Mexicans opened a wedge for them to pass, and Papa watched the dark eyes as he waded through.

Outside in the street Papa opened the rear door and Billy flipped the man inside. They climbed in and sped off down the street.

A quarter mile down Calle Ruiz, Papa turned to Billy and told him to pull over.

"Here?"

"Yeah, we're gonna dump this guy."

"Dump him?"

"You think I want to take him over the border? It's quiet here. Throw him in the alley."

Billy shrugged, got out and lifted the blond man from the seat. He carried him to the alley and dropped him behind a stack of old tires.

They crossed the border uneventfully, and Billy drove Papa directly to the aircraft, where he patched the wound with a butterfly suture. Billy then dropped off the rental car and within fifteen minutes was back and ready for takeoff.

Twice he asked Papa about Dotty's whereabouts and twice Papa explained he didn't have the slightest clue, repeating what the blond man had told him, and shaking his head in disbelief.

At ten p.m. they flew into Van Nuys Airport, where Papa promised to send Billy Whitelaw a check the next day. Billy asked if he could do anything else, make a few calls, hang around to cheer him up. Papa thanked him anyway and drove home.

One possibility had been eating at him since leaving Mexicali. What if Mason had killed Dotty and buried her somewhere? All the questions he should have asked the blond man began lining up before him. What if they *had* killed her! He reconstructed his conversation with the blond man, looking for holes and hesitations, the hint of a lie. Papa wanted him to be telling the truth.

He arrived home before eleven and spent two hours on the phone. Nothing had changed. He drank his bourbon too quickly and after an hour got sloppy during the conversations.

He sifted through the collection of stereo cassettes and selected Glenn Yarbrough's version of "I Wonder," a song his grandmother sang to him when he was very young. He drank more to kill the pain in his head and the pain in his back. And he thought about Dotty and didn't know what to think, so he drank more and changed the music and about three o'clock stumbled into bed and fell asleep.

The black phone woke him at two thirty the next afternoon. It was Robert Furey, Dotty's gynecologist.

"I'm calling you against instructions, Ralph," Furey said. "Dotty asked me not to but—"

"Where *is* she!"

"Cedars of Lebanon."

"I called there."

"She registered under her maiden name."

"Your idea?"

"No."

"She all right?"

"She's fine."

"Good. I'll be right there," Papa told Dr. Furey, and in less than a minute was dressed and headed for the car.

On the way Papa tried to figure out how he'd been duped. The key was Mason's phone call, saying he had Dotty, and the slap he heard. But Mason wouldn't let her talk. The bruise beside Rachel James' eye? Could that have been the slap he heard?

Richie Blumenthal was calling him on the radio.

"I got this crazy guy Elmo Sellers, kidnapped his own kid, jumped a twenty-grand bail to Hawaii. He's back. His wife called with the address. Two-oh-seven Fleet. West L.A. Get over there right away."

"Dotty's having the baby. I'm going to the hospital."

"On the way: Elmo Sellers. Two-oh-seven—"

"Richie, I'm *at* the hospital."

"Take your mind off it. Pick up Elmo Sellers. A mother's waiting, Papa."

"Get somebody else."

"I've tried." Richie broke into his high whine, which Papa knew was the preface to a major pitch. "You have my congratulations. Want a boy or girl? How 'bout both?"

"I'd like a boy." Papa turned the corner onto Fountain and spotted the hospital ahead.

"Yeah. A boy."

Papa could see Richie's huge cigar wagging in his mouth.

"Elmo Sellers has the kid with him, eight months old. A boy. Only a special person can pick up Sellers, Papa, you know? Somebody who understands. Understands what it means to *have* a kid and, also, how to *support* it. You got a grand already spent on that kid of yours. The birth. The hospital, the toys. It adds up. There's five thousand bucks for picking up Elmo Sellers. There's a mother waiting, Papa. Five!"

"On a twenty thousand bail?"

"How dangerous can a man with child be?"

"I'm at the hospital, Richie. I'll be hanging up soon."

"Seven thousand. Silk diapers. Private nurse. My ever-lasting gratitude."

"Richie?"

"What?"

"I'm parked. It was nice talking to you."

"All right. I understand. I only want you to remember one thing."

"What's that?"

"Two-oh-seven Fleet. Elmo Sellers." With that, Richie hung up.

Papa entered the hospital and took the elevator to Maternity.

Elmo Sellers was growing impatient. His wife should have been there long ago. The baby had been awake and crying for the last hour and a half. Sellers held it and burped it and rocked it, which only made things worse.

He had still not learned the knack of changing diapers. The supply of disposal diapers he'd bought at the market was almost exhausted. Sellers figured the baby had diarrhea. He prayed for constipation. He'd screamed at the baby to shut up, which made things worse.

At one point he considered running down to the market to call his wife.

He was irritated and bored; there was nothing to do, nothing to read, nowhere to look. Except out the window, which he did frequently.

18

The Ward

Papa checked with the maternity nurse, who called Dr.
Furey. Furey, a tall, gaunt man with a sad hound-dog face
and a droll sense of humor, came up shortly.

"How are you, Ralph?"

"Listen, how come you waited so long to tell me? I almost got killed down in Mexico looking for her. I thought
she was kidnapped."

"That's very funny."

"Yes it is and it's true."

"Before I gave Dotty a shot, when she was lucid, she
. . . but this is stuff she'll tell you herself."

"Tell me now," Papa insisted.

They arrived at Dotty's door, with its small window
through which Papa saw her. She was very white and her
eyes were closed. She held the bedcovers close under her
chin.

"What did she say?"

Furey hunched his shoulders and kept them there.

"She said you had a fight. You didn't want the baby."

Furey hesitated and peered into Papa's face.

248

"You sure you want to hear this from me?"

"I wouldn't have asked."

Furey dropped his shoulders and continued.

"She was extremely unhappy, didn't want you to know where she was having the child. Wanted to take it away from Los Angeles, away from you. She got nervous about a call she received while you were in Canada."

"In Canada, yes. Call?"

"She said it came from a police sergeant whose name she didn't recognize. She called LAPD and asked for him but there was no such person. She left the house immediately and called me. From what I gather, she did the right thing."

"So Mason *was* there," Papa mumbled.

Dr. Furey excused himself and Papa went into the waiting room where two men were playing whist on a card table.

Papa sat in a yellow armchair and watched the game. He leafed through *Time* and *Field and Stream*, looking at the pictures. He smoked and smacked his lips and looked at his watch a half dozen times. It was not yet five o'clock.

"Three-handed?" one of the men asked Papa.

"Sure," he said and joined them, pulling up the armchair.

They played in silence, during which Papa thought about Richie Blumenthal and the snatch he'd mentioned. He knew he'd go nuts hanging around the waiting room. He thought about the extra money he would now need and could make picking up—what was the guy's name?—Elmo Sellers.

He wondered if going after this Sellers was the right thing to do. Financially, it certainly was. After losing Ching and breaking even on Faust he badly needed to turn a dollar. An expensive new mouth might appear any minute. This Sellers meant five thousand dollars and he was less than an hour away. Papa could be back by eight. He didn't want to play whist with these guys anyway, not for three hours, and he didn't want to moon around the waiting room either.

He dropped from the game and went outside to call Richie.

"What was that address on Sellers?" he said when the bondsman came on.

"Two-oh-seven Fleet. Good boy."

"I'm leaving your number with the hospital. Relay any messages to me."

"You bet."

Papa called the West L.A. precinct for some backup. A guy like Sellers could be dangerous. This was no time for Papa to check out on the world. Damn poor timing, in fact. The watch commander told him there'd be a squad car at the address in ten minutes.

Papa rode the elevator to the ground floor and headed for the Plymouth.

PART IV

19

Sellers

Elmo Sellers dozed and when he awakened found himself in a drowsy middle ground. The recent past was with him now and by turns he felt heat and the throbbing headaches that followed.

Sellers sat on the round throw rug in the center of the room. Against the door was the barricade, a threadbare sofa with an armchair on top of it. On the window sill overlooking the street was a box of 22-caliber rifle shells; the rifle leaned against the sill.

Beside the window stood the bassinet in which the child slept peacefully on a faded brown blanket.

Sellers climbed slowly to his feet and on his way to the window took a handful of crackers from the box lying on its side atop the coffee table. He stepped silently so as not to wake the child.

At the window he dropped to his knees and placed both elbows on the sill. The street was empty of traffic. A half dozen parked cars hugged the sidewalks. From this position he was able to see the walkway leading from the street to the front door. He rested his chin on his arms and watched the entranceway below. A streetlight came on.

It took Papa thirty-five minutes to reach Fleet. He found number 207, a four-unit building with a single staircase up the center. It was typically run-down, and badly in need of a paint job. Eucalyptus trees grew everywhere on the street. Green and white paneled awnings shaded the windows of the apartment on the lower right. Flowers appeared in window boxes.

He called Richie. "Two-oh-seven Fleet," Papa said. "What's the apartment number?"

"Haven't got one. Is it a big place?"

"Four units. Sellers' wife didn't know?"

"No."

"Any calls from the hospital?"

"No."

Papa looked both ways down the street. "I'm waiting for backup."

"Good," Richie said. "Sellers is probably armed."

"I'd expect him to be."

Papa heard Richie open the metal cabinet behind him, then slam it shut. "Tony Bernardo," Richie said.

"What about him?"

"That's what I wanna know. We got less than a week, Papa. I don't wanna pressure you but it's been almost six months." Richie sneeze twice and blew his nose. "I don't have to remind you the money I got invested."

"Twenty-five hundred, I know."

"Not that far from the average national gross, twenty-five hundred."

"I can understand your predicament," Papa said.

"What I meant to tell you is I got a lead on Bernardo."

"Oh. . . ?"

"His parents been looking, too. Don't forget, they got everything they own riding on that punk. Lest I should be responsible for them going bust. Lest *you* should be responsible."

"Richie . . ."

"I know, drop the sermon."

"I'd appreciate it."

"Hey!" Richie was entering his tragic violet routine. "I see beyond the dough. We been together long enough for you to know that. I'm a barracuda. Of course I'm a barracuda! That's the business. I like people. That's also the business. *You* like people. That's why you're the best. I don't want no crazy mixed-up trigger going after my people. Look, if you don't snatch Tony Bernardo I'll understand. I'll sit here at the desk, psychologize my money out the window, and think about all the times you were good, when you brought 'em back, and the good times we had, I'll think of that."

"Me, too."

"Last week," Richie said, "I bought a motorcycle for my kid. I paid thirty-five hundred bucks. If you don't bring back Tony Bernardo I'm out six thousand dollars."

"The cops are here, Richie, I gotta go."

"You always cut me off. Neil Flaningam."

"Who?"

"Write this down."

Papa took the pen from his shirt pocket.

"Neil Flaningam. Twenty-two Belden Drive, in Hollywood Hills. You know it?"

"I'll find it."

"He knows where Tony Bernardo might be."

"Fine."

"The parents. They want to see this Neil. He didn't say nothing but they figure he was lyin'."

"Goodbye, Richie."

Papa did a U-turn and pulled up behind the squad car parked in front of Sellers' building.

A young detective sergeant got out and Papa explained the situation: the kid, the bailjump, kidnapping. The detective sergeant said a complaint had been filed by Sellers' wife.

They checked the outdoor mailbox and saw that the upper right-hand apartment had no name.

"Which doesn't mean a thing," Papa said. "He could be in any one of them."

Inside the building Papa knocked on the lower right door and stood away. A young kid in a baseball cap and sneakers answered.

"Your mother in?" the sergeant asked him.

"I can tell you what you wanna know." The kid's head bobbed.

"We're looking for this guy. Elmo Sellers's his name. He has a baby with him."

The kid's finger went up.

"Above us. I seen him come in. What's his M.O.?"

"M.O.?" the sergeant said.

"You know, his M.O."

"We want to talk to him, that's all," Papa assured him.

The kid wouldn't buy that.

"Sure you do. Anyway, that's where he is, right upstairs. That's where you can find him."

"Thank you," the sergeant said. "Go on back inside. We'll let you know what happens."

The kid didn't want to go back inside. He waited with one hand resting against the doorway.

"Please?" Papa asked him.

The kid pouted, then obeyed, closing the door behind him.

Papa and the sergeant started up the stairs.

Halfway up they heard a shot that sounded like a .22. Papa looked back at the sergeant and they pulled out their weapons.

At the top of the stairs a second shot rang out, which stopped Papa cold. "Oh, my God," he muttered and ran to the door. The door broke when he kicked it but didn't fall. Something was blocking it.

He and the sergeant used their shoulders to heave it the rest of the way.

Sellers' barricade moved aside and they pushed into the room.

Sellers was on the floor in a fetal position, blood coming from a gunshot wound under his left temple. The .22 was in his limp hand.

Papa knelt down to inspect him while the sergeant went to the bassinet, where the baby lay face down. He picked up the baby and turned it around.

The sergeant's grunt made Papa look up. He saw the officer holding the baby. A hole was in the baby's forehead. Blood was on the sides of the bassinet and the blanket covering the floor.

The sergeant began shaking. His hands trembled as he replaced the baby, wrapping it in the blanket, and returned to where Sellers lay.

The sergeant stood over the dead man. His face was streaked with tears. Finally he lifted his head and looked down at Papa, still kneeling beside Sellers.

"I'll call an ambulance," the sergeant said, and walked quickly from the room.

20

The Wait

The call came in forty-five minutes later. It was Richie who told Papa he'd received a call from the hospital.

"What did they say?"

"They didn't, except that you should get back to them."

"I wonder what the hell that means . . . Is everything okay?"

"I don't know. Was something wrong?"

"No."

Papa paused long enough for Richie to ask: "Hello? You still there?"

"Yeah, yeah."

"What about Sellers?"

"They're taking him downtown. He shot himself."

"Shot himself? Jesus, how come?"

"He also killed his . . ."

Papa froze. The child, in its crib, with the bullet through its head.

"Richie, I'll call you later."

Papa hung up and stepped on the accelerator. He was twenty minutes from the hospital. He passed phone booths where he might have called in but didn't because whatever Dr. Furey wanted him for—good news or bad—Papa wanted to hear it face to face.

He could not clear away the image of Sellers' dead child, and as his mind played tricks the picture of the child faded, replaced by another. He held a dialogue with himself. Hadn't Furey said Dotty was doing fine? Or was he lying? Why would he lie?

Papa broke all speed limits. He went through yellow lights and red ones. He nearly missed oncoming cars and cursed slower ones ahead of him. He leaned on his horn. He turned off the car radio and rolled up the windows. Sweat pored out of him.

When he reached the hospital he didn't bother with the parking lot, instead peeled into the red zone and scrambled from the car. He blindly bumped into people on the way in and cursed the elevators.

When the elevator doors opened he did not wait for the women to board first, and when they did enter told them not to push any buttons. He had to get to maternity, to his wife.

By the time he reached the floor he was convinced that Dotty was close to death.

He rushed to the desk and leaned over the counter.

"Dr. Furey," he said to the duty nurse. "I'm Ralph Thorson. He called me. My wife is expecting."

"Thorson," the nurse repeated.

"No, no. She's registered under her maiden name—Barras."

Papa tapped on the counter while the nurse checked through the patient list. She found it.

"Yes. Dorothy Barras."

"Is she all right?"

"Dr. Furey will be here in a moment. If you'll have a seat—"

"He called me! What did he want?"

"If you'll have a—"

"I want you to call him." Papa was shouting at the nurse. *"Now."*

The nurse backed away from the huge man with the menacing black beard and piercing eyes hovering over her.

"Mr. Thorson, I can't call him. He's in surgery."

"Surgery? What surgery?"

"I'm sorry—"

"Goddamn, I want to know . . ."

"Ralph?"

Papa turned and saw Dr. Furey coming down the corridor toward him. He watched Furey's eyes for some indication. There was none. He was all business.

"What's the matter, doc? Anything wrong?"

"Let's take a walk," Furey said, leading Papa away from the desk.

Papa's insides raced full-tilt as he tried keeping stride with the long-legged gynecologist.

"I'll be straight with you," Furey began.

"That doesn't sound hopeful."

"Sometimes," Furey explained, "the baby gets stuck and I have to pull it out feet or buttocks first."

"Breach birth."

"Right. And that's the situation with Dotty and the child."

"What about complications," Papa asked, not really wanting to hear the answer.

"Oh . . ."

"C'mon, c'mon. You want to be straight, be straight."

Furey halted at the end of the corridor and turned to Papa.

"Complications," he said thoughtfully. "Now, I'm telling you what *might* happen. The chances they will are thin."

Furey looked up at Papa who was staring him dead in the eye and continued, speaking rapidly.

"If the baby is removed fast enough it could die. If so, sometimes the mother will go into shock. Ralph, you don't want—"

"What else?"

"Heart attack, she could have a heart attack. Lungs could give out. She's breathing pretty heavily. Strain going on there. That's about it."

Papa made his connections, his pulse sped. He could feel it thumping at his temples.

"Give me some odds on Dotty's chances."

"I'm not a gambler, Ralph."

"Let's say you were."

Furey paused. Papa pressed him.

"You can't give me a rundown like that and not give me what kind of *chance she has!*" His voice boomed down the corridor.

"I don't know for sure until I start to operate."

Papa persisted.

"What about chances . . . now!"

"Fair," said Furey.

Papa froze, then spun around, marched two steps and turned back to Furey.

"Getting an answer out of you is damn near impossible."

"Ralph," Furey said, aiming a finger down the corridor, "go ahead and sit in the waiting room. Couple of fellows there have been through this four or five times."

Papa stood still.

" 'Fair,' you said."

"Fair."

Papa nodded once, turned and listened to his shoes club the linoleum as he walked slowly away.

The guys had their coats draped over chairs, shirt sleeves were rolled up, playing poker. Ashtrays spilled over on the table and the ashes swept over the edge. Somebody had brought poker chips. A bank of blue smoke hung five feet above the heel-marked floor.

A little guy in a blue pin-striped suit sat on a stack of magazines.

"How are you?" Pinstripe said to Papa. "You want in?"

"Might as well."

Pinstripe reeled off the details.

"The white chips are a buck, two for the reds. Blues are five. Three-raise limit. No check-raise. Five stud game. Nothing wild."

"I'm the bank," said the fat, frog-faced guy with sweat pouring off him and thick horn-rimmed glasses perched on his huge nose.

Papa sat down and passed three tens to Frog. Across the table from Papa sat a young kid in a cheap suit, and next to him a burly lumberjack type wearing a flannel shirt.

The Kid dealt while Pinstripe continued his story.

". . . So he surprised the hell out of us. When Crazy Eddie took over LAPD he blew the force wide open.

"Crazy Eddie moved through the ranks and made not one wave. Nothing. Mr. Calm. Nobody knew who the hell he was when his name came up for Chief. He took over and suddenly becomes a lunatic."

Pinstripe counted on his fingers.

"Proclamation number one: no fags on the force, says Eddie. What policeman is going to touch a mike that's been breathed on by one of those guys who just made love in a back alley? That's Eddie."

"King bets," The Kid said to Papa.

"Two dollars."

Pinstripe went on.

"The plane hijackers. Crazy Eddie said, and I quote, 'We'll set up a gallows on a big bus, drive it to the airport and give the hijacker a fair trial before we hang him on the spot.' That's our chief. I'm telling you, the guy's dangerous. Raise two."

The Kid dropped. Lumberjack called. The Frog dropped. Papa called.

"Juvenile crime rate," Pinstripe continued. "The reason for the rise in crime, according to Eddie, is woman's lib. Mom goes to work, her kid steals a car. Mom should stay home and the kid will too."

"I don't think mothers should work," Lumberjack said.

"You *like* Crazy Eddie?"

"He gets the job done."

Papa listened to them. He knew how crazy Crazy Eddie really was. He had talked to cops and crooks and politicians and D.A.'s and *they* knew how crazy Crazy Eddie was. Crazy Eddie was also very smart. He had played the game in his rise through the force; he stepped on no toes, did a solid job as far as anyone knew, except that no one knew solid Eddie Davis in those days. No one Papa knew knew him. He might have heard Eddie Davis' name. Might have. He wasn't sure. Neither did anyone know what happened to make Solid Eddie crazy. Suddenly, when he made Chief, he didn't have to cater anymore. That was one explanation for his craziness. Another was that he couldn't handle fame. It came too fast for him to handle. Whatever, Crazy Eddie became infamous.

Papa won the hand. Lumberjack dealt another.

"Call your four and raise you four more," the Kid said to the Frog.

"Raise? On what?"

"You callin' me or what?"

"Yes, call."

The Kid flipped over a third eight and the Frog sank into deep depression. He removed his glasses and wiped them on the yellow handkerchief dangling from his jacket pocket.

The round wall clock told Papa it was five to eight. Dotty would be going in soon.

Papa was up over a hundred bucks by eight thirty and became aware of the others watching him closely.

"What business did you say you were in, Mr. Thorson?" the Frog asked. "Cardsharp?"

"Two dollars," Papa said, pushing a red chip into the pot.

The doctor appeared at the door and said, "Mr. Clifford."

The Frog looked up expectantly. His eyebrows lifted and the glasses scooted down his nose.

"Come with me, please," the doctor said.

"Boy or girl?" Glasses said.

"Girl."

More depression. Glasses wanted to stay with the game. He slowly rose and, smiling sadly, shuffled out through the door.

"His fifth girl," the Kid announced.

Something dawned on Pinstripe. "Hey," he exclaimed. "He's the bank!" Pinstripe ran from the room and returned a few minutes later with the wad of cash.

Papa dealt and entered a head to head battle with Pinstripe, who had three eights showing. They both raised their limits and when they flipped over their hole cards it happened that Papa's full house beat the eights. All this in five cards and Papa raked in the pot, wondering if this were fickle providence working: hot at the card table, chalking up baby money, while Dotty suffered down the hall. God . . . he might leave the hospital richer by hole cards and poorer by . . .

He drove the notion back and passed the deck.

"Mr. DeCastro," the doctor called from the door.

Pinstripe stood and leaned forward, placing his fingertips on the table. "It's been interesting." He shook Papa's hand and nodded to the others. With that, the little man straightened up and marched out the door.

Soon afterward Lumberjack and the Kid were called out. The Kid, who inherited the bank from Pinstripe, passed out the winnings. Papa was ahead $150. Lumberjack was down a sawbuck. The Kid broke even. Glasses had been the big loser. Pinstripe made up for the rest.

Papa sat alone amidst the smoke and poker chips and

the cards strewn about the table. He sat with his back to the glass partition dividing the room from the hallway outside. He squashed one cigarette after the other in the ashtray and leafed through the magazines Pinstripe had been sitting on. The clock hands passed 8:45 and 9:00. His phantoms appeared and vanished and he drifted into melancholy repose, waiting in the deadness. Was Dr. Furey outside with the bad news, searching for a way to deliver it? Was the baby gone? Was Dotty? And if they were, why was he made to wait?

"Ralph."

His head shot up and there was Furey with his hand on the doorknob, a tired smile on his face.

"Congratulations. It's a girl."

They marched down the long corridor to the delivery room. When they reached the glass enclosure Furey raised his arm and aimed it in.

"Over there," he said. "Back row. Second from the left."

Papa peered into the luminescent room where thirty children gestured into life.

"How's Dotty?"

"She's waiting for you down the hall."

She lay beneath stark white sheets drawn to her neck. Her face was pale and lineless and the upturned corners of her lips portrayed a smile.

Papa crossed the room and stood above the bed. She felt his presence and her eyes opened.

"Hi, Papa."

"Hi, Babe," he said, reaching for her hand.

21

Tony Bernardo

Malibu. Where smugglers once sailed their galleons between high jagged rocks and moored in the granite coves. Malibu. Where gamblers long ago collected in slick Eastern suits and sat at tables with fishermen and grubby miners and the sons of wealthy men. Malibu. A violent town once inhabited by gunslingers and short-term sheriffs and castled rocks rising from the sea.

Papa rode the Pacific Coast Highway. It was late in the afternoon and the ocean gale hummed in. The windows were up and he listened to Verdi's *Falstaff* fill the car with woodwinds. He wore a heavy sheepskin coat; the temperature was forty-two and dropping.

He turned the Plymouth onto Topanga Canyon Boulevard and headed toward the peak. Back in the old days the road was a Chamush Indian trail where for eight miles braves etched a path between the half-fallen mountains and the shore.

He passed chimneys standing alone in old rubble where houses used to be. Nestled among folding hills were palaces dug into the earth, low-slung multi-leveled ranch homes

264

with pools and horses and high-powered telescopes peering off toward the sea. A late afternoon wind whipped through the canyon. The reeds bent away from the ocean. Crooked barren trees stood atop the hills in Gothic reverie.

Eight miles straight uphill played havoc on the car, still suffering from its Canadian experience. He prayed the damn thing would make it, and make it back.

The road swung back toward the ocean and a quarter mile further along Papa turned right on Fernwood Pacific Drive. He had followed Richie Blumenthal's tip and talked with Neil Flaningam, Tony Bernardo's friend, who was persuaded to tell him that Tony was holed up in the Moon Fire Temple. Papa had found out Tony's birthdate from his parents, and was pleased to note that the time was propitious for a snatch, astrologically speaking.

The Moon Fire Temple was the inspiration of stock-market speculator Louis Marvin, who constructed it in 1969 in honor of his belief that vegetarianism was the ultimate symbol of peace. A sign on the temple read: "If you love animals, don't eat them."

Papa parked at the white metal gate guarding the entrance, got out and started up.

Papa stopped three times during the twenty-minute climb. At one point he rested against a broken-down water truck, circa 1940, with a peace sign scrawled on its tank . . .

"I realized on the way that chasing up big mountains after little kids was not what I wanted to do the rest of my life. I'm getting old. That seemed like a hell of a thing to admit, I knew, but reality has a way of intruding itself. Men die young in my business. They get knocked off or they can't handle the financial insecurity. I've been lucky . . . and almost always broke. I could have been a rich man if I'd invested well and if the bondsmen paid me what they should have.

"Last year I could feel myself slowing down. I was getting tired. I got in more trouble than I'd ever been in. My ass was on the line with Paco Carrera and the Ching kid up in Canada. Ramsey called it testing the market: I went just so far and got out. Bullshit. I went too far and was *lucky* to get out.

"And, too, there are guys like Tommy Price whose death I felt responsible for. I might as well have pulled the trigger. And of course Jack Finnegan.

"One of the best indications of growing old is watching

the obituaries and reading about your old friends dying—
of natural causes. That doesn't do me any good.

"This bounty hunter-lone wolf jazz I suppose is romantic for other people but it's not for me anymore. I'd like to
retire and go into something else but I'm not exactly sure
what the something else should be. Office work would
surely kill me, and a helluva lot faster than what I'm doing now. I sometimes think back and wonder how it all
would have turned out if I had stayed with the juvenile
hall. Probably would have been making thirty-five, forty
thousand right now and with thirty years on the job been
ready to retire with a pension and a fishing rod and part
interest in a lodge in the mountains. But I have no pension, damn little security, so it looks like I'll just have to
chase assholes till I keel over.

"Beyond all that the baby came along. Part of whatever
I make goes into trust for the kid; can't see any other way
to do it. That was why I was so damn mad. Every time I
looked at Dotty's pregnant belly I could see myself chasing
after more pimps and hookers and dopers and anybody
else Richie Blumenthal had on the books. More of the
same. Having the kid made life—made *living*—more urgent.

"To compound all this the bailbond business is phasing
out. Already Illinois, Oregon, Texas and a couple other
states have done away with bailbonds. Unless there's a
serious offense involved the suspect is released on
O.R.—own recognizance—which means he hauls ass out
of town in a hurry. Illinois is totally screwed up because
of it but in the long run O.R. will turn out all right. Under
the regular bonding system the rich get out. The poor
hang around for months, sometimes as much as a year,
waiting for their trial date.

"Even in the California system there's no longer bail for
a misdemeanor and just about every crime these days is either reduced or plea bargained down to a misdemeanor.
I'd say within two years California, Arizona and Nevada
won't have the bonding system. The era of the bondsman
will be gone, and even Richie can finally retire.

"In truth, I'm tired of fighting old battles, like revamp-
ing the prison system. Most guys with any choice will
want to go to the federal pen which compared to the state
pen is a country club. Rehabilitation doesn't exist on any
level but federal pens are class joints. You get higher cali-

ber inmates there and a hell of a lot better treatment and food.

"Juries. Grand juries should be totally eliminated. They're a complete waste of time and taxpayers' money. They serve no purpose. They're supposed to determine whether a case should go to trial. Only one of five hundred cases don't go to trial. Grand juries are just another extension of the D.A.'s office or the Federal Prosecutor's office. And lawyers are the biggest ripoff artists in the world. They're scavengers. You might think for instance that the medical malpractice controversy is the doctors' fault, or the insurance companies'. The bad guys are in reality the lawyers. Insurance rates are hiked to pay legal fees.

"I talk about juries. One of the great injustices in the legal system is having twelve people who don't know their ass from a hole in the ground assigned to make a rational decision about another person's life. You can't expect them to, especially with the legal tricks and emotional hypes and faulty logic the trial lawyers fill them with. The only answer I can see is professional juries, men and women trained to filter out all that bullshit, who go to school and learn what ad hoc and ad hominem and "begging the question" mean. Professionals. There are professional lawyers and judges. Why not complete the circle and really make it a fair trial? It's a travesty to watch little old ladies in the hands of fast-talking trial attorneys. That's justice?

"And the battles go on and I keep picking up flakes who go to the joint and get out and I pick them up again, and again, and again. It gets to be one big revolving door and you hope when the door finally spits you out you land in one piece. The only problem is when you *are* spit out, dammit, if you don't want to head back in . . ."

The temple lay ahead on a small plateau. A concrete teepee, about fifteen feet high, faced him and behind stood a curved wall of the same material and height. In the center, the wall rose into an inverted teardrop where a heavy metal moon had been placed. Sprouting from the moon were twenty black metal rods of different lengths. They represented moon rays.

On the other side of the wall, facing west, stood a hut-like structure with flags and flagpoles rising from its roof, and beyond that, dropping a thousand feet straight down, the canyon wall, the Pacific pounding against its rocks.

Pets filled the temple grounds. Peacocks, a baby llama, Chinese chickens, a cow, a camel and Mutt, the vegetarian dog. The wall extended to the edge of the plateau, which meant Papa had to curl around it.

There was no way to know what lay on the other side. The wall blocked his view and the patch of earth that separated the wall from a thousand-foot drop was less than a foot wide. Papa pasted both arms on the concrete barrier and eased his body around it.

Finally he spotted the kid, seated cross-legged on a small wooden altar in the center of the open hut. He appeared to be meditating or asleep, both hands resting on his thighs, gazing out to sea.

The kid apparently sensed his presence and swung his head. His tired puffy eyes broke open and he leapt to his feet. A knife was in his right hand.

Papa made his way around the wall, and now stood facing Tony Bernardo.

The wind whipped against their clothes and Papa could see the kid was shivering in his ragged, dirty jacket. Bernardo looked as if he hadn't bathed in weeks. His hair was long and dropped in thick strands over his shoulder. He looked hungry. He held the knife, outstretched, at chest level.

"Who are you?" he said.

A dozen yards separated them. Papa's hands were jammed in his pockets.

"Ralph Thorson. Your parents asked me to bring you back to them."

"I ain't going back."

"I don't see why not. It's a helluva lot better than freezing your ass off."

Bernardo made no response. He held his ground. The knife wavered, though.

Papa shrugged.

"Let me explain the situation to you. In my right pocket there's a forty-five automatic, which makes your boy scout blade not worth very much. I'm cold as hell. If you run I'll have to chase you. I won't be able to catch you so I'll have to think about shooting you. Drop the knife, Tony. You're much better off."

"No way."

Papa motioned toward the altar.

"Drop it over there, and we'll head back to the car. The heater's working, and we'll have a nice pleasant drive back home. And don't argue with me because I'm getting irritated."

Bernardo turned and made it for the opposite corner where the temple wall hugged the edge of the plateau. There was no way out from that direction. He would have to storm by Papa whose huge frame blocked the passage. Bernardo looked at Papa. He started toward him, stopped, and shook his head.

He dropped the knife on the dirt and took three steps forward. And then he broke into tears. Papa kept his eye on the kid and walked to the knife, which he picked up and dropped inside his coat.

He came up behind Bernardo and placed a hand on his shoulder. The kid seemed to sag under the weight of it.

22

The Beginning

Richie Blumenthal had Tony's parents in his office when Papa arrived.

Richie offered them chairs.

"Now didn't I tell you Papa'd bring back your kid, didn't I?" Richie said.

No one said a thing. The Bernardos seemed embarrassed by it all, by the suspicion that they'd somehow failed with their son. All Papa wanted was his money and he'd go home.

"I just wanted you to see him in the flesh," Richie said, looking at Mrs. Bernardo. "He goes to court in three days. With no previous record, he might get a suspended sentence. All right. Everybody's happy. I got a paper here for you to sign."

Mr. Bernardo read it and nodded his approval. Mrs. Bernardo did not smile. She held the paper up to Richie's face and said, "What is this?"

"That's umm"—Richie read the paragraph—"you owe Papa five thousand dollars for bringing in your son."

"I can't sign," she said.

270

"Whaddya mean, you can't sign?"

"I'm sorry."

"Why not?"

"Five thousand dollars. We can't afford to pay him right now. Maybe later."

Richie dropped his head back and studied her. "Mrs. Bernardo," he said, "if he didn't bring your son back you would have lost your hardware store."

Mrs. Bernardo turned to Papa. "I'm sorry, Mr. Thorson, but for six months we have suffered. My husband has a heart attack. I have a nervous condition. I can't sleep. Antonio here, he's a criminal. We have paid enough. More than enough. Too much already."

Papa stood when she finished and looked over at Richie, who looked away.

"Mrs. Bernardo," Papa said in an even voice, "how much you've suffered emotionally I can sympathize with. That has nothing to do with our contract. You owe me five thousand dollars."

"For what? Gasoline?" Mrs. Bernardo said. Mr. Bernardo sat in his chair, head down.

"Gas," Papa agreed. "Time. I had to pay Neil Flaningam two hundred before he'd tell me where Tony was. I have to pay other informants for checking around. I had to go after your son, not knowing whether he was armed or not."

"My Tony has no gun."

"I didn't know that. He was arrested for armed robbery."

"I'm sorry, Mr. Thorson. My mind's made up."

"Mrs. Bernardo, we have a contract," Richie pointed out.

"I have not signed the release. I *will* not sign the release." With that she turned away from Papa and said to her husband, "I'm ready."

Mr. Bernardo automatically stood and slid one arm through hers. When they reached the door Mrs. Bernardo halted and turned toward her son.

"Antonio, will you come home when this is done?"

"Yes, Mama."

Mrs. Bernardo kept her eyes fastened on him. "You had better."

They exited and Papa could hear her heels clicking down the corridor.

"Tough old broad," Richie said, and turned to Tony. "You oughta know. Right, kid?"

"One thing *I* know," said Papa, "since I'm not getting paid right now"—he pointed a finger at Richie—"you get to take Tony to jail."

"I haven't got time."

"Neither have I."

They looked at one another for a moment and Richie said, "I know you're due some dough. Of course you are. Give me a figure."

"Five thousand dollars."

"Give me a realistic figure."

"Five thousand is very realistic."

"I don't think so."

"Richie . . ."

"Papa . . ."

Again they tried to stare one another down. Finally, in a gesture of hopelessness, Richie Blumenthal wrote Papa a check for three thousand dollars.

Papa pocketed the check, grabbed Tony Bernardo and left the office. He was in the street when he heard Richie call to him. He watched the little man shuffling down the corridor with a folder in his hand.

"Almost forgot. A seventy-five thousand case. I got it right here in my hands. Interested?" Richie asked.

"I need a rest," Papa explained, starting out.

"I'll give you . . . ten grand."

"No."

"Fifteen."

Papa shook his head. "Goodnight, Richie."

"Look at it. That's all I ask. It's easy. Quick snatch. Nothing to it."

Richie held open the folder for Papa's inspection.

"Capital Insurance sent it over to me."

Papa looked at the papers and the name of the fugitive: Robert Ching, Jr.

Richie continued. "This Ching used to be in Canada. Now he's outside Tijuana somewhere. The kid's rich old man has a restaurant . . ."

Papa turned and led Tony Bernardo down the crowded street. He heard Richie still going on behind him.

"Seventy-five grand bail! It's a cinch, Papa. The old man will show you exactly where his kid is. I'm telling you, there's no hassle . . ."

Epilogue

Seated on a stool behind his living room bar, Papa pours Jack Daniels and puffs furiously on his fiftieth cigarette of the day. His beard is newly trimmed and his light blue eyes that bore right through you dart here and there searching for a green piece of paper he held just a minute ago. He finds it, about to be ripped in half by his 18-month-old daughter, Brandi.

Headlining the piece of green paper is "The Bushwhackers," Papa's bounty-hunting organization, a brochure he has mailed by the thousands to bailbondsmen throughout the country, providing a complete service "from Application to Exoneration."

He has just returned from picking up a former National Football League lineman for bad-check writing. The time is six forty-five a.m. and he has not been to sleep in twenty-four hours. Dotty enters from the kitchen with Brandi's Diet, a mixture of vitamins, minerals, fiber and other nutrients that Papa has spent a year researching and concocting.

A steady flow of traffic has begun outside the window. Papa reaches up and closes the draperies.

"I would recommend to anyone wanting to be a bounty hunter to forget about it," he says. "It's one of those cyclical occupations that comes around every hundred years. The 'Wanted: Dead or Alive' guys served the purpose in the last century and faded. The cycle's about over for this century. Maybe in another hundred years the demand will arise for bounty hunters in space. Brandi's great-great grandson might jockey through the universe chasing after futitives.

"The business has had its advantages: irregular hours; not knowing where the next house payment is coming from; wonderful relationships with bail bondsmen; getting shot and stabbed every so often.

"I've made a lot of friends, some enemies, and out of good fortune and knowing when to go in or get out I've stayed alive in an occupation that has a ridiculously high mortality rate.

"It amazes me—and a helluva lot of other people—that I *am* still alive. I've taken my share of stupid chances. I'm a big target for anybody wanting to put a hole through me. I've done irreparable damage to my own body, thanks to Dotty's cooking, Jack Daniels and cigarettes.

"Somebody—I don't remember who—said it was my 'spirit' that's kept me alive. That's true. Which I translate as the code of ethics I live by; that's been essential. You have to learn it young, and you also have to learn how to bend, how to break a few rules and cover your ass down the line."

Papa's eyes are partially closed. Before him is a list of calls he should make to the East Coast, which he'll put off until tomorrow morning.

"Covering yourself," he repeats in a drowsy monotone. "That's a lot of what it's all about."

With that he hefts his three hundred pounds off the stool and makes his way around the bar. He kisses Dotty on the cheek and Brandi on top of her head and lumbers off toward the bedroom.

"Wake me up in a half hour," he says over his shoulder, and disappears around the corner.

The climax of *Rhapsody in Blue* trails him from the living room.

Sweet dreams, Papa.

DON'T MISS
THESE CURRENT
Bantam Bestsellers

RELAX!
SIT DOWN
and Catch Up On Your Reading!

Bantam Book Catalog

ere's your up-to-the-minute listing of over ,400 titles by your favorite authors.

his illustrated, large format catalog gives a escription of each title. For your convenience, is divided into categories in fiction and non- :tion—gothics, science fiction, westerns, mys- •ries, cookbooks, mysticism and occult, biogra- nies, history, family living, health, psychology, t.

) don't delay—take advantage of this special)portunity to increase your reading pleasure.

ist send us your name and address and 50¢) help defray postage and handling costs).